For Franc

Ballet
OF
THE CRYPT
DANCER

I thoroughly enjoyed your
Paris and Rome videos
this novel has scenes which
take place in both cities.
Although Mia + Gio may
find this story a bit scary.
Happy Vlogging

A.L. MENGEL

CRYPT DANCER EDITION

1

COPYRIGHT DISCLAIMER

BALLET

OF

THE CRYPT

DANCER

FROM THE TALES OF TARTARUS

A NOVEL BY
A.L. MENGEL

FOR BETSY

always a ballerina

FROM THE AUTHOR

Beloved Friends of 'The Writing Studio' (*aka The Wanderers and The Crypt Dancers*),

It's an interesting thing, the soul.

Some believe that the body and the soul are unified as one, others believe that the spiritual soul is placed into a body to have a human and physical experience. Yet still others believe in reincarnation: that souls return to new bodies and different lives after an "old life" and an old body has died. Upon death, that particular soul has lost its shelter, and transmigrates to a new shelter. At the precise moment when a birth is occurring, the soul travels outwards into the big and exciting world, and begins anew once again.

Ballet of The Crypt Dancer is not a story about reincarnation, but rather it is a story that examines the probability of the existence of the soul, as are all of my novels. **The Tales of Tartarus** series was the genesis of my writing career, and also the start of my journey, thematically exploring the mystery surrounding consciousness after death. That enigmatic theory could comprise one of the uncertainties of which I have had a deep connection with. I have always wondered, and still search for answers, and wish to discover what happens when we close our eyes for the last time. In the video series *#TheEraOf*, the fifth chapter entitled '*#Legacy*', the episode leaves the viewer with just that ultimate question. And exploring consciousness after death is certainly one of the biggest themes which surrounds all of my novels.

The story of *Ballet of The Crypt Dancer* first appeared to me in a dream.

I had a vision of a malevolent character who somehow had a connection with people in crypts. While the research from my 2017 novel *The Mortician* was still fresh in my mind, I was eager to get to work on the story, to at least plant some seeds, so that the idea would not be lost; so the garden of the plot would bloom. I had no idea at the time what the plot to the story would be. I also didn't know that it was the seedling for a new story in **The Tales of Tartarus**. I still thought, back then, that *War Angel* had been the conclusion to the series.

In all honesty, I still feel that *War Angel* is a conclusion to the series, and to Antoine's journey. But the new vision, and the new direction that I have been crafting with *Ballet of The Crypt Dancer* does not necessarily continue where *War Angel* left off. In fact, the story begins before the events of *Ashes* and overlaps the entire series. In a sense, this novel you are about to read is a new story in the genealogy of **The Tales of Tartarus.** There were characters – major characters – who needed their own stories to be told. And, while this book was in production, it was revealed to me that there were other characters that were part of the same journey of the series, which warranted a deeper exploration. The upcoming novels in this series should not be confused with the books of **The Astral Files** (which began with 2017's *The Mortician*). In that series, supporting characters of **The Tales of Tartarus** are explored in depth.

There is also an entire cast of characters who are appearing in the series for the first time in this novel. This has opened doors to new directions of storytelling, as the ancestry of the immortals of the original four novels expands in its blood lineage.

Now to the addition of the line which I address all of you fine and wonderful readers.

The Wanderers, and The Crypt Dancers, was the brilliant idea of someone with whom I am very close, and the idea asks all of the Beloved Friends of *The Writing Studio* to search deep within. The idea asks followers to determine how the aura of their soul may appear to them. And so I present the question to you, dear reader, as well. Do you feel that you are a wanderer? Are you on a seemingly endless journey, where the stepping stones are laid out before you, stretching out towards an infinite horizon? Or do you hold a deep fascination with the supernatural?

Where the appearances fail to be explained.

The path still remains for all of us.

And I ask all of you, dear readers, to join me in *The Writing Studio*. It's the "little nickname that stuck" for the A.L. Mengel Facebook page. We've grown over the years. And whether you feel that you're a Wanderer...or a Crypt Dancer...I can assure that you will find a welcome safe haven there.

Now, let's let the horror continue.

A.L.

BOOKSHELF

From The Tales of Tartarus

ASHES

THE QUEST FOR IMMORTALITY

THE BLOOD DECANTER

WAR ANGEL

From The Astral Files

THE MORTICIAN

From The Vega Chronicles

THE WANDERING STAR

THE EUROPA EFFECT

THE ARRIVAL OF DESTINY

BATTLE OF THE TRINITY

Other Works

THE OTHER SIDE OF THE DOOR

CURTAINS AND FAN BLADES

#WRITESTORM

#PAINTTHEWORLD

#THEERAOF (*Video Storytelling*)

#UNMASKED (*Video Diary Series*)

Tours

TAKE A JOURNEY (2018)

Ballet OF THE CRYPT DANCER

ACT ONE – THE IMMORTALS

THE *Crypt* DANCER (I)

THE JEFFERSON *Majestic* MASSACRE

ACT TWO – THE WITCHES

COFFIN *Voodoo*

Shadow OF THE WITCH

ACT THREE – THE CONVERGENCE

THE *Crypt* DANCER (II)   BLOOD+*Cross*

THE *Crypt* DANCER (III)

CAST LIST

ACT (I) THE IMMORTALS

RAMIEL

CRISTOFANO

MONSIGNOR HARRISON

CLARET ATARAH

THE COMPANY

DOMINIQUE

ACT (II) THE WITCHES

RAMIEL

CRISTOFANO

LaDONNA MASTUER

EMMALINE DE LA CROIX

GERET

QUEEN REYNALDA

GISELLE

THE COMPANY

ANTOINE NAGEVESH

DARIUS SAUVAGE

ACT (III) THE CONVERGENCE

RAMIEL

CRISTOFANO

MONSIGNOR HARRISON

EMMALINE DE LA CROIX

ANTOINE

QUEEN REYNALDA

GISELLE

PASQUALE

THE COMPANY

THE JEFFERSON MAJESTIC THEATER PRESENTS

BALLET OF THE CRYPT DANCER

(Les Ballerines de La Crypte)

Pirouette

Dust

Mustiness in the rafters

Chatter through shrouds.

Tight ribbon, squeezing clamp.

Throat —

Rise on platform as shrouds part.

Whispering thunder.

The sound of strings and timpani

And cool light.

A glide to first, second, fourth, fifth.

A swell; a hold; an applause.

Destiny.

ACT ONE

The Immortals

Part One

THE CRYPT DANCER (I)

There was a certain time, and in a certain place, when they knew that they were being hunted.

THE BLOOD DECANTER

THE CURTAIN RISES

One

RAMIEL ALWAYS WANTED to tell the story of The Crypt Dancer, and of the massacre, and of the witches.

But there was no one, for years, who wanted to listen. In the days before he became an immortal, as he wandered the outskirts of Rome, he had heard about the mystery of the everlasting kind. A young man preparing for the seminary, he wondered about the fascination with the immortals, those despised creatures. Why were they loathed so much? Was there an unseen threat towards humans which was insurmountable, inconsolable?

He found it unusual that there could be a population apparently impervious to death, and disease; that those eternally youthful could coexist with humans and seem to appear ageless, despite the passage of time. He witnessed some of the countless discussions about the immortals, throughout the city and across the world, that those with what was called "the dark gift" may be supernatural; ghosts, demons, wizards or witches…but certainly not human.

And must not be accepted into society.

As a boy, he would listen to the dinner table chatter, as rumors of another kind increased, about the threat of the immortal population, who lived in the same cities and countries as mortal humans did. But Ramiel had never encountered one of the legendary immortals directly until leaving his parent's home, when he left to join the church.

It was there that he discovered an apparent truth; that there was some certainty in the rumors. That there were those in the population who appeared ageless, as if frozen in time, yet otherwise indiscernible. He had matured into a young man of robust, yet slender build, and while he was in the priesthood, he watched the others. There were those who had angelic faces which far unmatched their chronological years; as a mortal man, his appearance was also youthful, strong, with brown shoulder length hair.

He could have been one of them.

But in those days, he wasn't.

There were those who harbored some of the characteristics which he'd heard mama and papa discuss with their friends at dinner parties when he was still a boy, while they were planning ways to extricate the immortals from society. Perhaps there was a jealousy, Ramiel had thought.

But certainly a fear of the unknown.

Immortals were eternally youthful, despite the passage of years, sometimes decades; charismatic, with the ability to convince one who is unsuspecting to become infatuated with their gifts and powers; and malevolent, with doctrines that must be followed unequivocally, bringing swift and cruel justice for those who disobeyed.

Ramiel's time with the church may have been a foreshadowing of the events which would follow; the monsignor was a loyal tutor, yet misguided.

And then there was Cristofano.

A fellow Italian, from Salerno, on the Mediterranean coast, Ramiel grew from a boy to a man completely unaware of their destined connection through the enlightened tapestry of immortality, and the secret society, the Inspiriti.

He knew nothing of Cristofano's existence, until he had been introduced to him while under service at the Sistine Chapel, under the guidance and tutelage of Monsignor Harrison. It was Cristofano who was the one who introduced him to the mysteriousness and pleasures of the Inspiriti, and immortality, and the dark gift.

And who transformed him.

Yet after Ramiel's days in Paris, which followed his time in Rome, and the massacre at the theater he had been destined to perform, there had been a period when his loneliness had consumed him. As if the immortals were secretly despised, his thoughts would frequently drift towards those who hunted them. It wasn't only those who burned the theater with angry, flaming torches; those who ignited the curtains and destroyed any immortal with fire who was unable to flee; it was, he thought, possibly a threat of annihilation which originated from their own kind.

But why?

It was those thoughts which brought him to America, not only to find an inner sense of purpose, but also to reach forward on his journey as an immortal and as a man.

He formed his story.

He knew some of the others who had comprised the cast at the theater, and some who contributed to the events of the massacre; the events were soul defining. What purpose could come from an immortal, dragged through the rear gardens in flames, who was unable to die? Whose consciousness would endure in the coffin, for eternity, with seldom relief from the lonely torment?

If any.

Where the dreams that he held, each night when he lay in a coffin, just as he was taught by his maker, were just simply dreams. That there was nothing on the other side that he could sample when he closed his eyes; that the dreams, tiny snippets of death, were simply that. And that his soul was just as darkened and stained as the others, and despite the many beliefs that he'd carried since he was a boy, the conclusion was that once he closed his eyes, in that sleep of death of which immortals were comprised, there would be a simple drift towards solitude, silence and darkness.

But there was death in the solitude.

The immortals burned in the massacre; the awareness was the punishment. When the flames charred their skin as it melted from bones, and the stench of burning flesh permeated the air, the immortals may have pleaded for the solitude of death, which in the torment, would be a respite, which the immortals would never receive.

Ramiel knew the story must be told.

The massacre happened.

The Crypt Dancer was real.

And the witches had evaded detection for years. But as he mentioned it to others, be they human or immortal, he got brushed off.

Until one immortal, Delia Arnette, knocked on the estate door in Coral Gables, in Florida, during his time in America. It was a southern city with brilliant green lawns and soaring, shaded oak canopies; hanging Spanish moss which swayed in slow afternoon breezes. A suburb of Miami that reveled in its plantation dreams.

The estate, in possession of the immortals for generations, was once occupied by Antoine Nagevesh, a coffee harvester from Sri Lanka who had been discovered and brought to America. Nestled on the corner of Andelusia and Anastasia, the soaring Corinthian columns were unmistakable from the streets, as the home was known as the mansion of luxurious overstatement by the locals.

Ramiel padded through the kitchen as he heard the door chime.

The foyer remained unscathed from the fire, yet the distinct smell of charred wood hung in the air, as sheets of plywood covered the winding staircase. Ramiel was occupying the estate to oversee the renovations. Antoine had left Miami, with his maker, Darius Sauvage, to return to their chateau in France, after the fire had devastated parts of the mansion.

As Ramiel parted the lacey curtains on the skinny, rectangular window next to the double wooden doors, he saw the small woman, the one who had been introduced to him as Delia Arnette.

She was one of the immortals who had originated from a coveted bloodline; one of those with the time gift, who possessed the ability to appear in different time periods across oceans and continents, in altered appearances – exhibiting variations in age, physical stature, and demeanor – which, Ramiel had learned, was a gift exclusive to those selected to the blood lineage of Claret Atarah, rumored to be the eldest of the immortals.

But the woman who stood on the long, wraparound porch, in between the columns, in front of the rocking chairs, did not appear as the same Delia that he had expected. Her hair, snow-white; her face, lined with wrinkles, and her short stature all brought on the thoughts which pierced Ramiel's mind. Had The Hooded Man gotten to her too? Was his global virus of wrath impossible for her to resist with its temptations?

She clutched her slender, black umbrella close to her chest.

She had been one of the most peculiar of immortals, Ramiel knew that for certain. He'd heard of her, back in his early days in Italy, not far from Rome. She was known, in the mortal communities in which Ramiel had grown and studied, that she was a woman who frequented Rome, and also Paris, and it was rumored that she was "one of them". When he was still a boy, and when he was infatuated with the immortals, he had heard Delia's name mentioned…even in the supernatural classes he had taken in secondary school which had studies of the immortal population as course electives.

It was Delia's name which had been mentioned, in the texts and the main doctrine, *The Code of the Immortals*, which had been published in an undisclosed location, by a mysterious publisher called Parchman's Press. And, it was told in the classes, that only one copy had been created, and that the book had supernatural powers. The students were instructed to avoid the book at all costs; that it was spawn from Satan, that only evil resided in the book. The book, which was housed in

Rome, Ramiel suspected, had not been the original, for it would have then diluted its power. But the book mentioned her, in several instances.

In the days when Ramiel had been studying the immortals, Ms. Delia Arnette had been youthful and vibrant, at least from the photos that Ramiel had seen. Most photos were crude, in black and white, and taken when the camera had just been invented. They were often in books, but sometimes in periodicals. Newspapers mainly. But she was young; elegantly styled hair, voluptuous lips.

That was how Ramiel viewed an immortal.

They were strong, forceful. Undeniably attractive, physically. The males endowed with a lush presence, muscularity and charisma; the females with the power of seduction, persuasion and supple physical features; voluptuousness.

The power of seduction, but more often persuasion, was a gift afforded to all immortals. It allowed them to take command of a room with ease. There was something about them with which most humans had become enamored. Those had offered myriad theories. Some had been that mortal humans harbored jealously towards the gifted ones who had been bestowed supernatural powers.

The immortals, though, had always been human at one point, and when Ramiel had first taken notice of Delia, he was a mortal human himself. And when he stood in the foyer of the Miami estate, as he watched the small, frail woman reach out for the lion crest knocker once again, he grabbed the bolt and turned it, slowly opening the door.

She nodded and smiled. "Ramiel, I presume. May I come in?"

Ramiel nodded and stepped back.

Delia took a cautious, slow step up the raised threshold onto the marble. When she stood in the foyer, Ramiel reached out and placed her umbrella on a round, marble table in the center next to a giant fern. She looked up, and scanned the room. "I see you are restoring Antoine's mansion to its former glory."

Ramiel nodded and ushered her past the table. The soaring ceiling was restored from the fire, and the massive crystal chandelier which hung in the center was one of the first items that Ramiel chose to replace. Antoine was back at his chateau in Lyon with Darius, and was aware that Ramiel was occupying the estate; Ramiel had been tasked with the repair and renovation, which Delia had confirmed while they exchanged pleasantries in the foyer.

"It's been a long time since the fire," she said. "A lot has happened since then."

Ramiel nodded. "That's why you are here, correct?"

She looked at him, smiled and nodded. "The fire, but so much more, my young one. So much has happened since the fires in Miami. We have much to discuss. Monsignor Harrison sent me, and I represent the Inspiriti, as you should know."

He nodded slowly.

He knew the answer to the question. Why she was here. He knew it, she knew it.

He didn't even understand why he bothered to ask.

It was Delia. She would know. And she would speak to those who would provide her the information she needed to make her decision. Ramiel was intelligent. All immortals were, at least from the human perspective, masters of their craft. Leaders in their fields. Corporate executives. Best-selling authors. Oscar winning film-makers, winners of the Pulitzer Prize and those who had been awarded the Nobel.

They stopped in the kitchen at a large, wooden breakfast table, and Ramiel gestured for Delia to sit. "Would you care for some tea? Geret has run out for a few things. But he should be back shortly. He can start a fire in the parlor once he returns. But for now, would you care for something?"

She shook her head. "No, I think I want to get started."

There was something about her exactness; the matter-of-fact way she entered the kitchen; she leaned on her cane, shuffling across the stone floors towards the table. To the casual observer, she was a senior whose quest was to maintain her independence. But Ramiel knew differently.

It was Delia.

She was immortal, and one of the strongest of their kind. From the coveted bloodline, as he remembered again. And multiple afflictions have plagued the immortal community in recent memory: first they became the hunted, as a figure known as The Hooded Man enticed them with a decanter filled with a venomous potion which had resembled blood; it was perceived to be a catalyst of salvation, but instead brought a swift demise.

The second plague was a different kind of pandemic for the immortal community. It was an attack on their own kind, from where they originated from — human beings. It wasn't to say that immortals weren't human, they were, but evolved. The immortals had been chosen to receive the dark gift, which made them different...and feared. The massacre at the Jefferson Majestic theater in Paris may have sparked the beginning.

Ramiel pulled out a chair and sat across from her. Delia steadied herself and placed her arms on the table. "I know the fires weren't caused by the coven."

Ramiel nodded. "That is correct."

"We have the fire here, at Antoine's estate. And the nightclub he operated on Washington Avenue."

Ramiel leaned closer to her. "Yes," he said. "Here. In Miami. It's still being investigated by the authorities, but you know how we're held with regards to our gifts and powers."

Delia nodded. "True. These fires could be a part of the mortal agenda." Her eyes fell, along with her voice. "It seems this has been an affliction of our kind for years. Attacks from all directions. It makes me think of the attacks in Paris, when you still had been a mortal. Fire as well. It seems they have discovered the element which is our weakness."

"Yet we are powerful. With many gifts."

"True," Delia said. "But people fear what is different. What they cannot control. They are still intelligent and resourceful. They've discovered fire, which can end our physical existence."

"But we still exist," Ramiel said. "We remain aware, even if our physical form fails."

"And that is part of the torment," Delia said. "These fires though. Here, in Miami. Could they have been a part of the witches agenda?"

Ramiel looked at Delia and his face shifted. "Agenda?" He leaned forward and hooked his black hair back behind his ears.

"Queen Reynalda has been on coffin sentence," she said. "Is it my understanding that she has been released?"

Ramiel paused and felt his heart pound in his chest.

Certainly Delia couldn't have known about what he and Cristofano did in Paris. On that rainy, blustery night, back when Ramiel had been a newly transformed immortal. When there was a secret meeting with the voodoo priestess at *Le Hotel Aristocrat* and then later, the exhumation at the cemetery, at *Père Lachaise*.

"You are thinking of the cemetery," Delia said. "The grave. And the coffin, be it as it may. I can see everything."

Ramiel caught his breath. He must remain careful until she can be trusted.

"And in the cemetery *Père Lachaise* was Madame LaDonna Mastuer's crypt, am I correct in that assumption?"

He nodded. "Queen Reynalda…"

"She has much reason to hold resentment towards the immortals," Delia said.

"She's an immortal herself," Ramiel added.

Delia stood, balancing herself on the table with her palms. She looked down at Ramiel forcefully, her eyes wide. "She has violated the primary rule in the code," Delia said, with an edge in her tone. "That severe of an offense against *our own kind* results in a coffin sentence for eternity! She should have remained in chains and in the dark silence of her coffin to consider her actions!"

Ramiel's mouth dropped open as he leaned back in his chair. She was passionate about the code. And quite visibly disturbed that Queen Reynalda had been released prematurely.

Delia eased herself back into her chair. "She should have *never* been released."

Ramiel eased his palms down on the table. He had not seen this side of Delia before. In the books and periodicals, she was always presented as a protector.

"I'm not placing blame on you for what has happened in Miami while you have been here governing," she said. "But, yes, I am a protector. And in this case, I am striving to protect my own kind."

Delia knew everything, but then that was one of her gifts. She received an extraordinary amount of gifts when she was transformed, so many years ago, back in Paris, when Vaudeville was in its infancy. But now, as she sat after losing her gift, after becoming mortal once again, as a frail, grey-haired woman, her powers had been as strong as ever. Her immortality had returned; and she had been retransformed. Her gifts had been bestowed once again upon her: mind-reading, time-travel.

Among others, Ramiel assumed, that he might one day discover.

"To answer your questions," Ramiel said. "That is what I must be doing now, correct?"

She nodded. "I have many questions."

"Very well then," Ramiel said. "I know the monsignor sent you. I'm willing to cooperate. And I'm not going attempt to stand in your way, or in the way of anyone else in the Inspiriti, for that matter."

"As you shouldn't."

Ramiel watched her hands, noticing that the skin was wrinkled and sagging; the veins protruded amidst light brown age spots. She looked up at him and he looked away.

"It was the decanter," she said. "When *The Hooded Man* had targeted the immortals, I had been a victim as well. You're familiar with what happened, are you not? You were in Rome and Paris. There wasn't nearly as much of an impact outside of Antoine's sector."

Ramiel caught himself again.

Of course she had discussed the assault of the blood from the decanter. And the scores of immortals who had lost their dark gift, who drank the crimson potion that *The Hooded Man* carried, seeking a redemption, but finding death.

"Yes, I am familiar with the situation. Antoine left Miami to return with Darius, who is aging rapidly. He isn't expected to live much longer."

He tried to think benign thoughts. But deep within his soul, he knew that he couldn't. He hadn't experienced the extent of the wrath that those in the Inspiriti had warned about, *The Hooded Man*.

"I was lured to the same false promise that countless other immortals had flocked to," she said. "The blood he carried was not a potion of salvation or redemption. My immortality was taken away from me. I aged rapidly as my body caught up with my soul."

"But you managed to survive."

She nodded. "Yes, I managed to survive. And we, all of us, really, we immortals who are left on this world – we do have vulnerabilities. And we have lost so many. Great numbers, that is apparent. But the deaths that have plagued us aren't the true death. The loss of consciousness, and awareness. The purported transformation of the soul. And a migration to the astral plane. We hold the torment of silence in the coffin. We cannot pass forward. Even more so, the finality of it all, is something that immortals have never had to deal with prior to that."

"The rapid aging and the finality of death."

She nodded. "Yes. The coffin sentences have been a part of the code for generations of bloodlines," she said. "And then there was the rapid aging. That is what brought us to a precipice during the wrath of The Hooded Man. The rapid aging, when we had always been ageless."

"Just like what happened to Darius," Ramiel said.

"And the death of too many," she said. "Far too many to count."

"Antoine knew when to leave."

"He left to tend to a dying Darius," she said. "And because of the coven. The witches had been taking over since before the wrath of *The Hooded Man*, and…then…."

Her voice trailed off.

The room became unsettled as the rain started to fall, gently pelting against the window pane. Thunder rumbled in the distance. She closed her eyes as Ramiel shifted in his chair. There was much hatred that had developed in recent years, a deep animosity for those who escaped the assault, like he had; Antoine and Darius escaped, perhaps for a different purpose, but likely so Antoine could mourn what would inevitably become the death of his maker.

Ramiel didn't understand the hostility between the immortals and the witches which developed while Antoine had governed the sector. But Antoine's leadership was blindsided by *The Hooded Man*, and the motivation for the assault to the immortal population remained uncertain. And so he chose to think about his own journey, of which Delia knew all of the details, no doubt.

She was powerful in that respect.

"I'm here because we seem to have a greater problem," she said, as she leaned forward. "More significant than *The Hooded Man.*" She commanded Ramiel's undivided attention.

"That's why they called me to Miami as well," Ramiel said. "Monsignor Harrison sent me and Cristofano to investigate the disappearance of the actors from the Jefferson Majestic theater."

"The one in Coral Gables? On Ponce de Leon?"

"Yes," he said. "After the massacre at the theater in Paris, there was a strong connection between the immortals who escaped. And those who disappeared."

Delia eased herself up with her cane and started walking around the expansive wooden breakfast table. "Antoine has lost his stronghold on this sector," she said. "Monsignor Harrison called me directly from Rome and insisted that I travel to Miami immediately, that the situation had become dire. But we are also discussing the coven. And the coffin sentences. There is much power in that respect, given to that individual, who carries the sentences out and upholds justice. But our relations with the coven couldn't be worse, and now Cristofano is missing." She stopped and looked down at Ramiel, who looked up at her and met her eye contact. "We have lost too many immortals to this," she said. "But all of that's not even the greatest concern."

Ramiel nodded.

"LaDonna Mastuer should never have been released either."

She returned to her seat, eased herself back into the chair, and sighed as her face fell. She shook her head slowly. "Why would she have been released? *Why?*"

Ramiel bit his lower lip, his eyes wide and unseeing, as the thunder crashed overhead, signaling the arrival of the storm, the torrent of rain outside, and the rush of the winds. Cristofano was his maker. They had been inseparable since he'd met him back in Vatican City, when he was still a young man of the cloth. But Cristofano sparked his creativity; it was as if Cristofano was his muse, and fanned the flames which had shifted his journey towards a path of artistry, painting and poetry, performance and dance.

Delia, though, grew quiet as the storm quieted. The rain pelted on the windowpane, as Geret carried some firewood across the parlor.

Ramiel remembered the nights in Paris at *Père Lachaise* and Cristofano's excitement when he pointed out the crypts which were rumored to contain immortals serving coffin sentences; those immortals, he had explained, were always aware of the dark solitude which surrounded them. Gagged and tightly bound in chains, their speaking was silenced and their movement was halted, but they could see the assault of the darkness. They could smell the wood decay over the years, decades and centuries; they would hear the deep, thunderous grating of the coffin as it slid into the cement cavern, the thud as the crypt was sealed and the footsteps as they walked away.

LaDonna Mastuer, the voodoo priestess who had been banished to a crypt for centuries, was one of the immortals who had deep connections with the coven, also to Queen Reynalda, and hers was one of the crypts, according to the Inspiriti, of which *must never be opened.* The chains may be able to contain her, Monsignor Harrison had told him one day while in the catacombs in Rome, but once unchained, she

42

would be the epitome of torment for the immortal community. The crypt must contain her, he said. Her sentence was for eternity as the ultimate threat to the immortal existence.

But there were interests greater than the monsignor's, and when Monsignor Harrison had had that conversation with Ramiel, he was a novice priest at the Vatican, and hadn't even been given the dark gift yet. It might not have mattered, in those days.

Cristofano, however, chose to ignore the warnings of the Inspiriti, and LaDonna Mastuer was destined to be unchained, released from the crypt, and to walk the streets once again.

The crypt came to haunt Ramiel in the days that followed.

When Delia had left and Geret had turned his bed down, he knew the coffin would call. Life beyond transformation had become a harbinger of darkness; his living in and renovating Antoine's estate might have been his call to remain with humanity.

I am the crypt dancer…

He paused in the doorway and felt a chill rush through his body. Geret placed his hand on Ramiel's shoulder. "Are you feeling alright?"

Ramiel nodded. "The grave is calling," he said. "I am making an attempt to hold to life and humanity…but it still rings in my head. The voice…the hiss. I can't get it out of my head. And it strikes without warning."

"Perhaps we should try to locate Cristofano," Geret offered. Ramiel slid into the massive bed. Geret drew the drapes closed as Ramiel pulled the covers up towards his neck. "I am holding on to human things," he said. "But the coffin is calling me."

"You've been saying that," Geret said, pausing at the door and turning to watch Ramiel adjust himself under the sheets. "Perhaps you have been abandoned, like the others?"

Ramiel stopped and looked over at Geret. "That's what you assume," he said. "But I am stronger than you give me credit for. I have the powers that I always held when I was transformed."

"You don't have Cristo's life force right now, with his whereabouts unknown," Geret said. "It's draining you. I can tell. I can see it in your eyes, on your skin. You need him around, right? Isn't that what you've been telling me?"

Ramiel eased himself up on his elbows, grunting as he did so. "Perhaps," he said. "There are connections between immortals that extend deeper than a soul connectedness. I don't want to digress."

"You can use me," Geret offered. He took a step into the darkened room, closer to the bed. Ramiel raised his eyes and looked at the young man. He removed his shirt, slowly, unbuttoning each button, downwards, watching Ramiel, locking eye contact. Geret still had his dancer's body, tight and taught from the days at the Jefferson. Ramiel hadn't expected Geret to follow him to Miami, but Geret did, and Ramiel was surprised. There wasn't much left for them in Paris, anyway, since Cristofano had gone missing.

"I am ready if you need it," Geret said, tilting his neck to the side. His jugular was engorged and Ramiel knew it would sustain him during the search. But Geret was still untransformed, waiting for his destiny, offering his sustenance to an immortal who had lost his way. Ramiel knew that he couldn't transform Geret, no matter how much he desired it. There would be far too much objection from Cristofano's jealousy, and if his maker were to reject him, then the draining of his lifeforce could become permanent. Ramiel leaned back in the overstuffed pillow as Geret removed his pants and slid under the sheets, raising his eyes and looking up at him. Ramiel sighed.

There was no use.

It didn't matter that he hadn't transformed him. Geret would never understand the plight of the immortals; the loneliness and rejection, unless he were to be transformed. Cristofano would never allow it. His maker had a penchant for evil. Sometimes Ramiel wished he had never met Cristofano. But if this had been his destiny, to receive the dark gift, then would he have met another immortal at some point in his youth? Would his building desolation remain, or had there been a misdirection in the guiding forces of his past?

Geret turned to face him. "Are you sure Queen Reynalda isn't behind this? All of this animosity towards the immortals?"

"Delia seems to think so," he said. "She mentioned earlier that the queen should have never been released from her coffin sentence. Kind of a subtle indication that I might be behind it."

"That's not true!" Geret said.

"Is it?"

"It isn't true," Geret said. "You have preserved your own kind since you were transformed!"

Ramiel sank deeper into the large, overstuffed pillow as Geret turned and snapped the lamp off. Ramiel sighed. "I've been involved with the coven since I arrived here."

"But Cristo told you to investigate them," he said. "You were acting under orders."

"It doesn't matter," Ramiel said. "It doesn't matter in the code. Cristo may have *suggested* that I involve myself with the coven. But the code doesn't care. I enacted it."

Geret crossed his arms and flopped on the pillow next to him. "Then the code needs to change," he said. "You had good intentions. You were trying to help your kind. Not hurt them."

Ramiel turned on his side to face Geret.

If he wasn't transformed soon, he would mature out of youth. Not much longer before he was middle aged. He was still quite attractive; not that middle aged and older people weren't attractive, but Geret still had the confirmation of youth on his side. Now would be the best time for him to be transformed.

Or he might have Delia's fate.

"I just can't forget the days at the Jefferson," Ramiel said. "And LaDonna Mastuer was chained in a coffin in those days. The massacre couldn't have been her. It may have been the mortals as Delia insists."

Geret turned and faced him as they made eye contact. "The case still remains unsolved."

Ramiel scoffed. "Oh, they've had their investigative trials in Rome, with the monsignor. For countless years. It's the *mortals*. They tore through the front doors with torches. The dissention between our two kinds has simmered with unrest for generations."

"And you are certain of this? That the mortals were behind the massacre?"

Ramiel leaned up on his elbows. "We were both there, Geret. Both mortals then ourselves. Remember those were the days before I was transformed myself. Certainly your mind can't have forgotten?"

Geret stood and walked to the door. Light filtered in from the hallway, spilling towards the bed. Geret turned back to face Ramiel as he appeared as a silhouette. "I have not forgotten," he said. "But generations have passed since the massacre, and immortal relations with the humans has progressed tremendously."

Geret turned, wrapping himself in the sheet, as Ramiel lay on his back, studying the ceiling despite the room being shrouded in darkness. His journey with the dark gift had always been masked with uncertainty. There were those in his life who made it seem that he had made the wrong choices, starting with his own parents; yet his parents never knew of his infatuation with the immortals, or the enlightened ones, as they were sometimes called. In the days when he was performing at the theater in Paris with Cristofano and Geret, some of his questions had been answered, which led to more mysteriousness. Ramiel knew that he wanted to do something which held a greater purpose. Perhaps the immortals were misunderstood? Had the mortal humans been threatened in some way, or some fashion?

Ramiel considered those answers, and a wave of disappointment washed through him, as he knew those thoughts had originated many years ago, and as he lay in bed with Geret, and heard the delicate, reassuring sound of his breathing against the dark silence as his human friend had fallen asleep, it appeared as though progress had not been made.

At least not in the respect that he had hoped from interactions with those when he was newly transformed.

When he was still discovering his true self in life, but after he had been selected and transformed, he'd heard of an immortal named Antoine Nagevesh, who'd been rumored to have a chateau in Lyon, in the inlands of France, just outside of the city, where the roads wound gently towards forests and farmlands.

In the earlier days before he had been transformed, Ramiel had only heard of France; he lived with his parents in the outskirts of Rome. The household was devoutly Catholic and regimented with traditions and belief. As a boy, he had only dreamed of the immortals who many claimed lived in the country; with talk that filtered across Italy, throughout his homeland, and tore through the population like wildfire, he discovered a new obsession. Ramiel thought of the early days, when he was still deeply infatuated with the immortals, yet had not been transformed.

He had been a loner, and a creative, a dancer and an enigma.

Little did he know, as he was still a boy in those days, and fascinated by the discussions he had overheard across dinner tables with generous servings of spaghetti, bread and red wine, that he would become an immortal himself.

"There is a rumor," he heard his father say. "That there is another population that is forming over in France. In Paris, and Lyon. That claim to be enlightened and immortal. That there are those who wish to deconsecrate the church?"

He heard his mother let out an exasperated sigh. "That cannot be true," she said, after a few moments of silence. "Italy *is* the church. And so is Rome. Why would they be concerned about some small sect of the population outside of Paris who disagree with them?"

"Because," he said. "These immortals. There are more of them than we realize. They hide quite easily, within our population. They have powers. It's easy for them to persuade good, decent people to follow the ways of darkness. I'm sure there are some living here, in secrecy. They are not as enlightened or innocent as they claim to be. They are the ultimate in evil. And debauchery. They conduct themselves against every moral principle that comes out of Rome! Don't you see? They are evil…and must be stopped!"

Ramiel stood in a darkened hallway which stretched out from the kitchen table, behind a door that he cracked open slightly, listening to his parents' dinner party discussion, and watched as the dinner guests observed mama and papa's discussion silently. He wondered how one segment of the population could be so hated.

He pressed the door open wider, letting a sliver of light in.

The adults were still talking.

"They must be exterminated," papa said, as he shoveled spaghetti into his mouth. He reached out and grasped a small glass of table red, and took a slurp. "They are not equal to us, Serena. They think they are superior. With powers that only they can seem to experience."

"They are vampires, are they? I've heard that mentioned."

Papa shook his head. "Vampires are part of superstition. And literature. These immortals are far more sinister. And real. They feed on humans…murder them without warning or motivation…other than the simple act to kill. They're demons. Monsters. *They must be stopped.*"

"They seek blood you told me."

"They do, at first. But then they transform to a darker, more sinister presence."

Ramiel watched as mama and papa sat, discussing what had become a deep interest of his over time. There had been many nights of dinner table talk; papa had grown closer to the church, and his penchant for the destruction of the immortals developed a stronger will throughout time.

"What are you going to do?" mama asked as Ramiel eased himself backwards. The sliver of light lessened as he huddled closer to the wall.

Papa scoffed. Ramiel could see he was flopped back in his chair, glaring at the others. He shook his head. "We have torches, Serena. We have been watching them now. You can tell where they hide, you know. They have their powers. And everyone seems to fall in love with them. 'They're so cultured!' they say. 'And they're so fascinating.'".

Papa took a breath, lowered his head. "We are going to burn everything down," he said. "Burn them out of our country. Let France deal with them. Better yet, send them across the Atlantic."

Mama gasped. "But how can you justify that? Are they murdering us? Killing us?"

Papa banged his fist on the table. "No! They seek blood! And recruit our young! Desecrate our church!"

Ramiel, though, didn't understand why papa had been so filled with hate. He stood at the threshold of the door, watching his parents between the tiny crack at the edge of the frame, and thought, the more that papa talked, the more the immortals sounded fascinating.

And he ate his dinner earlier.

It was past time for him to go to bed. He knew that. But he loved to listen to mama, and papa, and their friends who would come over for a late dinner with wine, bread and pasta. Their conversation was hateful, but intriguing, and he desperately wanted to discover more about the immortals, and the desire increased as papa's detestable analysis continued. For Ramiel had a yearning within; he felt purpose that night. Despite his tender age as a boy, his deduction was flawless.

He tucked his hands around his face and peered through the crack.

Mama carried a massive bowl to the table. Ramiel saw a cloud of steam rising from it. "Time to take this to Mariela. You know she is unable to cook right now." Papa nodded and picked up the bowl and stood. Ramiel took a cautious step back into the darkness of the hallway, but kept his ears trained on the muffled conversation through the door.

After a few moments, he slowly stepped back towards the crack.

"There's nothing wrong with France," she said, reaching towards the center of the table. Papa stood in front the of the table holding the giant bowl of pasta. Mama rose from the wooden bench on which she was sitting and reached for the pasta and meat. "Take all of it to her."

"It isn't France," he said, as their dinner guests sipped their wine and observed. "It's the immortals. They're *evil*. Like an infection. And they're not only in France. They are here in Rome as well."

Mama gasped as Ramiel eased his pressure on the door, closing the crack of light and shrouding the hallway in darkness. The voices became muffled and he was unable to decipher the chatter.

But that is how he knew.

His own perception had changed as he grew into adolescence.

During that same period, Ramiel had also heard of the immortals, and a group called *The Inspiriti*, and of high councils that sat beneath the Sistine Chapel in Rome, through the chattered rumors which struck through the human population in the city where he'd grown from a boy into a man. The immortals were an enigma, but they were there. The humans knew.

And, always knew.

Ramiel remained in his musings and memories long after Geret had fallen asleep. As he listened to the inhaling and light exhaling, the past came calling. When he thought of the days when he had been enamored with the immortals, yet still not given the gift, in the days before he had met Cristofano, he thought of his days in Rome, when he had left his parent's house, on a journey towards the church; at first glance to a lifetime of servitude and enlightenment, he didn't know at the time that the destiny held a different destination.

There was a man who held a mysterious connection to the immortals, a man who Ramiel had known about, and read about him in the papers. Ramiel wondered about how this man was closely linked to the immortals, yet a high ranking member of the church as well. In the days when Ramiel had matured into adolescence, he expressed an interest in becoming an altar boy at the Vatican, much to the delight of his parents. During that time, Ramiel spent his days at the Sistine Chapel, in close proximity to the priest, the man who was called Monsignor Harrison, who served as a mentor, convincing Ramiel to join the priesthood; it was the time was when Ramiel had learned in his tutelage that the title of monsignor had been a bestowment of authority and honor. But during those days as a boy, as he stood amidst the wooden pews, he crumpled a white dust rag and polished the back of the bench in a circular motion. He looked up as he heard the echo of voices approach, and set the bucket that he'd been holding in his left hand down gently and without a sound.

He ducked below the crest of the pew, and listened. It was a woman's voice.

Stern and forceful.

"I do not want Darius to approach anyone in Vatican City. He has far too much on his plate in Paris. And you see how easily he has gotten overwhelmed in the past."

Ramiel slowly peered upwards, shielding himself behind the back of the pew. He watched as Monsignor Harrison stood on the opposite side of the chapel, across the worship area, near *the door that he always must stay away from*, Ramiel had been told since he started. The monsignor's massive stature concealed who he was speaking with. Ramiel could not make out what Monsignor Harrison was saying, but heard the voices echo across the expansive chamber.

"And there is a call for Darius to develop another," she said. "He has been told numerous times."

"He was told by Madame Arsenault," she said. "I had her send the message while at Notre Dame. I sent her to Paris when I learned that Darius had been spending so much time there. But they hauled her away."

"Hauled her away?"

"Yes," she said. "I sent her to Paris to speak with Darius. To lecture him on the *Code of the Immortals*. Darius should know better than the way he's been behaving. He knows he must continue the blood lineage. So it has been written, so must it be done. An angry mob stormed the chapel and dragged her away."

"He could have a predetermined destiny, your grace. A calling which may be different than those others we have sent out to carry the immortals through the words of the code."

Ramiel jumped as he heard what sounded like a book being thrown on the floor, echoing through the chapel. "Absolutely not! When he was transformed, he agreed to the principles which dictate our kind. It clearly states that all immortals must carry on the blood lineage. We are too rare. It is imperative and it is not an option!"

The click of a lock echoed against the soaring ceilings.

Ramiel squinted in the dim light of the worship area, and watched as Monsignor Harrison and the mysterious woman disappeared into the bowels below the chapel. The door closed with a boom which reverberated upwards towards the soaring ceiling.

He sat up on the pew and flopped against the hard wood back.

He set the rag on the bench next to where he sat, took a breath, and sighed. He knew that something was going on. Down in the basement, it seemed. There were many mysterious visitors that always went down through the *door that he must always stay away from*, but there were never any answers to the questions that permeated his still young mind.

He had been warned by mama and papa to stay away from Rome; that the immortals had penetrated the sacred cities, and it appeared that they might have been incorrect. Hadn't there been centuries of an immortal presence throughout European cities?

But Ramiel had a mysterious connection to the immortals before he had been transformed. He held a desire to explore, and to be a part of what might, in fact, be something good.

Could the immortals be as bad as mama and papa had insisted they be?

Darkness enveloped Ramiel as he felt the twinge of sleep .

The memories of the chapel and the monsignor faded, as he could feel a heartbeat which he hadn't felt since before he was transformed. He turned on his side and watched the door. He hadn't first noticed that Geret had left the bed. Ramiel thought that Geret probably opted to sleep in Ramiel's coffin, as Geret had longed so for the immortal life. Ramiel turned and saw daylight filtering through the heavy drapes, yet he chose to rise.

He swung his legs out and felt the cool tile. Sleep would not be coming for him.

There were too many thoughts clattering through his mind. The discussion with Delia had been unsettling, but he understood its purpose. The disappearance of Cristofano had been equally upsetting, and he was afraid that his maker might have been subject to the wrath of Queen Reynalda. But the witches were a new part of the equation, for the time period when he and Cristofano had arrived in America, and when Antoine and Darius had left for Europe. The witch coven at Haddon House was unique and mysterious.

The immortals had never known of their presence for most of the period when Antoine and Darius had been in control of the sector; and Queen Reynalda, it seemed, appreciated the anonymity of their coven.

In the days since he and Cristofano had released LaDonna Mastuer from her crypt in Paris, there appeared to be a warming of the relations between the immortals and the witches, but many questions remained unanswered. Ramiel and Delia both were perplexed that Antoine seemed to be quite aloof when learning of the coven and the assumed intentions, particularly that the group of witches had been forming undetected under his and Darius' leadership.

Ramiel padded down a lengthy corridor.

The smell of soot still lingered in the air, wafting down from the upstairs as the workers carried charred sections of blackened drywall down the stairs. "Oh!" a small Hispanic man said, setting a large piece of burnt and blackened drywall down. "We were trying to be as quiet as possible. Master Antoine provided the foreman with a key to continue with the renovations while he was out of town. He said you'd be here."

Ramiel cracked a smile and nodded, continuing towards the back gathering room. As he approached the cellar door, there was a feeling of uncertainty that washed through him. Antoine had told him about the days at The Astral, the paranormal researching society in Coral Gables. It was when their proprietor had interviewed Antoine with the intent of writing a book about the immortal community in Miami.

Antoine said the book never got published, because the man had perished in the fires and the attacks.

The proprietor's name was Sheldon Wilkes.

Ramiel paused in the kitchen as he rummaged through the cupboard for the French Press. He knew the attacks in Miami were becoming more significant in the immortal community. The Hooded Man, and now the Reynalda Coven. The disappearances and the Massacre. Could the humans have been behind it? Or another, more sinister force?

He sat at the table with a steaming cup of coffee, and placed his head down in his hands. He ran his hands through his hair, pulling it back from the sides of his face. He stared at the coffee, examining the bubbles and foam on the top of the dark black liquid.

Delia had given him too much to think about.

She challenged him to revisit the days when he was still a mortal, and infatuated with their kind. She insisted he return to the days when he wasn't in a period of desolation and depression. And the days when he could remember the good in the path which had had chosen.

He still remembered the day in the chapel, when he was enamored with *the door that must never be opened.* His mind carried him back to those days once again and he took a sip of the searing hot coffee. He treasured the robust, hot liquid as it warmed his throat; and he leaned back in the chair, and closed his eyes.

Two

THE IMMORTAL WHO was known simply as Cristo, the one they had called Cristofano, from Salerno, on the Mediterranean coast of Italy, had known about the code. His maker had been wandering the street markets just beyond the delicate blue shores of the Mediterranean, and he knew that he was destined for the immortal kind. Cristofano knew from an early time that had had been assigned to carry the blood lineage from the moment of his transformation. He was a young man in Salerno, Italy, until the moment when he had caught the eye of his maker and had been transformed. Cristo, as he was called by his family and friends, was tall and muscular, yet somewhat lanky. He had long brown hair which spilled around his head like a fine blanket.

He had frequently walked the dusty stone streets of Salerno at sunset, when the sky was painted a brilliant auburn, and spent many nights on the edge of the Mediterranean, looking outwards at the mysteriousness of the sea, and back inwards at the warm checkerboard of the small stucco buildings rising upwards on the side of the mountain. His musings on the edge of the water had become a nightly ritual; he loved the call of the sunset. When the sky had enraged itself, if only for a short period. Perhaps it was to escape the dull solitude of his home, or the yearning for something more.

Cristofano knew little of destiny, nor did he care. He held an appreciation for the darkness which came after the twilight, when the moon would shine, and reflect its pale light across the buildings, highlighting the small, boxy stucco homes, like stones in a dark field. Even the mountains were indiscernible against the dark silent night; and then, as he sat on the bench, turning back around to face the still sea, as he listened to the gentle waves lap against the seawall, he heard them.

"We've been watching you."

It was a male voice. Soft, delicate, making a desperate attempt to provide assurance. But why?

He turned his head slowly and saw them.

There was a group of them, standing a few feet away from him, closer to the main thoroughfare, it seemed. He felt his heart pound. He had learned about them, studied them in school. He never thought that he would encounter them, especially in Salerno. But they stood there before him, watching, waiting. Saying they had been watching him. Had his studies brought him to their attention?

He opened his mouth to speak but found he couldn't.

There was a beckoning which resulted from their stasis; they stood, immobile, silent, waiting and watching, as he shifted nervously on the bench. This was the time. It was now or never. Could it be? Could these four figures be the immortals which he had studied for so many years in his youth? Would they transform him, and take him into their brethren, as he thought he one day might be?

He felt his eyes close, as his mind transformed towards the darkness. Tiny wisps of light soared past him as he felt the physical world wash away; destiny was ahead. He didn't believe in destiny, but there was something ahead, a light in the darkness, perhaps it was a hallucination, maybe they had drugged him, but why?

Why would they do that?

And why would he fall into a state of altered consciousness, in a dark, mystical existence, as wisps of light shot past him, unless they had wanted him to experience it?

There might have been some purpose behind their selection. He knew of the mysteries of the astral plane, and cosmic existence in otherworldly realms, principles of which the immortals were well versed. And in his studies, he remembered the mysteriousness of the Inspiriti.

The light grew larger.

He squinted, yet it would not gain focus. There was movement; darkness within the haze; it was as if a mist was concealing movement; as if he were looking through the lens of a distant telescope, soaring through the darkness at incomprehensible speed, but failing to reach the destination. Then came an unseen voice, harsh, deep, raspy…yet feminine.

You will be the chosen one…

And that was the precise moment he knew.

There was no greater mystery than that of the Inspiriti, and their choices; who they recruit may be as great a mystery as their own ambiguity. But he was the chosen one. He made an attempt to speak.

"But…who has chosen me?"

His voice sound small and tinny against the darkness, silent yet soaring with unseen winds; dreams of a nightmare and unheard sounds. Yet when he attempted to listen, the noise became more distorted, the image less focused. Not that it ever was.

You have been chosen to be the most coveted blood lineage…from the one who is our eldest. You must look forward, ahead of you. What you see will gain clarity, once you open your mind and accept. You have been given free will. But we urge you to choose wisely. The Inspiriti will be your guiding light. The force which will remain with you on your journey. And for the calling which you have for the immortals.

He watched the image and waited for it to clear. The dark image remained, movement in the midst of chaos, yet a sense of order washed through him. For what purpose had he been chosen?

You are a crypt dancer…

He felt his motion stop as the winds transformed to silence. The crypt dancer. The only bringer of justice to the kind. The one who carried the chains. The one who had the force to entomb, and the only immortal with the power to release.

Only those with your blood lineage have the power of the crypt dancer…and those who are selected are few…

"I…only have read about…"

You possess the knowledge. And the blood. You are the crypt dancer…

Cristofano felt breathless as his consciousness returned; he felt the hard cement of the bench beneath his back, physically. It seemed that he had not travelled anywhere. Had he passed out? Had it been a dream? As clarity returned, he thought of the images, and the voice.

You are the crypt dancer...

He caught his breath and lifted himself upwards on his elbows. How could he be the crypt dancer? There was the day that he'd seen the copy of *The Code of the Immortals*, years ago, when his professor had claimed to have a copy. Had his involvement with that placed him with a sense of the immortals? Were they actively recruiting him? Or was it a momentary lapse of reason?

The four figures were gone, and then he scanned the streets leading up the mountain. The tiny streets were desolate and quiet. He looked up towards the sky. The moon had traveled across the sky and was directly above the tiny sea town.

Time had passed.

And there was not much time left in the night. His roommates at the seminary school would be calling the residence if he didn't return before they awakened. In the days that followed, as the buzz of activity returned to the small, dusty streets, when Cristofano would wander towards the market on his lunch between classes, he would pass the bench by the sea.

He hadn't returned to the bench since that night.

There was as certain moment when he caught the eye of his maker, a certain woman who walked the streets of Salerno, Italy, where he had spent the majority of his young mortal life. It was a certain woman named Claret Atarah, rumored to be from ancient Jerusalem, and was thought to have a gift for time travel; she was a quintessential stranger in a strange land.

But Claret had spent most of her time browsing through the markets under tapestries propped with wooden stakes, examining the fresh produce. Cristofano would watch from afar, studying her movements as she picked up a melon and sniffed it. He watched as she would look back and forth.

"Look," he said. "Pasquale. Do you see her? She's been wandering through the market each day since the night I told you about. When they came to me. She's always walking through, looking at the fruits and vegetables, asking questions about the fish and meat, yet she buys nothing. She wanders through, looks at the goods, looks around, and leaves."

Pasquale shifted on the bench. He reached up and ran his hands though his thick, black hair. "What is unusual about that?"

Cristofano scoffed. "She never buys anything. And she seems unusual for Salerno. Not the type to be here."

"I don't know, Cristo," Pasquale said, as the woman stood in the middle of a crowd of market shoppers, facing them, from a distance, watching, standing and waiting. Cristofano felt his heart jump in his chest.

"I think she is watching us," he said, getting up carefully and slowly, easing himself around to the back of the bench. Pasquale turned around and shook his head. "Cristo, you are being fearful. How do you know she is looking here?"

Cristofano ducked behind the bench as he watched the woman. She stood motionless as the market shoppers wandered past her, around where she stood, as her eyes seemed to pierce in his direction. "She's watching me," he whispered. Pasquale stood and turned. "We are going to be late," he said. "And I think you are imagining things. I don't think she is looking at us. Or you, for that matter."

Cristofano slowly shook his head as he eased himself up and closer to Pasquale. "This happens every day," he said. "She is always there. It doesn't matter if you're with me or not. I see her every day, I tell you, and she is always doing the same thing. She always selects some fruits and vegetables, draws them up and sniffs them, and turns to look at me."

They started to head back to the seminary school, as Cristofano continued to turn his head, watching the mysterious woman, standing mysteriously still, watching in their direction, her head turning gradually as they headed further from the market square. "She's watching," he said, as Pasquale nodded.

"What are you going to do about it?" Pasquale asked. "Do you think she'll ever approach you?"

Cristofano watched as a building slowly concealed their view. He reluctantly turned towards Pasquale, as they walked back to their dormitories. Perhaps he was right. Maybe should would never approach him. He turned one last time, only seeing the edge of the brick building by which they walked, as a cooling breeze flowed inward from the Mediterranean, blowing his hair back. It didn't matter if she was still standing in the center of the market or not. He knew that he had a choice.

You have been gifted with free will...

The voice from the vision rang through his head, causing him to shudder. If he had free will, why did it seem that he was being pursued? Why did it seem that this mysterious woman was watching him, wanting him to see her?

Was it to acknowledge her presence?

Or was it simply an overreaction?

The next day, Cristofano sat on the same bench, just beyond the market, and looked between the pastel stucco buildings that rose from the sea.

He could see the woman from afar.

She had returned, just as she always did, at the same time. Their distant connection had become predictable.

He regretted bringing Pasquale. It seemed now that he thought he was making something out of nothing, but Cristofano couldn't help but feel his muscles tighten when he saw her. He remembered the vision. It might have been a dream, but he thought not. There were too many coincidences. There was a distant connection between them, somehow, in some way. He knew it.

He could feel it.

She was desperately trying to blend in, and he noticed her crimson hair. One of the characteristics that he always seemed to sharpen in the palette of colorful chaos which was the marketplace.

And her long, flowing black robe.

That was always unmistakable.

She reached out, picked up a large, red tomato, and brought it up to her nose. She closed her eyes.

Cristofano knew she was different, and her actions were no different from the previous days he watched her.

She only had been in town for a few days and nights it seemed, yet each day was the same. Her actions were caught by Cristofano, and then she would stand, motionless in the middle of the market as shoppers walked around her, watching him watch her. She spoke to no one unless out of necessity. Her Italian dialect appeared to be perfect. Yet there was something mysterious about her.

As Cristofano remained on the bench near the sea, he watched the mysterious woman as she finally made a purchase. She held out a small, brown satchel as the vendor placed the tomato inside. He gasped as she turned and headed in his direction, darting his head around as he peered out towards the crystalline blue sea. He could feel the beat of his heart thumping in his chest as he heard footsteps on gravel approach.

He closed his eyes.

"You have been watching me."

Her voice was deep, authoritative. About what he expected. But his mind was pierced with a picture of her opening her robe and ushering him inside, enveloping him with her warmth, but inside, the darkness enveloped him. He closed his eyes. There was a certain desolation to the blackness inside her robe. As if a chorus of wails had penetrated his ears, in a desolate crescendo which throbbed in his mind.

A flash of an oasis pierced his mind; it was a brilliant green garden filled with palms. He thought he was standing in the middle of a desert, yet there was a white mist which swirled before him and concealed his vision, as if it were a dream. But he could feel the wind blow lightly across his face, and the reality threatened to drag him back towards Salerno. He could still notice the salty sea air smell that he had always remembered. But he knew he was someplace different.

"Do not open your eyes," she commanded.

His mind revealed a group of men in robes stood in a clearing, they were speaking, he could tell, but it wasn't a language that he could understand. The men were gathered around one who wore a white robe who was speaking, yet he could not see their faces. The mist flowed at his feet, concealing the men, until he felt hands on his shoulders.

He opened his eyes and she stood in front of him, her robe clasped tightly. "Thirty pieces of silver," she said softly. "He was betrayed for just that sum."

He looked up at her.

Her eyes pierced as if silver, against her flowing red hair. He found himself speechless, as she straddled him, her black robe flowing outwards and spilling over the bench, as he felt her weight on his shoulders. "I have been watching you."

He gasped.

The woman remained shrouded in her robe and gazed downwards. He remained speechless as her eyes pierced his mind.

"Come with me," she hissed. Her hands appeared outwards from between the clasp of her robe; they were a fine ivory, far lighter than his own olive skin, and he wondered where she was from. The whispers on the dinner tables had said she was from Jerusalem, yet her skin was so light. As if the sun would pierce right through it; as if she were a walking ceramic doll; he felt her long, slender fingers, and then a sudden a buzz of electricity as she placed her hand in his.

She held a commanding presence, he could see.

And he rose from the bench as she took his hand, leading him towards her small bungalow, a small, shaded cement abode.

"Remove your shirt," she said, walking towards the small oven. She reached for several scraps of wood from a pile on the floor. As the door squeaked open, she placed the wood inside the small, dark chamber, and turned around.

Cristofano held his small, white dirty shirt, balled in his hands as she grinned. "Well aren't you just the epitome of what I am looking for," she said. "Now be the man that you so clearly are representing quite well and light the fire for me?"

Cristofano tossed his shirt on a small wooden chair and did what he was told. The accentuation of his olive skin and his taught muscularity gleamed in the fading light emanating from the windows. He felt a cool breeze blowing inwards as he worked on building the small fire.

He jumped when he felt the chill of her hands on his shoulders.

"Now then," she said. "What is the purpose of my visit, you ask? Why do you feel I have been watching you all these days?"

Cristofano turned around slowly, and she was revealed. She held her robe at her shoulders, revealing a china white torso and the rising of her breasts. "Now you know that. And I know you have been watching our kind for you entire life, am I correct?"

He nodded.

"Such a strong man you are," she said.

"I…" he stammered. "I work in the olive fields and help with the harvest."

"You are just the person we are looking for," she said. "Because I look into your mind, and I see the questioning. And the torment. You have a troubled mind, don't you?"

He stopped and watched her as she held her robe just apart, to reveal, yet also to conceal. He had held a deep fascination for her since she had arrived in the city, but now, he suspected, since she had been watching him, that she came to Salerno for the express purpose of connecting with him. Her advances weren't wantonly sexual in any means, but indescribably sensual. She ushered him to approach her, and he did.

He placed his arms around her as she pulled her robe apart, and he placed his arms around her back and she wrapped the robe around them, together.

"Now place your head on my shoulder," she said, as he felt his sex engorged and rigid. "The depth of your soul is determined by the influence of your person," she said softly into his ear, as she reached upwards and tilted his head to the side.

He cried out as he felt the pierce of her teeth and the warmth of his blood flowing downwards, spilling over his chest.

Three

RAMIEL FISHED HIS PHONE from his pocket as he brought his small, ceramic coffee cup to the sink and placed it on the stainless steel of the bowl. He heard the deep clump of footsteps and the clap of hammering above from the second floor. Perhaps they no longer felt the need to remain quiet since it was confirmed that he was awake.

The workers would still be at the house working on renovations for hours, and Geret hadn't risen yet, so he considered a day of research. There would be time, and since he had an assignment, he knew that he couldn't spend the days at Antoine's estate listening to renovation construction and waiting passively for Delia. She had wanted to continue their conversation, but in the meantime, he wanted to visit Ascension cemetery, as that was where he had been told there was a crypt that the immortals used exclusively. Perhaps there might be some guidance in that crypt, not only for the challenges that currently plagued the immortal population, but also as to Cristofano's whereabouts.

Ramiel knew the elders were wise.

Even if they had been sentenced in chains to the coffin, perhaps there might be a way that he could communicate with them. Seek their advice on how to proceed. But would they give it? Would there be a deep animosity for their chained, dark, eternal isolation?

He thought the risk could be mitigated with his prowess.

If he found a way to communicate with them, he would never release the chains.

Antoine had mentioned that the key was hanging inside the cellar door, but provided a stern warning. "There are coffins in that crypt from many immortals from generations ago who remain serving sentences. If the power of the crypt dancer was passed to you when you were transformed, and you aren't aware of it, you won't know how to wield it. And the power can betray you."

Antoine's words sent a chill down his spine as the cellar door creaked open. "I am not a crypt dancer," he said. "But I guard the crypt in this sector as I am the leader."

The memory of Antoine's words hung in his head as Ramiel pulled the hanging string, and the warm glow of an incandescent bulb yellowed the landing. Several rings of keys hung from hooks, but there was one key which stood out from among the others.

A violet amethyst crystal caught the light, and it seemed to reflect a blue aura across his face.

He reached up and stopped. *The crypt dancer will return…*

He shrugged off the voice when his phone rang. He reached into his pocket, drawing the phone up towards his ear.

"I have a letter to share with you," Delia said. "I need to return and speak with you again. I've been digging deeper into the Cristofano disappearance, but also the coffin sentences. Trying to determine how Haddon House and Queen Reynalda might be involved."

Ramiel cradled the phone to his ear as he lifted the crystal from the hook; his face shifted and he was surprised at its weight. "Involved? How so?"

"I'm trying to determine, once and for all, the witches' intentions. I'm suspecting they may have something to do with the coffin sentences. Some of their kind are immortals, you know."

"I have been told about Queen Reynalda. That she is bound there."

"And some of the others are bound and chained in the crypts. Those who are some of the most powerful and evil immortals of years past, Ramiel."

He paused for a moment. They had discussed that last night, but then, she would have an intricate investigation ahead of her given her position in the Inspiriti. "We have a multi layered problem which affects our kind," she said. "If you are thinking about going there, I must warn you against it. But I won't attempt to stop you if you do."

That, Ramiel also knew.

He held the crystal in one hand and kept the phone cradled on his shoulder as he navigated through the front door and down the steps towards Antoine's coupe. Now was the time. There was no sense in waiting, because waiting might cast the seed of doubt. He knew that going to the crypt that Antoine spoke of might not lead to finding Cristofano, but it might help in his pursuit to gain control of the Miami sector. Antoine had a lot to deal with, now that Darius had been cast back to mortality and might never return to the immortals.

The sun had started to set as Ramiel charged through the winding forested roads towards the outskirts of the city, towards Ascension. He slowed and turned onto Ascension avenue, and looked ahead. A crumbling stone wall rose from the edge of an equally untended sidewalk, covered with a shaded oak canopy. He pulled towards the side and cut the engine. Scanning the area, he looked towards the end of the street, which appeared to be a dead end.

WAXLEY MORTUARY AND FUNERAL HOME

Ramiel reached inside his pocket and touched the amethyst. Perhaps it had been Cristofano's influence in calling him an over-checker, or it might have been an innate need to feel secure in an environment that felt increasingly threatening. But he was an immortal. Cristofano's voice rang in his head, reminding him that he was not feeble, nor afraid. He was immortal, and generations old funeral homes, fallen into disrepair, would not be penetrating his thoughts.

He stood and looked up at the dark, crumbling structure, which served as a dark backdrop through the veins of trees. Antoine's instructions were to enter the cemetery through the hearse thruway; he saw a small, dirt path which cut through the overgrown foliage and split the forest. It wasn't much wider than a sidewalk, but wide enough for the hearses from the time period when this funeral home was in operation.

He jumped as he heard a creak from his left.

He shot a glance over towards the noise and stopped in his tracks.

The door was open.

He distinctly remembered it being closed when he had approached it.

At least he thought it was closed.

Was it?

He had heard stories about Waxley. But the amethyst in his pocket dictated a bigger cause.

Enter the crypt, Ramiel.

Do you have you the power? The courage to discover what lies within? Who lies in the crumbling coffins inside?

The voice reverberated through his mind.

The calling continued, like a babble which would never silence, a walk through the darkness of the forest that became eternal. But the crypt would be there, in an indiscriminate location, the crumbling stone, covered in deep, dark moss, shielded from the sunlight and shadowy in the darkness. But he knew the coffins would be inside. And the answers he sought would be bound and chained in those coffins.

It was as if it were the same as with Cristofano in the days in Paris, when he and the others in the dance company had fled the theater, when the massacre had struck without warning, mid-performance. The coffins were there as well. The secret crypts, scattered throughout the world, holding the immortals, bound to silence and desolation.

An eternity of silence.

He shuddered, reaching into his pocket, once again, touching the cool, smooth exterior of the amethyst. Why was he compelled to go to the crypt? The secret crypt which he hadn't known about until Monsignor

Harrison called him from Rome, insisting he locate the amethyst and locate the Miami crypt. That the answers he needed, the guidance that would restore an immortal stronghold in the sector, would be lying in a coffin in that crypt. There was no further instruction from Rome. "The crystal will guide you there," Monsignor Harrison had said. "Keep your mind open to all of the possibilities of the astral realm, and it will form your purpose, and your destiny."

"What about Antoine?" Ramiel asked. "Did he not know about the crypt?"

There was a moment of silence as Ramiel waited, holding the phone to his ear. "Antoine held a different purpose in the community," he said. "And now that his maker has been affected by the plague to our kind, his main directive has been to make every effort to preserve his blood ancestry. That is why I had you and Cristofano travel to America on short notice. There was no reason to keep you in Paris when I needed you in Miami."

"With all due respect, your highness, I was supposed to be here with Cristofano. He seemed fine until we arrived in New York. And then he started to exude hostility towards me."

"Hostility?"

Ramiel cleared his throat. "Yes, your highness. On the secret flight you arranged for us, he started to act resentful towards me." The monsignor's voice appeared to get more forceful, insistent.

"Resentful? How? And for what purpose?"

Ramiel took a moment to consider his answers.

Disloyalty to one's maker was one of the highest disciplinary offenses in the code. He didn't know why Cristofano would suddenly change his interactions with him, without notice or warning. He considered his actions, and his answers. "He wasn't hostile, I suppose. But the same night, after taking me here, to Antoine's estate, he told me he had something to do. To take care of. He left out the front doors into the night, and never returned."

"I see," Monsignor Harrison said.

Ramiel took a breath, held it for a moment, and released it as quietly as he could. The monsignor was taking a long time to add to his response.

"If he left you," he said. "And abandoned a specific directive from the Inspiriti, you know the ramifications."

Ramiel nodded. "Yes."

"Never mind it," the monsignor said. "I will take care of locating Cristofano on my end. I need you to focus on getting the amethyst from the estate and locating the crypt. As I said before, the crystal will guide you there. Open your mind and let it."

"Agreed, I will take care of it, your highness."

"Very good," he said. "Those coffins in there are centuries old. That crypt has been around longer than the city has been incorporated. A lot of answers there."

Ramiel stood in the forest beyond the mortuary. He turned, looked at the shadow of the Waxley Funeral Home in the background, and then looked outwards towards Ascension Cemetery. *The crystal will guide you there...*

The monsignor's voice rang through the silence as he headed through the mounds of dirt and empty graves. The moon was high, casting a pale glow against the headstones. The crystal would find the way, it said. He felt it's cool reassurance in his pocket once again. And then he proceeded, walking through the dug up graves in Ascension, his shadow cast a darkness which moved throughout the pale moonlight. Through the trees beyond the graves, there was a clearing. And in the clearing was a stone set of stairs, leading downwards into the Earth.

Just like he had seen in Paris.

Equally weathered, nearly identical, aged and hidden among the decayed brush and towering dark veins of the forest, which reached upwards towards the night sky.

The elders of this sector, no doubt.

There would be those immortals in crumbling coffins, who might have been lying in chains, bound in silence for centuries; before Miami had been incorporated as a city, before the cosmopolitan skyscrapers had dominated the landscape, the mansions and yachts. Before the boisterous nightlife, and before Antoine had developed and governed the sector for the Inspiriti, this crypt had been there.

You will approach...

He froze.

The voice of a woman; deep and forceful.

You will approach and have the power to release me...

The wind strengthened in the trees, as the foliage rustled. The moonlight faded as clouds raced across the dark sky. His heart quickened as he brought his hands up to his chest. Monsignor Harrison would not send him into danger, would he?

He stood at the base of the steps as the winds tore through the forest. He looked at the crumbling stone stairs, leading downwards into shadows, below the earth, towards a door; nestled between concrete walls, the dark moss reached across the stone and towards the door. Ramiel thought the door was mysterious, somehow inviting. His feeling of dread was replaced by curiosity, as his heart softened. He stopped in front of the rusted spires, which covered the glass and peered inside. He saw nothing.

The smudges of age concealed the darkness inside, yet he knew their ancestors would be lying there, perhaps listening.

Four

RAMIEL AWAKENED later in Antoine's room at the estate, in the large bed with the wooden spires, as the warmth of the sun reached inwards through the drawn curtains. Had last night been a horrendous dream? He swung his legs out over the bed, wondering what time it might be. He stood, and padded over to the window, stretching. It looked to be in the middle of the day. The sun was high in the sky.

The was a light knock on the door. "Ramiel?"

It was Geret's muffled voice.

He would be waiting with the car, as he'd instructed him to do yesterday. There was much on the agenda, there had to be more investigation into the coven, and the day appeared to be nearly half over.

Ramiel turned around as the door clicked open. Geret had the door open a small sliver, and peered his head through the crack.

"Delia is waiting for you in the foyer," Geret said.

Ramiel sighed and slapped his head. He had forgotten that Delia was scheduled to return to continue their discussion about Cristofano. Usually she would call before coming, which Geret confirmed that she had, and he said that he told her that Ramiel had planned on visiting the coven, but she said to wait. Their conversation was far too important.

After Ramiel hastily readied himself in the master bathroom, he headed through the foyer towards the front parlor. Delia was waiting, sitting on the main sofa in the center of the room. Geret had prepared a fire and some wine.

"I was thinking about visiting the coven today," Ramiel said as he took a chair across from her. Geret approached him and handed him a glass of red wine.

Delia set her wine glass on the table with a slight clink and looked up at him. Her eyebrows were raised, as she watched him. Ramiel knew that she was seeking more, but that was all he had thought about, at least when he had blurted it out to her. After a few moments of silence, and as Delia sank back into the sofa, he added to his statement. "I believe the witches have a deeper connection with the immortal community than what most believe on the forefront," he said.

Delia nodded. "I see," she said. "And how have you come to this conclusion?"

Ramiel shifted his posture and attempted to clear his throat, even though he didn't need to. He noticed that Delia had crossed her arms and could tell that he was stalling. "If I visit the coven, I think I can gain insight into Cristofano's disappearance."

His words hung over the room like a heavy blanket. Delia sat in silence on the opposite sofa, her lips pursed, glaring at him. The crackle and pop of the fire remained, along with a light rumble of thunder. A clock ticked in the foyer as Ramiel felt his pulse quicken. She had to be furious. Haddon House had always been considered off-limits, for as long as the Inspiriti knew about it.

Delia finally spoke. "We are not going to revisit the release of LaDonna Mastuer," she said. There was an edge to her voice. "But I recommend *against* going to Haddon House, Ramiel. That is the lion's den, I can assure you. The witches…they have power, Ramiel. Some that we immortals don't yet fully understand. And the magic and spells…"

"Are they more powerful than we are?"

"Their powers are different, Ramiel. Complex, and planet driven. I can't say that they are an enemy. But when a member of the coven receives the dark gift, it becomes an entirely different matter."

Ramiel looked down to his lap and clasped his hands together on his legs. Delia was right. Cristo had said that the coven was a powerful, unknown gathering of magical people, and that the understanding was limited. But Cristo also said that he felt that LaDonna and Queen Reynalda could both become allies to the immortals, if convinced. That was the hard part.

"Are you planning on visiting Haddon House to find out what happened to Cristo?" Ramiel looked up from his fidgeting as Delia pressed for further conversation. He nodded.

Thoughts of Cristofano drifted into Ramiel's head, tiny fragments of energy which danced through his mind, with determination, and a method of formative memories. They both had had formative life experiences which led them down the path of the quest for immortality. And when both Ramiel and Cristofano had been still mortal, they each felt the longing within themselves, the burning desire that something else was out there. That the physical realm wasn't the only state of existence. "Cristofano told me that in order to overcome a greater enemy, we must seek to understand them because we don't fully understand their purpose."

Delia crossed her legs and placed her hands on her knee, but did not follow up with another question. Ramiel knew that the discussion would take a turn towards the supernatural, because at that point, it was more about the immortals. He hoped she saw that. And most likely she did. He didn't bother speaking hastily, but rather took a slow sip of wine, watching her through the bulbous glass. He could see her blurred image through the center of the glass as he drank the maroon liquid. She was most likely listening to his thoughts.

Ramiel had his devout Catholic parents, yet he had a different philosophy of how the astral realm existed. There was the link to the immortals, and, to Ramiel, it seemed as though it was written in his destiny. That he and Cristofano were meant to have met, and intertwine their lives from a moment millennia in the past, when the doctrine had reportedly been written.

"*The Code of the Immortals?*" Ramiel asked after they had discussed the doctrine.

Delia nodded as Geret appeared in the doorway.

"I...remember first meeting him...Cristofano..."

"Close your eyes, Ramiel," Delia said. "When you do, I will be able to guide you through your memories."

And then he closed his eyes.

A blast of wind flowed past him as he opened his eyes to darkness. This was the moment, the one he had always heard of. There was something special about Delia. And minds. His mind, his thoughts, he felt her guiding hand. There was a vision which slowly came into focus; wisps of light which penetrated the darkness as they soared past him.

But he felt he was disembodied.

Adrift of the physical, now in the supernatural. Her guiding hand, and thoughts. Dreams which transformed into nightmares, but never entered the physical realm.

Do you see what I want you to see?

He concentrated on the vision.

He covered his mouth as the stench of decay permeated the darkness. *Will the vision clear? Is this where Cristofano is now?*

Thrashing limbs in treacherous, angry waters flashed before him, as waves cascaded towards the loneliness of desolate sands. The call of winds blew through unseen treetops, amidst the call of serpents and hissing, slithering demons.

A firebomb exploded outwards in the darkness as Ramiel felt his pulse quicken. "Delia?!" he called, but was only answered by darkness.

The vision cleared.

He stood on a clearing of sand, surrounded by darkness and raging fires; at the center was a massive steel gate, rusted with age, leading onwards to a deeper state of agony. He cowered as one of the fires exploded next to him, igniting the sand clearing.

Ramiel, Ramiel…what do you see? Is anyone out there?

He slapped the flames on his foot yet felt nothing as the bright orange fire extinguished. No physical pain. She had mentioned that. But the stench was overpowering. And after the silence came the wails. He could hear them in the distance. As he looked through the iron gates, back towards a darkness that appeared deeper than he could ever imagine, he could hear the screams. The wails of countless souls, tormented souls; the wails were coming from below.

But the gates remained closed.

Someone was out there.

He could hear them.

A shuffling in the darkness; a heaviness, a feeling of the rumbling of quakes, yet there was no discernable land beyond the small clearing of sand, illuminated by the flickering of the surrounding fires. But as he looked beyond, only darkness. He reached forward and grasped the gates, grunting with all of his strength, yet they remained closed.

The wails became louder as he released the gates.

Do not let fear bring you unwanted inhibitions, Ramiel. Move forward. You have the strength to proceed.

"Cristo!" he called out through the wailing screams.

But there was no answer.

My destiny calls you. It wills you forward. You will find a way. Ignore the chorus of wails. The screams and the darkness.

For through them you will find me.

The crypt dancer.

Five

RAMIEL THOUGHT about the past; when he was still a mortal. In the days before he had met Cristofano, before his destiny had been laid out before him, in a path of stepping stones, reaching outwards throughout an angry, endless sea; towards the horizon, farther than he was able to see.

It was years after Monsignor Harrison allegedly noticed Ramiel peeking and eavesdropping on his conversation, when Ramiel was still an altar boy, when Cristofano, a newly transformed immortal, took the journey from Solerno to Rome by train. Cristofano had received word from *The Inspiriti* that there was a new interest in a human, a mortal who had become infatuated with their kind.

Ramiel's eavesdropping had been frequent and warranted, as he discovered that the human in whom *The Inspiriti* was interested, was him. Or perhaps Monsignor Harrison allowed him to learn of their interest. Ramiel wasn't formally informed about Cristofano's visit to the cathedral, yet he managed to discover that another young priest would be joining them on the same day as he stood just in front of the altar, as he heard the echo of the atrium doors opening.

There wasn't a planned service on that day, and he turned in curiosity.

He watched from across the worship area in the darkness as Cristofano walked through the soaring wooden doors into the atrium of the cathedral, his silhouette lighted by the daylight which emanated from behind. Ramiel saw Monsignor Harrison padding through the pews towards the main doors.

The monsignor's heavyset frame waddled back and forth in the black vestments he was wearing. He looked up and waved enthusiastically. "Cristo! So long since you've come! Welcome, sir! Bon giorno!"

Ramiel sat quietly in the front pew, turning and watching, and hoped that his black cassock would conceal him in the darkened worship area. At the other end of the cathedral, he watched as the monsignor and Cristofano exchanged pleasantries.

Cristofano nodded. "You have sent for me to investigate a mortal for inclusion?"

Monsignor Harrison quickly composed himself. "Yes, well Claret only brought me here when I had just awakened. I wasn't made aware of any true assignment until recently."

Ramiel watched as they approached the office at the rear of the pews and Monsignor Harrison entered the dim light which emanated from his office door and nodded enthusiastically. "Yes! Yes! It's so rare that we are gifted with one of her direct descendants! A true pleasure indeed!"

But Cristofano's response had been inaudible.

Ramiel stood and walked in silence towards the edge of the pews, along the side with the stained glass windows. He had to get closer to them. He could hear them speaking, yet only was only hearing part of the conversation. It was about him. He knew. And if this strange, new visitor to the chapel was the one immortal who would be recruiting him for transformation, if the visitor was the one who would be enamoring him with their charisma, and tutoring him in their ways, he wanted to maintain an advantage by listening…even if he only thought they didn't know he was eavesdropping.

Ramiel maintained his silent approach and hid behind a stone column. He peeked around the rounded edge near the pews and watched them.

Cristofano stopped and looked at the monsignor. The priest's smile was broad and his teeth caught the light which filtered from behind him, for a moment while he turned his head. They headed towards the open office door, which cast a glow outwards towards the pews.

Cristofano stopped short of Monsignor Harrison's office. The monsignor dashed inside and started grabbing papers off of the desk hastily. "Please!" he said. "Do come in! Can I get you an espresso? Or perhaps a chianti instead?"

Cristofano shook his head and took one of the small wooden chairs in front of the monsignor's desk. Monsignor Harrison sat in his chair slowly, placing a pile of papers down on the floor. "So, your highness. You are visiting us for Ramiel, correct? From the message I had sent to Solerno?"

Cristofano nodded. "Claret sent me. You should have been well aware of that, shouldn't you?"

Monsignor Harrison cleared his throat again as Cristofano shuffled in his chair and crossed his legs. And then the silence in the office became awkward. Monsignor Harrison shifted again in his chair and tugged on his collar. "Well then, your highness, I must confess."

Cristofano looked up from his fidgeting and directly at the monsignor.

"I am ill prepared," Monsignor Harrison said. "I brought Ramiel on board because of his interest in Catholicism, but yes, I do know that he has expressed an interest in our organization…"

Cristofano raised his eyes and looked at Monsignor Harrison. "Are you sure of what his interests truly are?"

He scoffed. "I – I'm not sure…"

Cristofano slammed his palms against the arms of the chair. "But you didn't consider the instructions that Claret gave you?!"

Monsignor Harrison leaned back and raised his palms. "Now, now, Cristofano. There has been nothing from Claret or any of the overall governing sector saying that Ramiel was a mortal of interest. Nothing whatsoever."

Cristofano leaned back and scoffed. "Yet members of your own staff – and those who are right here in this chapel with you – have reported to Claret that Ramiel has been approaching them with questions. With knowledge he should know nothing *about.*"

"True, true. But a mortal of interest?" Monsignor Harrison leaned forward as Cristofano pierced him with his stare. "How could he know these things? He has been told nothing."

"Claret has been quite specific about her intentions," Cristofano said. "And Ramiel has been observed for years. It's time for him to be transformed, don't you think? That's why they have sent me, your highness. I've been chosen for Ramiel. He's been studied and I am the best fit for him."

The darkness enveloped Ramiel as the heavy office door closed quietly; a click echoed against the soaring ceilings.

Ramiel released his breath and leaned back.

He sat in the closest pew to the office door, and stared at the artistic murals and windows ahead of him on the side of the church, marking out the figures against the darkness. He took a breath and sighed. That man, that immortal, Cristofano, he was the visitor. There had been several conversations over the years when he had been at the Sistine; from the time he listened when he was an altar boy, polishing the pews, when he learned that there was an immortal named Darius Sauvage, who the mysterious woman, Claret, had wanted to recruit a new member, Ramiel realized that there was more going on below, in the catacombs, than most realized.

The immortals, though, were a group that brought him deep fascination and unexplainable intrigue.

Who were they?

Why were many humans enamored with them, yet others despised them?

He turned and watched the door.

They hadn't emerged, and now, he was shut out of the conversation.

He stood, navigated around the pew and into the side aisle, and took a few steps towards the heavy, wooden door on the back wall. There was nothing he could lose, he told himself. If he was unwelcome, the monsignor would tell him to leave. Even possibly have him excommunicated if he would be known to witness conversations which were classified for The Inspiriti.

But Ramiel believed they didn't know that he was listening. And already knew a great deal about the immortals, and The Inspiriti, and their plans for Cristofano. There were too many conversations that he coincidentally was able to listen to from afar, apparently undetected.

He approached the door.

He heard muffled voices inside for a few moments, and then they stopped. Did they know he was out there? His heart pounded as he heard heavy footsteps approach the door.

The door opened and Monsignor Harrison stood in the threshold.

His heavy stature was a silhouette in the light that spilled from inside the small room, and Ramiel noticed his stringy hair rising up from his expansive forehead. "Ramiel!" he exclaimed. "We've been expecting you."

His mouth dropped open as the monsignor smiled and nodded.

"This was a business visit," he said, reaching out his arm and inviting Ramiel in. "But you are welcome to come in and listen. Observe."

The openness confused him.

Had the conversations that he observed been planted specifically for him to discover? He slowly approached the room as he looked at the young man sitting in the chair opposite an expansive, paper-strewn desk and who promptly stood.

"I am Cristofano," he said as if he were simply stating a matter of fact.

He bowed slightly, and Ramiel noticed his dark hair fall forward in front of his shoulders. He was taller, about equally muscular, and almost devoid of personality. Ramiel had overheard earlier conversations where he'd heard that Claret had assigned him to the church to observe Ramiel's potential for the gift, and Ramiel assumed that when Claret sent him for an assignment, he must have been strictly professional. Cristofano's eyes suggested a deep, sensual personality. As he gazed deeply into Ramiel's eyes, he gestured his arm out to sit in the chair next to his, across from the desk. Ramiel cautiously headed across the small office, as Cristofano's eyes pierced him with every step.

Monsignor Harrison picked up on this and regained his composure.

He awkwardly cleared his throat and stopped just a few feet from Cristofano, as Ramiel slowly sat. "I know I am older than you in tradition," Monsignor Harrison said. "But I am from a different bloodline, of course, and Claret significantly outranks me. So I beg your mercy, your highness."

Ramiel watched as Cristofano sat. He turned his head towards Ramiel another time and smiled wanly, before returning his attention forward.

The monsignor sat at his expansive desk, leaning forward, watching the two young men. "I am somewhat stricken that I am sitting here, looking at both of you sitting next to each other, across from my desk."

Ramiel raised his eyebrows.

The monsignor planned this.

Cristofano nodded and turned to face Ramiel. "We are being paired with one another. I have a deep interest in the seminary, as you have, and we will serve the community together here."

Ramiel adjusted himself in the chair. "But…you…are you ordained?"

Cristofano looked over at Monsignor Harrison, who waved his hand outwards. Cristofano cleared his throat, and turned back to Ramiel. "I am not. But I am being paired with you. We will take a spiritual journey together. And artistic journey. I've been selected to be connected with you."

Monsignor Harrison leaned back and clapped his hands, rubbing them together. "Okay then!" As he talked he leaned forward to each of them. "Ramiel, you will be paired with Cristofano. You will have a spiritual connection with each other, I predict."

And then he focused on Cristofano. "I will not stand in your way."

Monsignor Harrison had given Ramiel the key.

After the meeting had concluded, and Cristofano had left the chapel, indicating that he would soon return, the monsignor began his nightly duties and closed the door.

Ramiel again found himself inside the darkened cathedral; his choices, however, were evident and clearly laid before him.

He could feel the cold metal of the key, as if he was drawing his hand deeper into the large pocket of his flowing, black cassock; he had held the key on his person every day since Monsignor Harrison had entrusted him with it. But this had been years after the day when he overheard Claret speaking with the monsignor while Ramiel was still an altar boy. Years had progressed while he was a member of the church.

He could still hear the choir practicing in the distance as their chorus of angelic voices reverberated against the rafters.

As a young man, during the days when his tutelage had developed him, and as he stood in the Cathedral, many years later, he stood between the pews, where he had hidden and listened to Monsignor Harrison, and looked again at the closed door.

He lowered his head and opened his palm.

The key glistened in the light.

Monsignor Harrison had placed trust in Ramiel, but Ramiel knew that there was a mysteriousness about the entire situation. Was he being recruited? If so, for what? And for what purpose?

The Monsignor was a simple mystery; the man failed to grow older. For that reason only, Ramiel suspected that the monsignor was an immortal. But had their despised kind invaded the church? Were the sacred sacraments at risk?

There was a simple mystery that fascinated him about the other members, and those who descended to the bowels of the chapel, down into the corridors of which Ramiel still had yet to explore. But he would always watch, as they would emerge through the door, and he noted that all appeared eternally youthful; some were clearly older than others, but all had a definite resistance to aging, as if each were frozen chronologically.

Ramiel held the key in the pocket of his long, flowing black cassock; he would always swear to himself that, after services on that particular day, when the worshippers had cleared, and the choir had practiced from far, he would draw the key from his pocket, and look down at it. He would always admire the key as it glistened from the light above: a large, silver skeleton key; larger than his open palm.

The mystery would be solved, he had hoped, from that simple, yet profoundly complex object.

But Monsignor Harrison had given it to him so long ago, it seemed. He had been holding it since that day, wondering when he might muster up the courage to open the door and venture inside. The key; an invitation of the highest order. He knew. The monsignor entrusted him with it.

And now, as he stood a mere stone's throw from the door, he took a breath. The time was now. No one was around to witness his curiosities; no one would probably care if they had seen him. He wore the cassock now; he had earned the privilege to enter through that door.

He held it just shy of the brass knob and waited, and listened.

There was no approach of footsteps.

He could hear the faint music emanating from the choir chamber across the cathedral for their evening practice. The rest of the church remained empty. Evening services were now long over, the Vatican was moving towards its Sunday traditions, and the seemingly silent slumber of the warm Rome afternoon as night slowly settled in.

He inserted the key, jiggled the knob, and drew the door open, outwards to darkness, taken aback by a blast of dark, cool air against his face.

He let his eyes adjust to the darkness, yet could not see much through the black void. From the light flowing in from the chapel, he could see stone stairs leading downwards into total blackness. The walls were plain, stone, reminiscent of a secret passage.

He did not know when he finally opened the once forbidden, mysterious door at the side of the chapel, but Ramiel was destined to meet an immortal named Cristofano, who was being recruited from Solerno to travel to Rome and join the staff at the Sistine Chapel.

But Ramiel had no inclination of the monsignor's intentions or the reason behind the assignment.

For he had never been told of another man of the cloth which he'd be paired. Although Monsignor Harrison had told him on several occasions that there would be a mentor assigned to him to guide him, Ramiel had never been told specifically told about Cristofano.

Cristofano, however, had been told of Ramiel quite early on.

When Ramiel was still an altar boy, hiding between the pews, watching Monsignor Harrison's and the mysterious woman's conversation about Darius in front of the door *of which must always remain closed*, he thought the monsignor caught of glimpse of Ramiel ducking between the pews in the corner of his eyes. He thought that his vestments were likely unmistakable in the darkness of the worship area, especially when dark clouds had permeated the outdoors. But the stairs led downwards before him; and he stood on the small landing, holding the door outwards with his arm, letting the fading, grey light spill inwards, but it revealed very little. The darkness, the black void was calling him.

The only way out is farther in…

There was a certain mysteriousness of the darkness, the blackness which surrounded him. But no matter how he tried to see what was before him, there was an utter denial. The change he sought…through his entrance to the unknown…was buried within his inactive thoughts.

He gasped as his heart pounded in his chest.

The door had closed; the darkness enveloped him and he looked down. The stone floor on which he stood disappeared. He watched as he saw the angry white crests of ferocious crashing waves against towering dark rocks. He cried out as he sank, downwards; he could smell the musty salty sea air, feel the race of the cold wind against his face…and the cries of desperation below.

He splashed in the water as the chill felt like knives driving into his skin. The water was putrid and stank of excrement.

Welcome to Hell! an unseen voice hissed.

He dragged himself up on the large, black rock, tearing himself away from the vice grip of the limbs. The torment. The pain of isolation. His eyes were wide with desperation. Had he died? Had he gone to Hell? Were the thrashing limbs the genesis of demons?

He collapsed on his back, flopping his arms to the side, panting heavily. He still stank of the sea. The wails still cried from the sea as the crash of the waves sprayed upwards against the sides of the rock.

He snapped his eyes open and raised his head as he felt a tremble on the ground. Looking ahead, he saw a seemingly endless, dark sea; he could see the pasty thrashing limbs reaching upwards in desperation, as the quaking continued.

A deep, grating, rhythmic voice penetrated: *You…are…destined for this…*

He propped himself up and leaned forward. There was a shadow in the distance. A shadow which appeared to be hovering back and forth…out in the distant sea…there was a presence which sensed his small body lying on the dark rock in the midst of an endless sea.

He gasped.

His mouth was suddenly dry and he grew desperately thirsty. "Water…" he croaked.

The waves continued their angry assault against the rocks as he felt the chill of the spray and the stink of excrement. But his eyes remained open as he watched the shadowy figure out in the distance.

You will always have plenty, the deep voice boomed. *You will drink forever of my blood…my sea of debauchery and poison will grasp your eternal soul for all of eternity!*

Six

RAMIEL AWAKENED and gasped for his breath.

He lay on the small landing, his feet splayed upwards on the first few steps which led up to the small stone floor, and he rested his head against the cool concrete wall. Had he fallen? Was he injured? He reached up and felt the back of his head, drew his hand around and it was dry. He leaned back and took a deep breath, closing his eyes. It wasn't too late to head back out into the chapel. To walk into the atrium and head out the front door. Monsignor Harrison would most likely still be in his office completing the weekly financials; the door to his office was closed anyway.

He opened his eyes and looked at the door.

The tiny, sliver of light from beneath the heavy wood illuminated the stone floor, yet provided little resistance the darkness. He shivered as the violent images remained in his mind...*the only way out is farther in!*

What kind of organization was this 'Inspiriti'?

Why did he seemingly lose consciousness once he entered the mysterious, darkened stairwell? Why did he have a vision that clearly was sinister…and evil?

Everything he had been told about *The Inspiriti* was encouraging; that is was an organization of enlightenment, and loyalty. One of purpose and inclusion, while remaining exclusive. His thoughts drifted to Cristofano, the young man who exhibited a desire to learn the ways of the cloth; he could see his lanky, muscular arms crossed when they had sat across from the monsignor, discussing the purpose of Cristo's visit.

Ramiel chose to press forward.

Because being in this church, with these enigmatic immortal creatures, may have drawn him in further towards their proposition of *the dark gift* ; he may be past a point of no return.

He stood at the base of the narrow stairwell and peered downwards. Darkness concealed his vision, but a tiny sliver of light emanated from below, a fragment of illumination. It most certainly was a door, he thought.

But what was on the other side of the door?

He reached above, but felt nothing save cool, damp stones with rough edges. And a musty smell to the air.

Nothing on the wall. No light, it seemed. He reached outwards and felt the cool stone walls, and steadied himself. If he was going to descend the stairs, and head towards the light, now was the time.

He who walks from the light towards the darkness, a destiny of desolation shall endure…

And then he paused.

The voice spoke as if it were the casting of a father in his mind, and as he carefully navigated the stone stairwell, gaining distance and approaching the sliver of light which shone across the lower landing and across to the faded paint on the wall, there was, it seemed, a warning.

There is no return once entering…

He paused.

Had this been the proper venture? Monsignor Harrison had given him the key. And told him that he had earned the right to go below. And the Monsignor had also said that he could do it in his own time. At his own pace, and with his own free will.

"Man was given free will," Monsignor Harrison had told him, in the past, after the daily services had concluded, when he was a novice priest. "One of the greatest gifts from God." Ramiel stood at the pulpit and folded the big, heavy Bible together as Monsignor Harrison descended the steps which led downwards towards the front pews, walking through soaring golden sunbeams which illuminated the church with light.

"And you, Ramiel, have free will as well, in what I am offering you."

The path towards darkness is paved with the bones of misfortune…

Ramiel shifted his face and lifted the heavy Bible in the crook of his arm and followed the Monsignor. "What is it exactly that you're offering me, your grace?"

Monsignor Harrison stood in the aisle and turned back to face Ramiel. "Well the keys to the kingdom, of course." He smiled and winked, letting out a small chuckle. As he headed towards the back of the cathedral, his voice reverberated against the soaring ceilings. "You just let me know when you are ready."

The monsignor disappeared into the atrium as the rear doors closed with a deep echo.

Ramiel stood at the base of the Altar, wincing at the weight of the heaviness of the massive Bible in his left arm, as the burn in his muscles took over. He knew. The Monsignor knew what Ramiel had always thought was a dark, distant secret. Yet he had never spoken a word of his curiosities about some of the members of the clergy who appeared never to age during his tenure. They never appeared a day older; never fell ill, and rarely made appearances during morning hours.

And they would be the ones who would always catch their eyes towards his direction, over the years, from when he had been an altar boy, and carried one of the heavy brass candle holders in the procession, to when he was promoted to carrying the golden crucifix, and to his early days in the priesthood.

There was always something mysterious about the members who would enter the door. A piercing stare, a knowing glance. As if they knew. As if they knew that Ramiel had been a chosen one, perhaps chosen by Monsignor Harrison, but for what purpose, Ramiel hadn't fully understood. And then, there was the key which the Monsignor had given him in full confidence. That Ramiel would keep what he was to discover in the bowels beneath the Sistine Chapel a secret; one that he would take with him to his grave, forever.

But then, at the base of the landing, after carefully navigating the dark, stone stairwell, he stood in front of the closed door. He looked down, and could scarcely make out his feet from the sliver of light that emanated from below the door. He closed his eyes and listened. There were muffled voices emanating from the other side of the door, but he couldn't determine what was being discussed.

There will be no return...

He reached out slowly and grasped the heavy, metallic door knob, and held his breath.

The chatter faded away.

Enter the door and enter the darkness...from whence there shall be no return...

Bright lighting flooded the small stairwell and Ramiel held his arm up over his eyes. As his eyes adjusted, he slowly lowered his arm and took a single step forward. A long, empty corridor wound gently around towards the distance.

The voices, it seemed, must have been part of his imagination, perhaps? A projection of the voice within his head? But what he heard in the hallway was desolate silence. And the eerie call of mystery, shrouded in a cascade of closed wooden doors, lining the stone exterior walls, each containing something, that much he knew, but something that Monsignor Harrison chose to protect. And to keep a secret, of which the penance for divulging would be a swift and final damnation.

The key drew heavy on his pocket as he made his way into the center of the corridor, and stood, watching the hallway watching him, waiting to be explored, wanting to draw him in deeper...

The only way out is farther in!

But that was years ago.

And Ramiel had only known when Monsignor Harrison had explained to him what that conversation was about, which he had witnessed back in the days when he was a new altar boy. Ramiel remembered knocking on Monsignor Harrison's heavy mahogany office door.

The knock reverberated across the soaring ceilings of the chapel with deep thuds.

"Enter."

The Monsignor's voice was muffled, yet authoritative. Ramiel was then new to the cloth; his altar days were behind him, but he had yet to graduate to the mass. The heavy door creaked open slowly, and Monsignor Harrison sat in the middle of an expansive, dark wood desk, in the middle of a small, smoky studio. He hovered over the desk, as a massive Bible stood next to him as he furiously wrote on a large sheet of parchment paper.

Ramiel cleared his throat.

"I know why you're here," Monsignor Harrison said, without looking up from his work. Ramiel heard a clock ticking in the background but could not locate it.

"I…" and then Ramiel paused. He thought the sound of his own voice seemed small, tinny. Grossly inexperienced, it seemed. He could feel the beads of sweat form on his forehead.

Monsignor Harrison let out an exasperated sigh. He looked up at Ramiel and removed his glasses. "I have told you before, Ramiel. If you wish to enter the door, you must be sworn to *absolute secrecy*. There will be others, that is for certain. Others who you will see below the chapel in those corridors. But what you will *see* and *hear* will be far more important to guard with your life than wondering who gains access."

Ramiel sat on one of the small wooden side chairs across from the Monsignor's expansive desk. Their eyes locked as the Monsignor appeared to be studying him. At least that's what Ramiel thought. But the elder sat back in his high back chair, and took a breath. "Well then, Ramiel. Why are you disrupting my work?"

"You have my word," Ramiel said. "If you give me the key…I will guard it with all my being."

Monsignor Harrison sighed. "Very well then, leave me please."

Ramiel stood slowly as Monsignor Harrison returned to his work. The elder said nothing as he turned and headed back towards the worship area; and as he headed forward down the center aisle of dark wooden pews, he turned towards the right and saw the door. Why it was inside the church remained a mystery. And why Monsignor Harrison even presided in a role of authority was another question which seemed to lack an answer.

But as Ramiel stood in the stark corridor below the chapel, he hoped that the answers to his questions might lie behind one of the closed doors that lined the exterior wall. He reached into the pocket of his long, flowing black cassock, and held the key in his hand. It was the key to the kingdom, Monsignor Harrison had said. But what kingdom lies in the bowels of Vatican City?

And what purpose warranted the secrecy?

Ramiel caught his breath as he heard the click of a lock in the distance. He shot around. The door was closed. He lunged forward and grasped the handle. "Damn!" he slapped his thigh and spun around, leaning his back against the wall. He scanned the corridor, yet it remained empty and silent. His chest was thumping as he felt a stream of sweat glide down his cheek.

He dared not call out.

But who was on the other side of the door? He turned his head to the left as the cool stone rubbed against his cheek. The door was closed. Locked. He drew his breath in and listened. Could there be footsteps ascending the stairs?

But he heard nothing.

He looked down in his hand. The key. A wave of relief washed through him as he exhaled. He carefully placed the key back into his pocket as a door creaked open in the unseen distance of the long, winding corridor. He snapped his head in the direction of the door as his heart thumped and throat tightened.

He was either going to face what was down there, or he was going to use the key. Monsignor Harrison had told him that the choice was his, but once he made the decision, there would be no return.

"Hello?" His voiced cracked and sounded tinny against the reverberation of the stones. He paused and listened, and wondered if there would be an answer.

And then he heard footsteps.

The sharp clap and echo of what could only be heels on concrete, getting closer, determined, and approaching, yet still out of sight. His heart pounded as the clapping steps came closer, and he clamped his eyes shut. *The only way out is farther in…*

The steps approached as he held his eyes tight, the sweat dripping from the sides of his head. His face felt hot and flushed as his chest pounded. And then the footsteps stopped right in front of him.

"They are ready for you now."

He had heard that woman's voice before. He knew it sounded familiar. And as the steps moved beyond where he stood, he slowly turned his head around and opened his eyes. The woman did not acknowledge him, but her voice had haunted him for years.

I do not want Darius to enter these chambers. I do not want him to leave Paris. Is that understood?

As she drew a gleaming key from her purse and slowly opened the door, Ramiel caught a glimpse of her flowing black coat and crimson red hair as she disappeared through the doorway.

Seven

THERE HAD BEEN A TIME when Claret did not wonder why *The Inspiriti* had chosen their secret dwelling to be underneath Vatican City in Rome; yet there had been a dream when she had been sleeping, the once forever-sleep in the coffin, in the graveyard to which she would always return, and sleep, close her eyes to nothingness hoping to be pierced by night thoughts, only to arise and awaken once again three days later like the same Christ she had known from her days in Jerusalem.

Her connection to the cup had been bestowed upon her when she had still been a child, back in the days when she would hide behind the flowing branches of the olive trees in Gethsemane, when she would listen to the men in the garden. They would gather there each evening, especially as the time drew near to the crucifixion. But it was the cup, and the power, that she sought, and gained…and then she found the gift; bestowed upon her when she had grown into a young woman, and as she matured her hair turned the color of blood, and some of the immortals had deemed that was a curse from her theft of the Christ cup.

But she paid it no mind.

And when she discovered her manipulation of time, she quickly rose to power in the immortals. Her unique gift allowed her to govern myriad sects of immortals, across oceans and throughout the expanse of time, for she had been rumored to be the oldest of the immortals. But those were rumors which permeated the immortal communities from the early days.

During the era when she was heavily involved in the operations in Rome, her position of stature was secured and solidified in the immortal community, yet conversations with Monsignor Harrison in the small chapel office proved that he always remained an adversary. "Do not lecture me!" he said. "I have the entire community under control!"

She balled her fists on her hips. "Darius remains without a successor. His bloodline will die with him if he commits any sort of crime against the immortals. And it seems that he has been quite volatile since he was a human. But then, that would make sense, wouldn't it?"

Monsignor Harrison raised his head as Claret fished a long, white cigarette from a brass clasped holder. She flicked the lighter, drew in, and exhaled a cloud of smoke. "Darius met with Madame Arsenault just recently, as you know. She was hauled away by an angry mob but Darius escaped. They didn't even acknowledge him, thankfully." She stood and circled the chairs across from the Monsignor's desk, as she continued to draw on her lengthy cigarette. "I sent Madame to inform Darius that he needed to have a successor. A son, preferably. But at least a daughter."

Monsignor Harrison sat back in his chair and scoffed. "What is the significance of a son?"

She looked down and glared at him. "I am the eldest, am I not?"

He shook his head slowly.

"And I don't need any others who will challenge me for that role," she said. She sat back in the chair. "Delia has been a thorn in my side for centuries."

"Yet you created her."

She shook her head and tossed her cigarette on the floor. She let out an exasperated sigh. A plume of smoke rose up from the thick, plush maroon carpet, as she stamped a heavy black boot and ground it down.

"That will require a substantial cleaning fee," Monsignor Harrison said.

Claret leaned over the desk. She slammed her palms down. "Delia does not understand her place in this community. And you...as my governor...must not grant her any exceptions! She must continue to abide by the rules of this organization. I may have created her, yes, but she has been rebellious ever since. My bloodline is loyal. My bloodline does what is expected of them. You understand that, don't you?"

Monsignor Harrison nodded. "Of course. And I will keep her under control, your highness. Now what about Darius?"

She took a breath and exhaled heavily. She shook her head as she grasped the heavy brass doorknob. "There is one out in Badulla that Darius should evaluate. A coffee harvester in Sri Lanka. He seems to show some promise."

"In Sri Lanka?"

She nodded. "His name is Antoine Nagevesh. He has a certain connection to our world. But Darius would have to be sent to transform him. He's still young. It may not take much convincing. But Mr. Nagevesh is quite intriguing. A prostitute for the entertainment of tourists."

"What is his connection?" Monsignor Harrison asked.

"Antoine has a gift," she said. "A cerebral connection to the Astral plane. There's been a selection since his birth, it seems. And there are others, Monsignor. Numerous humans around the world who have a destiny of earthbound immortality. And advancement to the Baal. We must locate them. We must strengthen our kind."

"And then I will be sure that Darius is instructed to head to Sri Lanka."

She nodded as she opened the door. "He must go. If Darius refuses, there will be consequences. The code is clear. The blood lineage must, and always must, continue. Madame Arsenault will not have died in vain."

Monsignor Harrison gasped. "She –"

Claret sighed. "You know that I will bring her back. I have a protégé who I have bestowed the power to end coffin sentences using his judgement. I have great faith in him. But for Darius, get him to Badulla. His future depends on it."

Eight

THERE WAS NO UNCERTAINTY about the genesis of *The Inspiriti*, or of Claret, or of the others who formed her inner circle of immortals. There was, however, a deep wonder of their origins; of the dark destiny from which they had been chosen and born into.

There had been no uncertainty because it was published in *The Code of the Immortals*.

Darius Sauvage was the immortal who Claret and Monsignor Harrison called the *vampire extraordinaire* among the immortals, as if it were a term of endearment. He always wore his long, dark hair tied back behind his head, and this day was no different. He had remembered the early days after his transformation when Tramos, his maker, had entered his small bedroom in the early hours of the morning; he remembered the blood on the sheets.

He could never forget the bright red blood.

But now, his separation from his maker Tramos, who the immortals had called 'the conqueror', had been long coming and continued through the years, decades and centuries. Darius knew that he needed to continue the bloodline. But when he was lost in the streets of Paris, performing in the days when Vaudeville was at its infancy, he would walk along the sidewalks, listening to the chatter and boisterous laughter in the background. He stopped and stared up at the moon.

The white sphere shined a pale, blue blanket across the city, and as he approached the livelier blocks where the glitzy shows were held, he sought the guidance of the moonlight. He wondered if the life of an immortal was the correct path.

If he had been making the right decisions.

If only he had the will, and the proper judgement to carry his decisions forward, then he might receive the right of passage that he so craved. He knew that Claret demanded the bloodline be carried throughout time. And that the dark gift – of which he was selected – could be stripped from him at any time. And that if that were to occur, he would become a mortal once again.

He recalled *The Code of the Immortals*.

He was told about it shortly after he was transformed.

Shortly after he befriended a fellow immortal, Delia Arnette, whom he met after they had performed in the same Vaudeville show, he found himself sitting in her Paris flat. She had mysteriously grown old, which Darius thought nothing of, given that he learned that she was a time traveler. She sat across the parlor from him, telling him about the book that all immortals must read and follow.

And as Darius drew it from the bookshelf, Delia watched him. He looked over at her and she had a pained looked on her face. Her snow-white hair hung down towards her waist, as if it were an enveloping blanket. But Darius knew that she was a time-traveler; an immortal with a special gift, even more so than the dark gift that had become the standard for life eternal.

There was something, Darius knew, about the time travelers. They had a special purpose, a drive brought on by the other-worlds, an assignment which Darius believed he would never fully understand.

"Parchman's Press," he said, as he thumbed through the heavy hard cover, flipping a few pages inwards.

"They've been our publisher of choice over centuries," Delia said, with a slight croak in her voice. "And I've come here, Darius, before you've created another immortal, to remind you of the code. And I know you will comply."

Darius sat in a nearby chair as he paged through the book, staring at it intensely.

"You must contribute to the blood lineage," she said. "The random transformations must stop. I came here because the time travelers have noticed you struggling."

Darius looked over at her and returned his attention to the book.

"I'm afraid I don't know how many times I can traverse time again," Delia said. "Our powers are not infinite, you know."

"But I am with you here. In Paris. And I have been, Delia."

She nodded and leaned on her cane. "Young Delia. A far less experienced Delia. But still knowledgeable. And still in possession of the time gift. You don't see her around, do you?"

Darius shook his head as he paged through the book without giving it much attention.

"I have overtaken her," she said. "Because she has a different mission. As for myself, I have risen to a position of great authority. And when I was informed that there might be a struggle to fulfill the code, it was apparent that I, personally, had to visit you."

Darius sighed.

She hung her head and rested on her cane. She took a deep breath and sighed. "There is too much that I cannot tell you. Not right now. But know this. You must, *must* create another. An immortal of importance. It's written in your destiny, Darius. There's a mortal in Badulla who is destined for our kind. He is a coffee harvester. And he is destined for your guidance. And together, you will achieve greatness."

"How do I find him?"

"Let your destiny guide you," she said. "But always remember. His name is Antoine. And you will find each other. That, you will."

Darius opened the pages of the book, towards the chapter that discussed transformations. "It says here that each immortal must contribute to the *survival* of the immortals."

"Yes," Delia said.

"And the failure of securing a suitable carrier of the blood will result in a coffin sentence not less than four centuries."

"That is why I've come to you, Darius. These are doctrines that have been in place for thousands of years. Even during the ancient days of Claret, when the immortals were merely a rumor, these rules had been spoken. That is, until they were written down, and published, so all of the immortals across the world could speak in one voice."

Darius closed the book and sighed.

"There's another," Delia said. "Who might be able to assist you with locating the one in Badulla — Antoine — that is where you will be sent. But the other immortal is also now here in Paris, and his name is Ramiel. Cristofano is his maker. Ramiel is the one who appears to have a charisma that Cristofano seems to lack. And Claret knows that, but she assigned him in a very specific role. And important position which has been needed for generations but never filled. And for that role, the charisma isn't needed. But Ramiel, Darius, very well could be the assistance you need to get Antoine recruited and transformed. Ramiel harbors the same enigmatic personality that I believe…and Claret believes also…that Antoine may possess once transformed."

A delicate deep roll of thunder sounded from the outside as Darius gently laid the book on the table. He stood and extended his arm out, as Delia slowly rose, balancing her weight on her small, wooden cane.

"Think about it, Darius," she said. "If you make your way back to Lyon from Paris then you can contact Ramiel and satisfy the doctrine."

"Will…he…even…"

She sat back down. "Remember how I work. There will be others who will influence your destiny as an immortal who may not have been transformed yet. They may not even have been born yet. But they remain important in your journey. That is why I returned to this time to speak to you. Antoine is your destiny. But there are others as well. Take my advice, dear Darius. Continue your bloodline. It will serve your purpose one day."

Nine

AS RAMIEL EXPLORED the catacombs beneath the Sistine Chapel, the secret network of hallways that reached outwards in a web of darkness and deception, he held his breath for a moment and listened. Nothing but silence. As he walked slowly down the corridor, as his footsteps clapped against the concrete flooring, he thought that maybe, just maybe, he might discover his destiny within the walls of these dark and secret caverns.

There were torches which lined the walls, burning.

They seemed to have an infinite supply of fuel, or wood; but in these corridors, in these dark catacombs, it seemed that there was a feeling that certain natural laws no longer applied. Ramiel proceeded as the warm glow reflected on his face. He slowly shuffled one foot in front of the other, approaching the first closed door.

Someone was certain to be in those rooms, he thought. The call, he felt, was real.

He knew that certain chapel staff members had entered these chambers; some never emerged. His curiosity had gotten the best of him as he slowly approached the first closed door. It had an elegant curved brass handle, which glimmered in the dim, flickering light. He reached out, and paused, stopping just short of the handle.

He listened.

There was a babble in the unseen distance.

A caterwaul, it seemed. Faint, yet pleading. It sounded male, a bit deeper in sound, but it could have been female. Further in, it was for certain. Down the corridor, into the darkness, into the unknown, there would be the source of the wailing and babbling.

The mysterious voice.

And then he heard the voice of father. Speaking to him.

And he remembered the days when he had still been a boy, in the days when he was sent to the chapel, and to board, and be schooled, and never to be seen or heard of again in his home city.

Are you father? Are you the babble? The wailing and the moaning? Is that you? Are you calling me from your coffin?

Ramiel recalled the passing of his father for several years after he had been ordained a priest; there had been no sense of grief until then. He remembered the feeling of numbness, the days of staring through the stained glass windows, watching as the sunlight emanated through the colored glass, reflecting a colorful patchwork on the stone floors. He would stand and stare out at the pews, even as the parishioners would enter the chapel, trickling in on Sunday mornings. He would stand in his flowing, black cassock, waiting for Monsignor Harrison to emerge from the vestment room in the far corner, demanding that he dress.

But as he stood in the dark, mysterious corridor, his hand open, waiting, still, just short of the curved brass handle, he shook off the ghost of father. "You are not here," he muttered under his breath. "And you never were. I may have mourned you silently. But what I was truly mourning was our disconnection. And what might have been but never was."

He grasped the handle.

Listen to father...

"Go away."

He pushed the door open as a small, dark, stone room was revealed; in the center was a coffin made of glass. Candles lined the perimeter, spaced apart methodically and sitting on the floor, around from the edge of the door, onwards behind the coffin. But Ramiel was drawn to the coffin. The candles flickered through the glass like lights through a layer of mist. The coffin, though, wasn't empty.

And his heart started to pound in his chest. *Father, is that you? Father are you there? Are you calling me to this dark destiny?*

He stared at the coffin.

And watched as the flicker of the candles reflected on the glass, concealing who was inside. But there was a darkness to it, as if the occupant were dressed in dark burial dress; shoes, for certain, would bring an unfocused shadow towards the end of the coffin, for the feet were closest to where he stood.

Ramiel figured that he could approach the casket and see who was inside, but had a deep suspicion of who it might be. These underground corridors had a mind penetration which he had never experienced before. Of a dark destiny; of walking through passages of mystery and uncertainty, through the unknown. But the coffin, he knew, was a different story.

For the story of the coffin, as he stood, watching the flicker of the flames reflect on the glass, seemed to know precisely what he was thinking.

And longing.

And missing.

And the story knew he didn't need to know who lay in the coffin. For these catacombs already told him, and knew what his story always *was*.

Come forth, Ramiel. You must approach.

He stopped.

There it was again.

The voice, the babble, the wail.

It seemed so far before, so close at the moment. As if the voice was in the same room, as if the four stone walls had a cerebral connection with his mind, and his past. But he didn't want to approach the coffin, the glass rectangular *bara* as he had always known it to be called. Supple white satin lined the interior; an elegant resting place for whoever was inside.

He took a breath and exhaled.

He couldn't understand his desire to approach the coffin, his curiosity to look, but it was overpowering. Would it be father? He had died so many years ago. Would he be a piles of dust and bones?

From dust you come, and to dust you shall return.

He remembered reciting that, over and over, in the chapel. Spreading the dark ashes on each parishioner's forehead with his thumb, making the Sign of the Cross; but down here, it seemed ashes were different.

Long before Darius had accepted Delia as a guest in his small flat in Paris in the days of Vaudeville, Ramiel stood in the secret underground catacombs in the Vatican, many years before, staring at a glass coffin, hearing the ghostly spoken words of his father, beneath the Sistine chapel.

The coffin.

He stood staring at it, entranced by the reflection of the flames on the glass. He wished he hadn't entered this room. There was something knowing, yet sinister, about the reflection and the flames. The plain stone walls. The candles which line the walls. Something familiar, yet distant. It was as if it were recalling a past life, with all of the disappointments and regrets which had come with it.

For the room knew him too well.

He was remembering papa, in the days when he had still been a boy, and he was wishing that there would have a been an opportunity to know him, to live with him, to be his son. For papa was a busy man, a provider for his family; a proud and concerned man.

And he had little time for Ramiel.

Ramiel stared at the coffin, going deeper into a trance, as the flicker of the flames danced on the glass. His eyes remained open as he watched the fiery reflections, yet his thoughts carried him back to that night with papa.

On the night they lost him.

It was when papa's concern had gone too far; and those whom he despised, the immortals, who had been living underground in the deep mountainous caverns in southern Italy, chose to venture into the city that night.

For they had a score to settle.

And the immortals had heard of papa.

They heard of the rumors he'd started, at the tables of the cafes. Papa would speak while sitting at the bars, and the other humans with whom he spoken, sometimes over dinners that mama lovingly prepared. People began to listen to papa. And the people of Salerno started talking, and the immortals quietly listened. It became papa's death sentence.

Ramiel remembered the night vividly.

As if it were a painting which remained untouched throughout time, he could still see the blood streaks on the stone floor, and still hear the shaking and pounding of the front door. Papa ran in from the kitchen. "Go away muggers! *Go away*!"

The door splintered inwards as a group dressed entirely in black tore inside, knocking papa on the floor. He winced and cried out as he struggled to get up. Ramiel ducked into the kitchen, letting the door close silently as he heard his mother screaming down the stairs. "Ramano!" she cried as those who wore black crashed through the hallway, knocking down tables and throwing chairs. Ramiel cracked the door. One took his hand and slashed it across mama's throat as Ramiel caught his breath. A stream of bright red blood gushed outwards as she clutched her neck and dropped to the floor with a thud. He bit his lower lip as tears welled up into his eyes, until he could taste the warmth and saltiness of blood. He retreated into the kitchen as he heard papa cry out.

And then a deep thud.

He gasped and ran through the back door, out into his mama's garden, rushing through the soaring tomato plants. Did they know he was there, watching in the kitchen? As the mysterious intruders in black murdered his parents in front of him?

He ducked down behind several thick, full plants and looked back at the house, listening. The night was silent and still, a sharp contrast to the chaotic bedlam that had befallen inside the house. But he dared not go back inside. Mama and papa were there, lying in the front corridor, both dead, lying in pools of blood. And they would not be calling him back inside.

Not anymore.

He waited and felt his heart pound in his chest, and grabbed a small wooden garden stake. He looked at the windows, as the light still burned inside, and saw the kitchen table through the window.

Mama? Papa? Are you there? Or are you now looking down on me from Heaven?

He gasped as a dark shadow moved across the window. They were still inside.

He snuggled down into the tomato plants, as the garden concealed his small body. There was a chill developing in the air, and he started to shiver, but nestled in further. Would the bad people wearing black leave? He felt the warmth of tears run down his cheeks as he lay in the bushes, watching his house for as long as his eyes would allow. For not before long, the sun would be rising and the sky would fill with light, and Ramiel knew that in the daylight, the house would not seem so scary. And he could go inside, and look for mama and papa, and maybe everything will have been just a bad dream. But there was another side of his mind which kept seeing the intruders wearing black.

Watching mama's throat get slit.

And hearing the thud of papa's body falling on the floor in the deep slumber of death.

Centuries later, when Ramiel was in America, thoughts of papa flooded his mind, as he stood in the desolate night, steps from the skeleton of the Waxley Mortuary.

Papa was there.

He could feel it; sense it.

He turned away from the door of the crumbling mausoleum as the silent night was interrupted by the mating call of southern toads. As he looked ahead towards the cemetery, he saw the reflection of the moonlight against the hanging Spanish moss . There was something peculiar about the funeral home, it seemed. Something about it which did get into one's mind, thoughts, and memories. But Ramiel listened to Cristofano. "You are an immortal! You are stronger than that! You fear *nothing*!"

But the words seemed distant now.

He looked at the door, open just a few mere inches to darkness. But the darkness had called. A blotch emanating from within, against the fading daylight and crimson sunset and shadows, he knew that there was a reason for the darkness. It was something which he had never thought he might be able to address; but then, as he stood at the crumbling front steps, he took a deep breath and exhaled.

He knew what was behind those doors.

It wasn't fear or horror.

There was a sense of something missed. As if he was being called to go through the doors, and when he stood and made an attempt to peer through the opening into the darkness, thoughts of his father pierced into his mind. There was the coffin. He remembered the glass coffin and the burning candles. Forever etched into his mind from when he had visited the catacombs beneath the chapel in Rome; when he had still been a mortal. But it seemed, that, perhaps, the feelings of despair and rejection had remained with him, despite his transformation to immortality.

For immortality, at the forefront, and despite the grand desire it had become, was flawed. There was no secret answer. No consideration for the possibilities which might befall those who were betrothed to the code.

"Papa?"

Antoine had been right.

The funeral home had an interesting purpose, an enigmatic power. He hadn't felt so close to papa in many years; the days in Italy, oceans away from where he stood, seemed much closer to him as he navigated towards the crypt.

As the leaves and twigs crunched beneath his feet in the pale moonlight, his thoughts returned to the exploration of The Inspiriti, and the catacombs with their similar enigmatic power to see within one's secrets.

As if he had just done so, he was standing in the catacombs beneath the Sistine Chapel, entranced by the flames reflection on the glass coffin. It was time. He had to approach and look inside.

Come inside Ramiel.

He took a slow step forward.

Now was the time to face his fear, and listen to the voice of papa. The darkness inside the coffin could only be him. From a small boy who was denied the chance to say goodbye to either of his parents, when his last memory of them was through the shroud of the rising plants in the night air under Italian skies, to a young man, who had a deep fascination with the immortals, the idea of living forever, and the prospect of becoming an outcast of society. Immortals were feared and tormented, and that notion had an effect on Ramiel that he would carry, perhaps eternally, if he were to be transformed.

He stood above the coffin and gasped.

Papa's eyes were closed; his bushy dark hair framed his face as Ramiel had always remembered. He stood for a moment, gazing at the image of papa, forever frozen in time, the lips and eyes closed, eternally silent and forever without sight.

There was a light knock on the door as he looked up from the coffin. He wiped a tear from his cheek, and looked at the door. It was still open, and in the shadow was a large, dark figure, waiting patiently and silently as Ramiel stood next to papa, his hand on the cool glass of the coffin lid, waiting for something to be said.

"Ramiel," he said.

Monsignor Harrison.

Of course.

"I see you've used the key I gave you."

Ramiel looked down at his clasped fist. The key gleamed within it, a shimmer of silver against the warmth of the candle light.

"And you entered this room, which is what I would have expected."

Ramiel removed his hand from the coffin and turned to face Monsignor Harrison. "This isn't real, is it?"

The monsignor stepped forward, into the dim, flickering light, and tilted his head to the side. He drew his arms behind his back. "It's as real as you want it to be."

Ramiel looked down and shook his head. "All this. All of this. It's not staged?"

Monsignor Harrison moved a few steps closer and shook his head. "No. This is all…yours."

"Mine?"

The monsignor nodded as he finally approached the end of the coffin which was closest to the door. He took a breath, and looked back up at Ramiel. "You see," Monsignor Harrison said. "When one is invited to these chambers, there is already a spiritual connection. And when you accept the offer, that connection deepens."

"Yet I was drawn through the first door."

"That you were," Monsignor Harrison said. "But there are many doors which follow. As the corridor winds towards the darkness, it makes a deeper representation of your state of mind."

Ramiel paused.

Why had Monsignor Harrison recruited him to enter these chambers? Was an exploration of the chambers of his thoughts in order? "What does each door represent?" Ramiel asked.

Monsignor Harrison took a step back and held his arm out.

Ramiel approached him where he stood at the far end of the chamber. Monsignor Harrison spoke as Ramiel craned his neck and looked out and down the corridor. "Other doors," the monsignor said. "That is where the answers will lie. Doors which lead to chambers in which we hold important discussions. And investigative trials. If you choose to go down this path, you will see."

Ramiel raised his eyes and looked up at Monsignor Harrison. "If I choose?"

The priest nodded. "Yes. The choice is yours. You are being given a choice that many are denied. Is this the journey for you? Only you can provide that answer."

Ramiel thought of the night back when he lost mama and papa. When he had been hiding in the garden. And he knew, even as he stood in the mysterious room with the glass coffin in front of Monsignor Harrison, that he had a fascination with immortals. And he appreciated that the choice was ultimately his.

Ramiel took a step closer towards Monsignor Harrison. "So you are saying," he said. "That I will live forever? That I will never see this?" He gestured down to the casket with his arm.

"If you uphold the doctrines," Monsignor Harrison said. "If you follow the code."

Ramiel shifted his face.

"It's the *Code of the Immortals*," the monsignor said. "Every immortal must adhere to it, or receive punishment. Throughout our global community, there has been a number of those who were rebellious, but that would never change the code. For that doctrine was established in the genesis of the inspiriti, when the immortals were at their fewest and finest, and when those who have received the most coveted gift – the time gift – would have entered the immortal race."

Ramiel gasped. "So it's true!"

Monsignor Harrison caught his breath in his throat as Ramiel walked towards the coffin. He spun around to face the senior priest. "You are immortal?! How is that even possible?"

He did not answer.

Ramiel took a few steps closers to Monsignor Harrison and extended his arm back towards the coffin. "But I asked you about all of *this*. How did *this* happen? It's like these catacombs have entered my mind? Have they not?"

Monsignor Harrison let out a small chuckle. "What you see here is what is within," he said. "You can explore the dark corridors all you wish. But you will not discover anything down here that isn't already within you."

Ten

IN THE DAYS AT THE SISTINE Chapel after Cristofano's visit and introduction to Ramiel, and after Ramiel had explored the ghosts in his mind in the catacombs below, Cristofano had returned. It was in those days when Ramiel was attempting to tutor him in the spiritual traditions of the cloth.

Now that Ramiel knew of the catacombs, and the power within the dark corridors below, there was an intensification of his fascination with the immortals. When Monsignor Harrison had finished with him in the chamber of the glass coffin, he had told him about Cristofano, that the young immortal would be assigned to him for a short period, and that he had a special mission.

When he became an immortal, Ramiel wished he hadn't known about Claret.

In those days, the others had talked about her. But in the days when he had first encountered his Priesthood he saw Claret in the days when he was eavesdropping on the conversation in the chapel with Monsignor Harrison, and Ramiel remembered the name Darius. When

Cristofano, the one who he had encountered first in Rome, and then again in Paris, was the one who had been deemed another rebel by others in the immortal community. Cristofano was like Darius, it seemed. Those were the days when Ramiel and Cristofano were living in Paris. Then, Rome was just a memory, when the Priesthood was behind him, and *The Inspiriti* had come to govern his life.

The days in Rome incessantly burned into Ramiel's mind.

It was in the days when he had been at the Sistine, and the mysteriousness of Claret had consumed his very existence. It was when the sermons he gave had warranted an unexpected call into Monsignor Harrison's office at the rear of the chapel.

"Ramiel, Ramiel," he said. "What are we going to do with you?"

Ramiel scoffed and slumped the chair across from the desk. "You told me to speak about my spiritual musings. About my interpretation of the world."

Monsignor Harrison slammed his palms against the desk. "And did I not *tell* you that the secret was to be guarded with your *life*?! Your ultimate *existence*! We have absolutely nothing to do with them! Are you trying to expose us?!"

Ramiel hung his head down. "Never, your highness. I took the oath. I will protect us."

Monsignor Harrison shook his head and leaned back in his chair. He released an exasperated sigh, and looked up at Ramiel. "Then why are you saying there's an imposter in our midst? They have nothing to do with this! Can't you see that?"

Ramiel raised his eyes and nodded. "I will not do it again."

Monsignor Harrison sighed and shook his head. He leaned over the desk and returned to his work. "You are on probation," he said, looking down. "Consider this your first warning. I hope I didn't make the wrong decision when I gave you the key."

But Ramiel did not think about his errors in the sermon when he was leaving the monsignor's office. He closed the door silently, and as the image of Monsignor Harrison hunched over the desk, working on his next sermon, was shut away, he turned and faced the soaring chapel.

The sun had set, and it was difficult to discern shadows from light.

The chapel, it seemed, was a good thing. Cristofano had become an immortal, yes, but he was a rebellious Priest who seemed to be completely against what he was reportedly preaching. And now he wanted to go to Paris? It was all so bizarre. At least on the forefront. Cristofano had a spontaneity which Ramiel envied. As he spent time with the rebellious priest, he learned that there was growth, and development in that. It seemed as if Cristofano was recruiting him.

And Antoine – he had heard of Antoine on more than one occasion.

There had been rumors circulating during the years when Ramiel was a young man, not yet transformed, of the leaders which had emerged in the hierarchy of the immortals – Antoine, his maker Darius; Tramos and Claret, and many other members of the immortal community who rarely surfaced outside immortal connections, however remained mysterious among the human population.

Ramiel was no stranger to these rumors.

And he was still a mortal when his dream of dancing and Paris became a reality, when he left his tiny home in Italy, he had a dream to dance among the Paris performers although he first entered the priesthood;

the pointe ballerinas who he watched as a child, when his mother took him to the city, just a single time, to watch the grand performances. And it was then that he fell in love with dance.

And performing.

He had dreams of a dark figure who would approach him in his dreams, a mysterious character who spoke to him…not in words, but a state of mind. He would awake, shoot upwards in the bed, as the sheet would fall from his bare chest, slick with a layer of sweat.

But in those days, before the performances at the theater, Ramiel was still mortal, and hadn't yet received the dark gift of immortality. He hadn't known then that it was his destiny, that living eternally was his providence. In his mind, and throughout the years when he grew from a boy to a man, he always knew that he was a performer. That he sought to entertain. And perhaps, enlighten. That the ovations were like a drug which rushed through his veins, coursing through and giving him purpose, and meaning, and waking him up to the liveliness of Paris.

The lights and the cosmopolitan soar of the network of the low-rise buildings reaching outwards from the River Seine. Not far from *La*

Cathedrale de Notre Dame, sat the Jefferson Majestic Theater; it was a gargantuan artistic masterpiece, framed with gold spires and guarded by gargoyles. The massive doors soared upwards at the entrance, reaching toward rosette windows, which Ramiel thought were unusual on a theater, as opposed to a cathedral, but thought they were stunning regardless.

When the doors rumbled outwards, a soaring atrium was revealed; the expansive windows rose in columns up through the exterior walls, framed by rosettes, and gold statues, and spires. And then the smaller doors, which led towards the orchestra seating, sloped downwards towards the stage, down to the orchestra pit below, and the stage above.

Ramiel knew the theater quite well when Cristofano entered his life. It was long before the days of the meetings of the High Council of the Inspiriti in Rome, when Ramiel had next encountered Cristofano, at the Jefferson Majestic in Paris. They danced together in the nights performing pointe ballet in Paris when the two had become fast friends, until Cristofano revealed the secret he harbored.

On the night of the massacre.

There were the nights leading up towards that fateful performance, when Cristofano would stand next to Ramiel as they dressed in their tights and pointe shoes preparing for a performance. Ramiel watched as Cristofano pulled his long, brown hair back behind his shoulders.

"What did you have to tell me?" Ramiel asked.

He looked at the young dancer, and admired how Cristofano embraced both masculine and feminine traits. But there was something mysterious about him…and when they walked together towards the Parisian cafés, he had turned to face Ramiel. "I told you I would tell you at the performance on Friday night," he said. The chill of the winter lingered as Ramiel notice the small cloud of vapor emit from his mouth when he talked. He pulled from Ramiel's embrace and twirled on the sidewalk. The hour was late and the streets were wet, and reflected the brilliance of the full moon.

"Cristofano!" Ramiel said. He stopped twirling and looked over at Ramiel. His eyebrows were raised.

"Why can't you tell me now?" Ramiel asked.

Cristofano approached Ramiel and placed his arm around his shoulder. "Because after Friday night's performance, I will tell you everything. I know…and I have to be sure that this is what you want."

"What I want?!" Ramiel scoffed and released Cristofano from his embrace. "You have been telling me about this deep secret of yours since we met. Why can't you just tell me now?!" Ramiel crossed his arms.

But Cristofano did not tell his secret that rainy night on the desolate streets of Paris.

For as he'd instructed, he would tell Ramiel everything on the night of the performance. He said he wanted to wait until after their show, when the theater was full, when they bowed for their standing ovation that they would certainly receive, and then Cristofano would take his hand, lead him back towards the dressing areas, and reveal his secret.

But not that rainy night in Paris on the wet streets which reflected the moonlight.

"Come with me," Cristofano said. "Come to my flat. There's plenty of wine there. I can let you know all about my past. And how I came to be. At least in this phase of my existence. But my secret…that I will reveal after our performance."

Ramiel looked at Cristofano who returned a warm smile. The hour was late and he knew that they should part ways. But there was just something about him that Ramiel was infatuated with. "I can't come back to your flat," he finally said. Cristofano's face fell. "Why on Earth not?"

"Isn't dawn coming soon?"

Cristofano shook his head and let out a chuckle. "It is," he said. "But if you come to my flat, we can spend all of tomorrow resting. And you want to hear about my past, yes?"

Ramiel nodded.

But there was something about Cristofano that caused hesitation. And still yet something in his eyes that seduced him into saying yes. He'd not accompanied another man to his flat ever before, but that night, that rainy night in Paris he did. And when they approached the brownstone walkup, Cristofano laughed nervously when he fumbled with the key. Perhaps he was less of a threat than Ramiel previously thought. But still, there was the mysteriousness about the man. Some unseen force that was drawing him closer…a yearning need to discover more about this mysterious Cristofano.

"We are in!"

Cristofano leaned his bodyweight against the door as it forced open with a deep scrape on the cement below. Once inside, Ramiel noted that despite its shortcomings, the building must have high rent. The chandelier above the foyer was fitted with electric lights – the latest thing – and the bulbs were burning a soft incandescent glow.

"One level up," he said, and dashed up the metal staircase taking several steps at a time. Ramiel stood in the foyer and looked up, at the maze of stairs leading upwards, squaring off the soaring atrium. Cristofano leaned over the railing several floors up. "What are you waiting for?!" he called down.

Ramiel hesitated as he felt his heart thump in his chest.

He hadn't known Cristofano for that long. But as Ramiel heard the click of a lock and the creak of a heavy door opening, he ascended the stairs, and watched Cristofano disappear into the dark recesses of his flat. "Come in! I have wine!"

Ramiel stood at the top of the steps and looked down the lengthy hallway. Similar plain black doors lined the corridor, and all were closed save Cristofano's, at the end, where the steps wound up towards the third floor. The small window at the end of the hallway, just next to Cristofano's door, cast a glow of moonlight that reached inwards towards the darkness like an enigma.

"Come in, Ramiel."

Cristofano called from inside the flat, as Ramiel slowly approached the open door. It was late. The city was sleeping, the moon was full and high, and he wondered what he was doing out so late with his fellow dancer.

He looked down.

His feet were at the threshold.

Ramiel…are you there? Ramiel…are you listening?

The voice was Cristofano but the flat was dark and silent. Perhaps he glided towards the back room, for he knew, and the entire dance company knew that he was a philanderer. Ramiel knew that blatant seduction would be involved. And then there was a chime; as if church bells were ringing in the dark silence of the night…and then, the plain, stark walls of the Paris flat transformed before his eyes.

Ramiel looked up.

A pair of eyes were watching him from the opposite wall. In the darkness. And the silence.

"Cristo?"

His voice reverberated against the darkness yet there was no answer. "Cristo!"

Ramiel…come forth…

And then the pierce of coffins and crypts flooded his mind. He was no longer standing in Cristo's flat, he was in a field of stone crypts, under the shroud of darkness, and taking steps in tiny stones with rising weeds under the moonlight. He was surrounded by the rising stone crypts, listening.

The call of crickets from the distance. The heaviness of the humidity against the chill of the night air. But there was something different. He questioned the reality he was in. As if he stepped across the threshold and out into a cemetery. For it was then that Ramiel knew. That Cristofano had an enigmatic aura because he was destined to. Or perhaps that he somehow had fainted? That he was lying on the floor in Cristo's building, and that this was all in his mind?

A horrendous dream.

Of stone crypts. And the whispers of the dead. He heard the gravel crunch beneath his feet as he stopped and held his breath. There was a whisper. From deep in the catacombs. His heart thumped as he squinted, trying to determine the source of the whisper. It was indiscernible, but there.

He scanned the area.

Each crypt rose from the ground like a small stone monument, some with crosses above, sloped roofs, statues of angelic cherubs and scripture.

"Cri – "

His voice caught in his throat as the whisper loudened, coming closer to him through the graves.

This is not it. This is not the night of my death. I can see my death and welcome the grave but not now, not tonight.

But the whisper called him closer, deeper towards the crumbling small mausoleums, surrounding him with their mystery, pulling him forward with the unseen force of a desolate whisper, which he could not understand…but somehow seemed drawn to.

And then he closed his eyes.

This was not the cemetery back in Italy, beyond Salerno, where the mountains rose from the Mediterranean; back in the days when he was still a boy, running through the streets with fresh baked loaves of bread, requested by mama, because she had been ill and could not bake that day.

But the mirror in their small apartment was the one where he'd first heard the whisper.

Ramiel!

He paused, looked at the mirror, and sighed. He saw that a painting of Vlad the Impaler hung on the far wall, surrounded by a gold framing.

The immortals couldn't have been vampires, yet they sometimes drank blood?

He remained infatuated, yet inquisitive.

Cristofano hung his head. "My immortality is the curse of youth; my mortal destiny is the fruit of wisdom."

Ramiel looked up from where he lay, on the bed, watching Cristofano across the room, sitting in a side chair. "The gift you have been speaking of is a curse?"

A rush of light came towards him, surrounded by darkness, shrouded in mystery. The tapestry had been woven, wrapping him and swaddling him; the light and the warmth had been proven forces he could detect, yet the voice remained unspoken, the eyes without sight, the hearing without a tremble.

He soared forward; a spirit, without physical form, his eyes saw nothing, his ears only heard silence. But he knew he existed. His thoughts remained charged; and the darkness, though penetrative, and without remorse, failed to penetrate his mind.

You are of the bloodline...

Cristo's voice boomed from an unseen source; there were clouds racing beneath him; angry, swirling, electrified with flashes of light. The winds tore against his face. As he opened his eyes to the visions below him, the thrashing of limbs below, beyond reach, downwards, inwards, falling eternally, through viscous binding of souls, lost in an eternal embrace, thrashing with torment, racing through stones.

The crypt dancer walks with the divine, the petulant, the penitent in pursuit of glorification...

The eyes opened before him; nestled between darkness and racing clouds; gasses billowing upwards, charging towards beyond, and mystery, but the eyes watched. They could see although he remained blind, if only to himself. He could hear the wails and the screams below; the splashing water, desolation and desperation felt upwards, yet it remained in the sea.

There is no loss; only uncertainty. And a desire for isolation, abomination. Do you honor the code?

His eyes shut tight as the thoughts pierced his mind.

You are.

Crypt dancer.

Part Two – Act One

THE JEFFERSON MAJESTIC MASSACRE

One

AFTER RAMIEL AND DELIA had their investigative conversations regarding the fate of the immortals at Antoine's Miami estate, not only in America but throughout Europe as well, and the mysterious disappearance of Cristofano, without warning, Monsignor Harrison had called from Rome. He insisted that both Ramiel and Delia travel to the chapel immediately so he could perform exploration procedures of his own on Ramiel, in an effort to gain further understanding of how Cristofano could have vanished so quickly, without warning.

"He's the crypt dancer," Monsignor Harrison had said over the speaker. Ramiel and Delia sat in the back gathering room of Antoine's estate in Coral Gables as the monsignor had a pained look on his face. "The bringer of our justice," he said. "And my abilities appear useless when I attempt to contact him telepathically. I need Ramiel here, as soon as possible, so I can perform the Atarah procedure on him."

Ramiel looked up from a steaming cup of coffee and over at Delia.

"It's harmless," she said to him. "It won't hurt...but you'll think that you dropped acid."

"Come to Rome tonight," he said, as Delia returned her attention to the screen and nodded. She looked back over at Ramiel, who dropped his eyes and nodded. He took a slow sip from his coffee cup and Delia looked back up at the screen and nodded. Monsignor Harrison quickly signed off as Geret appeared in the archway.

"I will take care of things here, Ramiel," he said. "Go. We must find out what happened to Cristo."

Within hours, Ramiel and Delia were boarding a commercial flight from Miami to Rome, and once the plane landed while the sun was rising over the Mediterranean sea, they gathered their luggage from the First Class section just after the plane had taxied to the gate at Rome International Airport. Ramiel watched as Delia carried a bag and rollaway, determined to do it herself, and he watched her glide through the airport effortlessly. She turned. "And I am immortal," she said, cracking a smile.

Ramiel nodded. She was reading his thoughts again.

It didn't matter what they had flown to Rome at the last minute for, Ramiel knew. He'd heard about investigations which took place in the very same catacombs which he had become infatuated with during his short time in the priesthood. But now, the walk through the doors of the Sistine would have a different tone than in the days of the past and the priesthood.

Cristofano had disappeared.

He was the crypt dancer.

Without him, there would be no way to serve justice.

He had to be somewhere on the planet. But where?

While Ramiel had made an effort to locate him, he also knew that there would be an inquisition. As the sedan pulled up towards *La Piazza San Pietro*, a flock of pigeons scattered. Delia touched his arm as he placed his hand on the door handle. Delia looked tired, but her face was shifted with worry. "You've never been interviewed before, have you?"

Ramiel's face fell and he shook his head.

"Very well then," she said. "The monsignor can get…testy…when asking questions. Most commonly, he is looking for an opportunity to read your mind. He has the ability to discover thoughts that you may not even be aware of."

Ramiel considered his time in his younger days, while still a mortal priest at the chapel. Monsignor Harrison was much warmer and friendlier than Delia was now indicating. Had he changed for the worse? "Thoughts I wouldn't be aware of?"

She nodded. "Once we've been transformed, what we call our sleep is quite different than what we experienced as mortals before transformation. There will be things that your mind will experience – sometimes in this plane of existence, but most often in another – which can be stored in places which only those like the monsignor have the ability to discover."

Ramiel released his grip on the door handle and leaned back into the seat. "There are others like him?"

Delia looked ahead and shifted her mouth, as if she were deep in thought. "There were others, yes," she said, nodding. "But I do believe that Monsignor Harrison is the only immortal currently who has that ability. The others…"

"The others are serving coffin sentences?"

"Or dead."

Ramiel exited the sedan, he always thought it strange that an immortal could die. It didn't really make them an immortal, did it? As Delia explained to him as they walked across the plaza, surrounded by a circumference of soaring, white columns, was that everything does indeed have an ending point.

Even immortals.

Nothing in the physical realm is eternal, she had said, no matter how much a species can strive for it. "And when we call ourselves immortals, we are, in a sense," she said. "Take The Hooded Man, for example. In the days when he pursued our kind, a way was found that can end us."

"Antoine said he is writing about that in a book he is calling *The Blood Decanter*," Ramiel said. "His account of the assault of The Hooded Man. He was telling me about it before he left for Paris. Showed me part of the manuscript. It's uncanny that both he and Darius have become accomplished authors, writing books about the immortals."

He walked steadily towards the chapel, seemingly unaware of the throngs of tourists taking photos and scattering birds. The immortals were, in fact, immortal. Yet flawed. There was a darkness which each possessed; not so much born into darkness, but many had a yearning for redemption and a better cause. And after Antoine returned to his chateau in Lyon, there had been a return of Ramiel longing for Cristofano's companionship.

He paused at the soaring wooden doors.

He looked up at the spires; the light and clouds silhouetted the chapel, bathing it in darkness, as if it were angry. It looked down on him as if he were tiny; a disobedient child who had left to pursue dreams of burlesque and debauchery, following a life of sinful transgressions.

One of the heavy doors creaked open and he returned his gaze ahead of him. The light highlighted Monsignor Harrison's face. He was wearing the casual hooded gown, but he appeared disheveled. Ramiel noticed that his hair was untended, and his eyes were red, puffy.

It looked like the monsignor had been crying.

He reached his arm out and gestured for him to enter. Ramiel turned around as Delia appeared behind him, her face also appearing solemn. They followed the monsignor inside the darkened church.

"We've received word from France," he said. "Antoine notified us to say that Darius is dead."

Ramiel gasped. "They didn't get to him in time." He looked over at Delia, whose head was lowered. Ramiel pressed for an answer. "They couldn't restore his gift like they did with you?"

She bit her lower lip.

Delia looked up at him, her eyes pained. She slowly shook her head. Monsignor Harrison turned back towards them. "No, I'm afraid," he said, with touch of sadness in his voice. "It's just like you said. They didn't get to him in time."

"Yes," Ramiel said as the three of them paused at the door which led downwards towards the underground catacombs.

"What does Antoine plan to do?" Delia asked.

Monsignor Harrison slowly opened the door and ushered them down the stairs. "He plans to inter him at the Inspiriti crypt in *Les Enfantes*. I don't know if Antoine is going to attempt anything like he did when Darius been sentenced to the coffin."

"Resurrection?" Delia said. "I don't know. I don't think he wants to give more reason for the demons to pursue him."

As the lower door to the corridor opened, the flickering torch light cast a warm glow on their faces. "And we also have the mysterious disappearance of Cristofano. Which is why I called for you both to come."

Ramiel felt a chill as he remembered the last time he was inside the catacombs. The memories of papa would always be there, and when he walked past the room he so much remembered, the glass coffin was not there; the candles were not burning. Brown cardboard boxes were now stacked on the sides of the room.

Monsignor Harrison led them deeper into the catacombs as the corridor wound towards the left, where several wooden doors lined the wall, each closed. He opened one and gestured for him and Delia to enter. There was a small, rectangular wooden table in the center. It could have been an altar, Ramiel thought, but the plain, stone room which it inhabited was unorthodox.

"You will lie on this wooden table," he said. "I will connect these to you."

He held up a series of shiny metal probes, which were reflective when they caught the light. Delia moved closer to Ramiel as he gasped. "Those pointed ends," he said. "Look like daggers…"

Delia looked and reached up and placed her hands on his shoulder. "It's part of the process," she said. "These connect to your bloodstream. That is how you live now, Ramiel. Your blood is life. It's *your* life. This is how he will investigate what still lies deep within your soul."

Monsignor Harrison raised his eyes and placed the probes down on the table. "There will be some pain, I'm afraid. Some spilled blood. But you must understand…we have to make a record of this information that you hold inside."

Ramiel's eyes widened.

This was not part of the discussions. Pain and spilled blood was not touched upon. But as he looked at the pointed probes, he saw how they caught the light and reflected it back towards him, as if there was a deeper purpose. A calling for something greater. A walk towards the light. As if in some way, that gesture would provide a sense of guidance for the others, for the immortals, and the humans, but most importantly for himself.

Ramiel's attention shifted from the probes back up to Monsignor Harrison. "Do you consent?"

Ramiel took a slow, deep breath and released it. "If I don't," he said. "What then?"

Delia squeezed his upper arm. He looked down and saw her pleading eyes.

"You know the code," he said. "And the ramifications for refusal to assist one's bloodline in a time of desperation."

Ramiel knew it well.

With Cristofano missing, there would be no immortal that could carry out the sentence, was there? Still, as he looked down again at Delia, who pleaded with him to accept the investigation, to use the free will he had been given to help his kind, that he was their only chance for salvation. That his blood would provide the answers which they sought, the understanding of the sacred ones.

Claret's blood ancestry.

The most coveted of the immortal kind.

"Do you consent?!"

Ramiel gasped as Delia looked over at the monsignor. He was leaning over the table, glaring at them. There was an edge in his voice which Ramiel had never heard in the past. "I do not have all day," he said. "You must consent and if you don't…"

"If I don't then it's only a matter of time, correct?"

Monsignor Harrison straightened his posture and crossed his arms. "This is for the good of the immortal community," he said. "A crypt dancer will find you," he added. "No matter where Cristofano may be, or what might have happened to him. It may not be sooner, but rather later, but a crypt dancer will find you."

He was right.

Delia released her grip on his arm and stepped back. She looked up at him and looked directly in his eyes. She knew it, and so did he, that the only way to locate Cristofano was to complete this procedure. It was something which Ramiel had never experienced before.

He looked over as the monsignor lined the four probes up on the adjacent small table. As Ramiel looked on, the monsignor picked each up and explained the purpose of the probes. He started with the smallest two. "These two are for your wrists," he said. He then set the small probes down and picked up the larger one. Ramiel watched as the giant, reflective pointed object caught the overhead light. "For your ankles," he said. "And the last one there…for your heart."

Ramiel inhaled deeply through his nose, his lips pursed together. The crucifixion wounds of Christ. Delia moved closer towards him and placed her hands on his upper arm. "It's the only way," she said. "He needs your blood to complete the vision. You won't die, you know that. You're immortal, and you can survive without blood in your body. But you are in Claret's blood lineage."

"It's the only way," Monsignor Harrison said, laying the probes out on the side table in an orderly sequence.

Monsignor Harrison waited patiently as Ramiel and Delia looked at each other. Ramiel knew that he was part of the sacred bloodline of immortals, the time-traveling ancestry, the all-knowing, the seers, the descendants of Claret Atarah of Jerusalem. She had partaken of the blood on the night Christ was betrayed by Judas in Gethsemane. And she was the first of the immortals.

The most powerful.

The blood would reveal what happened to Cristofano, Ramiel knew that. He'd been told in the past that he was part of a special ancestry, he and Cristofano, and also Delia. That they were rare in the immortal world.

He nodded as Delia stepped back.

"Remove your clothes," Monsignor Harrison said, as he worked to prep the probes. Delia took a seat in a nearby folding chair, as Ramiel undid the top buttons of his shirt. All eyes were trained on him as he drew his arms out of the shirt and dropped in on a nearby chair. He crossed his arms over his muscular chest as he felt the chill in the air.

He looked over at the Monsignor who nodded. Ramiel's belt clanked as he undid the clasp, and then the top button of his pants; he drew down the zipper and pushed his pants down to his ankles.

"Place them on the side and lay on the table on your back," Monsignor Harrison said.

Ramiel stepped out of his pants and draped them over the back of the chair. He looked over at Delia once again. She sat, watching, her legs crossed, leaning on her cane. He looked over at the wooden table and wondered why she couldn't find another way to determine Cristofano's whereabouts. Certainly there must have been a way that wouldn't seem so blasphemous?

"I have been through this," Delia replied quietly.

Ramiel looked back towards her and she gave a knowing nod. She was reading his thoughts again. As he lay back on the table, the Monsignor had instructed him to extend his arms outwards and cross his ankles. Ramiel closed his eyes, took a breath, and sighed. There was no use in resisting.

This quest for knowing was going to happen, whether he liked it or not.

"I will connect the heart probe first," Monsignor Harrison said. "When the blood leaves you will lose consciousness and leave this realm. But you will feel no pain."

Ramiel felt his eyes getting heavy, as the room felt distant. It was as if he were traveling through a tunnel, as their voices increasingly seemed farther away.

The only way out is farther in...

A deep voice penetrated the silence, and in the background, within the darkness, he heard the squabble of voices; words were spoken which he could not discern. A clatter of the chaotic ramblings spoke to him, yet as he drifted further within, as the darkness enveloped and wrapped its limbs around him, as he floated farther downwards, he heard the piercing of clarity.

Destiny...

And then he saw an opening.

Looking downwards, there was a the movement of clouds, yet the vision was different. His time in the coffin was an assembly of dark purpose, unfounded travesty which traveled throughout and teased his senses. But this was different. There were no wails of desperation, no thrashing pasty limbs. This vision was different. And he knew, still within his senses, that Monsignor Harrison would be waiting in the room in the catacombs, Delia would be by his side, and they would be monitoring his progress, looking into his mind.

As he looked downward, the revelation came.

Amidst the sea of low-rise buildings, nestled with the tiny lights and rolling mist, he saw the golden spires reaching upwards through the white vapor. Images of Cristofano flashed through his mind. His smile juxtaposed with his petulant demeanor permeated the swirl of the clouds, as if nestled between the spires, and waiting, beckoning him. His eyes were blue, as they always were.

There was something different about Cristofano.

It wasn't the same Cristo who he had come to follow, and love, and dream about when he wasn't in the same room or the next coffin. But it was the Cristofano he remembered from generations past; the immortal who nurtured him, tutored him, after recruiting him. It was the days in Paris which he remembered, and as the clouds parted, and the mist retreated, he saw the spires, undeniably, of the Jefferson Majestic, from the reach of the spires and golden gargoyles, he saw the theater from the perspective he never would have imagined in the days when he had performed there.

It was the days in Paris when Cristofano had captured his infatuation and imagination; when Cristofano had ignited his passions for performance, artistry and dance. The one who rescued him from his youthful uncertainty and pushed him towards his destiny, charging him with a confidence he never knew he had.

It was those days at the Jefferson Majestic that there was a fondness, a mysteriousness, but also, considering the time in a different frame of mind, there was a sense of loss. And, now realizing, those days, before Cristofano had transformed him and given him the dark gift, that his sense of questioning had been warranted, when he was mortal, and desiring immortality. Yet while he hovered above the theater, he looked downwards and viewed the past as if on film — a celluloid version of the days past, of the performances and the ballet, and of the autocratic style of Madame Arsenault who insisted that the show be impeccable.

Years had passed since the moment that Cristofano had given Ramiel the dark gift in his small flat in Paris to when he hovered above, wondering where his maker might have gone. He looked down at the streets below.

It was in those days when Ramiel was in pursuit of his dreams of performing, of dancing.

They had been dancers then and remained dancers throughout their joining, before they parted. After years in America, they had ventured from Rome to Paris when many in the immortal populations escaped America to return to Europe. In the days when witches were hunted in the new world, immortals themselves became hunted also. At that point in time, Ramiel knew that Cristofano had the time traveling gift, which Claret had given him.

"We need to start dancing again," Cristofano said as Ramiel exited the jetway into the Charles de Galle terminal. Cristofano drew a cigarette from his breast pocket and shook his head.

"Are you referring to now? In this time? Or are you planning one of your journeys again?"

Cristofano scoffed as they entered the crowded terminal.

Despite the early morning hour, the airport was cluttered with travelers, and Ramiel and Cristofano darted through the crowds. After the driver waved at them as they headed down the escalator, the driver claimed their bags and they charged through as the doors slid open with a slight hiss; the large black Mercedes sedan was waiting at the curb. An olive skinned man dressed in black stood in front of the passenger door with his hands clasped at his waist.

Cristofano quickly approached the man and placed the back of his hand gently on his cheek. "Angelo." The man nodded and smiled politely as Cristofano leaned in closer to his ear. "Take us to the mausoleum," he whispered.

Ramiel saw the interaction between Angelo and Cristofano, and he felt a twinge of uncertainty wash through him.

The only way out is farther in…

The voice hissed through his mind and he shuddered.

He closed his eyes for a moment and listened to the hum of the traffic charging through the terminal. Things were different now. So much time had passed since Cristofano had given him the dark gift; the immortals were now under assault from a mythical figure called *The Hooded Man*. It seemed to have been occurring over generations, but the immortals don't celebrate lives lived in the same way that mortals do. For lives of the immortals encompass so much more, yet are weighed with dark torment, and uncertainty, and passions that generally are never quite fully understood.

But now, it was time to return to Paris.

America had been a challenging period which Ramiel would always remember, but now it was most definitely time to return to Paris.

The power couple – Antoine and Darius – who had governed practically the entire American sector of the immortals, were now in trouble. Antoine fled his base in Miami, and traveled back to Lyon with a dying Darius, who was infected with a fallacy of redemption. But redemption, Ramiel thought, was what all immortals seek at some point in their existence. It did not seem so out of character for an immortal to seek a sense of purpose.

And meaning.

Ramiel stood on the airport baggage claim sidewalk. Cristofano rushed towards the other side of the Mercedes and slapped his hand on the roof as he was about to duck inside the back seat.

"Ramiel! Wake up!"

Ramiel opened his eyes.

Cristofano's eyes were wide and his face shifted with anger, which was not uncommon for Cristofano and his temper. Ramiel sighed, grabbed his rolling case, and nodded as Angelo accepted it from him and lifted it into the trunk. Ramiel sheepishly turned and opened the back door, bending down and looking inside at Cristofano, who sat on the other end of the back seat with eyes that seemed to pierce him.

Ramiel slid into the dark, smokey leather.

They sat in silence as the car accelerated with a dull rumble. Ramiel settled into his seat and looked out the window as the sleek sedan pulled away. After a few minutes of silence, Cristofano tapped Ramiel on his forearm. Ramiel turned over to face him. Cristofano's eyes were wide and stood out as white orbs in the fading light at the opposite end of the dark interior.

"You know," he said. "You said that you would stop that."

Ramiel looked over at Cristofano. "Stop what?"

Cristofano scoffed and shook his head back and forth. "Don't try to pretend that your bloodline will protect you. We have seen what you have been orchestrating with the witches back in Miami."

Ramiel looked at Cristofano, as he placed his chin in his hand and looked out the window. He knew not to respond to Cristofano's assumption, even if his intentions were noble. There was a lot of Claret in him, that was apparent. He didn't know what he'd done over the years to upset Cristofano, but there had been a change in their relationship. As if Cristo had some deeper purpose. And as Ramiel settled back into his seat for the ride, his thoughts drifted to Antoine and Darius. Antoine was padding around their large chateau in Lyon, another evacuee from the American assault of The Hooded Man. The figure had become was a torment to all of the immortal community.

And as he closed his eyes, he thought of the time when he had met Delia Arnette for the first time, back in Paris, when he had still been a young dancer for the ballets; it had been years after his time in Rome and the church. Cristofano had come and taken him out of that life of service. And when he was in Paris, he knew that he was a performer. An entertainer and showman. That was something that Cristofano had gifted him. He discovered who he truly was.

On the night that he remembered, Delia had joined Ramiel and Cristofano for a glass of wine in his Paris flat. "I am the crypt dancer," Cristofano said. "At least that is what I have been told."

Delia was young and robust; at the height of her prime in Paris. Fiery red lipstick, a matching tutu with fishnet stockings. She scoffed at what Cristofano said. "Is that what you've been told?"

Cristofano raised his eyes towards her as Ramiel looked on.

"I've been told that the Claret blood ancestry dictates this purpose," he said, as he took a sip of the deep red wine and stood. "Now you must excuse me. I have some business I have to attend to at the theater. I will return soon."

Ramiel and Delia watched Cristofano's sudden departure as a pop emanated from the fireplace; the flames reflected on the shine of the bulbous wine goblet left on the nearby table. The Beaujolais had been quite robust, yet smooth and velvety. It served as lubrication for the terror of the conversation, which Ramiel knew was coming. Delia would press him, as soon as the door closed.

He leaned back in a large, overstuffed cranberry side chair. The fire popped again as it started to die down. He balled his fist and rested his chin on it, exhaling deeply through his nostrils. "I can scarcely remember the night I met Cristofano. He was always so penitent.

Except when it came to the performances at the Jefferson. He's unapologetic in that theater. He has a passion for performance. And illusion. Sometimes with him, it's difficult to detect reality."

The woman who sat opposite him, on the other side of an expansive, mahogany round coffee table, held her wine in her lap. Her eyebrows were raised, but she didn't appear too inebriated. "You do know that was the site of the massacre? Right? Am I correct?"

He nodded.

"Do you know why Cristofano would feel the need to go there now?" she asked.

Ramiel's eyes fell as he looked down in his lap, as if the answer was located there. Ramiel didn't know everything there was to know about his maker. Sometimes, he was thankful that he didn't.

He shook his head.

But he did know that Cristofano was a crypt dancer. And that there were possibly others. But could a crypt dancer be corrupted? Were they always allegiant to the code, regardless of personal gain?

Ramiel sighed, looked back up and studied the woman.

It wasn't the first time they had met, but he imagined it wouldn't be the last.

Cristofano seemed quite close with her at times. Others not.

In the past, Cristofano had spoken of Darius incessantly, who Ramiel had never met. He talked about his discussions with the time-traveling Delia, and how they talked about Darius, and some new "recruit" from Sri Lanka named Antoine; they spoke of him as if he was the new savior of the immortals. He had told Ramiel that Delia had made the prediction that *The Hooded Man* would nearly wipe them to extinction. Ramiel scoffed at the prospect; but that wasn't why she was here. And it probably wasn't even the massacre, either, for that matter.

"And what about Cristofano?"

Ramiel adjusted himself in the chair and set his glass on the table. "I don't know what happened to him, Delia. He just isn't the same as he was before the massacre. After the fire, we escaped – several of us – to the Paris crypt. He said the elders would protect us, which I didn't know how they would, given they were bound and chained. But we stayed there for quite some time. Resting with the elders. Eventually, he took me back to his quarters, and I was transformed. I spent quite a bit of time with him. But I'm not really sure where he went after that. It was as if his mind changed. It's like he just disappeared."

"Just like the others," Delia said.

Ramiel nodded.

Delia slowly stood and he got a quick flash of the older time-traveler.

Her flowing dress rustled.

Ramiel saw that she was old; according to her prediction, *The Hooded Man* must have gotten to her too. But Ramiel sat and held the stem of his glass, watching her. She was an old woman, pleading with him to leave Cristofano.

That a horrific plague brought on by a hooded imposter with a crystal decanter affected the entire immortal community around the world, and that Cristofano would be somehow involved. "Involved? Why would he want to annihilate his own kind?" Ramiel asked. He took a sip of the Beaujolais and treasured the warmth as it flowed down his throat.

Delia's eyes fell. "I'm afraid I cannot tell you," she said. And then she looked up and looked at him directly. "But I can tell you this. It will happen. *It will.* And there is nothing that you or I can do to stop it, nor should we try. This is a dark destiny of the immortals, which cannot, which should not, be stopped."

Monsignor Harrison stood next to Delia as they watched Ramiel. There was no movement beneath his eyelids, but they could see the rise and fall of his chest. Delia looked up as the monsignor shook his head and sighed. "You told him to leave Cristofano," he said. "Why did you do that?"

She sighed, got up from the small folding chair she had been sitting in, and stood on the opposite side of the table. Drops of blood ran down Ramiel's forearm from his wrists. Monsignor Harrison reached down and adjusted the probe attached to his right wrist and raised his eyes, looking at Delia. "Any thoughts as to why?"

She inhaled though her nose, pursing her lips. "Cristofano's attitude towards Ramiel changed over the years," she said. "As if he harbored some resentment towards him."

"But an immortal is forbidden to abandon his maker," he said. "The code clearly states that."

Delia looked down at Ramiel.

He looked like a corpse. His skin was pale, it was normally a sweet olive complexion from his Italian heritage. The heart probe was buried deep within his chest; it appeared as if the dagger has been plunged deep through his heart. A large transparent tube extended from his chest and bright red blood flowed towards a clear glass holding chamber on the opposite side of the room. Monsignor Harrison turned his attention back to the monitors next to the chamber.

"Cristofano abandoned him," Delia said quietly, watching Ramiel's motionless body as the blood flowed through the tubes. "The code is equally as clear about the ramifications for that as well."

Monsignor Harrison looked up from a monitor filled with indiscernible text. "There are some indications of your investigations with him," he said.

Delia eased herself over towards the monitors, balancing on her cane. Monsignor Harrison noted that there were some additional visuals coming through the noise, that perhaps, as if there was a form of electronic voice phenomena taking place, that perhaps the blood would answer their questions. But it was supernatural, nonetheless.

Delia watched the screen.

The text continued to flow outwards from a deep, billowing cloudy atmosphere. As if the storm in Ramiel's mind were inconclusive, yet, mysterious and inviting.

"I...see wine," she said, slowly, squinting her eyes. "Something is coming through. Yes. I see it. The reflections of a glass. Flames on crystal, perhaps? And a tipping bottle. I see a fire..."

And then they watched as the vision came through...

…Ramiel watched as Delia placed her glass on the table with a delicacy that he had not seen before. She sighed, looking downwards. His attention was not broken, nor had she moved, until a pop emitted from the fireplace as Geret stoked the fire and dropped another log on the flames. Thunder emitted from outside as Geret drew the heavy drapes closed.

"A storm is coming, master Ramiel," Geret said.

Ramiel sighed himself. "Delia?"

She slowly raised her eyes. They were wide and pleading. She slowly shook her head, but Ramiel knew. There was a difference in her tone when she spoke of Cristofano. As if he were destined for something darker than what Ramiel could fathom. And now, he felt helpless. As if there was absolutely nothing that he could do to control or prevent it.

"Let's change the subject," she said. "Let's discuss the massacre."

"At the Jefferson?"

She nodded.

Ramiel knew the topic would arise.

That's what he thought the initial visit was about. Earlier, when the door chimed, he had not expected a small, frail, white-haired woman to be standing there, leaning on a cane. And he was even more surprised when she had asked to come in, that she was an immortal, that she had been sent to warn him about something magnificently horrific.

But the theater house slaughter, that was of a different caliber. It could have been an inside job. How could one comprehend the immortal community attacking itself? And murdering hundreds of innocent mortal humans? The memories were cemented in his mind.

The atrium doors crashed open while in act three.

Cristofano stopped his pirouette and gasped as chaos and screaming tore through the audience. They appeared as dark silhouettes behind the raging fires of torches, rushing through the theater, igniting the tapestry, charging through the scurrying crowds.

Ramiel caught his breath as the screams emitted from the seats; the mob advanced and charged forward, igniting the stage curtain. "Death to the immortals!" a man screamed.

"Be gone the cursed evil ones!" a woman said.

As his thoughts were thrust back to the present, Ramiel felt a solitary tear stream down his cheek. He looked over at Delia who leaned forward, reached across and placed her hand on his knee. "I know they are painful and fearful memories," she said. "But as we discuss them, things might start to make sense."

Ramiel scoffed, reached up with his arm and wiped his cheek. He shook his head. "We are not evil," he said.

"No, we are not," Delia said. She leaned back and settled into the couch.

Ramiel looked directly at her. Her eyes were pleading. She knew the pain. She had experienced it as well.

"Why do they despise us so much?"

Delia tilted her head. "You mean humans?"

Ramiel nodded.

Delia sat for a moment as Ramiel took another sip of his wine. The fire continued its crackling, and the clock ticked. "That's a question that rarely receives an answer," she said. "We are different, we have certain powers that people don't quite understand, and because of that, we can be perceived as monstrous. Even if we aren't. Although some of us are."

"Yes, some of us are. But many of us seek the same redemption that others search for."

Delia nodded. "And there are despicable humans as well, many who are quite evil."

"So why do they hate us?"

Delia sighed. "I may have the same blood in my veins that you do, Ramiel, and we may be seers. But there are some things that just aren't possible to be seen. We can't always explain the hatred in the world. Why it's there. Why only some hate. And kill. Just as there are good and bad people, the same goes for the immortal community."

"Why we have crypt dancers," he said.

"Yes. Now the massacre."

Ramiel sighed.

She was bound to bring it up.

Those days at the Jefferson Majestic in Paris. When he and Cristofano had only known each other for a short while, in the period just after they had been together at the Sistine Chapel in Rome. It was the time before Cristofano had transformed him, and if Cristofano also shared the same blood from Claret's lineage, why did he not foresee the massacre?

Delia may find answers as they sit and travel back to those days. And he knew it was her duty to investigate the matter.

"So then," Delia said. "Let's start from the beginning. Let's go back to the days in Paris when you were youthful and still mortal. Do you remember them?"

Ramiel nodded as Geret hurried to the table and refreshed their wine. Ramiel reached for the bulbous glass and sank back into the chair, as Geret returned to the bar.

"I used to perform pointe ballet nightly in the Jefferson Majestic, but not that night. Not the night of the massacre."

Delia sighed. "Yes, not that night. But are you telling me the truth?"

Ramiel took a sip of wine and swallowed slowly. He stood, watching Geret, who stood at the bar polishing glassware. "We all have our loyal manservants," he said quietly. "Hopeful mortals, looking to obtain the dark gift. Because, you know, Delia, that being mortal appears to be a curse, it seems. Geret here latched on to us after one of the performances." Ramiel looked up as Geret joined them and sat on the sofa across from Delia. "Isn't that right?" Ramiel asked.

"Oui!" Geret exclaimed.

Delia leaned forward, turned and looking at Geret. "But you are not immortal now?"

Gerets face fell and he shook his head. Delia looked across the table at Ramiel. "You never transformed him?"

Ramiel shook his head. "Cristo and I disagreed on it. I mean, I had no issue. And I know that I need to continue the bloodline. It's been explained to me repeatedly."

Delia scowled and then turned towards Geret. "And where are you from?"

Geret clasped his hands together and shook his knees back and forth. "I am from Marseille," he said. Ramiel buried his face in the wine glass but maintained his stare at the others.

Delia nodded. "And when did you come to Paris?"

Geret hesitated. "I…it was years ago now," he said. "I was a very young man then. It was when I had heard of the show. Of the ballet. *Les Ballerines de La Crypte.* All of the controversy, and the rumors that it was a production by the immortals, had reached all the way down to the south coast. I'd already heard about immortals. But at that point, I knew that I wanted to become an immortal."

Ramiel set his glass down on the table with a clank as Delia raised her hand. "So what brought you to Paris?" she asked. "The desire to become an immortal? Or to perform at the theater?"

Geret cast a nervous glance over to Ramiel. "It was both," he said. "Word had spread that the theater productions were of the finest that people had seen, anywhere. The most magnificent costumes, astounding acting and dancing, and a mesmerizing orchestra."

"I see," Delia said.

"And then also," Geret said. "I met Cristofano and Ramiel here, and they took me under their wings."

Delia looked over at Ramiel. "Why haven't you transformed him?"

Ramiel shook his head and scoffed. He leaned back in the chair and tugged at his collar. Her words grasped him like a vice. "Must I do everything for you?" She lunged across the sofa and plunged her teeth into Geret's neck. He cried out, falling back as she straddled him. Blood poured from his neck, down his white uniform, pooling on the couch.

Ramiel reached up and touched his chin, gasping as he drew his fingers away.

Blood.

Bright red and hot.

He looked up at saw Delia move away from Geret's limp body, as blood poured down her face and white blouse. "You have his blood," she said in a breathless tone. "You have his blood."

Ramiel reached into his mouth and felt that hot sweetness. He put his fingers in and drew them out, looking at the fresh blood. "I…"

Delia shook her head. "Just put him in a coffin. He should have been transformed a long time ago."

Ramiel looked over at Geret's limp, drained body. His skin was pale, more so than ever before. He knew that if he didn't place him in a coffin, he might die. But he was torn in his own emotions. How had Delia managed to transform him at a moment's notice? And give him his blood?

"He is your bloodline," she said. "But that is the last time I save you from the Code. This will protect you from a coffin sentence. Now go do it." As Ramiel gently picked up Geret from the sofa, Delia headed towards the hallway. She turned and called him. "Where is a powder room? I must clean myself up."

Ramiel heaved Geret's limp body up in his arms and looked down at his eyes. Fresh blood spilled from his mouth and his neck. "Third door down the hall," he said, without removing his eyes from Geret's lifeless face.

"He is your creation," she called after she had disappeared down the hallway. "He is of your blood. Now see to it that he is properly reared in our ways."

Ramiel carried Geret into the foyer and stopped at the cellar door. He sighed and placed him gently on the floor and opened the door. The door swung open and he felt the cool, musty air penetrate the foyer. As he stooped down and eased his arms underneath Geret's back, he thought of Delia's line of questioning about the massacre.

And when Geret joined the dance company.

As he descended the stairs, he could still remember the night when they had been practicing on the lit stage. He had looked up when a young Geret walked slowly down the aisle of the descending orchestra seats; and Ramiel looked up and instantly locked eyes with the young man. He stopped as Cristofano spun towards Ramiel and nearly crashed into him.

"Fresh meat!" Cristofano said, his eyes widening. He giggled, doing a trio of pirouettes and gliding towards the other side of the stage. Ramiel paused, hugging himself, watching the young man. "Most likely Italian. From which part?"

A heavyset woman dressed in black clapped her hands and charged across the stage. "Are you here for the auditions?" She stood at the edge of the stage, which ascended from the rows of small, wooden chairs.

The young man stammered and placed his bag down on a nearby chair. "I...am Geret Moretti. I heard the call for auditions."

She scoffed. "From as far away as Rome?" Her voice boomed with authority and echoed from the soaring ceiling.

He nodded slowly, and stood, clasping his hands at his waist. "There is much talk around Europe that this is the premiere theater with the best productions."

She glared at him from across the stage. "Do you have your own shoes?"

He hung his head. "I spent all of my money getting here."

She balled her fists and placed them on her waist. "Then how will you do pointe? This production calls for pointe ballet."

He looked up and his face brightened. "I dance barefoot."

She scoffed and threw her head back in laughter. "You honestly do point without shoes? How do you get on the tips of your toes?"

"I do it quite well, I believe."

She glared at him for a moment and snapped her head towards stage right. A group of female dancers huddled on the side. "Alandra. Find him a pair of shoes that fit. We do not dance barefoot here. You will not leave blood on my stage. Now drop your bag backstage and join us here."

He picked up his bag as Alandra glided over to the side steps to greet him as the woman turned towards him once again. "I am Madame Arsenault. You will always listen to me or you will be removed. There are no second chances. Do you understand?"

Ramiel watched as Madame Arsenault headed towards the back of the stage and clapped her hands. "One, two, three…together!"

As Ramiel fell back into formation, he kept looking over towards Geret as he and Alandra disappeared through the heavy black drapes towards backstage. There was something about Geret, he thought. Something alluring, mysterious. And Ramiel felt, deep within his soul, that Geret might be a kindred spirit. Ramiel knew that Cristofano was an immortal, and Ramiel desired the gift, yet Cristofano had not yet given it to him. Did Geret share the same curiosities that he did?

As Ramiel's thoughts were cast back towards the present, as he was carrying Geret down the stairs into the cellar. The memory faded, and as he stepped on the cool, stone floor; he knew that Geret had finally received the gift he had been seeking so many years ago. He placed Geret on the floor and reached up for the string. The incandescent bulb glowed a dull yellow, and revealed the small, wooden coffin in the corner. Stone walls rose upwards, and despite the dampness of the cellar, it was the quintessential place to transform. The same coffin I used, he thought. Geret would appreciate this when waking to his own dark existence. There was a certain nostalgia for using his own coffin.

Save your best thoughts for your time in the coffin…

He grasped it and the lid creaked open. A dark red satin interior which looked like blood in the dim light; Ramiel reached down and straightened the pillow. He picked up Geret, and gently placed his body in the coffin, crossing his arms over his chest. After he was snug in the coffin, he looked down. "Rest well, Geret. My son. My creation. When you arise, you will have new senses, and a new perspective. I am sorry that I was weak and didn't respond to your transformative desires. But I will promise you this: when you awaken, I will conjure up all of the powers that I have received to help you transition from your life resembling a vampire to your life as Baal."

He knelt down, closed the lid, and sighed.

It would be a long few days.

He had grown accustomed to having Geret around. He was a loyal manservant, and both he and Cristofano enjoyed his presence and his body. But now, when Geret is born anew, will he have changed so drastically?

Only time would tell.

He stood, reached up and pulled the string as the cellar was again bathed in darkness. "Rest well, my friend."

His shoes clumped as he ascended the stairs, and once he emerged in the foyer, Delia stood in a fresh blouse, her arms crossed. "Are you ready to continue our discussion?"

Ramiel closed his eyes and nodded.

"Alright then," she said. "Let's return to the parlor. You need to tell me about your time at the Jefferson with Cristofano and Geret."

As Delia returned to the sofa, the fire had begun to die down, but Ramiel ignored it as he sat quietly in the side chair across from her. He looked at his wine glass, as it sat on the table exactly where he left it, and over at the bottle of Beaujolais sitting across the room on the bar, precisely where Geret had left it. He cleared his throat.

"I remember…"

Delia looked up as the last embers of the fire emitted a pop. Ramiel looked down and shook his head. "Too much torment," he said.

"After the massacre?" Delia asked, looking up at him.

He turned to face the fire, propping himself on the mantle with his hands. He hung his head down. "Cristofano should have never taken me there. To the cemetery. I wish I had never even known about that place."

"And what about Geret? Where was he during this time?"

He had a flash of Cristofano and Geret chasing each other throughout the backstage corridors, nude, before the female dancers had arrived. "He had a special relationship with Cristo."

Delia leaned forward. "Define that."

Ramiel shrugged. "Cristofano took an instant liking to Geret. I think that's how Geret came here. Cristofano seemed that he wanted to become a maker."

"He hadn't at that point?"

Ramiel shook his head. "I don't believe so. I hadn't been transformed yet then either. But then, Cristofano only shares intricacies about himself with me which he chooses to reveal. Nothing more. Many times, I am left to compose my own assumptions and draw my own conclusions, whether they are correct or not."

"Did Cristo ever take Geret to the crypts? To the cemetery?"

"No," Ramiel said. "That was one thing he never did. For many nights, Geret remained at the flat with me and Cristo. We all slept together during the days in a massive bed with robust mahogany posts, and performed at the Jefferson at night. Until the massacre, that is."

And then Ramiel closed his eyes, as his thoughts carried him back to the Jefferson once again.

He saw himself, looking downwards at the dusty stage floor. He was sitting at the rear against the black wall, in the midst of the black, heavy hanging curtains, and Cristofano was next to him, his toes bleeding.

Geret was still dancing with the women in practice, but looked over at them repeatedly with a worried look on his face. Ramiel dabbed at Cristofano's bleeding toes with a damp white towel.

"Fold it over again," Cristofano said. "Put some pressure on it to stop the bleeding."

Ramiel raised his eyes and looked over at Cristofano. Cristo hung his head downwards, his brown locks concealing his face.

There was a certain sadness there. Cristofano looked up and their eyes locked, a direct stare that Ramiel knew was a beckoning. But he had been used to being in Cristo's seductive embrace, for even on nights when they performed together, as Ramiel would pirouette across the stage, and lift the women in the air, as he would look to the left, Cristofano would be waiting amidst the massive, heavy drapes. He would always say that he was awaiting his cue, and he certainly could have been, but Ramiel would shudder at the pierce of his stare.

He let Alandra down as she glided across the stage as the audience cheered. It was the final performance, that night. As he looked out into the audience, they rose to their feet, and the chorus of applause continued. He watched the theater, at the scores of people, laughing, cheering, loving the performance.

He squeezed Alandra's hand as they prepared for the bow, and looked towards stage right at Geret, who took a deep bow.

You will always bow farthest. Cristofano's voice would hiss through Ramiel's mind, each and every night, as he would glide to center stage with Alandra. Cristofano would waiting amidst the heavy, hanging drapes, he watched as the audience rose to their feet. Ramiel could feel the pierce of his stare on the back of my neck, for Cristofano was the understudy.

You must always bow, he would say. *Thank them for their attention. And their awe.*

Ramiel craned his neck to the side as he felt the light touch on his shoulder. As the curtain dropped, and the chorus of cheers silenced, he turned, and Cristofano stood in front of him, his eyebrows raised. There was a certain mysteriousness about his understudy, that was for certain. Ramiel locked eyes with Cristofano. As Ramiel slowly headed towards stage right, and when he reached the hanging black drapes, he turned, and gasped.

Cristofano was still standing in the middle of the stage, watching him, his eyes wide open and piercing. Ramiel could feel the chill of the back of his neck. *You will not leave this theater...*

Ramiel looked over at Geret as a chill ran through his body. The curtain fell and the dancers dispersed. Yet Cristofano had disappeared. Geret approached Ramiel as the women headed backstage towards the darkness. "Where did he go?" Geret asked, moving closer towards him. His eyes were wide open and he was looking around the stage, as the lights dimmed. They were center stage together, as Geret fell into Ramiel's arms, eyes wide.

Embrace...the crypt...the coffin...will guide you...

An unseen voice hissed as the lights went dark and the women dancers screamed from backstage. Ramiel held onto Geret tighter as he snapped his head towards backstage.

He saw Alandra's white costume amidst the darkness running towards them.

"What happened Alandra?!" Ramiel said as Geret released his grip.

He could scarcely see her in the darkness, but he could see the reflection of tears against the slit of light emanating through the curtains. "What is it?! What has happened?"

"Hurry!" she cried. "Come! It's Dominique! She has collapsed and is so hot!"

Ramiel rushed as Alandra led them towards the darkness of backstage. The women huddled and he could see Dominique's legs splayed out, shaking, from the slivers of light that filtered through.

"Move aside!" Ramiel commanded. He knelt down as several of the dancers backed up. Geret rushed forward and knelt next to him. "Where is Cristofano!? And what happened to the lights!" He turned to Geret. "Go…see if you can turn on the lights. Go now!"

Geret leapt up and rushed further backstage.

Dominque's legs and arms were thrashing.

"Get something to protect her head!" he said, as the dancers rushed towards the prop room and grabbed a small pillow. Ramiel reached down to remove her shoes and winced as he started to untie the ribbon. "She's burning up! I can barely touch her!"

"He was here!" Alandra said as she fell to her knees next to Ramiel.

"He who?" Ramiel asked as he winced, yanking off her shoes. He reached his arms around her waist and guided her towards a nest of small wooden chairs. Geret appeared with several flaming torches and nestled them in the wall holders as the flickering light revealed Dominique's skin. "That's all we have!" he said.

Yet Ramiel paid no attention to Geret's failure to turn on the lights, nor did he care that the younger dancer appeared with torches to light their way, and that he had placed him in unused holders which had been in the theater since before the electric light.

He focused on Dominique. He pulled one of the chairs out of its formation and placed her down on the floor. He looked up as Alandra rushed past them.

"Alandra!" he called out.

She turned and slowly approached them. Her mouth dropped open as she saw Dominique through the shadows of the flickering wall torches. "Is she ill?!"

Ramiel shook his head as he bit his lower lip. He returned his attention to Dominique as he reached his hand up to the back of her neck, and cried out.

"What is it?!" Alandra fell to her knees and leaned forward toward her fellow dancer.

"She's burning up!" Ramiel cried. "I nearly burned myself!"

Alandra hesistated when she brought her hand closer to Dominique's cheek. "What is *wrong* sweet one? What has happened to you?"

But her eyes closed.

"Get Madame Arsenault," Ramiel said. "I will stay with her and lay her down."

"But you'll burn! You just nearly did!"

Ramiel shook his head. "I will be careful not to touch her skin." Alandra locked eyes with Ramiel, and as they broke their stare, Ramiel watched as she looked down at Dominique. The two of them had studied together. Ramiel had known they were close, and as he watched her skip away, he noticed her face fall towards her friend; the sparkle in her eyes had faded, yet there was a sense of determination that she exuded.

Alandra had Dominique's best intentions in her heart, Ramiel knew without equivocation. But Dominque's collapse had been so sudden. And her falling on the stage. There was too much now that had become uncertain. There wasn't really anything else to consider, when it came to the dancers.

Her thrashing before them. And her skin. He watched in horror as it grew a deep crimson, and appeared to glow in the flickering light from the torches. As Geret joined him, the other dancers gathered around as Ramiel slowly reached his hand out. He drew it close to her skin and cried out. "She's literally *burning!*" He turned to Geret. "What happened to Cristofano?!"

But Geret was never able to answer the question.

Dominique burst into flames as they spilled backwards. Ramiel felt the assault of the heat bursting from her burning body. The flames tore upwards from her body and shot up the curtains, reaching their way upwards towards the ceiling.

And then there was the sound of clapping from deeper backstage, with the approach of footsteps.

"You're all such grand performers."

Ramiel looked towards the sound of the voice. Cristofano. He leaned against the wall in his dark leotard and tights. He crossed his muscular arms and watched them as the fire thrashed heat upon them, yet no longer spread.

"Touch her," he said.

186

Ramiel looked at Dominque, engulfed in flames. "What is happening?"

Cristofano scoffed. "You don't see?" he asked. "It's all performance. It's all an illusion. We're here to entertain, aren't we? We put on costumes, practice until our feet bleed, and for what?"

Ramiel looked at Dominique as Cristofano spoke. "We create an illusion of reality. The theatergoers don't see this backstage area. They don't see our practice, our bleeding toes, our pulled muscles. They see only what we *want* them to see. They will gasp in awe at our artistic beauty...and revel in the music and the grandeur...and when the curtain falls that illusion will end."

He waved his hands as the flames extinguished.

The dancers gasped and everyone watched as Dominique started coughing. Her skin was intact, unburned, and seemingly unharmed. "We always perform, and always entertain," Cristofano said. "But we must *all* adhere to the code, at all times." He looked over at Dominique. "Isn't that right my little sweet dancer?"

The thud of footsteps approached as Cristofano turned and the heavyset imposing feature of Madame Arsenault moved into the flickering light as the dancers eased themselves back slowly. Madame Arsenault's face was grimaced in a scowl as she slowly approached Dominque.

Ramiel looked up at her as she pursed her lips together and looked down at the dancer as she gasped for air.

She scowled. "Take her to the coffin," she said with deep authority. And then she turned towards the huddling dancers. Ramiel felt Geret grip his arm more tightly.

"Let this be a warning to you all. Don't let this illusion be the end of your fear. If you disobey the code you will be sentenced to the coffin! Now go!"

The dancers gasped and retreated down the hallway past her and where Cristofano stood. She turned and looked at Ramiel and Geret. "As for the two of you," she said. "You are both still mortal. Illusion is reality once you receive the dark gift. Embrace it. Live and feel it. For the code is the only thing that will save you from the crypt."

Two

DELIA AND MONSIGNOR HARRISON both sat in front of the monitors, watching the visions as they penetrated the noise. Delia leaned forward. "I believe there is going to be a continuation of our discussions," she said. "I'm seeing the same visions." She looked over at the Monsignor, whose head was raised towards the monitors. "Do you see the glass? Do you hear the faint chime of a clock?"

Delia sat back and folded her arms as they both watched and listened…

…Ramiel leaned forward grabbed his wine glass from the table as Delia looked on. A grandfather clock chimed in the background.

Ramiel cleared his throat. "On one particular night, I was walking through the dusty gravel pathways past the alleys between the brick midrise building. In the shadows of Paris."

"Where were you headed?" Delia asked.

He shook his head. "Maybe the theater. Perhaps Cristo's flat. But I frequently took these walks. Guided by the stars. The night sky had a certain lightness to it; the moon, it was a certain presence which I had always known since I was a boy. On that night, I felt the jut of the cold stones on my bare feet, as I hung my point shoes around the back on my neck by the ribbon."

Ramiel continued telling Delia about the days at the Jefferson Majestic, as she sat, and listened, taking notes furiously.

Ramiel sat back, closed his eyes, and listened to himself as he remembered...

...As Madame Arsenault clapped her hands together, Cristofano slinked to the backstage and slumped against the wall. Ramiel rushed to his side. "She does not mean what she says," he said, as Cristofano draped his arms over his legs, a scowl on his face. "Your pirouette's are divine!"

"But they are off."

Cristofano slumped down on the floor, and untied the ribbons from his shoes. As he removed them, the blood on his socks seeped in to the bright white material. He had been working hard, that Ramiel knew. He wanted to be the lead, that he knew as well. But Madame Arsenault was unforgiving for error. Every move must be precise. The lifts had to be perfectly marked. Married to the music with precision and perfection.

She would accept nothing less.

The women gathered at the far end of the stage as the music hit a crescendo. Ramiel sat next to Cristofano, as he hung his head down between his knees. There was a certain aspect of failure which he could never accept, that much Ramiel knew. But besides that, there was a certain aura of mystery which surrounded the mysterious dancer who had captured him in Rome. An allure which Ramiel couldn't quite explain. Mysteriousness surrounded him, in a blanket of uncertainty, which somehow, Ramiel seemed to find fascinating.

The clap of heavy heels approached, and they both looked up.

Madame Arsenault had her hands on her hips. Her lips were pursed and her eyes wide. "You will not be in tonight's performance if you do not pirouette with the others! Across the stage! Now, let's go!" She clapped her hands and stood just in front of them, and looked down at Cristofano's feet.

He shook his head. "I cannot, dear Madame. I am bleeding. The pain is unbearable."

She closed her eyes and drew a deep breath in through her nostrils. "If you choose this," she said. "Monsieur Boucher will not pay you. You know this. He only pays for those who dance."

He sighed and closed his eyes.

Ramiel watched him, listening to his heartbeat. There was a certain silence that washed over them, sitting there, their feet searing in pain, their legs splayed out before them.

Ramiel reached down to undo his ribbons; he nestled his shoes off of his feet, and winced.

His toes were bleeding as well.

But as they chose to sit this performance out, Madame Arsenault's decree was extraordinarily clear: they would not be paid.

For Monsieur Boucher did not pay dancers who failed to dance. The show must go on, he would always say.

His voice would boom and carry upwards towards the rafters as the dancers would stand in the center of the stage, huddled together sheepishly, their stark white costumes a brilliant contrast to the dark flowing curtains which surrounded them.

"We are ready to open the doors!" he boomed.

Theater staff lit the torches on the sconces as the massive doors creaked open. A flood of chatter filled the air, as Ramiel looked out and onwards towards the sea of small, wooden seats. Ladies wore their finest flowing gowns; corseted at the waist, bulbous skirting billowing outwards. The men removed their top hats and escorted the ladies in as the first row violins started playing a single note in unison: the performance was about to begin.

The deep breath of the cellos wafted beneath the shrill violins, joining in a solitary chorus, as the men and women rushed to their seats. As a timpani boomed, the flooding of the rolling beat cascaded throughout the soaring atriums, and the audience fell into a hush.

The curtains slowly parted, and Ramiel stood center stage, awaiting his cue. The trumpets would sound, and the first pirouette would begin. But it did not matter how long the music would play, nor that he would hit the marks with precision, or that the lifts would send the audience into a state of awe.

Ramiel looked to the left just after Dominique glided out from his arms, gliding across the stage. Cristofano was there, waiting between the heavy, hanging black drapes. *It doesn't matter if you miss your mark or not. There will be no consequences from tonight's performance. The audience will say nothing.*

Ramiel froze.

For the stage felt different.

It wasn't the muted feelings, or the numbness of his feet as the pointe shoes were tied too tight. The ribbons were always too tight for these performances. But the music faded way.

Ramiel watched the audience watching him; he saw the sea of the reflections of their eyes against the darkness of the theater. They were watching him. Intently. With purpose, it seemed. But he froze.

Center stage.

His arms would not move, nor would his legs. But he still had his faculties. He saw the small, flickering flames of the torches on the walls towards the back of the theater. Their flames reflected against the heads of the audience, seemingly frozen.

He looked outwards towards the rear orchestra seats.

The doors crashed open as a torrent of wind rushed through the theater; the torches blew out in the ferocity of the winds. Ramiel shuddered at the crashing of the doors, and the deluge of the winds…yet the audience remained frozen.

Still there was a chorus of screams from backstage as the curtain fell with a deep thud.

It was what Cristo spoke of. Cristofano, and his bleeding toes.

There was something about Cristofano. He'd always been the first billed; never the understudy. But tonight, he was gone. Minutes before the performance.

And the curtain fell.

Ramiel heard screams from the theater. He felt his heart thumping in his chest. For the audience certainly was no longer frozen, no longer mesmerized by the dancers.

His heart thumped in my chest.

It was as if the dream had transformed into a nightmare; a dusty rendition of the unison of minds, as each entity sat obediently in neat rows, facing the stage, yet the theater was filled with the wail of screams.

"Ramiel!"

The theater was empty; he stood on the stage, the curtain had risen, and the seats had no people in them, and the torches had been extinguished. Had that been a terrible nightmare?

He was in costume.

"Great performance Ramiel!"

It was Dominique from stage right. She stood, gathering her bags, holding a feathered mask in her hand. "The masquerade is to start soon!"

Ramiel knew that the entire dance company would be attending, except him and Geret. There was a degree of exclusivity to the event; one had to possess the dark gift in one form or another. Cristofano had become an interesting flat mate and friend, but he and Geret remained in mortal human form.

"Ramiel!"

A male voice from above.

He looked up towards the rafters; in the darkness, he could see a silhouette. Movement; a billowing waistline. Wearing a costume. Of course he would be. Tonight was the masquerade.

"Ramiel, look up at me."

He could recognize Cristofano's voice anywhere. It had a certain depth to it; he had the confidence of a leader, mixed with the spontaneity of youth.

Ramiel looked up.

There was a flash of him standing outside of Cristo's flat.

The voice, he remembered. When he used to stand on the landing above the door, looking down at the small café umbrellas below, he would always look down and welcome Ramiel when he arrived back after his long walks. On that moonlit night, the landing remained empty.

As Ramiel pulled the door open as the heavy frame ground against the stone walkway, he trudged up the quiet stairs and thought of the masquerade ball. And the sense on longing to be included, to be considered an equal among the immortals.

To receive the gift; to be bestowed with powers which he could use for good.

He wanted it.

Ramiel thoughts returned to the present when he had stood on the stage. He could see the edge of Cristofano's arm in the darkness; there appeared to be some feathers on his costume, yet in the upper stage darkness in the rafters, he could see little else.

The dancers had scattered back to the dressing rooms to prepare their costumes for the ball, and Geret had joined them in the hopes that he might be invited.

Ramiel knew that he wouldn't.

Ramiel looked up when he heard Cristofano's voice calling from the rafters. As he looked up, Cristo looked down; his face was angelic, it seemed. As if he were a china doll. Reflective of the light. Ramiel had only met him earlier that season, his name was Cristofano. Different personality from the Cristo he had known in Rome at the chapel; this version of him was changed. A passionate performer, without a doubt. Continually enigmatic. And he had taken Ramiel to Paris to be in the production of *Les Ballerines de La Crypte*.

But tonight, there he was, in his mysteriousness and mask.

The reflective ceramic was lined with colorful feathers; a skin resembling a pale skull. Cristofano stood above on the rafters, looking down at Ramiel, with his own china mask, staring downwards as Ramiel stared at the mask on the dusty, quiet stage.

"Are you going to come with me tonight?"

Ramiel paused.

He had thought the masquerade was by invitation only. "You mean..."

"The crypts," Cristofano said. "Not the silly party. To the crypts, of course. I have much to show you there."

Ramiel snapped his head to the left as he heard the distant racket of the front door locks clicking into place. They didn't have much longer until they would have to spend the night in the Jefferson. "I've thought about it, yes."

He heard a rustling above and looked up as the long wooden rails wobbled back and forth. Cristofano was gone. Heading down to the stage, no doubt. It would be only moments and they would be standing next to each other. His rugged masculinity would be emanating from behind his mask. Ramiel could sense him. And smell him.

"You told me you would come."

He approached Ramiel and stood by his feet. Ramiel felt his heart race in his chest as he looked at the skull mask; he could feel his hot breath emit from the brilliant red lips. He would have thought Cristofano a monster, if the colorful feathers hadn't foretold of a lighter persona.

Cristofano took a step back, extended his arms and took a slow bow. "You are the mysterious one, Ramiel! You are profoundly inquisitive…yet dramatically cautious. Now will you accompany me to the crypts as we had discussed before?"

He stood across from Ramiel, nearly a foot away, and he could hear his breathing. The thump he felt might have been his heartbeat. But there was no time for matters of the heart in Cristofano's perspective, he deduced.

Ramiel gasped as Cristofano lunged forward and hugged his arm around his neck. Ramiel closed his eyes and sighed, resting himself on Cristofano's taught, muscular frame. There was a certain masculinity to his muscularity, yet his movements were sleek, and had a degree of femininity, or perhaps that of a feline; for this was ballet. His virility remained profound; his bicep crushed the back of his neck as Ramiel gasped. Cristofano dropped his mask and flexed his arm in a rigid ball of muscle, pressed against Ramiel, pulsating, throbbing, and he looked up into Cristofano's eyes.

"You are coming with me tonight."

He grabbed the back of Ramiel's hair and yanked his head back.

He gasped as Cristofano leaned forward in front of him, his long hair concealing the fading light of the dusty stage.

Ramiel gasped.

He wasn't prepared for the pierce of his fangs, or the warmth of the blood as it ran down his neck, and down his chest, staining his brilliant white stage costume.

Cristofano pulled back as viscous red blood dripped from his mouth. "You must come with me now, or you will die," he said. "I can leave you here right on this stage. Or chain you into a crypt and no one in this theater will question me."

Ramiel opened his eyes, yet his vision was clouded, blurred; wisps emanated from the lights above, as his eyes filled with the tiny, bright flashes of stars, drown in water as the warmth of tears streamed down his cheeks.

"Now of course, you must spend some time in the coffin," he said. "We all do, we always have. And when you awaken, you will have a different set of senses: your vision and hearing will be heightened, yes, but you will be at the genesis of your transformation."

A lock clicked in the distance as Cristofano pulled away.

Ramiel slumped downwards in a pile of white linens as Cristofano walked to the edge of the stage, looking outwards, towards the empty dark seats. Ramiel could scarcely keep his eyes open as he watched Cristo raised his head and studied the ornate gold detailing on the ceiling. Cristofano he didn't need the lights to be on, for that was one of his gifts. He could see in the dark, like a feline.

He turned with a smirk. "We are locked in here, aren't we?"

Ramiel struggled to nod, at the brink of death, and clutched his chest. The white linens were stained bright red with the spill of his blood, and he attempted to stand, but was too weak.

Cristofano watched him and scoffed. "I could leave you here," he said. "Or we could go to my flat and I could finish the transformation. Right now, you've simply lost a great amount of blood. You need the gift to save you."

Ramiel looked up at him, and the fuzziness took over. Cristofano started dancing across the stage, twirling in pirouettes as Ramiel held to consciousness with a mere thread. The movements were graceful as he glided back across the stage in a second triple pirouette.

Ramiel struggled to lift his head as he saw Cristofano glide towards where he lay.

He danced towards him, his arms flailing outwards like a butterfly; his legs, reaching forward, in a muscular stampede, his tights revealing the roping muscles under the fabric. His pointe shoes clapped against the hardwood.

As he approached, Ramiel felt his eyelids grow heavier. He felt disconnected yet somehow cared for; he could feel Cristofano's muscular arms lift him from the stage floor, as the linens fell to the ground. He could still feel the warmth of the blood running down his neck and chest, and despite closing his eyes, he felt movement, as if he were being carried.

But there was time for one last bow. Ramiel felt the dip, and managed to open his eyes, as he saw the seats in front of him, as he felt a falling downwards, followed by a quick lift back up. Cristofano had to take one final bow before leaving the theater.

He was the penitent performer.

Late and after the performance, in Cristofano's flat, Ramiel stood at the edge of the room, holding on to the heavy, dusty, wooden frame, and watched as Cristofano slept.

The mysteriousness of his lover was pronounced. And substantial. Cristofano had only provided a small portion of his personality, it seemed. But Ramiel knew that his past ran deeper. Far deeper than what Cristofano had been willing to share.

Ramiel didn't know the specifics of Cristofano's transformation. But as his own maker, Ramiel knew, now, during his own period of gestation into Baal, that there was a time when Ramiel wondered if Cristofano had other, more sinister intentions. There was always the story of The Crypt Dancer, of which Cristofano had told him, on that rainy, humid night in Paris, after the performances at the Jefferson, when he was following him deeper into the cement maze of rising monuments in the darkness well past the midnight hour.

Cristofano walked ahead of him. The faint light from the candle he carried cast a warm glow against the rising stone monuments in the early morning darkness.

"There is a myth?" Ramiel asked. "A legend, you say?"

His boots crunched on the gravel as Cristofano stopped in his tracks. He turned around slowly as the glow from the flickering candle bathed his face in a warm light. His faced shifted. "It's no legend," he said. "It is real."

Ramiel watched as Cristofano turned and looked out to the sea of stones. "There are many immortals," he said. "Buried beneath these stones." And then he turned back to face Ramiel. "But that is the way and the law. Of the immortals. There are those who are sentenced to coffin time for injustices." He turned back to face Ramiel.

"There is an order," Cristofano said. "And those who commit crimes against their own kind have several levels of punishment. These here are serving lighter sentences."

"For what type of crimes?"

Cristofano took a breath and turned away, walking forward again. Ramiel followed. "There's a number of things," Cristofano said as the gravel crunched beneath their feet. "Any crime against an immortal – a threat of death, an exposure to mortals...we must protect our kind, Ramiel."

"What's the worst punishment?"

Cristofano stopped as the gravel crunched beneath his feet. He turned slowly and faced Ramiel, who stood behind him. "Death by crucifixion," Cristofano said. "Golgatha in Jerusalem. Sacred ground, as you may know. Crucifixion on those grounds ends an immortal. At least those of our kind. Bathed in darkness, we are."

Ramiel gasped. "So we aren't truly immortal, then, are we?"

Cristofano shook his head and turned away. "Oh we are. But everything ends, eventually. We can evade sickness and death, for as long as our own behavior allows us. But I've been warned of a coming pandemic for the immortals."

"A pandemic? How is that possible?"

Ramiel watched Cristofano as he lowered his arms to his side. The candle nearly caught his pants on fire, yet Cristofano remained unaffected, and his pants never caught aflame. He hung his head down for a few moments, and then slowly looked up at Ramiel. "I fear I've told you too much."

Ramiel scoffed and approached him, placing his arm around his shoulders. "What are you talking about? Who has told you this?"

Cristofano raised his head and looked out towards the sea of monuments in the cemetery. He raised the candle as the fire cast a glow on the crypts. "I cannot tell you any more specifics," he said after a few moments of near silence. Cristofano's words danced through the rising smoke from the flame. And Ramiel pressed Cristofano to continue, for he knew that they didn't have much life left in the candle. Wax dripped in small puddles on the ground.

"Who told you this?"

Cristofano looked back over at Ramiel. "There are some of us who are able to foreshadow events. And move through time. In this case, there is a rumor, but it can't be substantiated."

Ramiel scoffed and shook his head. "A rumor? It's a rumor now?"

Cristofano grabbed Ramiel's forearm. His eyes widened. "Now just you wait!"

Ramiel gasped and fell back, catching his balance.

"I have many duties!" Cristofano exclaimed as he waved the torch around, illuminating the monuments and crypts in a warm glow. "And *this* is part of my duty! Which I am showing to you. But just forget what I mentioned to you. It may not even happen. But here...this...is what I came to show you."

Cristofano headed forward several steps and stopped, holding the torch in front of a double crypt. He drew the torch towards the upper compartment, and Ramiel leaned forward to see the etching in the stone, yet it was far too weathered.

"LaDonna Mastuer," Cristofano offered.

Ramiel looked up at Cristofano, who remained transfixed on the crypt. The warm glow from the candle reflected on his face. Ramiel leaned back, watching Cristofano stare at the grave, holding the torch, waiting.

"Who is she?" Ramiel finally asked.

Cristofano broke his trance. "Only one of the most powerful immortal witches in the history of our kind."

Ramiel looked at the crypt.

It was worn, weathered, and the etching on the stone was indiscernible. But Cristofano knew. Of course he would know.

"So you asked me about my duties," Cristofano said, as Ramiel looked up at him. He carried the torch closer to the stone crypt. "Ms. Mastuer here was bound and chained and sentenced to coffin time in the 1500's."

Ramiel gasped. "She's...alive...in there?"

Cristofano nodded, as he moved away from the crypt and closer to Ramiel. "For hundreds of years, she has been sentenced to that coffin in there, in torment, as she lay in chains, and darkness, with no hope for escape."

"What...why?"

Ramiel sighed. "What did she do?"

Cristofano nodded as the flames bathed his face in a warm, orange glow. "Crimes against the immortals are not taken lightly," he said. "She was a powerful witch," He said. "And still is. In the time she was alive, she would hypnotize immortals and lure then into her coven and annihilate them."

Ramiel gasped and shook his head. And image of the claws and clutches of a group of witches dragging screaming immortals through dark, deep caves, further into the bowels of the Earth tore through his mind. "Why...why would she...she's immortal herself, isn't she?"

Cristofano drew the candle closer to the dank, nameless stone crypt. "She was very powerful," he said. "Her immortality is something of mystery. When she walked the streets in Paris, she was rumored to have a powder...or potion...which held supernatural power."

Ramiel shuddered and felt a chill rise through his body.

Cristofano continued. "Punishments are designed to fit the offense, as is in the human society. But we, as immortals, design our system. There's the Blood Lineage, which is a significant factor for us all."

"And where do I fit into that?"

"You are mine," Cristofano said. "And I am Claret's. So that is your bloodline."

"What about further back than Claret?"

Cristofano shook his head. "She is the ultimate," he said. "There is no going farther back than her."

But Ramiel watched as he drew the torch back closer to LaDonna Mastuer's crypt. Her coffin sentence. And when he watched Cristofano kneel on the ground, and drive the torch into the ground, he looked at the crypt.

LaDonna's resting place for centuries.

But she wasn't really at rest. Like Cristofano had said, she had committed some sort of crime against the immortals to warrant being bound and chained, and sealed in a coffin for all of enternity?

"I am reading your thoughts," Cristofano said. "And what you are thinking is true. She *did* commit crimes against the immortals that warranted this sentence."

"But she was a witch? What did she do?"

Cristofano nodded slowly as he stood. "That is the twist," he said. "There's multiple layers about her. How she was a witch has to do with her history as a human. And a mortal. But how she became *immortal* is the mystery that I have been assigned. And that is why I will be freeing her."

Ramiel paused. "Wait...you are letting her out?"

Cristofano took a small bag from his back and let it drop to the ground with a clank. He bent down over the bag, rummaged through it, and looked up at him. "Yes, I am."

Ramiel felt a wash of uncertainty flow through him. "What did she do, Cristofano? What did she do to warrant this sentence?"

Cristofano scoffed and let out a laugh as he rummaged through the bag and took out a pickaxe. He looked up at Ramiel and stood. "I have the power and the authority to raise any immortal from a coffin sentence."

"You've been told to do this?"

Cristofano shook his head, and slammed the pickaxe on the edge of the crypt, where the face fused with the frame, and a shower of sparks rained down on the rocks below.

"But…when was she supposed to be let out?"

Cristofano continued his assault on the crypt as the sparks shot into the dark night air. "I don't know exactly," he said. "It was never shared with me. But this is what I am here to do. This is what I've been *told* to do. And I do what I am told."

Three

ON THE NIGHT OF THE MASSACRE, the crowds lined the sidewalks for the premiere curtain call of *Les Ballerines de La Crypte*. It was long after Cristofano had revealed LaDonna Mastuer's crypt in *Pere Lachaise* and the winter clouds have covered Paris like a blanket.

The show was ready; the newspapers called it "a musical like none other" and the chatter across Paris debuted the show as the most anticipated and discussed in many years. There were rumors about the cast and crew of the Jefferson Majestic, that the immortals had been known to reside in Paris and most of France with a distinct level of discretion, which was common practice for the immortals in those days.

Snow fell as the sun sank in the horizon, and the temperature was the coldest that Paris had seen in years. Those who were lined up along the sidewalk huddled in heavy jackets and fur coats. The ushers swung the doors open as the ticket takers tore the guests' tickets and handed each a program. The activity in the atrium carried through the slit in the heavy, wooden doors, across the empty seats, down towards the stage, and the hanging, heavy maroon curtain. Geret peered through a slit in the drapes, looking outwards across the seats, towards the heavy doors in the back, in the darkened area underneath the mezzanine, and watched the people mingle in the atrium with cocktails and top-hats.

Ramiel approached him and placed his hand on his shoulder. Geret turned around. He'd already been to makeup and his eyes were wide.

"Don't worry," Ramiel said. "It's just opening night jitters. They'll pass. They always do."

His face fell. "It's not that," he said. "I've been excited for this since I was a boy. It's not jitters." He turned and parted the curtain, peering through once again. "It's just...something doesn't feel right about tonight. Something's off."

The heard the approach of footsteps.

Cristofano gently slapped both Ramiel and Geret on their arms. "Something's off? What on Earth is that nonsense?"

"Geret has a bad feeling about tonight," Ramiel said.

As they spoke, Madame Arsenault charged through stage right, clapping her hands, as the dancers hastily gathered around her. "We are thirty minutes from curtain!" she said. "Everyone must do one final run-through in the back and listen to the orchestra!"

She snapped her head in the direction towards Ramiel, Cristofano and Geret. "And you three! I expect your lifts to be *perfection*!"

Cristofano stepped forward. "They've been perfection and only that."

She banged her cane on the stage floor. "The over confidence is unbecoming of you, Cristo. And I would imagine Claret would be none too pleased of your behavior."

Cristo scoffed and turned to the others. Ramiel shrugged his shoulders. Geret's eyes were closed as he was peaking to himself, practicing his moves. "Let's try to keep him calm," Ramiel said. "It's his first show. He's young."

Dominique approached them.

"You're on borrowed time, Dominique," Cristofano said, as he headed further backstage. "I will allow you this one last performance, and that is all. Then justice must be served."

They all followed him.

"What is it, Dominique?" Ramiel asked. And then looked at Cristofano, who pulled up his tights near rows of colorful hanging costumes. "What did she do, Cristo?"

He glared at Ramiel as he put the finishing touches on his costume. "That is none of your concern," he said. Ramiel looked at Dominique, her brunette hair was tied neatly in a bun, the makeup was flawless, and her tutu billowed outwards from her waist. She fidgeted, and then held her arms down her sides as she lowered her head towards the floor.

"It's the look of guilt," Cristofano said. "We all understand the code. Failure to adhere to the code brings a sentence in the coffin. Doesn't it, dear Dominique?"

She nodded slowly. "Yes…the crypt is my destiny."

Geret's face lit up. "You will go willingly?"

Dominque slowly raised her head, looked over at Geret and Ramiel, and nodded. "Yes."

Cristofano moved forward, preparing to head to stage left and wait for his cue as a timpani sounded from below the stage. "Dominque knows she must serve her sentence. And since you and Ramiel have not yet been transformed, I will explain to you. A coffin will be prepared just for her, she will be wrapped in chains, and when she closes her eyes, mortals, like you, will assume her dead. She will be buried in a crypt until her sentence has completed."

Ramiel watched as Cristofano disappeared between the hanging heavy, black stage curtains. His solo was about to begin, and the words that he left him and Geret to consider were cast with the weight of boulders; Dominque had followed Cristo, leaping forward, her arms extended outwards, with a dainty glide, her pointe shoes remaining silent on the wooden floor.

"Cristo!" Ramiel called. But he did not hear, as the cue of the timpani swelled, and the lights brightened, and Dominque flew forward. He could see the sea of faces beyond the dancers, and watched as Cristofano lifted Dominque into the air, as they glided across the stage to a swell of cheers from the audience.

Geret tugged at Ramiel's puffy white sleeve. Ramiel looked over at him and could see the wide eyes, a look of terror. He bit his lip and shook his head.

"Look at them," he said, as Ramiel saw what Geret was pointing to. "Behind the orchestra," he said.

Beyond Cristofano and Dominique's gliding across the stage, he looked, beyond the sea of faces, towards the rear of the theater, under the shadows of the mezzanine, through the glass doors, people were gathering. Torches were lit.

It was time for the company to join the stage.

In the back corridor, Madame Arsenault banged her cane on the floor as the remaining dancers scurried into position, and Ramiel and Geret soared forward, as the audience bolted to their feet in a roaring applause. But as the company took formation in the center of the stage to bow for the first act, Ramiel got Cristofano's attention. He nodded out towards the doors, where the crowd had swelled. There were more torches.

The wail of screams emitted as the lights went out.

Glass shattered as the shadows erupted with fire, silhouettes ran down the sides of the theater, igniting the curtains with the roar of bright orange flames, which charged upwards and reached across the ceiling.

"Down with the immortals! *You are all from Satan!*"

Madame Arsenault gathered the dancers as they fled the stage, rushing towards the back areas. "Come with me, girls, come with me!"

They screamed as a mob rushed through the side doors, crashing into the backstage corridors. The dancers shrieked and rushed into the back dressing areas while Madame Arsenault reached her arms outwards. "Come to me my dancers! I will protect you!"

But the mob continued their advancement as more tapestries, costumes and curtains caught in flames.

Ramiel and Geret rushed towards the dancers and Madame Arsenault, but Cristofano grabbed them and held them back. "No!" he said. "It's too late for them! Come with me! I have somewhere we can go!" Geret starting coughing from the smoke, waving his arms. "I...can...hardly...*breathe*...!"

Cristofano grabbed them both and lifted them by their shoulders, levitating upwards. Ramiel looked down and saw the scattered crowds as the fire ravaged the room; men and women screamed in agony as their flesh melted from their faces, the terror rose like the dark, black smoke, as the assaulters carried the torches along the perimeter, and continued the burning, as Ramiel and the others levitated at the crest of the ceiling, they catapulted through the burning rafters, through the searing heat of the flames, the choking grasp of the smoke, and chorus of screams below.

Geret's eyes were closed, but Ramiel continued watching the torment below, as the flames engulfed the theater; he thought of the others. And the immortals. The dancers who had desired the dark gift, and who may never live to receive it. He felts Cristofano's arm tremble.

"I cannot hold it any longer! We must descend!"

Cristofano eased them down in the rear of the theater. Several of the dancers were in small groups huddled in the area, their costumes covered in soot, their tutus torn, tears streaming down their cheeks, holding each other, their heads bowed. One of the dancers looked up and saw the three male dancers. "Madame..." she struggled to get the words out through sniffles and tears. "Madame..."

The dancers screamed as a flaming figure tore through the back door, engulfed in flames, screaming and stumbling through the yard. The dancers stumbled backwards and cried out.

Ramiel grabbed Cristofano's arm. "Wake up Geret!" he said. "They are out of control! The building is collapsing! Can you get us somewhere safe?!"

Cristofano gestured towards the dancers, cowering as Madame Arsenault collapsed to the ground, the flames engulfing her; and Ramiel watched as the smoke billowed upwards towards the sky. "Then find a way to save them!"

The thumping of footsteps approached them as Cristofano leaned over and breathed into Geret's mouth. Footsteps thumped in approach down the rear corridor. Ramiel craned his neck around towards the door. "Cristo!" he whispered. He tapped his shoulder. "Cristo!"

Geret's eyes opened.

"They're almost here," Ramiel said. "Where can we go?"

Geret sat up in a fit of coughing as the mob charged through the back doors, past Ramiel and Cristofano. The dancers leapt to their feet and emitted a chorus of screaming, as the mob charged back towards them, waving their torches, chanting "down with the immortals! You are from Satan! We banish you to hell!"

"Follow me!" Cristofano whispered.

Ramiel assisted Geret as they crawled behind the bushes, in an attempt to block out the wailing of the dancers and the roar of the fire. As they approached the end of the theater, Ramiel looked upwards. Flames roared upwards from the roof, as the crash of timbers and crackling wood crashed above them. Cristofano turned to face them. His eyes were wide. "Let's go!" he yelled. They cleared the brush and ran. Ramiel picked up Geret in his arms, as the young man draped his arm around his shoulder; and Ramiel maintained his course.

He heard the screams behind him, but only Cristofano existed. They ran down the streets, and into the dark alleys, through the low rise brick buildings, into the trees at the edge of the city, as the lights and activity flashed by them.

They ran towards the darkness, as the winds howled above them and the trees swayed angrily. The clouds raced across a dark sky, highlighted by the pale blue moonlight, in an seemingly eternal darkness which held its grip upon them.

Cristofano continued but slowed his pace, which Ramiel welcomed. Geret roused and lifted his head, looking into Ramiel's eyes. Ramiel saw that the young man appeared to be much more alert.

"Do you think you can walk?"

Geret nodded, as Ramiel let him down. Cristofano turned, panting. "We are out of danger," he said. "But we still have a ways until we reach the crypt."

Ramiel watched as Cristofano leaned to the left, looking past Ramiel. Footsteps approached as Ramiel felt his heart pound in his chest. He watched Cristofano, his face stern and his eyes piercing, as he tensed. Ramiel grabbed Geret and held him close to his chest.

"Who goes there?" Cristofano called.

"Wait!"

The voice was feminine, small and shrill against the silence of the night. "Wait for me Cristo!"

Dominique fell against Cristofano. She was panting, breathless and stained with soot, her eyes wide with desperation. "I barely escaped...my...everyone's *gone*!" She buried her face in her hands. "They're all dead! Burned to ashes! Every last one of them!"

Geret covered his mouth with his hands and looked up at Ramiel. "Who would do something like this?!"

Ramiel's face fell and he shook his head, and then looked over at Cristofano. "There are those who hate us," Ramiel said. "We immortals are hated by some across the world, despite the gifts we bring."

Cristofano's face softened. "Come on, everyone. We have to move forward. The crypt will protect us. They can sense us through the trees. Been doing it for years. But they can't find us in the crypt."

Cristofano led the group as they followed, walking at a slower pace. The sky was lightening as Dominique and Geret walked arm in arm, and Ramiel watched Cristofano lead the way. There was something about Cristo which Ramiel could not place; he was a difficult immortal to read; almost impossible to understand. But, at times, despite his forceful and domineering exterior, Ramiel could tell that Cristofano had a caring, deep within, that would pierce through his layers of darkness.

He was a protector of his kind.

And he knew, despite Geret still being mortal, that the young man would be loyal to the immortals; he did not share the same misconceptions about the immortal kind which the mobs of humans did.

Cristofano stopped at a clearing, extended his foot and brushed the dirty, dead leaves away. He lifted several sheets of old, rotting wood, revealing a set of weathered, stone stairs, which led deep into the ground. "We'll rest here," he said. "It could be some time before the city is safe for us to return to."

Dominique helped Geret towards the stairs. "What about Geret?" she asked. "He will need water…and food…and we cannot transform him in this condition."

"There are plenty of provisions," Cristofano said, descending the stairs. He placed his palm against a panel on the door, and it lifted, revealing darkness. He turned and extended his arms.

"Behold, the crypt," he said. "We will be safe here from all harm."

Cristofano headed inside the darkness and started rummaging in the corner, as Ramiel remained outside. Dominque assisted Geret inside, and they sat in the middle of a stone floor. Cristofano lit several candles, bathing the small, stone room in a warm glow. Ramiel remained in the doorway, looking at the flickering light glow against shelves of wooden coffins.

Cristofano leaned down, and grabbed a candle. He held it up, and carried it around the crypt, as the others watched. The flickering light revealed the wooden coffins, resting on the stone shelves. "These are the eldest," he said. "Those who have been chained, bound in coffin sentences for centuries. We will rest among the protection of our ancestors."

Ramiel entered the crypt and the door slid downwards as the sky was lightening and the sun was rising. The darkness enveloped them, save the flickering candle light.

"We are being hunted," Cristofano said. "As we have been for centuries, and as we will be for centuries to come. The ancestors listen, and they will protect. This crypt is only known by those who are in the Inspiriti, and our presence here will alert the members back in Rome."

Dominique raised her head as she and Geret settled on the floor, laying down. "You have the time gift?"

"My maker does," Cristofano said.

Dominique turned and looked over at the coffins. "Can you release them?"

Cristofano's face fell. "No," he said. "We stay here, and their presence will protect us."

Ramiel sat and joined the others. It was going to be a long wait, it seemed. There was no telling how long it would be until the streets of Paris would be safe for immortals again, perhaps never. He looked at Cristofano, who lay back himself, closing his eyes. Ramiel waited, watching the door. He assumed that no mortal would have access to the crypt, or even know its whereabouts, but despite Cristo's words of reassurance, he couldn't help but feel hunted.

THE CURTAIN FALLS

ACT TWO:

The Witches

Part Three

COFFIN VOODOO

One

THE MASSACRE was far from their minds as they waited in the safety and solitude of the hidden crypt. Ramiel watched as Cristofano would awaken and leave, sometimes once or twice in a single day, giving the command to the others to remain in place and wait while he ventured out into the apparently hostile territory; yet Ramiel could scarcely remember the threat of the mortals. The animosity was there, Cristofano had reminded him on multiple occasions, from a segment of the human population who hunted the immortals.

He thought of papa.

On the nights back in Rome, when papa would hold his pasta and wine dinners with mama, they would host neighbors and others around town, to discuss the necessity of stamping the immortals out of existence permanently. They thought the immortal population was a threat to anything good and decent; a blasphemy to the church, and a force that must be destroyed, no matter the reason.

He looked over at Dominique, who was huddled in the corner, her knees drawn up close to her breasts, her eyes closed, seemingly content and possibly asleep. And then Geret, the only mortal in their group, yet to be transformed, but desiring the dark gift of immortality. Certainly now, would he want such a curse? To be banished from society, in an apparent feat of jealousy from the mortals?

The time seemed long, as they sat, and waited for Cristofano to return; Geret had his provisions and the others sat and waited. And then, Cristofano said they could leave the crypt. Enough time had passed since the massacre, he said. They could return to Paris, go to Cristofano's flat, and plan their next course of action.

"I've received instruction from the Inspiriti, Dominique," Cristofano said, as Ramiel raised his head. "Your sentence will still be carried out, despite the massacre."

"What about the others?" Dominique asked.

Cristofano stood as the heavy door slid open to bright sunlight. "When I was gone, I returned to the theater. Madame Arsenault's bones still rest in ashes in the back gardens. The others are gone. Dead, most likely. There have been many shadows lately."

"The dark ones," she said. "I know them well."

"And you will serve your penance," he said. "Then they won't come for you because the time in the coffin will save you."

Cristofano signaled for the others to join him as he waited at the threshold to the crypt. "Our ancestors have protected us," he said. "Those enduring the most stringent of coffin sentences still wield the power to guard those who share their blood ancestry."

Ramiel walked next to Geret and followed Dominque and Cristofano. The woods looked far less threatening in daylight. The sunlight was deceptive; there was little warmth and the forest was a network of dead branches. When a gust of wind tore through the treetops, Ramiel put his arms around Geret in an attempt to keep him warm. "I am the only mortal here," he said, looking up at Ramiel. "When will I be transformed?"

Ramiel looked into his big, brown eyes, appreciating his eagerness to receive the dark gift himself and become an immortal. "You have to be certain," Ramiel said. "Without equivocation. The gift will find you."

"I am certain," he said, a note of confidence in his voice. "I was sure that this was the path I wanted to take from the moment I stepped in the Jefferson."

"There has to be more," Ramiel said.

"More?"

He nodded. "Yes. We immortals are challenged with broadening the bloodline. Our ancestry is of the utmost importance to our elders, those who are still walking the earth. Some of the eldest are in Rome. Others in the middle east, and here in Paris. But despite their physical distance, they all remain in close contact. And the code is held in the highest regard."

"I am ready."

Ramiel turned and eyed Geret. "You must be selected," he said. "There is nothing else I can do about it. The code is what it is. That is what makes the gift sacred. Mortals are given free will, and when the time comes for you to receive the gift, you will know. And your maker will know too. We all must continue the blood ancestry, so as long as you continue your desire to be a part of this, it will find you."

Cristofano stopped as the others looked up. He turned and ushered them closer to him. "We're not far from the theater," he said. "Some time has passed since the massacre, but I am going to warn you. There has been little done. The theater is still a burned out wreck. There is destruction everywhere. Burned out rafters. The roof is caving in. It's like the city has ignored everything. The massacre, everything. As if it never happened."

Dominque's face fell. "And yet they caused it."

"They will always despise us," Cristofano said, as Geret raised his eyes and looked over at him. "We have something which they can only dream about, and yearn for."

"What is that?" Geret asked.

"Immortality," Cristofano said. "The power to live through centuries, experience multiple generations. We have the dark gift, which many may fear, yet many embrace. There's been a quest for immortality throughout millennia. All across the world and through human existence. There has been a fascination with us, yet at the same time, a fear. We hold gifts and powers that they never would have as mortals."

"Gifts that only we can give," Dominique added.

"And with that comes power," Ramiel said. "Some fear power, not all, but some. Others are threatened by it."

"But many are threatened by what they don't know. What they fail to understand," Cristofano added. "And from those who are different."

Geret nodded slowly, looking downwards as they proceeded. His eyes were slits. "Is that why they – I mean we – attacked the theater?"

"There could be multiple reasons for that," Cristofano said.

The group stopped as they saw the remains of the Jefferson Majestic in the foreground. The small forest concealed the greatest damage; but

Ramiel knew what lay in the rear gardens. He lowered his head and closed his eyes, thinking of Madame Arsenault. She was a fierce instructor, a forceful immortal, and a profound influence on his artistic creativity. No one deserved to die in flames. He couldn't imagine the agony. But Cristofano had said that she was one of the immortals from an elder bloodline. If she were immortal, would she still be lying in the gardens, her body charred and partially decomposed...yet in agonizing, eternal pain?

Ramiel watched as Cristofano paused in front of the small, thick cluster of trees as they stood, listening. Just beyond would be the streets and avenues of Paris. The sun was setting, as the sky ignited in a crimson palette.

"Let me go first," he said.

Ramiel and the others waited as Cristofano proceeded through the trees. They could see his white shirt and the silhouette of the billowing sleeves through the dark veins of the branches. Ramiel watched as Cristofano hung his head, shaking it slowly back and forth. Could Madame Arsenault still be there? How would she be able to recover from such a forceful torment to her body?

But as Cristofano navigated further towards the charred remains of the theater, there was a sense of despair which washed through the others. Geret leaned against Dominique, as they fell into each other's arms, and Ramiel felt a steady force rising within, as he watched Cristofano move from the trees, into the garden and turn back towards them, waving them forward. As they proceeded, slowly, their feet shuffling through the remains of dead leaves and listening to the snap of small twigs against the otherwise silent dusk, he felt his stomach squeeze into a knot.

And his breathing quickened, as he felt a tightness in his chest that he had never experienced before, watching Cristofano, as he stood motionless in the center of the charred, desecrated gardens. Ramiel saw the remains at Cristofano's feet. Ramiel watched as Cristofano raised his head and looked over at them as they approached. A smell of charred wood and smoke hung in the air. Cristofano raised his left arm. "Stop everyone," he said.

The others stood behind Cristofano as Ramiel reached up and placed his arm on Cristo's shoulder. He turned his head slowly.

"What is it? What do you sense?" Ramiel asked.

Cristofano turned back forward. After a few moments of watching the smoke still rising into the clouds, he spoke. "There's still movement there," he said.

"Where?" Ramiel asked. "From inside the theater?"

Cristofano nodded slowly.

"Who is in there?" Dominique asked, as she and Geret moved closer to the others.

Cristofano turned forward again. "There have been rumors," he said. "Rumors that the mysterious and mythical 'crypt dancer' haunts the theater."

"But you are he," Dominque said, after a few moments of silence.

Ramiel watched as Cristofano remained fixated on the remains of the theater. He could tell by looking at his maker that his mind was churning. Cristofano was likely right. There might be another force inside the theater, yet it might not be what they expect. Ramiel turned and looked at Dominique and Geret, who waited nearby, and waited for instruction from Cristofano and Ramiel. Dominique reached around Geret's back and gave him a squeeze, lovingly caressing the side of his hair. She looked back towards the two immortals. "If there is a dark force inside the theater, we cannot risk Geret. Not when he hasn't been transformed."

"And it makes no sense to attempt to transform him now," Cristofano said, while looking ahead at the dark, crumbling skeleton of the building.

Ramiel knew.

And despite that the pressure fell on him to create a new immortal to continue the bloodline, Cristofano was correct. Given the state of Paris, there would be no safe haven for Geret to properly transform. He could hear the distant shouting. The mobs still ran the streets. Immortals were no longer welcome in the city.

"It's not the mob that I fear," Cristofano said.

The others moved closer to him and listened.

"It's the shadows," he said. He stooped down and rested on his feet. The others looked down at him as he continued. "It results from the envious nature of the immortals. And the eternal desire to supersede another's gifts and powers."

They fell silent as Cristofano dug into the ground with a stick. The mood had taken on an aura of uncertainty. Ramiel considered his maker's words and thought about the shadow demons he was referring to. Perhaps there was some logic to Cristo's hesitation.

"There's a competition?" Geret asked, breaking the silence.

Cristofano turned to face the young mortal man. Dominique looked at him and nodded. "We immortals have been plagued with envy from our inception," she said.

Geret shook his head as Cristofano stood and tossed his stick aside into the brush. "That doesn't seem to be the case at all, from my perspective," Geret said.

Ramiel took a cautious step forward as Cristofano scoffed, raising his eyes up towards Geret. "Do you honestly think you can understand the rivalry between those with the dark gift?"

Ramiel extended his arm between them. "Cristo," he said. "He's just inquisitive."

Cristofano snapped his head in Ramiel's direction and glared at him as Geret took a step back and raised his hands, his open palms facing Cristofano. "I...I..." Dominque placed her hands on his arms and drew him back towards her. "Don't worry," she said. "You will learn."

Ramiel looked at Cristofano as he calmed. There was an uncertainty in his disposition, not only from Geret's comment, but also from the entire situation. They watched as Cristofano stood once again, dusting himself off, and looking directly at them. "Dominique," he said. "You know we must go below the stage. You know what's down there."

Ramiel looked over at Dominique as her eyes fell. She hung her head. "Yes, Cristo. It's the only way."

As Cristofano started to proceed, the others slowly followed and Ramiel caught up with him. "Cristo," he said. The dark skeleton of the charred remains loomed ahead through the remaining gardens and trees. "Cristo!"

Cristo stopped and turned, exasperated. "What is it, Ramiel?"

"Why do we have to go? Why do we have to go there?"

Ramiel watched as Cristofano shook his head, making eye contact with him. He was looking down on him, as if a father was looking at a child who should have known better. But Ramiel could only speculate. He knew that there were certain areas deep within the theater, below the stage and performing areas, which had been rumored to transport those who ventured into the darkness.

Ramiel felt a chill run through his spine.

Cristofano stood in the center of the garden; the stench of burned flesh remained in the air. He hung his head down and closed his eyes.

The others gasped as the burnt corpse gurgled. Dominique covered her mouth with her hands as tears welled up in her eyes.

They stopped looking at Madame Arsenault's remains when they heard a whisper emanating from inside.

"What...did you hear that?" Dominique wiped her cheeks as they gather closer to Cristofano, who stood in front of the other three, as if the protector.

The immortals who have perished under your hand will rise victorious over your soul's destiny!

Dominque shrieked as she grabbed the back of Cristofano's shirt and cowered behind him. She squeezed her eyes shut, shaking her head dramatically. "No, no, no, *no!*"

Ramiel bent down as Geret held her from behind, making an attempt to comfort her. Cristofano remained facing forward, as the clouds swirled angrily above. "This has become your journey, Dominique. They have come for you. For your penance. For justice..."

231

Ramiel watched as Dominque released her grip on Cristofano's shirt. He knew that there would be no other way to avoid the sentence, her time in the coffin was required by the code.

"The Dark Ones have come for you, Dominique," Cristofano said. He bent down, placed his hands on her arms, as she opened her eyes and looked up at him. "It is time." Her eyes were red as tears streamed down her cheeks. She slowly nodded.

Ramiel gestured for Geret to join him as Dominque slowly stood.

We have come for you…

She shuddered as the voices hissed from within the theater, as Cristofano stood next to her. Ramiel and Geret watched from behind as they slowly approached the charred remains of the theater. As Ramiel trailed behind them with Geret, he watched as they slowly ascended the rear stone steps; Ramiel looked up as the dark spires still rose up into the clouds, undamaged from the fires. Down towards the doors the wood frame was crumbling and charred black, it still smelled of soot and smoke and decay, but he knew the interior…the rooms below…would have far too many shadows.

Ramiel and Geret rushed to catch up as Cristofano and Dominque disappeared into the darkness. He turned and gestured for Geret to follow. "Let's not lose them," he said. "It's pitch dark in there."

Geret nodded and they emerged into the rear corridors of the theater. From his memory, the back hallway would lead ahead up towards stage right, but there was no discerning any type of indicators. Beams from the upper levels had crashed downwards in the fire, blocking access ahead.

"Cristo! Dominque!"

No answer.

Geret stopped next to Ramiel as he called again. "They literally just walked in here," he said. Ramiel hesitated moving further inside the darkness.

The only way out is farther in…

He gasped.

They were speaking to him.

Was it a warning, perhaps? Or an invitation?

The doors which lined the opposite side of the corridor remained closed, charred black from the fire yet their steel and determined presence remained. The doors which he had never thought he would enter. The mysterious entryways which Madame Arsenault, and Cristofano and the remainder of the company had said never to enter; those steel doors must always remain closed.

But as he squinted to see in the fading light, a clap of thunder resounded from above; and just as the rain began to fall, he saw the final door in the lineup. It was open, just slightly, still resting against the frame, and then he suspected where Cristofano and Dominique may have gone.

Down below, towards the mysterious unknown; where the shadows would live and breathe and speak. To the caverns and the war between shadows and light, where the entrance to the netherworld would remain, guarded and locked, surrounded by candles and chains.

"Stay with me," he said to Geret as the young mortal joined him. "There are shadows everywhere."

Ramiel approached the door as Geret kept close. "Those doors have never been open like that before," he said. "There's something sinister down there, isn't there?"

Ramiel turned, making eye contact with him, and nodded. "If you ever are transformed you will know," he said. "You will read the code. And abide by the code. Or you will receive the same fate as Dominique."

The door slowly opened with a deep, rumbling creak. Ramiel closed his eyes and took a breath.

"What did she do that was so horrible?"

The piercing rattle of clanking chains emanated from the darkness below as Ramiel opened his eyes and looked back towards Geret. "She was at great odds with her maker," Ramiel said. "Blood was shed. But in the immortal community, bloodshed has no fatal consequences."

"What happened, Ramiel?"

"I know few details," he said. "But there was premeditation. She is not as innocent as she seems. Her history is long, and her bloodline is diverse, but she had always been rebellious when it came to her maker. She failed to create herself, and...I don't know if it was a fit of rage...or if it was truly premediated as Cristofano claimed." He took several steps down heavy, stone earthen steps. "The code was written with great clarity. Rebelliousness in general is a characteristic that many immortals share. But it's forbidden against elders. And in Dominique's case, punishable by coffin sentence."

"Why wouldn't Cristofano burn her like when he showed us the illusion backstage?"

Ramiel scoffed. "Because death would not be a punishment for an immortal who violates the code," he said. "Fire will end most immortals; you saw that first hand when the humans torched the theater."

"And Madame Arsenault was still aware? Of her burned and charred corpse?"

"She's not a corpse," Ramiel said. "I don't know what Cristofano plans to do with her. She's been lying in the garden since the massacre and there are ways to resurrect her…"

"But?"

"The demons come."

Ramiel returned his attention to the darkness as the sound of the chains grew louder.

From the top of the steps, they could see little in the darkness save the warm, flickering light of wall torches. He heard screams in the distance. This was never an experience to witness, he thought. He'd heard of instances when immortal sentences were carried out by the crypt dancer; when the violator was mortified and tortured and humiliated for their transgressions against the immortal kind.

The code.

It was the violation of the code, Ramiel thought.

But he could hear her voice, through the darkness. And if the voice inside his head was correct, if the only way out was truly farther in, then why did he feel such reservations for proceeding?

Would there be a horrific scene so incomprehensible that he would regret his transformation?

It couldn't be, he thought. As the screams emanated from deeper within the darkness, he heard the chains rattle and he fought the resistance to descend the steps downwards to the earthen floor.

And then he saw the coffins.

Piled in corners, plain wooden coffins, stacked towards the ceiling, neatly in rows. The dark wood reflected a gentle flickering of the flaming torches which lined the walls, breathing whispers of days when there was far less judgement in their community. The coffin used to be a symbol of comfort, of transformation. Now, as he looked at the reflection of the flames in the dark polished wood, the representation had changed.

The symbol of the coffin had become that of a prison; a holding place for rebellious immortals who had violated the code. A place of dark isolation and torment. For some, it lasted an eternity. Cristofano was the harbinger of these feelings. Yet, as the doctrine had been written, he was simply fulfilling his duties as the crypt dancer. But could he have been corrupted?

They proceeded beyond the stacked coffins and Geret gasped audibly.

Dominique stood unclothed in the center of a small clearing. A coffin lay on the dirt floor next to her, as Cristofano stood in front of her, arms crossed, a stern look in his eyes.

She cried out as blood ran down her back.

Ramiel watched the scene play out before them, as he slowly placed his arms around Geret, pulling him closer towards his chest. This was the scene he had only heard about; he had only read about it in *The Code of the Immortals*, and there were few who spoke of it. During the trial of The Dark Ones, the crypt dancer would preside, but judgement would always be rendered ahead of time.

He had only heard about the shadow demons."

When the dark shadows transformed, elongated and tore towards her, the penalty had begun. A torch burned on the wall next to Dominque, as Cristofano cast a long shadow on the dirt floor. She turned, whimpering, her wrists bound in chains, as the shadow moved closer towards her. Cristofano bent down towards the dark corner and lifted a long, reflective chain, which rattled against the stone walls. Her whimpers echoed throughout the chamber as Cristofano tossed the chain in the shadow, clanking. The darkness wrapped around the metal and shot towards Dominique; she cried out at it wrapped around her, tearing into her legs, and around her back, as bright red blood poured from her. Cristofano's voice charged deep.

"As the crypt dancer, I hereby sentence you to an eternity of silence, torment and torture in the coffin. Your awareness will remain with you as the crypt is sealed. The darkness and the demon will silence you. May you find peace in the pursuit of a death you will never find!"

Her screams were silenced as the shadow wrapped around her head, as her eyes were wide and pleading. She collapsed to the ground, writhing, as Cristofano bent down and picked her up, placing her in the waiting coffin.

"The demon will bind you for eternity."

He extended his arm as the lid slammed into place, and six nails lifted from the ground and pierced the lid, tightening it into place.

Ramiel stood with Geret and stared at the coffin. Cristofano hung his head and collapsed onto the ground, sitting with his legs raised, and his arms draped over his knees. He hung his head down and closed his eyes.

He slowly released his grip on Geret, watching Cristofano.

The sound of crying emanated through the darkness, as the torches flickered and the shadows retreated. There was something about Cristofano. Ramiel thought that the duties of the crypt dancer must take an emotional toll. Cristofano had been friends with Dominique when they danced together with the company on the stage just above where they stood. But if the theater was the cover for a justice operation for disobedient immortals, then what would come of it, now that the theater was in ruins and most of the immortal cast has been burned and their bodies decimated.

He knew his maker had a heart.

Somewhere, deep within, the blood still flowed in his veins. The crypt dancer was forceful and driven, bound to the code yet there was a sense to protect inside, Ramiel could see.

The code, however, dominated.

Two

IN THE DAYS LEADING UP TO the massacre and fire at the Jefferson Majestic Theater in Paris, Ramiel and Cristofano spent their days in each other's arms in bed in Cristofano's expansive and elegant flat; at night, they walked the streets of Paris together, wearing fine suits, and top hats, and canes, and continued to do so despite the passage of time. Geret remained with them as well, and became loyal to them. Cristofano had yet to transform Geret, and neither had Ramiel, despite Geret's pleading.

After the massacre, which had become a pivotal moment in the immortals' existence, a sense of abandonment and despair started to overtake the immortal population of the city. The days turned into weeks, and the weeks turned into months; the snow melted and the remains of the Jefferson Majestic were finally demolished. The Inspiriti sold the land to the city, and contacted Cristofano, advising that all immortals vacate the city and choose other areas.

The massacre had been an attack on humanity by their own kind.

The rogue mobs who stormed through the theater doors that fateful night knew that the theater was owned and operated by immortals, with links to the Inspiriti in Rome, but the massacre had truly affected their own kind. The audience had been humans who were there enjoying the production. The immortals had escaped, they always do. And had they not, the perception that fire would not hold the power to bring an immortal to death was a fallacy. The sear of the flames might damage tissue in a grotesque fashion, yet an immortal, incapable of feeling physical pain, would endure much mental anguish as the sentence, of justice, would endure for days, nights, months and centuries. Should a massacre occur by fire and flame, the body would be destroyed.

Time progressed as the trio remained in Paris, when the theater became just a memory.

They frequented *Pere Lachaise* and many times the same crypt, which Cristofano had taken Ramiel and Geret the night of the massacre. They would revisit multiple times, taking the same stone steps which would descend down into the ground, to the concealing door with clouded glass with rusted spires, where Geret would cup his hands around his face to look inside at the crumbling coffins on the stone shelves.

"This is the crypt of our bloodline ancestors," Cristofano said when they had spilled into the crypt on the night of the massacre.

While the days and nights progressed to a more modern era, Ramiel and Cristofano appeared frozen in a time period with which they both held a deep connection. And as the sun was setting over the western horizon, they walked down *Quai de Gesveres*, along La Seine river, towards where the Majestic theater once stood.

"Many years ago," Cristofano said. "Generations it seems." He looked up at the light across the dim sky. "I think it's time to move on, Ramiel.

What do you think? Perhaps Paris has become somewhat dull and unpolished?"

Ramiel looked up as throngs of revelers exited a posh hotel in front of them.

"We could travel to America too," Cristofano said. "In fact, I think it's imperative that we join the progress over there. Antoine's chateau in Lyon has been closed for quite a while now. The Europe scene has been transforming to far too much governorship from Rome, it seems. At least over there, we could stretch our legs for a bit."

"And you want to go to Miami, like Antoine?"

"We have some more work to take care of here, first, before we go," Cristofano said. "But Miami would be an ideal sector. It's quite polarized. And they have the coven there. Seems to be a threat."

"A coven?"

Cristofano hugged Ramiel closer to him as the small clouds of vapor emanated from their mouths in the chill. "Witches," he said. "There is a long history, centuries really, of the immortals and The Inspiriti in Rome. There are several who are serving coffin sentences."

Ramiel felt a shudder run through him.

How many layers were there to the tapestry which Cristofano appeared to be weaving?

"Antoine has been in Miami for years now," Cristofano added. "But the sector has been in turmoil. He's in need of our aid."

Ramiel cocked his head to the side. "I don't know...you really think he is?"

"Darius is with him," Cristofano said. "Antoine resurrected him, but in doing so, he opened a portal. A gate. A means for the demons to pursue him. Especially Asmodai."

"And our purpose…is to help Antoine?"

Cristofano paused as they arrived at the *Le Hotel Aristocrat*.

Ramiel looked up as they navigated the rising old buildings, which looked to him like stacked, colorful pastel dominoes. The hotel was nestled in the midst of buildings, providing no indication of the soaring, rounded dome inside.

He guided them into the cool atrium through a set of black iron gates, boarded by heavy hanging drapes, and they were swiftly met by two smartly dressed doormen. Cristofano danced ahead and twirled in the lobby. His eyes were wide, his smile was bright and brilliant, and he remained dancing to an unseen orchestra, as the other guests backed away from him.

"Don't you see Ramiel?!"

Ramiel approached and folded his arms. "I want to go to America. I want Geret to come with us."

Cristofano stopped spinning and approached him, placing his cool hands on Ramiels chin. He looked up and acted as if he were on a drug. "We still have work to do here before we go! Don't get ahead of yourself." He sung and twirled towards the front desk. He stopped and froze at the edge of the desk and reached out and caressed the young woman's cheek. "I am expected," he said, and flipped around to look at Ramiel.

His eyes were wide, there was a look of excitement on his face. Ramiel looked at him in a state of perplexity. Cristofano had always been rather gay and giddy. But tonight, he was somewhat different. Like an excited child running down the stairs on Christmas morning, Cristofano had a look of amazement and wonder about him as they headed towards the rooms.

"I will finally get to stretch my legs!" he said.

He twirled back around and reached his arms outwards. "And you will assist me from the very beginning," he added.

"Cristo…I haven't even seen you so excited…over a group of travelers from Haiti?"

He lunged forwards and grabbed Ramiel's lapels. "Not *any* group of travelers! It's the Mastuers! They are one of the strongest voodoo dynasties in the Caribbean!"

Ramiel didn't understand the fascination with voodoo. "How are we involved in all of that? Magic and spells?"

Cristofano backed away from the reception desk and approached Ramiel, who stood further back in the lobby sitting area. "Don't you see?" Cristofano asked. "There's a connection with everything. Have you ever heard of LaDonna Mastuer?"

Ramiel shook his head. "No. Should I have heard of her?"

Cristofano reached out and placed his hand on Ramiel's shoulder, and then dropped his head down. "If only I had tutored you more," he said. He looked up as his face brightened. "She is a master priestess," he said, as his voice lowered. "And she is entombed *right here* in Paris! Don't you see?"

Ramiel's face shifted. "See what?"

"*She isn't dead.*"

And then Ramiel realized what Cristofano was trying to tell him. It wasn't that he wanted to pay respects to a figure in witchcraft lore, but that, at some point, there was a crypt dancer who had carried out justice with Ms. Mastuer. It wasn't the responsibility of the crypt dancer to know all who were serving sentences of entombment across the world, but it could certainly be researched. Cristofano, it seemed, had done his research. Ramiel watched as Cristofano released his grip on his shoulder, maintaining eye contact as he spun around. Certainly, he had his reasons for contacting the Mastuers. Was he attempting a negotiation of some sorts?

Ramiel sighed.

Cristofano, though, had been difficult to discern.

Ramiel leaned his face back, watching as Cristofano wandered off towards the guest room hallways.

Cristo had the smell of blood still on his breath. He had been hunting, which was out of character for him in recent days, especially during the years of the massacre. But now, he had been speaking with different tongues; Cristo was quite convincing about the trip to America. But also with the crypts…and his fascination with the Mastuers.

He turned as they approached a large set of dark wooden doors. A dark man in a black suit stood at the side of the door, his arms clasped at his waist, wearing dark sunglasses despite the late hour. He stood and stared outwards, but Ramiel knew that he was aware of their presence.

Cristofano glided up towards the man and he snapped his head in his direction.

"We are here about LaDonna," Cristofano said as Ramiel joined him at the door.

The man leaned down close to Cristofano's face. He backed up a few steps and held up his arms. "Is Madame there? Is she inside? She sent for me."

"*Tann isit la.*"

The man opened the door slowly and eased himself into the darkness. Ramiel tapped Cristofano on the arm and shrugged his shoulders.

"Wait here," he said. "Creole."

Ramiel nodded as the woman who could none other than the current Madame of the Mastuer voodoo dynasty emerged from the darkness. Her dark skin contrasted her white, flowing dress. She crossed her arms and looked at Cristofano, over to Ramiel, and then back. The tall man retook his position at the side of the doors as Madame raised her eyebrows and looked up at Cristofano. "So you are the one your Claret has been telling me about?" She balled her fists and leaned them on her waist, as Ramiel noticed her forceful demeanor; Ramiel assumed that she was high ranking from her commanding tone and presence.

"Claret, yes," Cristofano said. "I am the one who can help you with LaDonna."

She is buried in a crypt and is crossed in chains. She is a threat to the immortal community worldwide.

Ramiel stopped for a moment, as the words hissed into his mind, and watched Cristofano, who remained enthralled, and polite and pleasant. Madame nodded slowly but didn't say a word. She turned and gestured for them to follow her into the room, in which the curtains were closed and the room was shrouded in darkness.

Ramiel and Cristofano followed her as they walked into a massive suite. The curtains were drawn tight, shutting out the light from the day and the city outside, and candles were burning, lining tables throughout the room. Madame found herself a spot on a small couch, in front of a glass coffee table covered in burning candles, as her subjects surrounded her. The warm flicker of the candles reflected on their faces.

Ramiel and Cristofano were shown to two small side chairs and they sat hastily. Ramiel and Cristofano made eye contact as Madame cleared her throat.

"You are here about LaDonna."

Cristofano turned towards the priestess and Ramiel heard him take a deep breath through his nostrils. It was the first time he'd seen him with a hint of nervousness.

"Yes," he said slowly. "It's my understanding that she rests here in Paris, am I correct?"

They saw the reflection of the candles against Madame's face as she slowly nodded.

"There's a deep…history…with that, and us. The immortals, I mean."

Ramiel looked down and pursed his lips. Cristofano appeared nervous. What was he getting at here?

"There is," she said slowly. "And what makes you think that we are going to discuss specifics about our high queen with two immortals?"

Cristofano looked across the chairs at Ramiel. He shrugged his shoulders as Ramiel glared at him.

"We want to release her," Ramiel said. He didn't even realize what he had said until he'd said it. He had potentially just committed the most grave of sins against the immortal code in a split second. He shot a glance over at Cristofano, who looked over at him with an approving tone. Would both of them be banished to the coffin for centuries, if not longer?

Cristofano leaned forward in his chair. "She has the power to resurrect," he said, as Madame and her followers looked on. "A power which we have sought for generations, but have never found. We made a mistake, clearly, when she was banished to the coffin."

Ramiel struggled to keep his mouth shut when he listened to Cristofano.

Was he selling the immortals out to the Mastuers?

Three

THERE WERE NIGHTMARES about Cristofano, and in the days that followed the massacre, he went to Rome for several days. There were those who believed he was not the malevolent character that he always claimed to be; in fact, it was over the centuries that he'd been far worse. He was the dark child of Claret, but not in the physical sense. Her gift of time-travel took her through myriad cities and centuries.

She had been to modern-day Rome, during the time when The Inspiriti was investigating the wrath of The Hooded Man, when Cristofano sat on the back bench of the courtroom. He knew there had been punishment of Claret by crucifixion…but that is where the obsession began.

How long had she been governing the immortals?

He knew then that the immortals knew that Ramiel had yet to be transformed, that he was a human ally to the organization of immortals which existed in the bowels of the Sistine Chapel in *Citta del Vaticano*, but the appearance of Claret was both unexpected and came in a torrent of supernatural phenomenon.

Cristofano had been listening to the trials; Claret was punished with crucifixion, there was no more physical being to pursue him.

Or seduce him.

Yet when he turned, and as the Inspiriti council remained forward facing, and focused on the words of Monsignor Harrison, who stood at a pulpit in the center of the council tables, the voices drowned out. He gasped as he saw a hand reach around the side of the door frame, as if searching for him, as if beckoning.

Cristo…come out to the corridor…

Cristo.

Mama had always called him that, before she passed. But the voice had hissed, it was not mama. *Cristo!*

And then as he watched the door, the hand retreated into the darkness, yet the door remained open…just a crack.

Mama was on the other side of the door. She stank of the grave and there was dirt caked in her hair. Her face looked rotten as the skin hung in flaps, exposing her dry and bloodless skull. "Come out into the corridor, little Cristo…"

There will be solitude and peace when you have your time in the coffin…

He shuddered, hung his head and squeezed his eyes shut.

There would be no visions of mama. Not at these proceedings. It was destined to be a plea; he had to commute her sentence.

"Cristofano, you may approach." Monsignor Harrison sat in the center of the pulpit, surround by the High Council on either side. He looked down at him, with a stern look on his face, one of the elders, looking down at the son who had failed to follow directions which he had been given. The monsignor looked down and thumbed through some paperwork. His file, no doubt.

"I have all of the reports from the Jefferson massacre," he said as he continued to examine the contents. "It says here that Madame Arsenault was the leader of that sector, yet you had a special role."

Cristofano nodded. "Yes. I was given specific instructions from my maker about the purpose behind my transformation."

"Claret Atarah?"

Cristofano nodded. "Yes. We had many discussions when she was preparing me for the role. She told me about the origins, and the history behind the purpose of the role. And why she had selected me for it. The council was never made aware of this?"

There was a murmur which flowed through the crowd, as Monsignor Harrison leaned closer to his closest subjects.

He was holding a conversation which Cristofano could not decipher from the movement of the monsignor's lips, but he already knew what it was about.

Claret was gone, and there was only one way to receive an answer.

He knew that he held the power to resurrect; there was a certain aspect of his blood ancestry which had taken him years to determine.

"Claret was in close contact with the council before she was destroyed," Monsignor Harrison said. "And it was for good purpose. I know she was your maker. You have the sacred blood lineage, that you do. But her transgressions warranted her punishment."

Cristofano thought of Claret. "Shouldn't we all be offered redemption if we are willing to change?"

The monsignor remained silent, and Cristofano thought of the last time he was with Claret, in Rome. She had stood with him, outside the chapel, her lips pursed. She brushed her red hair from her cheek as she drew deeply on a cigarette. Cristofano noticed the bright red lipstick stain on the filter.

The skies above Rome darkened, painted with wisps of orange through an angry cover of dark, swirling clouds. Claret walked across *La Piazza San Pietro*. The deed was done. Antoine would be transformed. The perfect puppet, a buffet of evil tyranny would begin; for the prophecy against the immortals must be fulfilled. And all of the pieces would soon be in place.

A flash of lighting crashed down towards the cathedral, igniting flames on the spire as the winds tore across the plaza. Claret turned, smiled and headed towards the edge of the road. She closed her eyes. This was all too easy. Each piece was being put into place, and then, she would know, that there was a certain purpose of her animosity.

Thunder crashed overhead as a chorus of screams rang in the distance.

She opened her eyes one last time as the steeple crashed to the ground below. She turned around. A mass of people stormed the front of the cathedral as flames tore through the falling steeple.

The protection…of the grave…will become a welcome destiny. The same darkness, the solitude…the silence.

She looked up, watching the flames engulf the cathedral, as the people carried buckets of water, hoisting it across a line connected with arms, and long flowing cassocks, as the clatter of indiscernible squabbling fought against the howling of the winds and thunder.

She drew another cigarette from her pocket, and placed it in her mouth slowly.

The massacre.

And the flames.

The chaos and the torment would never end there. For what Ramiel didn't know, nor did Cristofano, or Darius, or Antoine, was her true intentions. And those intentions were never revealed. For Claret remained a mystery throughout the history of the immortals. As it was always known, she was a fierce leader who led through others. She was feared, and rumored to torment, and torture, and have no regards for anything…or anyone…save herself.

But there had been a warrior who rose against her, another immortal who had insisted through oceans of time that Claret did not have the best intentions of the immortals in her heart. That she had a sinister plan…but why?

The immortals were working on integrating themselves into society.

To work in unison with their human, mortal counterparts. To live harmoniously.

But Claret, as the immortals had discussed in hushed uncertainty, had always appeared to work against that. And then there was the darkness. The never ending sunset, and the impact of the swirling, angry clouds that always seemed to draw inwards. And the storms, the anger and the torment which rained downwards on the immortals.

It was their dark destiny for which they had each been chosen.

It was not a different purpose than that any woman or man, for they each had free will as well. Yet for the immortals, there was a certain purpose, a draw, a yearning for something darker. And more sinister. And none of them were immune.

Claret blew a cloud of smoke which caught the wind and flew away. She stood and watched the pathetic mortals struggle across the plaza with overflowing buckets of water, hoisting them on the flames which tore downwards, to no avail.

And then she caught a glimpse, and the voice, of one who could be Monsignor Harrison. An immortal, her Governor, helping the mortals save their building, their symbol.

She tossed her cigarette down and stamped it out with her heavy black boot as the skies opened up, and rain fell in torrents.

"There you go," she said. "And enjoy the aftermath your highness."

Ramiel watched Cristofano as the Mastuers indicated their expectations about LaDonna's release from coffin sentence. He watched Cristofano watching them, and from the look on his face, Ramiel wondered if Cristofano was still present in the moment. The look on his face said that Cristofano's mind had wandered. Perhaps to the past. And most likely to Claret. For his maker had a significant power which remained. Her fate, on a wooden cross, at Golgatha, after the trials, bothered Cristofano. Ramiel noticed it.

The Hooded Man came in a robe, with a decanter, and a false promise.

Ramiel remembered the trials and Monsignor Harrison's outbursts. "He promised salvation and brought us *death*!"

Was Cristofano attempting to clear his maker's name?

As the meeting with the Mastuers concluded, they exited Le Hotel Aristocrat to the rising sun. As they walked back to the flat, where Geret would surely be waiting, Ramiel thought of the days when the Jefferson Majestic had been a burned shell. He thought of the stacked coffins, the dark shadows that wielded the chains.

And how Dominique had been entombed for so many years.

There was still a great deal of anger running through Cristofano's veins, it seemed.

When they returned to the flat, Geret welcomed them and they all retreated to the bedroom with the gigantic wooden spires.

Geret tore into the sheets like a boy, as Cristofano kicked off his pants and fell onto the pillow. Ramiel stood, watching them, and admiring the love that was shared between the three of them. Geret would have to be transformed soon, if he was to have any shred of youth left for the gift.

After Ramiel eased himself under the sheets, he listened to Geret's soft breathing, and heard nothing from Cristofano, which he expected. He sank his head into the fluffy pillow, and thought of Dominique.

He saw the Jefferson Majestic.

It was crumbling; the massacre had already taken place. And then he realized it was the day after they had gathered in the bowels of the theater.

Dominque's coffin was carried from the charred remains of the Jefferson Majestic theater the following day as a crowd gathered on the streets to watch. News had circulated around the city that one of the performers had perished in the massacre that had befallen the dance company just days prior. The doors to the theater remained open but charred and blackened; the crowd gathered on the steps which led downwards to the street, yet the scent of smoke and burnt embers remained in the air.

When the coffin emerged, the crowd erupted in a polite applause.

Dominique had been beloved.

Ramiel, Cristofano, Geret and Alandra stationed themselves at each corner of Dominque's coffin and hoisted it upwards in front of the crowd as their cheers swelled. When Cristofano leaned over and quietly reminded Ramiel that she could hear the crowds, neither of them were aware that Dominque actually *was* listening to the crowds that had gathered to send her off, and although she was bound by a shadow demon and chained, she could still feel the warm tear that streamed down her cheek.

"They loved her," Cristofano said, as they slowly descended the steps. Ramiel nodded and returned his attention to the stairs.

As one of the premiere dancers in Paris, when word had traveled that she had perished in the massacre, those people who were not threatened by the mysteriousness of the immortals, but rather intrigued, came to surface. It was rumored that the Jefferson Majestic dance company was comprised and directed by immortals; that there were those in Paris who refused travel to Rome. That the rumors of the immortal kind who were taking over society in small, discreet increments had originated from Rome, and that the Italians were threating, murderous and barbaric.

But the Parisians, who lined the steps and sidewalks as Dominique's coffin was gently carried down the street, further towards *Pere Lachaise*, were those who were boundlessly fascinated with the theater and the dance company; they adored the elaborate productions which Paris had not seen previously. And those who had comprised the company, including Dominique, were revered by this sector of Paris society.

Ramiel watched as the crowds parted as they carried the coffin further down the street towards the cemetery. Some were weeping, many threw roses as the coffin passed.

He craned his neck outwards, around the front of the coffin, and saw Cristofano's profile. "Hey!" he whispered.

Cristofano glanced his direction and raised his eyebrows but said nothing.

"Are we taking her all the way to the crypt? With the elders?"

Cristofano shook his head. "The Artistic Dance Society wants to hold a ceremony honoring her contribution to the Paris ballet community. We'll be placing her in an Inspiriti owned single crypt in the cemetery."

"And she will hear it all? The ceremony I mean. She is fully conscious and aware of what's going on?"

Cristofano turned his head and made eye contact with Ramiel. "I would imagine that she could. It's a gift, really. The gift I give the immortals. They get to experience their own death. And more often than not, they are able to witness – at least through the darkness and confines of the coffin – the outpouring of emotion. And they can see, for certain, how much they were loved. Or hated. In Dominique's case, she was beloved."

"But then what happens?"

Cristofano slowly nodded. "Well, after that, the punishment begins. The outpouring of love and ceremony only lasts a short while. And then life does go on."

Ramiel faced forward once again and considered Cristofano's words. That Dominque was chained in the coffin, lying demon bound, listening to everything. She probably was listening to their conversation. And also to the outpouring of love and appreciation.

After the ceremony had concluded and the sun was sinking in the sky, Ramiel stood, leaning against a cool, stone crypt, watching as they slid the coffin into the dark chamber, as a small crowd on onlookers hung their heads.

Cristofano approached him. "She heard that," he said, as Ramiel felt a chill in the air. "And when they seal it…"

"There will be darkness and silence," Ramiel added.

Ramiel opened his eyes.

He eased himself up on his elbows, looking over towards the others. Geret had left the bed, but Cristofano remained on his back, and motionless, on the opposite side of the bed.

The sunlight shined through the window above the desk, which indicated that it would set soon. Not much longer and Cristofano would awaken and emerge. Until then, he appreciated the silence.

When he looked over at his sleeping maker, Ramiel remembered the days when he didn't wish for silence.

In his thoughts, Ramiel saw himself stand and watch Cristofano dance in the street as the burning embers from the Jefferson Majestic still remained in the air. He twirled and stopped, as Ramiel's shoes slid on the gravel. "Must you dance?"

Cristofano looked up at Ramiel. He held his pose as his eyes remained wide. "Don't you see?"

"See what?" Ramiel asked as he regained his footing.

"The massacre *had* to happen," he said. "Yes, dancers had to die. The building went down in flames. But don't you see? There will be so much uncertainty between the immortals and the coven. The witches will be blamed. It would make sense, wouldn't it?"

Ramiel stopped and raised his head towards the sky. He could see the bright and brilliant pale blue moon in the sky as it casts a glow on them in through the fight of darkness. "It doesn't make sense to me at all," he said, as Cristofano resumed his pirouettes, splashing in puddles from the fresh rainfall. "And you...don't you fear that the immortals will be blamed for this?"

Cristofano stopped just next to Ramiel. "From the mortals? The humans?" He tossed his head back and laughed. "It doesn't matter what *they* think of us."

"Or with what *we* do," Ramiel said.

"Yes," Cristofano said. "Simple, silly little Ramiel. The mortal who has always held a deep fascination with our kind. Isn't it about time that you held your fascination...somewhat deeper?"

Ramiel folded his arms, and looked up towards the sky. "It looks like there isn't much time."

Cristofano scoffed. "Oh don't you worry," he said. "Come with me if that's what you want to do."

And then, Ramiel followed as Cristofano ran ahead, turning and gesturing for Ramiel to pick up the pace. "Come on!" he said. "I have somewhere we can go!"

As they headed towards the edge of the city, where slender paths wound their way through soaring dark forests, Ramiel saw, in the infant light, the edges of crypts rising from the blackness which they walked through.

"I have a crypt in there where we can go," Cristofano said as twigs snapped under his feet. He moved closer. Ramiel could feel the chill of his breath as he felt a chill run down his spine.

"Are you going to come in with me?"

Ramiel stammered. "I – we are going into a crypt?"

Cristofano grinned. "Suit yourself," he said. "But if you have the true fascination which I believe you *do*, then you will want to accompany me in the coffin."

Ramiel took a breath and sighed as Cristofano patiently waited. "I have all the time in the world," he said. "But my offer will expire when we reach the crypt down *there*."

Ramiel looked outwards through the cemetery, at the rising crypts, looking like small silhouettes of a cityscape, as if they were giants walking through, looking down at the masonry, the rising angels and crosses, as daylight threatened.

Cristofano stopped at the final crypt, at the edge of the forest, as the daylight heightened at the edge of the horizon, igniting the sky from an incoming brightness fading out towards a deepening dark blue. "We will wait in here," he said. "After I have drunk of you, you will die here. But by sunset, you will resurrect in a new life."

Ramiel thought of mama. And of papa. And of the glass coffin in the catacombs beneath the Sistine Chapel. He could see Monsignor Harrison's warm, smiling face before him. There couldn't have been a way that Ramiel was an immortal, it seemed, back then, when he was a young priest and even before, when he had been an inquisitive altar boy. But in the days Ramiel spent in Paris, with Cristofano, the penetration of the immortals throughout the world had been more apparent.

He learned that the immortals were not that dissimilar to humans; there was a sense of government and order, despite their quest for secrecy and discretion.

"You need to make a decision."

Cristofano's voice pierced Ramiel's thoughts. Perhaps there was a tinge of frustration in his words, but Ramiel couldn't ascertain for sure. He looked at the light reaching across the sky.

"If you are taking this step," he said, "then the time is now. Once I drink of you, you will be intolerant to daylight until you transform further. You and I will lie here, in this crypt, together, while you change, until the sun sets and the skies return to darkness. And then you will awaken, and you will be in your new life. Your new immortal life. Where you will never die."

"Unless I have a coffin sentence."

Cristofano hung his head. "It is up to you to avoid something like that. Coffin sentences are only enforced with those immortals who commit crimes against their own kind."

"And if I don't?"

"Then you have absolutely nothing to worry about." Cristofano leaned down and grasped the marble cover, grasping it out. Ramiel looked down and saw the dark outline of a coffin inside. "We are both going to fit in there?"

Cristofano reached down and dragged the coffin out as it grated against the concrete. He removed his shirt, and Ramiel looked at his naked chest; he tossed his shirt inside the crypt. "We will both fit," he said. "In the coffin, we become one. Our limbs will intertwine. Our blood will run in joined veins."

When Ramiel's thoughts were cast back to the present, as he lay in the heaping bedsheets, Cristofano remained silent and immobile. There would be little relaxation, it seemed.

Paris, 1592

THERE WERE RUMORS ABOUT LaDonna Mastuer's sudden disappearance which had circulated among the immortal communities. But during those days, in the dark days of Europe, when the wooden coffins were carried out from each of the small walk ups, there was a period of questioning.

"My daughter will travel to Port-Au-Prince," LaDonna said, as her heavy frame leaned back the small, wooden chair. A fire crackled in the corner as the flames cast a warm glow on her face. "We are few in number here," she said. "I will always be her maker, I am the true Voodoo Queen."

The others who sat around the room, watching her, and listening to her, slowly nodded, but no one spoke.

"And when she returns," LaDonna said. "She will travel to the western world. The New World. And take our ways and traditions with her. But she will have plenty of time to build her principles there. And in the New World. Beyond Haiti, it seems. To where mother voodoo rests in New Orleans."

Monsignor Harrison sat in large rouge colored high-backed chair across from LaDonna. He leaned back, and watched her as she watched him. "She was an important investigation," he finally said. "Her coffin sentence was imposed and will not be changed."

LaDonna took a deep breath through her nostrils as she placed her hands on her knees. "The Queen Madame is very important to our operation," she said. "I implore that you lift her sentence."

"Crimes against the immortals will not be tolerated, period." He stood and lifted his top hat from the table. "Now, if you may, I must return to Rome." He walked to the door as the servants swung the glass doors inward. "We have one member of our kind who has the authority to release those from coffin sentences. But it is only him. And his maker holds the gift of time manipulation."

"Where is he? Where do I find him?"

Monsigner Harrison turned as he started to head out the door and placed his top hat on his head. "He has not been created yet," he said. "She manipulates time. And while she has informed us that a coffin sentence releaser would be a member of the immortals, she has not given us a time period. All I know, Madame, is that he is coming."

She rose from the sofa and approached him. "You cannot do it? You cannot travel to New Orleans and release her."

He shook his head. "I do not have the power."

She scoffed. "Certainly someone does."

"Indeed," he said. "But the only one with the power now is her. And I guarantee you with the utmost certainty that she will not release your Madame. Now if I may, good day."

Centuries later, in Paris, after he and Ramiel had awakened at sunset, Cristofano grabbed a heavy, metal pickaxe and placed it in a brown satchel with a long shoulder strap. Geret waited in the kitchen, nursing a cup of steaming black coffee, as Ramiel appeared in the doorway from the darkened master bedroom. Cristofano swung the bag over his shoulder and raised his eyebrows. "Let's go, right?"

Ramiel froze as he watched Cristofano turn and head to the door.

The Queen Madame is very important. The Queen Madame has the ultimate power to resurrect. If you release her, that power can be yours. But if you disturb her she must be convinced to help you.

LaDonna Mastuer had created the powder to resurrect; Ramiel knew why Cristofano wanted it. For that powder, which could be taken as a potion, would give him an ultimate power.

A negotiating tool which no immortal had ever seen or experienced.

Cristofano paused with his hand on the doorknob. He looked down for a moment, and then turned his head over to face Ramiel. "It's time to go, Ramiel. You are coming with me. I am not doing this alone."

Ramiel took a few steps forward and stammered. "I – I – "

Cristofano slammed his bag on the floor as Geret watched them with a concerned look on his face. "As your maker I command you!" Cristofano said.

Ramiel hesitated for a moment, and then joined him. Cristofano swung the door open and charged into the hallway as Ramiel looked in at

Geret, who sat at the kitchen table, holding his cup of coffee in front of his chest with both hands.

"Be careful," Geret said.

Ramiel nodded and joined Cristofano as the two rushed down the stairs together. They emerged into a chilly Paris evening. The sun had just sunk below the horizon, and despite the orange hue towards the west, the darkness had penetrated and the streetlamps were lit.

Cristofano hoisted the bag to his other shoulder as he slowed his pace; the two navigated through crowds of tourists and busy cafes.

He looked over at Ramiel as they approached *Rue de l'Abreuvoir*. They waited for traffic to cross. Ramiel studied the opposite side of the street silently. It wouldn't be much farther to *Pere Lachaise* and the anticipation of being in the cemetery again with Cristofano, among the crypts, sent a chill through his body. He scarcely understood how Cristo could be so dismissive of what seemed to him like a grave risk. He was truly the crypt dancer, no doubt.

"Ramiel!" Cristofano said. "Snap out of it!"

Ramiel broke from his musings as they crossed to the opposite block, towards an alley of rising brick buildings, and away from the crowds.

"What are you concerned about, Ramiel?"

"It's what we're about to do," he said. "For both of us."

Ramiel could tell they were closer to the cemetery as the sounds of the streets quieted, and the silence was overtaken by the calls of crickets and toads, under the cover of the dark veins of tree branches.

"Elaborate."

"She has a power that immortals seek," Ramiel said. "I understand that deeply. But should the immortals have that power?"

Cristofano stopped.

He turned and faced Ramiel, looking him in the eyes. Cristofano had a look on his face which told him that there was some uncertainty running through his veins; Ramiel could see it in his eyes. "We need this," Cristofano said. "The Hooded Man has nearly destroyed Antoine's sector over in America. You understand that, don't you? The decanter was filled with blood that brought death...not the salvation it promised. A total false prophet. And we immortals deserve our redemption."

Ramiel placed his hand on Cristofano's shoulder. "But should we wield that power? What are the consequences if we do?" He slowly removed the bag from Cristofano's shoulder and placed it on his own. "I will carry the weight for you, my maker. Now lead us there, to her crypt. But think about the ramifications of this practice. We don't know how she is going to react when we open her coffin!"

Cristofano turned and ran into the cemetery. "We are releasing her chains!" he called. "We must resurrect our fallen!"

Ramiel secured the bag against his torso and ran into the cemetery. The pickaxe bumped into the side of his chest with a heavy thud with each step. Once he was through the massive wrought iron gates, he stopped, peering inwards through the rows of crypts; private mausoleums which rose from stone walkways and rose into the night with crosses and angelic sculptures atop.

"Cristo!" he hissed into the silence.

Ramiel slowly proceeded as a swirling layer of mist covered the stones, as if he were walking through a layer of fresh fallen snow. The moon was shining; the night was growing older. He watched the edges of the small crypts, for a hint of a leg, or a shoe, or a glimpse of a foot as Cristofano likely was dancing through the cemetery, maintaining a flippant attitude, wandering through, careless, yet his eyes earlier told Ramiel something different. That there was a deeper uncertainty than Cristofano was showing.

"Let's go!"

Ramiel felt a sudden jolt as Cristofano appeared, from behind the crypt, a smile across his face. "It's just simply amazing that you walked right to LaDonna. As if your steps were guided."

Ramiel shook his head and dropped the bag to the ground, as the mist billowed outwards.

"You may have more promise than I originally thought," he said. He stooped down and reached inside the satchel for the pickaxe. Ramiel watched as he drew it out into the night air, as it caught and reflected the moonlight.

Cristofano turned and faced the crypt, as Ramiel stooped down and joined him. "It's been unmarked intentionally," Cristofano said. "To keep it from the Mastuers. They could easily break her out of the crypt."

"But could they release her? From the chains?"

Cristofano paused for a moment to consider Ramiel's question. "There's much power in their magic."

Cristofano clanked the pickaxe against the crypt cover to LaDonna's tomb and it pierced the quiet night. Bright orange sparks rained down on the ground as Ramiel took a step back. "And so that is how the rift between the immortals and the witches started," Cristofano said.

"Through the voodoo?"

Cristofano clanked the pickaxe on the crypt once again and nodded. "There's a deep connection with the coven that's emerged in Miami," he said. "Connections to Port-au-Prince. And then also to Rome. And now New Orleans."

"LaDonna though..." Ramiel said. He felt a chill run down his spine. "She holds the powder. The potion."

Cristofano stopped and stood back. He dropped the pickaxe on the ground. "I'm releasing her because I have the power to do it," he said. "Her power of resurrection will give the immortals the upper hand in a sector that is struggling. Miami. And the coven. If we hold that power over them, balance will be restored. We will release her, and then we will travel to America."

Ramiel took a breath, in and out, through his nostrils, as he glanced at the crypt and then looked down at the ground. Cristofano had always had a rebellious nature about him, but this venture seemed out of character even for him. Release a known voodoo practitioner, who was given an eternal coffin sentence for crimes against the immortals? Could the crime simply have been the power she possesses?

Cristofano continued piercing the edges of the crypt face as bits of stone rained to the ground. He turned and tossed the pickaxe to the ground, easing his hands into the edges. "Help me," he said. "It's heavy. We have to lift it out. Call on your strength."

They grunted as the crypt face grated out of the cavern. They dropped it on the ground with a deep thud. They peered inside the dark, dusty tomb, and saw years of webs and debris surrounding a crumbling wooden coffin. "It's disintegrated around her," Cristofano said, as he reached inside.

Ramiel felt his heart pound as his eyes adjusted to the darkness; he could see the mound, the muddied chains wrapped around her. Her feet, of which the shoes had worn away, perhaps by infestation.

But she was there.

The clothes remained; dirtied and sullied, torn with holes and fragments of debris and soil.

Cristofano dragged the splintered wood out, resting her body on one of the boards as Ramiel assisted. She was free. Ramiel looked down at her body, dirty yet nearly perfect. The chains wrapped over her legs, up across her torso, and yet, her face was concealed. A dark shadow.

"The binding of the shadow demon," Cristofano said. "They hold the chains in place. I will release the demon and she will be free."

Ramiel sank to his knees as Cristofano lay her out on the ground. "LaDonna," he said quietly. Ramiel could see the outlines of her face, her mulatto skin, beneath the shadows which wrapped around her face and across her head. "LaDonna," Cristofano said again. But her eyes remained closed, sleeping in silence like death.

"We will release you on one condition," Cristofano said. "And I know you can hear me. We want the powder. And the potion."

Ramiel watched as Cristofano placed his hands over her face, in the dark shadows. He closed his eyes and raised his head upwards, towards the sky as the shadows released, levitating in the air, rising upwards and disappearing into the darkness.

They both looked down.

Her eyes remained closed; her face was round and plump. As if she were sleeping. Some had speculated that immortals on a coffin sentence experienced a hibernation of sorts; a combat of the desolation of the darkness and silence which proved to feel eternal. Or that in the case of LaDonna Mastuer, perhaps she had a spell, or a powder, some magic to give her the compassion of death?

Her eyes slowly opened.

They eased themselves backwards and maintained steady eye contact with LaDonna. She slowly moved her arms and legs, gradually, as the chains fell to the ground, disintegrating.

Cristofano eased himself forward as she opened her mouth, attempting to speak. Her voice was gravely, grating.

She coughed as dust and dirt blew out of her mouth and throat.

"I...will give you your potion...on one condition," she croaked. She bent her arms slowly, easing her palms on the ground, struggling to lift her body.

Cristofano knelt next to her, assisting her into a sitting position, leaning her against the side of the crypt. "Yes? What is it?"

She erupted into a fit of coughing.

After a few moments, she leaned her head back on the cement, and closed her eyes. Ramiel watched her chest heave in and outwards, as her body resumed the intake of air. "I have been fully aware and listening that entire time," she said, slowly. "About the actions in Port-au-Prince. And Miami."

She opened her eyes and looked up at Cristofano, over at Ramiel, and back to Cristofano.

"Take me…to America."

Part Four – Act Two

SHADOW OF
THE WITCH

One

MIAMI WAS KNOWN, in the immortal community, as the Devil's city.

In the days when the Hooded Man brought an assault on those with the dark gift, the crystalline jewel on the tip of Florida had been the epicenter of the assault. They called him a false prophet; a bringer of unkept promises. His identity was concealed by a long, flowing robe, and darkness maintained his anonymity. And across the city, as the sun shone throughout brilliantly, casting shadows on the streets which the skyscrapers dominated, there was a house which had a different architecture than most of the Spanish Mediterranean style of homes.

Victorian style homes were rare in the modernistic art-deco feel of Miami, yet Haddon Hall remained a prominent fixture walking distance from Villa Vizcaya, beneath the shaded oak canopies, which filtered the assault of the searing afternoon sun. At the sidewalk, the wrought iron fence which surrounded Haddon House offered a supreme view of well-tended gardens; many of the plants and flowers were native to Florida – Hibiscus, Bird of Paradise, mixed with bright yellow Milkweed and Lavender.

The house was formidable; a wooden staircase led to a wraparound porch lined with rocking chairs, floor to ceiling colonial windows, and glass double doors.

Many were blissfully unaware that this historical monument was home to the largest coven in South Florida.

Emmaline De la Croix, mature, blond, demanding of elegance, wore a long, black fitted dress, and glided her hand across the dusty keys of the black grand piano, as her heavy heels clumped on the hardwood. The strings were setting up on small wooden stools in the far corner of the parlor, as Giselle parted the heavy cranberry colored drapes.

The brilliant Miami sunshine flooded the room.

Emmaline looked down as the long beam of sunlight reached its way across the floor, as if searching for guidance. And purpose.

But she knew that the house remained dusty. And captured one's imagination, the desolate corners of one's mind. There was too much torment, it seemed, as she headed out towards the massive foyer.

A crystal chandelier hung in the center.

There was silence in the walls. The walls were painted a deep cabernet, surrounded by gold paint and wallpaper trim. And there was also a deep, smokey mysteriousness to the dark mahogany credenza, nestled next to the wall just next to the door – which led downwards.

To the cellar.

She paused and listened.

"I can hear him," she said. There was a faint babble which emitted from below. A desolate, desperate voice of a man.

A rattle of chains.

She snapped her head over towards the man standing in the foyer. He shuddered back and clutched a clipboard close to his chest. "You told me that these walls would be sound proof." She glared at him, as her eyes pierced.

The contractor held his hands up. "Please madame," he stammered. "I...I..."

She flung her arms down to her sides. "I must entertain in this house! Dignitaries. Corporate executives. You assured me these walls would be silent! I cannot hear that constant *babble!* Giselle!"

She clapped her hands together as the contractor followed Giselle's movement with his eyes, wide and pleading, uncertain as he bit his lower lip. Giselle stood next to Emmaline. "Yes madam?"

"Get the dogs."

Giselle scurried towards the back as Emmaline approached the contractor. "You know what we do here," she said, as she reached out for his clipboard. She slowly drew it from his grip. "And you've been sworn to secrecy." She circled him as his eyes followed her. "But you've done a...miserable job it seems. I can still hear that babble. Now how...and please to tell. How am I able to receive guests?"

"Uh...I..."

A growl emitted from the far end of the foyer as Emmaline stepped back. Giselle appeared with a pair of Dobermans, standing next to her, side by side, in an obedient formation.

The contractor looked at the Dobermans and took a step back. "I assure you ma'am. Your secret is safe with me."

But the shadows were far and long. The contractor had no choice but to submit, for her power was exquisite, like the dance of a flame in the twilight…there was a purpose for her actions. A dream of a nightmare of sorts; a moment when visitors would drop on the floor just after they crossed the threshold.

Her smile was infectious.

Like a virus.

There was no need for her to speak, for Emmaline would always have Giselle call off the Dobermans and escort them back to their pen. The other servants would scurry into the foyer with mops, buckets of water and scrubbing brushes, and clean up the mess.

Emmaline lit a cigarette, inhaled deeply, and closed her eyes. They would never learn, it seemed. She watched as he was carried across the foyer, down towards the back corridor, and towards the basement door. His eyes were closed, she saw, but she knew he would contribute to the babble. She exhaled a cloud of smoke, hugging her arms across her chest, and looked up towards the carved crown molding; she closed her eyes and listened to the babble in the distant lower level.

She sighed.

She crossed the foyer to the basement door, as her heavy footsteps thudded on the hardwood. She reached out and smacked the door.

Bang Bang Bang!

"Hey! You keep quiet down there, you hear?!" The door shook in its frame as the babble stopped.

"I'm not going to keep reminding you!"

As the babble had quieted, Emmaline knew that it would begin again soon. It was too late to hire another contractor; she had been in contact with Antoine, the immortal who was the leader of the Miami sector in their group. He was scheduled to arrive shortly, and had a proposal. He would certainly be upset to hear the chains in the basement.

Indeed.

She picked up an ashtray from the side table in the nearby corridor and stubbed her cigarette out. It would have to wait, she thought.

"Giselle!" she called.

She appeared in the doorway, her hands clasped at her waist. She bowed her head for a moment, and then looked up at Emmaline expectantly, her eyes wide. "Yes ma'am?"

"Make me a martini," she said. "And be sure to use the good vodka this time. Extra olives, of course."

She made her way to the adjoining parlor suite, waiting for Antoine's arrival.

Across the Atlantic in Rome, in the cavernous offices beneath the Sistine Chapel, Ramiel stared into a steaming black cup of coffee. A white towel hung around his shoulders, and his hair was wet, hanging downwards over his shoulders, partially covering a muscular chest. Monsignor Harrison sat at a computer terminal across the room, his glasses were up on his forehead, as he furiously scrolled through screens of data. "You have an extraordinary history!" he exclaimed.

Ramiel turned slowly to look over where the monsignor sat, as Delia approached him with a wet towel. "You'll need this to cool yourself," she said, as she patted it on the sides of his face.

Monsignor Harrison got up and placed his glasses back properly on his face. He approached the others, who remained close to the wooden table. "It's an unfortunate side effect of this procedure," he said. "We are still perfecting it, but the blood removal helps us analyze your mind, since with the dark gift, your blood becomes your mind."

Ramiel slowly nodded as Delia continued patting him with the cold towel.

"Anyway," Monsignor Harrison said. "Rest up and rest well. Now that we have the data, we won't require any more of your blood." He looked at Delia. "You will be flying back to Miami?"

Delia nodded. "Yes, after a few day's rest. Ramiel is too weak right now. He needs to recover."

The monsignor nodded as Ramiel looked down and examined the steaming brown liquid in his cup. Cristofano was still missing, but he had hopes that the analysis of his blood would provide some clues, some evidence, of his maker's whereabouts.

His mind felt foggy and the room felt distant as his eyes grew tired. He held the coffee, debating if he wanted to take a sip, or to lie down and take a rest. He placed the cup on the table, leaned back in the chair, and closed his eyes.

He remembered the sweet, smokey aroma of the coffee he had had when he was speaking with Antoine, before he arrived at the catacombs, up in Lyon at Antoine's chateau.

He inhaled the aroma through his nose and closed his eyes. "Tell me, Antoine, I cannot consider the options of isolation like that." He leaned back in his chair and looked across the table. Antoine was stroking his new, lengthy goatee, his eyes piercing.

"I've had no contact with them," he said.

Antoine rose from his chair as Ramiel looked up at him. Antoine had changed, he had a different perspective, on life, and the life of the immortals, it seemed, after losing Darius. But these were uncertain times, and the sense of security that had once wrapped around the chateau simply washed away in an instant. Antoine stepped down from his role in Miami, and told Monsignor Harrison that he was no longer interested in traveling back to America.

"The witches are taking over," Ramiel said, as Antoine leaned against the stone countertop. Antoine looked up, stood straight, and crossed his arms. "Then let them."

Ramiel stood and approached the opposite side of the counter. "Certainly you can't abandon the entire population like that!"

But Antoine did.

There was too much pain from the assault and the loss of Darius, that Ramiel knew that Antoine didn't want to return to America any longer. He didn't care about the witches, and what they did…or even if they would come into power.

But there was simply no use.

Ramiel knew.

For he knew that he was of the bloodline of The Crypt Dancer, and there was a vision of death that he always seemed to embrace. Bodies in crumbling caskets, waiting to rise and be immortal forever.

After the meeting at Antoine's chateau, Ramiel stood at the edge of the forest. The night sky had just risen as the moon cast a pale glow on the ground. Through the trees. It was just through the trees, and Darius would be buried there, in the family crypt. Dead as a mortal, his body rotting in a casket. And then he heard a voice from behind him.

"Ramiel."

The voice was familiar and masculine.

From the distant past, it seemed, but he remained facing the forest, and he listened for the voice again while focusing on the dark spines of the trees, dark reaching limbs against the pale blue moonlight.

"Ramiel, I have come to help you."

He looked up at the source of the voice, but only saw the darkness of the trees. He scanned the area, yet saw no signs of the voice. The moonlight bathed the forest in a pale light, yet the darkness between the trees fought for dominance. He stood and watched the trees in the distance, listening, as he shifted on his feet, the leaves and twigs crunched beneath.

"Ramiel I have come for you."

It was a whisper.

And closer.

There were few moments in his immortal life when he felt his heartbeat quicken, yet he dared not speak. A light breeze cooled his warming face, as he took a breath and held it for a moment. It was time to attempt to relax.

Cristofano never told Ramiel what happened to LaDonna Mastuer after they assisted her to their flat in Paris in the wee hours of the morning, as the morning sun was just starting to brighten the horizon. Geret was reading a book on the couch, and looked up as he saw them assisting her inside, taking her to the bathroom to bathe her, and search for clothing that was appropriate to the modern era; she was exhausted from the entire experience of a centuries-long coffin sentence, and spent days sleeping in the spare bedroom as Cristfano started packing suitcases for both himself and Ramiel.

"I left the pickaxe in the coffin," Cristofano said to Geret when they had first arrived back at the flat.

Ramiel assisted Cristofano with everything, the bathing, the packing, and checking on LaDonna's condition. But then one evening, when Ramiel was awakening as the sun set in the sky, Cristofano was gone. All Geret knew was that he and LaDonna left, and Cristofano didn't return until the following day – alone.

Ramiel knew that Cristofano, like Claret, was a time-traveler, and he made the assumption that he had the ability to relocate LaDonna to America in that fashion. He didn't question Cristofano's judgement, but he worried about it. Had their release of a sworn enemy to the immortals sealed their fate of future coffin sentences of their own?

On the plane, Ramiel sighed as he heard the announcement of their arrival in New York. He opened his eyes and leaned over towards the window. The small white crests on the waves in a sea of blue gray was below their plane, but after a few minutes, he listened to the rumble of the jet engine. He watched as the ragged edges of sand and green rose up from the water, and then he looked up.

She was a magnificent gift from France, he thought.

As the plane started its descent to JFK, he leaned back in his seat and looked over at Cristofano, who lay back in his seat, eyes still closed. Ramiel reached out and poked his arm.

Cristofano fluttered his eyes open. "You know never to rouse an immortal from rest, don't you?"

Ramiel let out a slight chuckle and faced forwards again. "We are about to land." Cristofano leaned over and looked out the window as the terrain grew in size. "That we are," he said. "And Antoine is scheduled to meet us at the terminal. It's still a long ways down the coast to Miami, but given what has been happening here it's important that we keep a low profile."

Ramiel nodded, and gazed out the window again. The cabin crew made their final announcements and the plane roared to a landing. As they navigated the jetway, Cristofano shifted his bag from one shoulder to the other. "There's too much going on right now," he said. "I know you wanted to use your powers. And I did mine. But we cannot attract the attention of The Hooded Man. Antoine was pleading with me to come. And now, we are regulated to behave as if we are mortal. But you can do that, right?"

Cristofano turned and made eye contact with Ramiel. His eyes were stark white, open, wide, and inviting. It wasn't like the Cristofano back in Paris. But he knew. Ramiel knew. That there wouldn't always be the time to use the powers; that the powers must sometimes be suppressed in the pursuit of anonymity. And he understood that. But as they exited the terminal to the chaos of New York traffic and the pungent smell of exhaust, Ramiel longed for the simpler days when they were both new to the gift in Italy.

There had been so much uncertainty back in those days, but he remembered them both discovering and embracing their powers. Now, the immortals were in torment, and Monsignor Harrison had sent both of them to assist Antoine with the government of his sector.

The uncertainty now was much greater.

Ramiel stood back as he saw Antoine's silver Mercedes coupe pull up towards the baggage claim. Cristofano waved as Antoine charged out of the driver's side door. Ramiel watched as Antoine ran around the car and up to embrace Cristofano.

"It's been so long!" Cristofano exclaimed.

Ramiel scoffed and stood back as he watched Antoine fall into Cristofano's arms. And then he felt a twinge of empathy as he watched Antoine and Cristofano interact. He could see the reflection of tears on Antoine's cheeks, and then he knew. Antoine actually wanted to succeed. But now, after losing Darius, and a short return from Paris on a separate flight to remain discreet, Antoine seemed as though he might want to move on from Darius' death and assist with getting the sector back in working order.

It was possible that Ramiel and Cristofano's trip should never have happened.

Cristofano had a soft place in his heart for Antoine, a coffee harvester from Sri Lanka, who had roping muscle and an insatiable appetite for tourist hustling. In the past, when Monsignor Harrison and Madame Arsenault had informed Darius of Antoine's presence, a group of immortals had been selected to travel to Badulla ensure Antoine's recruitment.

Yet still, Ramiel remembered the days in Sri Lanka when Antoine had been selected. Delia had time travelled to Badulla to evaluate him. Ramiel and Cristofano had also traveled there, and Ramiel spent the night with Antoine before he was given the gift.

"I am certain that you want me to strip," Antoine said as he navigated the bed. Ramiel sighed, leaned against the wall, and listened to the boisterous activity in the café below. Cristofano and Delia were patiently waiting by the bar, and he was certain that they both knew what was happening.

It was not his destiny to transform Antoine. That remained for Darius.

But it was clear that Antoine needed to be transformed.

He was a lost soul. Selling his body to tourists for sexual favors. It was all so clear, so apparent. As he watched Antoine approach the small, plain table next to the pillows, he crossed his arms. Antoine dropped his pants and slid into the bed.

"Come join me," he said, burying his face into the pillow. "Just make sure to pay the bartender before you leave. Or they will find you."

Ramiel took a few steps closer to the bed, looking down at Antoine, with his face buried in the pillow, huddled under the covers, waiting. Antoine remained motionless.

"There will be someone who will come for you," Ramiel said, breaking the silence. "But it won't be for this." He turned. "Not for these simple pleasures."

But Antoine didn't move.

"Antoine? Do you hear what I am saying to you?"

The covers ruffled as he turned around slowly. His face shifted.

"You don't want companionship? Then why did you take me up here?"

Ramiel sighed and shook his head. "There is a specific reason why I am here. And my associates. We are trying to deliver a message to you. That someone will be coming for you. And soon. But you have to grow up, Antoine. These surroundings do not befit you. We think you are lost right now. And we are coming to take you out of that."

Antoine shuffled under the covers. "You have to fuck me if you come up here," he said, his voice muffled. "That's the house rules."

Ramiel approached the bed and knelt down next to where Antoine lay. "Would you just stop it? I will pay the bartender. But I am not going to do anything to you or with you."

Antoine turned towards Ramiel and raised himself up on his elbows. His eyes looked big, brown and questioning. "So why are we up here?"

Ramiel shifted on his knees. "Someone will come for you. Take you out of all this. We are here now to make sure you are prepared for the transition."

Antoine looked down and fidgeted.

"You've been here for years now, selling yourself for the pleasure of tourists. We are here to make it stop. We have a proposition for you. To live life eternal. And only embrace sensuality, not this barbaric thing you are offering yourself up for here in a seedy, dusty room."

As Ramiel was carried back to the present in New York by a cab driver leaning on his horn, he watched as Antoine released his embrace, fidgeted and waved towards Ramiel. Certainly they would not all be riding in that small coupe. But as Cristofano leaned against Ramiel's shoulder, Antoine sped away.

"He had been living in the condo for months before they returned to Lyon and before Darius had passed."

Ramiel looked up. "In Manhattan?"

Cristofano's eyes fell and he nodded. "They've sent a car for us. Antoine wanted to greet us after his own flight and make sure that we knew that. But we aren't driving. There is a private airport in Virginia where a plane will be waiting for us."

"What happens when we arrive in Miami?"

"Antoine said he left instructions with his house servant at his main estate in Coral Gables," he said. "But while you were dreaming, Antoine informed me that he was flying back to their Chateau tonight. Antoine has a private jet booked to Frankfurt. As for us, we will receive further instructions once we arrive in Miami."

Ramiel leaned on his rolling bag as Cristofano took a few steps towards the edge of the sidewalk. Had he been wrong about Antoine? Why did he make the trip on a separate flight simply to fly right back to his chateau? It didn't make sense to him.

The chorus of rumbling engines and honking horns filled the air, but all seemed distant when he watched Cristofano. There was something about him that he always knew and trusted. But then, Cristofano gave him the gift, and this was the life that he had accepted. No longer were the days and the nights in Solerno, or Paris for that matter.

This was America.

And the rules were different. Antoine had made that apparent when he called them saying that his sector had become increasingly challenging to manage. But when The Hooded Man surfaced, the situation had to be addressed.

Claret was the prime suspect for masterminding the assault, but what was the motivation?

And there was no assumption that Antoine and Darius might evade Claret's wrath by escaping to Lyon, it was a mere certainty that Antoine was accepting reality; that he knew that Darius was dying and he wanted to bury his maker by their chateau, the place that was always their home. The home that their loyal servant Giovanni lived in full time, regardless of where his employers chose to reside, and maintained the enormous residence. And now that Darius was gone, what was Antoine's motivation to suddenly return to France?

Why would Claret allegedly attack her own kind?

The questions mounted.

As they piled into a large, black SUV, Ramiel still ran the questions through his mind. It did not matter that the driver introduced himself as an "ally". He wasn't one of them. It didn't matter that they left the JFK airport in dark tinted windows and secrecy, for they would always have to remain discreet. Everyone they encountered in this new sector would be a suspect for deception.

Antoine's mansion in Miami was still distant from their location; all the way down the coast. They were still hours away from the estate in Coral Gables.

Ramiel never understood why he and Cristofano couldn't get a direct flight into Miami, but Cristofano insisted this was the best way. "Given the climate there," he said. "We have to keep a low profile."

But *The Hooded Man* had torn through so much of the immortal community in America that Ramiel wondered what they would be coming to. Antoine and Darius had left Miami, sequestered themselves at their New York condo, fled to Europe, towards the apparent sanctuary, it seemed, and now he and Cristofano were here to pick up all of the pieces and put the sector back together. And with Antoine's loss of his maker, Ramiel knew that they would have no choice in the matter.

The ride to Virginia was long and tiring, and Ramiel felt his eyelids grow heavy as he watched the driver navigate the heavy traffic of New Jersey and the neighboring states.

It was several hours before they would even be close to the airport, where the private jet would supposedly be waiting to shroud their arrival to Miami in secrecy.

He looked over at Cristofano and his head was tilted back and his eyes were closed.

Ramiel leaned his head back, closed his eyes, and listened to the rumble of the roadway as his thoughts carried him deeper into the darkness.

He saw an image.

A vision of *The Hooded Man*: the mysterious cloaked figure approached him in the darkness, as the long, flowing cloak surrounded him; and he levitated on a cloud of swirling, white mist.

Drink from my decanter...

He could feel his heart pound in his chest, a feeling that he hadn't felt in many years, not since the days before Cristofano had transformed him.

Wake up!

His eyes fluttered open and he saw Cristofano leaning over him. "We're here," he said. "Let's go."

They rushed from the car to the plane in the shroud of darkness. Ramiel scanned the horizon and all he saw was darkness. Cristofano explained that they were well west of Washington, D.C., and the tiny airport was rarely used anymore. But a sleek black jet waited for them on the tarmac, and Cristofano bolted up the stairs as the driver handed their luggage to the attendants.

Ramiel followed and he looked at the swanky interior; gigantic leather seats lined each side in the front, and a lounge was in the rear. Far more opulent and larger than they required. Cristofano glided into a seat in the rear lounge and ordered a whisky on ice, and after the attendant swiftly handed it to him after mere seconds, he took a sip and looked up at Ramiel, who slowly lowered himself in a seat across from Cristofano.

"Keep a low profile, Ramiel," he said, and took a bigger sip of his drink. "Everyone is a suspect. You don't know how anyone will react to our presence. If you thought the massacre in Paris was transforming, The Hooded Man's wrath in Antoine's sector dwarfed that."

Ramiel considered Cristofano's words as the plane started to taxi towards the runway. He looked back as Cristofano was settling into the massive leather seat, preparing to close his eyes. "Antoine is writing a book about it, isn't he?"

Cristofano opened his eyes and slowly nodded. *"The Blood Decanter.* Yes."

As the small jet accelerated and shot into the sky after take-off, Ramiel watched the sky lighten towards the east far off into the Atlantic horizon. He felt his eyes grow heavy.

Mid-way through the flight, Ramiel opened his eyes and watched Cristofano let out an exasperated sigh and raise his glass, shaking the cubes. The flight attendant hurried over to the wet bar and grabbed the decanter. The plane jolted and some of the amber liquid spilled. "My apologies sir!"

Cristofano shook his glass after the flight attendant refreshed his whiskey. The flight attendant headed back towards the wet bar; he replaced the liquor and swung the cabinet closed. "Gentlemen," he said. "I suggest you both fasten your seat belts. The captain is informing me that the air is rough all the way down the coast."

Ramiel raised his eyebrows and cast his glance towards Cristofano, who leaned forward, took a sip from his whiskey, and gestured for Ramiel to lean closer.

"He just thinks we're rich executives," he whispered. "So let's keep it that way."

Ramiel leaned back in his chair and pulled his seat belt tight around his waist. No need to worry. Let the plane go down. He looked up at the flight attendant as he took a seat himself, his face shifted with concern. He watched the young man as he tapped his fingers on the armrest, alternating between looking over at Cristofano and Ramiel, and then back out the window.

"Remember, you are immortal," Cristofano said, as Ramiel turned and settled back into his seat, making an attempt to ignore the thrashing of the sudden turbulence, as his eyes felt heavy once again. He glanced over at Cristofano, who took a sip from his whiskey.

"We might be immortal but our bodies aren't impervious to damage. Or destruction."

Ramiel shook off a groggy feeling, opening his eyes as the plane descended towards Miami International Airport.

The sun was rising in the east, as the first wisps of delicate pastel pinks and oranges soared across the dark, but swiftly lightening sky. He'd been sleeping; an unusual thing for him to do in the dark hours, but when he noticed Cristofano settling into his seat after sipping his whiskey, Ramiel thought it was the best thing to do to pass the time.

The plane had met them in the rural Virginia airport, right on schedule, but it did not take off until the early hours of the morning. "As I said before we took off, we must keep our arrival the utmost secret," Cristofano said, as the plane taxied to a terminal towards the south, reserved for private plane arrivals. Cristofano ordered one last whiskey, and Ramiel studied the ice cubes as they clinked against the crystal, floating in the amber liquor.

He sighed and leaned back in his seat.

"Do you honestly think that Antoine doesn't care that we are in America?"

Cristofano raised his eyes and looked across at Ramiel. "Of course he cares. Don't be ridiculous."

"What about the immortal community down here?"

Cristofano scoffed as he handed his empty glass to the attendant. The plane eased to a stop. He stood as Ramiel looked up to him. "There aren't many of them left," he said.

"Then why the secrecy?"

Ramiel leaned forward as the flight attendant looked up at him, his eyes wide and pleading. He couldn't help but feel nervous.

"Delia will be meeting us shortly," Cristofano said. "She's already back. Sent a car for us. We'll have a few hours rest at Antoine's estate, and then will have to head to Haddon Hall to meet with the coven."

Ramiel tried not to hear his words as he looked out the window, and saw a large, black Mercedes sedan waiting for them. Sent by Delia, no doubt. They climbed inside and headed south, towards Coral Gables and Antoine's estate on Andelusia Avenue, on the corner of Anastasia. As they stepped inside, Cristofano typed the code for the beeping alarm, and Ramiel took a few steps inside, through the expansive foyer, and looked up at the massive crystal chandelier which hung above the rounded staircase. Plywood concealed the upper level.

"Make yourself at home," Cristofano said, as he opened the front door. Ramiel spun around and watched as Cristofano held his hand on the brass handle. He was leaving already?

"I have some business to take care of," he said. "I will return."

And the door closed, and Ramiel was in the unfamiliar mansion alone.

Two

THE CLOCK TICKED in the foyer as Delia and Ramiel stood inside the threshold of Haddon Hall. The housekeeper had called for Emmaline and they heard her heavy footsteps approach, determined, methodical thuds on the hardwood.

They were the footsteps of authority.

Emmaline stood in the door, and Ramiel thought she was much taller than he had imagined. She wore black boots, which he assumed were zipped up high, but her long, flowing dress concealed them. At first glance, she might appear naïve, but as the Supreme, Ramiel assumed that she was far from that. Her powder blue, lacey dress flowed outwards as if she were a southern belle, but she spoke in a firm, authoritative tone.

"You have told me that there was an imposter, am I correct?"

She joined the others from the coven, as all three sat on a large, ornate cranberry suede sofa, and studied the two immortals who sat in matching side chairs across an expansive glass and wood coffee table. A vase of bright white lilies sat in the center, and Ramiel leaned to the side to get a good look at the witches.

They didn't seem like witches in the least, he thought.

Three women, dressed in traditional southern bell gowns, all flowing light pastel colors, billowing outwards as they sat, waiting for tea to be brought to them on a silver tray, lined with white doilies, and sugar cubes with mint syrup and lemons. Ramiel was interrupted from his musings when he saw one the of the staff members carry the tray in, navigating the round circumference of the table. He placed a cup carefully in front of Delia, and then Ramiel, and then poured the amber liquid into each cup in the opposite order. He offered sugar and mint, and when neither Delia or Ramiel accepted, he approached the witch who sat in a blue flowered dress, to Emmaline's right, and then to the witch dressed in black on the opposite side of the sofa, and then Emmaline herself. After the tea had been served, Emmaline picked up her saucer and the others followed.

Delia cleared her throat. "This is…"

"Just tea," Emmaline said, while taking a sip, looking over at Ramiel. He looked down and studied the brown liquid in his cup. Potions had been prevalent for the immortals, after the assault of *The Hooded Man.* Ramiel looked up and saw that Emmaline continued her piercing stare.

"So tell me about this man," she said.

Delia looked over at Ramiel and raised her eyebrows. Ramiel adjusted himself in his chair and placed his tea down. "Well," he said. "We received word while in Europe, and arrived in Miami just last night, so our information is second hand."

"That's fine," Emmaline said. She took another sup of tea. "But the two of you asked to come here to speak with us because Antoine and Darius lost their control of the sector?"

Delia nodded and inserted herself into the conversation. "We know much more about this assault than Ramiel is letting on," she said. "We have numerous immortals at higher levels of the hierarchy who are investigating the origin of *The Hooded Man.*"

"And who is he?" Emmaline asked.

"Some call him a prophet," Ramiel said.

"A prophet?"

Ramiel nodded and took another sip of tea. "Yes," he said. "Initially, he appeared to immortals who had a sense of loss, or loneliness. He would approach them as a hooded figure, and entice them with a potion that would promise them redemption."

"Redemption?"

"True immortality," Delia added. "In the code, the dark gift can be taken away from immortals. But with the redemption gift, an immortal can achieve true immortality, when the gift cannot be taken away, from any source. It would be a true sense of eternal existence."

Emmaline shot a glance at Delia. "And what of this true immortality? It's a promise from this figure?"

"*The Hooded Man* was a farce," Delia said.

Ramiel leaned forward as Emmaline slowly looked back at him. "His potion was a poison. It was an enticing blood which made the false promise of salvation and immortality, yet brought death."

"How?" Emmaline asked.

"It would strip the immortal of the gift, rendering them human once again," Delia said. "A blaspheme of the Christ blood, with the exact opposite effect and purpose."

Emmaline took a small sip from her china cup and set it back down on the table. "I see," she said. "And what is your proposal for us?"

Ramiel looked over at Delia and paused.

From her conversations with Antoine, and how much detail she had placed in her discussions with Ramiel, it seemed that Darius had been correct: there had been a period of rapid aging, of the formerly immortal body catching up with the aged soul, and a final and mortal death.

Delia cleared her throat as the room grew silent. "Well," she said. "The best way your coven can assist the immortals is by being transparent about your intentions."

Emmaline raised her eyebrows and leaned back in her seat. "Our intentions?"

Delia shot a glance at Ramiel, who nodded.

They watched as Emmaline sat and considered Delia's request. She picked up her steaming cup of tea and took a sip, raising her eyes and looking at both of them directly. She took her time enjoying the hot liquid, then she slowly placed the cup back on the table and rose from her chair. She walked over towards the far end of the parlor where a black baby grand piano sat in the corner, surrounded by lengthy windows framed with heavy floral curtains.

She sat at the piano, and turned to face them, her legs crossed, her arms folded over her chest.

"LaDonna Mastuer has a lengthy history with this coven," she said. "And we have been in existence for many centuries. When the coven learned that she was chained in a cemetery in Paris was when the strife began."

"She's a voodoo priestess," Delia said.

Emmaline raised her hand to silence her. "Now that you have found it prudent to *release* her, she has returned to the coven. And we will keep her here in safety."

"We need her," Ramiel said. "That's why her sentence was thwarted."

Emmaline glanced across the room towards the other two witches who sat across from Ramiel and Delia, remaining silent. "Anastasia," she said. "Gretchen."

They looked up expectantly.

"Will you both head down to the basement and tend to what I asked you about earlier? I can still hear things wafting up through the rafters." They rose from the sofa and both nodded to Ramiel and Delia, and walked out of the room hastily, closing the glass double doors quietly, as Emmaline stood and walked back over towards Ramiel.

Ramiel looked up and watched her, as her eyes looked down upon him, their gaze locked – direct, focused and determined. He had heard about Emmaline.

She was the Supreme of the coven, a leader who appeared soft on the exterior, yet was solid and relentless in actuality. She pulled another side chair close to Ramiel, sitting next to him, as Delia watched nervously. He knew that the witches held powers, potions and spells of which the immortals held little knowledge or understanding. But he knew that the power that LaDonna held could transform the immortal community; a sense of power could be restored after the wrath that befell their kind in recent times.

She smiled politely. "You really must excuse me," she said in her delicate, southern drawl. Ramiel noticed her brilliant straight white teeth as she spoke. "Do you hear anything?"

She reached for a long, slender brown cigarette from a golden case on the table in front of them as Ramiel and Delia looked at each other for a moment. Delia shook her head slowly as Ramiel turned his attention to Emmaline. She placed the cigarette in pursed lips and struck a match, as the flame ignited and burst to life. She inhaled deeply and leaned back in her chair. "You have to understand these old houses," she said. "So much noise that comes from the cellar, you know."

Delia looked at Ramiel with a confused look on her face.

And then he knew.

There was a distant wail.

Not unlike the babble that he'd heard in Rome, there was a desperation to the call which he hadn't heard before. A clanking of chains, as if there were a reason for the dark destiny which they now found themselves in.

He knew the stories.

He had read *The Code of the Immortals.*

There was formidable truth in that book; as if the pages were the stepping stones of progress, the forward movement of the immortal kind. But here, in Haddon Hall, he watched a witch. He watched her look at him coyly, and smile, draw on her cigarette, and blow a cloud of smoke upwards into the air as she called on the maid to place Beethoven on the gramophone.

She called their attention to the babble, to the call, to the wails, and the rattles, and then she watched them. Their reaction. For they knew. Cristofano had disappeared. Ramiel had not seen him since their arrival in Miami.

Ramiel looked at Delia, and she had a knowing look on her face. Cristofano's disappearance might not have been coincidental.

ACT THREE:

The Convergence

Part Five

THE CRYPT DANCER (II)

One

RAMIEL FELT A DISTANCE from Cristofano which he had never felt before. There was a peculiarity to his disposition on the night that he left, Ramiel felt, and then he thought about papa, in the days back in Rome, during the days when he had still been a boy, listening, watching through the slit of the door. He remembered how he stood in the darkened hallway when mama and papa had been entertaining friends over spaghetti dinners with aromatic sauces and red wine. He longed for the days when he could speak with papa once again; when he returned to Antoine's estate after departing Haddon House with Delia, he closed the door with a click, which reverberated through the empty mansion.

The loneliness washed through him as he padded towards the kitchen. It felt like a simple metaphor for what he might be living; the loss of a father, the sense of a maker's abandonment. Cristofano would not die, he said to himself, over and over, as he prepared to retire. He removed his shirt and tossed it on the side chair in the guest room, and chose to sleep in a bed. It was time to regain some sense of self-reliance. Cristo's disappearance lacked a motivation. Or a reason.

Yet, as he slid into the cool sheets and reached over to snap the bedside lamp off, he could scarcely remember when he had opted to retire before midnight. It had been years and decades and centuries of night dwelling, not because he had to; he was not a vampire, and he could move about at any time he desired. But here, in this bed, on that particular night, in a friend's mansion that was big and cold and unfamiliar, he felt the sense of loneliness creep in. And when he felt the heaviness take over and the effort to keep his eyelids open became greater, his thoughts went to Cristofano, and Italy, and when he had taken Ramiel to the cathedral, and the catacombs…

In the days before Ramiel and Cristofano left for America, Cristofano took Ramiel to Italy by train to Salerno.

Cristofano had insisted that they immediately drop off their luggage as the *Luci d'Artista* was in the oldest section of the city; the quaint bed and breakfast was close to the monastery where Cristofano had studied theology. After they had dropped their bags and returned to the thoroughfare, Ramiel looked out towards the sun setting over the warm waters of the Mediterranean, its fire reflecting on the serene waters in a palette of brilliant auburn.

They would not have far to walk to the cathedral.

Ramiel remembered the church, and the cloth, and the years with Monsignor Harrison, who undoubtedly would be in nearby Rome, at the Sistine, governing his council, ruling the immortals, bound by the doctrines of the code. And then, in Salerno, Cristofano would be taking Ramiel to the *Cattedrale di Santa Maria degli Angeli,* the church of Cristofano's youth.

As they approached the portico and soaring bell tower, Cristofano quickened his pace, leaving Ramiel to follow. He could tell that his maker had a sense of pride, as Cristofano danced and glided across the courtyard, surrounded by the arches and columns of the portico. "This is where I began," he said, as he twirled to a stop, his feet crunching the gravel. Ramiel approached and saw his wide eyes, and then he scanned the area. The cathedral was magnificent; a towering centerpiece of Salerno. Cristofano opened the heavy door, which he explained was Byzantine bronze, and entered the darkened chapel.

Ramiel stood in the worship area, in the front of the pews, where the steps led downwards, below the altar, to the crypt. Cristofano eased his bag down from his shoulder to the floor and grabbed the two torches he had brought for the catacombs below.

"Claret," he whispered into the darkness. "I know you are hiding down here!" Ramiel looked upwards at the expansive ceiling as Cristofano's voice echoed.

"She wouldn't answer you if she were," Ramiel said as he descended the stairs slowly. Cristofano held his torch towards the opposite wall. "There's a rumor circulating that she is trying to punish the immortals."

"Extinguish her own kind? To go against the own code which she enforces? Whatever for?" Ramiel scoffed and joined Cristofano next to the crypt. A row of massive white candles reached towards the ceiling, nestled on gigantic gold candlesticks which were taller than he was. "Whatever for?" Ramiel looked up and noticed that the candles had never been lit.

Cristofano knelt downwards and drew his torch closer to the gate. "Look there," he said. Ramiel knelt down and peered inwards. A small crypt, nestled in a wall of crumbling brick, with a small stone door.

"There he is," Cristofano said. "Saint Matthew. Resting here for all this time. Now all I need to do is resurrect him…and then…"

"And then you will…"

Cristofano held out his torch and Ramiel took it. Cristofano gave a light kick to the bag as the tools inside clanked. He knelt down and rummaged through the bag and looked up at Ramiel. "Claret will do what she is destined to do. And for that she will be crucified."

"The Law of the Inspiriti."

"Yes," he said. He reached inside the bag and pulled out a rusted pickaxe. He gave one more look up and winked at Ramiel. "Borrowed this one from Antoine." And then he slammed it on the edge of the crypt. Ramiel jumped as the crash echoed in the dark, empty cathedral. He watched bright sparks shower to the dusty stone floor.

But as Cristofano continued his assault on the crypt, Ramiel carried his thoughts back to the days when Antoine had again entered his life, when he had been a new immortal and Antoine had discovered him walking the lonely, tree-lined roads on the outskirts of Lyon; he was somehow drawn to that area yet could not understand the reason. No matter how hard he tried.

But during those days, it was rumored that Antoine still roamed the streets at night. He would walk through the small shops and purchase nothing; sit at a sidewalk café with a single cup of coffee and never take a sip. He would simply stare…off into the distance…towards the horizon, watching the auburn strokes across the sky as the sun sank below the horizon towards the west. Ramiel remembered those days when Antoine came to Europe, for there was a connection, it seemed. No, rather, it was for certain.

Ramiel watched his feet, in the worn loafers, and took a step on the crumbling pavement. The trees soared upwards towards the sky on either side, as the pale blue moonlight filtered downwards. Each step. One foot in front of the other, he had always learned, while still a child outside of Rome.

His mama, the sweet portly woman, who he had seen through the narrow, stucco walls in their house on *Via del Corso*, rarely heard him when she would pad through the kitchen, hovering over a large, steaming stockpot.

Ah, the sweet aroma of the fresh marinara.

Ramiel could still smell her cooking…but then, in those days, when he remembered heading into the house, he knew that there was an evil entity from which his mother needed to be protected. He would lie in his bed at night, bathed in sweat, and he could still remember the heaviness of the humid air which enveloped Italy each night off the Mediterranean.

The house was quiet.

He lifted the small blanket and let it drop to the floor. He swung his legs around and watched the window. The curtains blew inwards with a light, passing breeze. He slowly walked across the dusty, stone floor, as he studied the moonlight which filtered inwards, casting a glow on the floor against the silence of the tiny, dark room.

"I want to dance, I want to perform." He had told his mama that over a heaping plate of spaghetti earlier that same evening. He reached towards the center of the table and tore a piece of bread from the loaf. Mama looked up from her plate and reached for a glass of chianti. "You have to study that craft," she said. "And Paris is no place for a young man like you."

He slammed his palm on the table as mama jumped, nearly spilling her wine. "Ramiel! Stop!"

He leaned back in the small wooden chair and crossed his arms. "I must go to Paris. I must."

"Paris is no place for you. You can perform in Rome if you like. But not Paris. Never Paris. Your grandfather must be turning in his grave. And don't tell papa. Never tell him."

He looked up at mama, who returned his stare. Without breaking her stare, she slowly reached for her wine. "It's time for bed, Ramiel. There is nothing more to discuss."

But later that night, when the house was silent, when he heard his mother quietly crying in her room down the hall. Her father had been buried in a small, wooden coffin just days before. Ramiel knew that mama was in pain, but she remained faithful to her son. Could he respect her wishes and remain in Italy?

And, once at the window, he looked down towards the narrow alley below, looking downwards, and saw Cristofano, standing on the sidewalk, swinging a pickaxe. When he was looking outside his window, he knew nothing of the figure who would appear at his window. He did not know that his destiny was to meet the mysterious figure in Rome.

He knew then, in his childhood bedroom, that his destiny was carved for him, from the moment of his birth. He wanted to leave for Paris and perform; he had to stopover in Rome to meet those who would help form his destiny. The path was long, and far-reaching, toward a horizon; a path which he felt he may never see the farthest away stones, but they remained part of his journey, and his destiny. It was those in his life who he encountered, and interacted with, who helped shape who he was, as an individual, an immortal, a destined leader of their kind.

When he remembered looking down, out from his boyhood window, in the alleyway below, he remembered the mysterious figure who would walk the streets. And Ramiel understood how he was drawn to him.

It was Cristofano.

Before Ramiel had met him, in Rome.

Ramiel understood now.

He remembered watching as Cristofano swung a pickaxe, dancing around with it, swinging it in the air, lifting it as if it were a ballerina. And then Ramiel's thoughts were carried back to the cathedral, to the dark, dusty church, watching his maker crumble through stone, to the solace of one Saint Matthew; a rumored immortal, a body uncorrupted.

Was Cristofano rebelling against Claret?

Ramiel awakened covered in sweat.

He felt the heavy comforter as it was wrapped tightly around his body, up towards his neck, completely unnecessary in Miami. He kicked the covers down with his feet, and relished the cool air against his sweaty, muscular chest. There was much to be learned about his immortality, it seemed. Despite his transformation years ago, back in Paris, when he and Cristofano shared the flat together, he had been under the impression that he would be a night-dweller, a blood-drinker.

As he discovered over the decades, that couldn't be further from the truth. And in Miami, alone for the first time that he can remember since he was mortal, he was feeling more human than he had ever remembered feeling since he was transformed. He swung his legs onto the cool stone floor, and padded to the kitchen; the door chime rang, startling him. He was shirtless but wearing pants, so he thought it acceptable that he answer and see who the caller was.

He pulled back the hanging shears on the slender windows which surrounded the front door and saw an equally slender man on the front porch. His jet-black hair was slicked back, he wore a dark suit and red tie, and he stood, tall and imposing, on the front porch with his arms behind his back. Ramiel clicked the lock and slowly opened the door.

He smiled and nodded, keeping his distance. "Ramiel," he said. "Do you remember me?"

Ramiel paused for a moment, standing on the threshold, looking the lanky man up and down, while squinting at his face. There was a degree of familiarity, for certain. And despite his gifts, he was unable to place any moment in the past when they would have met.

"May I come in?"

Ramiel slowly nodded and stepped back as the man stepped up into the foyer and rounded the large center table. Ramiel watched as the visitor looked up at the hanging crystal chandelier; his gaze then settled upon the plywood covering the first floor. Ramiel noticed some of the black charred crown molding near the top of the arched staircase. The visitor lowered his head and looked over at Ramiel. "You know, it's a shame what they did. This place has been so magnificent over the years. It's the old Perez mansion. Have you been in Miami long enough to remember the Perez family?"

Ramiel shook his head.

The visitor put his hands on his hips and scanned the room as Ramiel kept a close eye on him. "Anyway," he said. "Before your time. Ask Antoine about it, sometime, if you can. The head of the International Bank of Venezuela used to own this house. Hernan Perez. But ask Antoine. He knows all about it."

The visitor turned back to face Ramiel.

"How can I help you?" Ramiel finally asked, after a few moments of silence.

The visitor appeared flustered for a moment. He reached his hand out. "Where are my manners?! I deeply apologize. I've been acquainted with Antoine for many years now. Ned McCracken here."

Ramiel slowly reached out his own hand, maintaining eye contact with Ned. His hands were cold. Clammy. Seemed to be a match for his smile and pasty white skin. Ramiel released his hand and rubbed his palm on his pants.

"I am the chosen mortician for the immortal community," Ned said. "I've been placed in Miami to personally oversee the operations of the crypt, and also was called by Antoine to Lyon to handle the proceedings for Darius. Antoine does seem to be taking that pretty hard. I haven't had the gift for long, however I would imagine that it might be quite devastating to lose one's maker."

"Losing one, or being abandoned," Ramiel said. "I don't know which is worse." He thought of Cristofano and his disappearance shortly after their flight had landed at Miami International. And now, he was here, in an unfamiliar estate, alone, searching, the fate of the immortals in his hands, the uncertainties of the coven's intentions on his conscience.

Wake up! He could hear Cristofano say it now. *Put on your big shoes. Your adult pants. Stop being a petulant child and accept your responsibilities!*

He brushed off the thoughts.

"So why I am here?" Ned asked. He straightened his posture and clasped his hands at his waist. "I'm here because you've been to Waxley Mortuary, haven't you?"

Ramiel nodded.

"And you visited the crypt in Resurrection Cemetery, haven't you as well?"

"Yes," Ramiel said.

"What were you looking for? You were looking for Cristofano?"

Ramiel studied Ned. He didn't understand how the two of them could have never crossed paths over the years when he had accompanied Darius to Sri Lanka to oversee Antoine's transformation, yet Ramiel had never been to Miami before this trip. Antoine had confided in Ramiel over the years, and when Darius had lost his gift, when Darius had rapidly aged, Ramiel had been there. When Darius had passed, Ramiel had assisted with removing the body from the chateau and taking it to a secret location to prepare it for burial.

He looked at Ned.

The dark slicked hair and pasty skin had a degree of familiarity.

Ramiel remembered the afternoon in Lyon, at Antoine's chateau, just after Darius had passed. And then he knew. How had he forgotten? Had the intensities of the coven – and losing Cristofano – become so encompassing that he failed to recognize Ned when he saw him?

"There is a new mortician there now," Ned said, as he sat on a small upholstered bench on the side of the foyer. He again looked up towards the second level. The construction had almost been complete upstairs; there was nearly no evidence that a fire had even occurred in the mansion save the charred crown molding. With Antoine back in Paris, and Ramiel overseeing the estate and the Miami sector, Cristofano was, once again, nowhere to be found. Ramiel wandered to the adjoining parlor and sat on a white sofa near the fireplace.

"Like I said," Ned said, as he rose and joined Ramiel near the fireplace. "There is a new mortician there now. He took over for me after I had received the gift."

Ramiel nodded. "Yes. Antoine explained everything to me before I left Paris."

"I see," Ned said. "Well did he tell you what the coven has been planning since Cristofano released LaDonna Mastuer?"

Ramiel had a feeling.

His mind returned to the night when he had visited the crypt with the amythyst that Antoine had instructed him to take. The Queen, Reynalda, held a specific interpretation of the doctrine which all immortals must uphold. But now, as he stood in front of Ned, a friend of Antoine's and Darius' who he'd failed to meet over the years, Ramiel was forced to reconsider his judgement. Was venturing to the crypt of the immortals a lapse in his own judgement?

He'd already been associated with the coven. He and Delia had already visited Haddon Hall. The witches. The coven. They were all there. And now, could there have been a deeper purpose within them all? The witches would have control over the sector after the wrath of The Hooded Man.

Ramiel raised his head and looked at Ned. "Isn't the Waxley Mortuary a historical building now?"

Ned nodded.

"Who owns it now?

"The city," Ned said.

"And who is this mortician?" Ramiel asked.

"His name is Jacob Benjamin," he said. "He arrived at Waxley under the most peculiar of circumstances, it seems. But his presence won't disturb us. Or what the witches want. LaDonna's power is significant to the coven, with the ability to resurrect. The immortals need that power to recover from the assault of The Hooded Man."

"The amethyst hangs just inside the cellar door," Ramiel said.

Ned nodded. "And you went there," he said. "But who you encountered is what the council in Rome has been concerned with."

"Why have they sent you? Why didn't they send Claret, or even Delia, who's right here in Miami?"

Ned cleared his throat. "I've been tasked with the protection of the crypt and mortuary while Antoine is away in Europe," he said. "Delia has her hands full with the investigations of the coven and Cristofano's disappearance. And although I am a newly transformed immortal, my connections with Antoine and Darius go back years, and there had been an establishment of trust."

"I see," Ramiel said.

"But the concern the council has is about Queen Reynalda. She appeared to you that night, didn't she?"

Ramiel slowly nodded.

Ned clasped his hands together, lowered his head, and inhaled deeply through his nostrils. He looked up at Ramiel and released his breath. "You do understand the ramifications of her power, don't you?"

Ramiel fell silent for a moment. He'd heard about Queen Reynalda over the years, while he was still a mortal, Cristofano had mentioned her name. She was equally as legendary among the immortal community as the Mastuer dynasty. Queen Reynalda, however, was an elder, an immortal, and a witch – a potentially lethal combination. She was quite charismatic, which was a gift often bestowed upon newly transformed immortals – yet her powers from witchcraft and extensive knowledge of potions proved to be a formidable threat and a greater power.

Later that same evening, Ramiel creaked the door open to the Waxley Mortuary and Funeral Home and took several cautious steps inside. His conversations with Ned seemed so far away; distant, yet he could remember every word that they had exchanged.

He peered through the rusted iron spires of a nearby fence as he heard footsteps approach. The pale blue moonlight reflected on the mounds of dirt which reached back towards the threshold of the dark, mysterious forest. The footsteps stopped just behind him. He turned and could see LaDonna's flowing white dress blow delicately in a passing breeze, set against the dark solitude of the night.

"Is everyone here?" she asked, scanning the area.

Ramiel nodded.

"Then where are they?"

"Ned is waiting in the front…just in front of the main steps. Cristofano is still missing. And Pasquale is parking the car."

LaDonna nodded. "Very well then. We will go to her grave and she will live again."

Thunder rumbled in the distance as the winds increased in intensity. Ramiel shivered, to his surprise. Feeling the chill in the air was not something that he had felt since his time in Paris. Since he had been transformed, he always knew what the chill meant. And LaDonna had been on a coffin sentence for good reason.

Lighting crashed as his mind cast back to the *Pere Lachaise* cemetery in Paris. On that night in Paris, when LaDonna was set to live once again, Cristofano's eyes were wide and pleading. "Get back, Ramiel!"

Ramiel jumped back as thunder crashed above. Cristofano dropped his pickaxe as lighting struck the rusted steeple at the crest of the crypt roof. "She's angry!" he cried.

He dragged Cristofano towards the edge of the trees as the crypt shook. The cover cracked through the middle as Cristofano cried out. "Rise forth! Only the blood of your maker can resurrect you!"

Thunder crashed as Ramiel's thoughts were thrust back to Resurrection Cemetery just next to Waxley Mortuary.

He started back towards the building, the dark, decrepit shadows of the crumbling structure in the darkness, through the dark veins of rising tree branches. His feet crunched through dead twigs and dried leaves, and he heard LaDonna closely following him.

"Ned!" he called into the silence.

No answer.

They approached the old structure, the old, abandoned funeral home, the place where Ned once governed. "Ned, are you there?!"

They stopped at the rising stone steps as he emerged, slowly, from the darkness; he opened the heavy, wooden door, as the moonlight shined on his pasty white face. "We are here," he said. "Pasquale parked the car in the hearse loading area on the other side. It's a direct route to the cemetery from that side."

Ramiel was starting to feel that he was in over his head.

Now that Ned had contacted him, in a city which still felt foreign to him, why would Ned suddenly feel the need to visit the crypt? And he insisted they open it and venture to the crumbling coffins inside.

LaDonna wore her graceful white dress, and as he followed her deeper into the forests which surrounded the cemetery, he noticed the wind catching her clothes, and her aura seemed bright, as if she had already been to where he was concerned they might be forced to venture.

"Hades is the termination of all life," she said, turning back to face him for a moment.

"Will the powder work?" Ramiel asked.

The leaves and twigs snapped beneath her feet as she stopped and turned to face Ramiel. "The powder will work," she said. "The powder always works. It has worked for centuries, and it worked until I was bound with the shadows and wrapped in the chains…"

Ramiel lowered his head.

She was right.

The immortals held an insecurity which he never clearly understood. In his mind, he heard the familiar voice of his maker.

I am mere steps away, Ramiel. In the realm of shadows, where the evil and tyranny meet in a destiny of darkness.

"Where we all go when bound by the shadows," LaDonna said slowly as they reached the crypt. The wrought iron gates were a familiar sight, as he stood, looking inside, as the crumbling coffins were stacked neatly in open stone rows.

"Your maker," she said. "The one they call Cristofano, is there. In Hades Pass. In the culmination of the sea of souls, he is there. Amidst the thrashing limbs splashing in the putrid water."

Ramiel gasped. He had read about Hades Pass in *The Code of the Immortals*. It was the purgatory for banished immortals; a destiny of darkness, of which few could emerge. "Cristofano is there?! How did – what did –"

"Cristofano made his choice," she said. "We are all given free will. But to him, there was a price to pay for his transgressions. If you want to find him, you will enter the crypt; I have a coffin just for you. You will lie bound with the shadow demons. Just as I have. And with this powder I will make a potion. And you will find Cristofano. In Hades Pass."

Ramiel turned to face LaDonna.

She stood, as her flowing white dress reflected the pale blue moonlight. He looked down, and she was holding a small jar with a white powder inside. She was the powerful one. More so than Queen Reynalda, it seemed. If, perhaps, she was the true leader of the coven. The Mastuer dynasty had been right to desire her release from the crypt. The power she wielded could bring the immortals to their knees. Ramiel looked back inside the crypt and studied the caskets of the elders. Each one, bound. A shadow demon reserved for each of them. And Cristofano had the power to release them.

Yet did not.

This was the moment which brought a sense of dread, and as the rusted wrought iron doors opened with a deep creaking, the smell of death and decay hung in the air. He paused for a moment as they stood in the dank, musty crypt. He looked at the coffins, and listened to the silence. Was there movement?

Was there a rattle of the chains which bound them?

Not even a whimper, a cry for help was eternally silenced by the shadow demon. A dark, tormented existence, for those who were bound in their eternal penance. He noticed one coffin in the corner, on a mid-rise stone shelf, which appeared newer than the others and painted in gold, adorned with several colorful jewels on the lid.

"Queen Reynalda," she said, and then pointed out a nearby coffin, in the darkest corner of the crypt. "And the one for you."

Ramiel felt his heart pounding in his chest, as she placed her jar on Queen Reynalda's coffin. "The powder will take you there," she said, as she bent down. The coffin grated against the stone as she slowly dragged it out into the open. Ramiel looked down at the coffin as she lifted off the lid. The dark red satin was dusty and covered with dirt.

He felt a chill run through his body.

"Your coffin," she said. "Lie down inside and I will give you the potion. It will not end your life, but allow you to explore Hades Pass and when it wears off, you will awaken in the coffin. This will allow you to experience what your subjects see, hear and feel when their sentences are carried out. But in Hades Pass, there you will find Cristofano."

He knelt down next to the coffin and looked up at LaDonna. She reached for the jar, and he eased himself inside, sitting for a moment with his legs raised. The satin was cool, damp. Clammy. The stench of decay permeated the air, as the mustiness of the fabric which surrounded him overwhelmed his senses. As he lay on the hardened pillow, he looked up, as LaDonna hovered above the coffin, stooping down, cupping her hand above him. She lowered her head and removed the cork with her teeth, and poured a small amount of the white powder into her open hand, placing the jar on the floor and recorking it.

"Breathe it in," she said. "You will sleep the slumber of death. It will take you there. Your mind will guide you through the darkness."

She held her hand close to his nose and mouth, and he took a deep breath; the delicate powder clouded into his body, and he felt the grittiness in the back of his throat.

"Now lie down," she said. "And I will replace the lid."

$T\kern-0.3em_{wo}$

THERE WAS A CERTAIN MYSTICISM about The Crypt Dancer.

And how the rumors of the mythical figure, which circulated through the immortal community about the mythical figure; were similar to those rumors of *The Hooded Man,* which had circulated in the same communities in years past.

Yet the inaction of the immortals sealed their doom.

In the current period, The Crypt Dancer, as he was known, was an equally mysterious part of the immortal community.

Coffin sentences had been a regular threat to the community. Yet the harbinger of those sentences were self-inflicted: the code had been true, followed to its core, and adopted by all. Any crime against the immortal kind would be punished with swift punishment.

Ah, those nights in Paris.

In the days when the sunlight had faded through the network of low-rise apartments, the dusty neon signs that hung on the edge of brick corners cast a pale, faded blue glow against the dirty sidewalks.

It was Paris at night, a night when he had thought he was meant to embrace. It was a night, however, that he could not. He failed to fathom its massive fog of interpretation; for the mist had been heavy, wet, and a damp nightmare across his cheeks.

He missed Cristo; his heart felt heavy.

The darkness provided no solace as he closed his eyes; he listened to LaDonna replace the lid with a thud, and he felt the grating as she pushed the coffin back into place.

And then the silence ensued.

Yet for him, it was different.

There were no chains, no shadow demon which bound him. But he could feel the effects of the powder, as he struggled to remain with consciousness. She had instructed him not to fight it, to let the powder gain control of his senses. And that by doing so, he would experience the visions which his mind would display for him; the introspective journey would commence.

And, then, there was darkness, until he saw himself, and Cristofano.

Ramiel watched as Cristofano stopped at an unmarked, plain stone crypt, which rose from the ground at the same height as the others, with more ornate markers and artistic statues. He paused and looked down at the crypt as Ramiel stood and watched.

Cristofano looked up and at Ramiel. "You know why I do this?"

He shook his head.

"It's because I have control. I've been given the power. To raise our own kind. And the judgement…to know when we need it the most."

Ramiel stood and watched Cristofano as he raised his palms against the stone crypt cover and closed his eyes. There would be no need for primitive tools; Ramiel knew, Cristofano was the chosen one. Claret was his maker, and all of the immortals talked about his mysterious presence among their kind: he was the only immortal in existence who could release a coffin sentence.

The coffin sentence.

Innocence lost.

And the darkness, the solitude and the clamp of the cement cover being shoved into place. But the coffin, it seemed, was a catalyst for the experience of the supernatural. For one, when they listen to the coffin scraping deeply along the concrete as its pushed into the crypt, would find a more significant sense of purpose.

For the meaning of existence has then changed.

There was no longer a call for the physicality; for the dream that existed outside the crypt. The dreams had been transformed into nightmares, and the call of the crypt remained. There was a removal of clothes. And the signs which covered a true person, an actual purpose.

The death was real.

The dining was coming on the horizon.

Yet others, who embraced that purpose, whose thoughts remained soaring across multiple plains, feared the clamp and thud as the call to the poison of life which inoculates the soul. But would life be considered a poison?

Or perhaps the threat of mortality?

The crypt slammed closed with a deep thud as the coffin shook.

The silence ensued, although the faint clap of footsteps could be heard faintly, in the distance, leaving the grave. Eyes closed, darkness envelops.

The shot of light surrounding the senses, for the senses existed under a veil, and only the thoughts remained. Lying in a coffin, arms clasped across the chest, eyes closed yet a sense of place.

And purpose.

But the darkness did not remain for eternity. For the chorus sounded at a certain point, when the thoughts resounded with despair, which descended towards humility.

His eyes closed, and then there was darkness.

The methodic deep roar of approaching ocean waves filled the darkness; the call of the surf, the gentle waves in a deep, methodic tumble towards the sands.

He could feel the dampness on his cheek.

As he opened his eyes, he still saw nothing. But his senses, it seemed, appeared to be returning. LaDonna had been right. The powder must have worked. Although he remained in the shroud of darkness, until he felt a rush of wind against his face.

The putrid smell of rotting corpses.

And then the light filtered in.

His eyes struggled to focus at first, yet he could see racing dark clouds above in an angry crimson sky. And then there were the voices. The babble; the wails of multitudes. Despair set in; loneliness. It was as if he were on the beach alone, listening to torment, and then when he looked outwards at the sea, the waves angered, rushing towards him as he sat up.

He opened his mouth, dry, cracked, overcome with a deep thirst. The sulfuric stench coming from the water provided no image of being quenched, but his throat remained parched with dehydration. "Water," he croaked slowly.

A shadow approached him slowly, a dark figure which projected the hope of relief, an offered thirst quenching.

I can bring you water.

But the water failed to come. His mind thrust himself into a feeling of the approach of danger; of monstrous intensity, a deep, methodical thud.

Ramiel leapt to his feet and ran as fast as he could, given the limitations placed on his power. *Never look anyone in the eyes in Hades Pass,* LaDonna had warned. *If you do, you risk an eternal sentence in the Sea of Souls.*

He looked up and watched as Queen Reynalda stood at the precipice of Hades Pass; she stood on a rising mountain of rock, her arms raised as the angry clouds swirled above her. Ramiel jumped the stones as the bodies writhed and wailed in the putrid waters below; he collapsed back on the beach as the cool, damp sands burned his face.

"You will not return!" the Queen boomed. *"Hades is your home now!"*

But he knew that there was hope. Back in Paris, back in Miami, when the Jefferson Majestic had been the sanctuary of the Crypt Dancer; the one who betrothed justice upon the immortals, the one who could release them from their torment. Ramiel looked upwards towards the sky, watching the swirl of the clouds before him, the angry red flashes, and listened to the deafening grating of Queen Reynalda's movement. He snapped his head around and saw she was descending the distant, dark mountain as a desperate female voice grated near the shoreline.

"Ramiel!"

He scanned the area and searched for the source.

"Ramiel, save me!"

His heart pounded, but he dare not answer.

"Save me, Ramiel! Only you can! I am trapped in the waters. In the chill…*I can hardly breathe*…"

He studied the shoreline and saw the cake of dirt on her red hair. She opened her eyes and looked up at him. There it was. The windows to her soul; a revelation of her past, and where she had been through the rivers of tears which she now cried. There was a purpose to her existence, and her crimes. A different season for each, they always say. We're all from the same cloth, yet different tapestries, it seemed.

But she was there.

Her eyes beckoned, watching him watching her, as he stood on the cool sand, after the winds had quieted and after Queen Reynalda had retreated, there had been that single moment.

For the first time, he saw Claret.

She wasn't the same evil being who dictated the actions of the immortals. It wasn't the same demon who cast her assault and her leading them to a certain death, through lies of a promised redemption which was never delivered.

It was the eyes of a Claret who had not yet been transformed.

Do not look into her eyes!

He could hear LaDonna's warning repeat through his mind. *Do not look into her eyes. She will drag you into the putrid sea!*

But he still saw her.

He saw the image of a girl in Jerusalem, who wandered through the dusty marketplaces, searching for her parents who had abandoned her; it was of her fascination with the Christ cup and the power which it contained. It was on that night, in the small hut next to Gethsemane, that she had stood on the small, wooden stool, watching the men, as they sat on the floor, around a small, wooden table. It was long enough for all of the twelve men to sit around.

"Do this in My remembrance."

She raised to her tip toes as the stool leaned towards the clay wall of the hut. As she leaned her bodyweight against the wall and balanced the tipping stool, she rested her face against the cool edge of the opening. She hoped they didn't see her. Yet as she watched them, as she watched the loyalty of the men, she focused on the cup.

The cup of a carpenter.

In her mind, while still a child, she held the wisdom of which few are gifted. The predictions she carried with her had already made themselves known at that tender young age. But she knew that she was destined to have that cup.

"Save me, Ramiel! Spread your wings and be the angel you were destined to be!"

He watched as the writhing pasty white limbs dragged her under the surface, as Ramiel gasped for air. Thunder crashed overhead as he fell backwards. He winced at the chill of the water as it splashed on him. \

Hell is frigid, LaDonna had said. *It will all be extreme. The heat, and the cold. The torment and the loneliness.*

A voice called through the chaos of the winds and the waves.

It was distant, yet seemed masculine and familiar. He struggled to ignore the pierce and the chill of the water as it spilled over the rocks, and propped himself up on his elbows. The splashing of the deserted clouded his vision. But he heard the voice calling once again, in a fit of desperation.

"Ramiel! I can sense you are there. Help me! Save me!"

And then there was a revelation.

The images tore through his mind like a cloud of fire, igniting his memories. He saw his face, looking up at him with wide eyes, when he had stood in the atrium of the Sistine Chapel in Rome. When Monsignor Harrison had stood and commanded their friendship.

"Cristo!"

Ramiel's voice sounded foreign against the hiss of the winds. Dark clouds raced above him in a crimson sky as the winds had abated to a whisper. "Cristofano!"

The sea had silenced as Queen Reynalda had retreated.

The limbs had ceased thrashing as a sense of calm washed through the area. But Ramiel knew that the calm would be short lived, and attempted to lull him into a false sense of security. For he knew the purpose of hades was trickery and deception; that if he assumed that the threat had abated, he would be sorely mistaken.

Queen Reynalda had retreated from her perch, but where did she go?

The ring of dark mountaintops had a movement about them; they were far yet still close, moving yet still. Antoine had stood on the same sand, viewing the same mountains, in front of the torrents of the sea, and the screaming wails of the deserted.

I...am the Crypt Dancer...

Ramiel paused.

The voice was familiar.

It could have been Cristofano, yet the voice sounded feminine. Of a different realm, with a purpose that Ramiel could not fully understand. He watched the mountains as they drifted back and forth in the distance, opening valleys just as quickly as closing them.

"I am coming for you Cristo," he said.

He took a step towards the sea but hesitated.

Was hades beckoning him further?

Did the disappearance of Queen Reynalda serve as a purpose for him to proceed?

He waited.

Spirit was a different experience than body.

The visions returned as Ramiel felt the force of the heavy air holding him back on the stones. He saw them reaching far out into the sea; he could see the stones grow smaller as they reached outwards, towards the sandy brown mountain where Queen Reynalda would appear, as the crests of the angry waves and the stench of the sea of death over powered the cries of lost souls and the thrashing of the limbs, reaching upwards, finding nothing but stale, putrid air and searing heat just above the frigid waters.

He forced his way forward, and the visions resumed.

Paris.

In the days of the Jefferson Majestic Massacre.

He could see the lights and the night and the throngs of people gliding along the sidewalks; the cafés and dusty little used book shops. And the cemetery, the rising stone monuments against the night sky, and the small crypts.

He saw it all well.

Ramiel watched as Cristofano glided deeper into *Père Lachaise,* through the winding darkness of which the rising stone crypts reflected the pale moonlight, he paused. Cristofano spun around. "What is the matter, Ramiel?" He tilted his head to the side as Ramiel's footsteps crackled on the gravel.

"You raised LaDonna. You see what that brought us. Now you are raising Dominique?"

He scoffed and turned. "She has done nothing wrong," he said as he continued deeper into the cemetery.

"Except the massacre. Certainly you remember that."

Cristofano paused. "She had nothing to do with that." He turned slowly. "But yes, Ramiel, I do remember the massacre. And do you remember what has befallen us since then?" Ramiel felt the cold blood rush through his veins as Cristofano's voice carried an edge. "Certainly you remember what Antoine went through. And Darius. And the rest of our kind with the assault of that man in the hood who carried a false decanter!" He lunged forwards as Ramiel cowered back, but Cristofano raised his hand, slowly collapsed it into a fist, and retreated.

"You clearly have your own objective," Ramiel said. "Releasing those who are serving a sentence is an abuse of your power. Regardless of how much we loved Dominique, she must serve her sentence. It's clearly written in the code."

Cristofano scoffed. "Oh, the code! There you go with the code once again! Don't you understand, Ramiel? A crypt dancer possesses the judgement gift. We can make a determination to end a sentence, or not."

"We," Ramiel said.

He took a deep breath and watched as Cristofano leaned on a nearby crypt, looking upwards towards the stars. After a few minutes of silence, he spoke. "You see those stars up there, Ramiel?"

Cristofano turned and raised his eyebrows, but Ramiel didn't answer.

"There's a purpose behind them," he said, as he turned and looked back upwards. His voice trailed off slightly as Ramiel sighed. He watched as Cristofano seemingly studied the night sky, perhaps searching for purpose, an internal reasoning of which Ramiel felt he might never fully understand. But Ramiel stood behind Cristofano, and leaned further back on the same crypt, watching his maker watch the sky. And then Ramiel knew. The answers may never appear to him. For Cristofano had a duty placed on him by Claret – a responsibility which no immortal ever would want. And then Ramiel watched him hang his head down. And wondered if Cristofano knew. If he realized that releasing those immortals from coffin sentences to receive a personal elation might not always yield the desired results.

Ramiel felt the warm hands of empathy wrap around his heart, and debated whether to approach and comfort Cristofano. He had so much of Claret in him. And Claret was gone, and Ramiel knew that Cristofano had become a lost soul. For even though Claret had her nefarious intentions, she was his maker. And an immortal without a maker can easily become a lost soul. Ramiel felt the need to step forward and place his arms around Cristofano, but, could he?

He felt a twinge of desperation as he watched Cristofano hang his head.

"Cristo?"

Ramiel thought his voice sounded small, and tinny, against the solitude of the cemetery. Cristofano remained facing forward, and Ramiel could tell from the curvature of his back that his arms were still crossed; his head still hung downwards, and then Ramiel watched as he saw the silhouette of Cristofano's arm reach upwards, towards his face, and move across it, outwards. Could he have been wiping a tear from his cheek?

Ramiel bit his lip, moved forward, and then hesitated. Cristofano had never proved welcoming of his comfort. And this particular night, he may not be any different. Still, Ramiel reached his hand out, and held it just behind Cristofano's shoulder. There was still a remnant feeling of his time in the clergy, and an innate need to console. He understood that Cristofano recently lost his maker, and while he may not understand his grieving, would Cristofano welcome his comfort?

He drew his hand back slowly as Cristofano straightened his posture and cleared his throat. He turned for a moment. Ramiel saw that his eyes were slightly red, his cheeks were a touch wet. "Just come with me," he said. "We came here for a specific purpose."

Ramiel watched as Cristofano turned and headed deeper into the cemetery. He knew the purpose for this mission. The Hooded Man had almost completely wiped out their kind. And there was strength in numbers, they both knew that. Yet Ramiel never achieved clarity on whose orders that Cristofano operated under. He had the authority to end coffin sentences, yes, but at what cost? Would raising the immortals who had earned their fate through a desecration and betrayal of their own kind have good intentions to transform towards the better good of the immortals?

Ramiel watched as Cristofano glided down the wide path, framed by the rise of the stone crypts; he watched his maker as he danced beneath the pale blue moonlight, falling into a trio of pirouettes. This was it, Ramiel thought. The dance had begun, the ballet, the eternal walk thought the cemeteries, drawing on coffins of the immortals, interspersed throughout the purpose of the graveyard, the people, and the humans. For in the midst, there were the immortals. Listening. And waiting. For the crypt dancer to come. And open the seal. The ballet of the crypt dancer, it seemed, was only at the first act.

Ramiel's consciousness was thrust back to Hades Pass as thunder crashed overhead. He closed his eyes for a moment as he felt the chill of the putrid water washing over the stones on his bare feet. He could hear the deafening roar of the winds, the desperate cries from the sea, and the limbs splashing through water, from which the lost ones might never emerge.

"They are preparing!"

Queen Reynalda's voice boomed over the torrent of winds, the crash of thunder, the howling coming from the lost souls. Ramiel opened his eyes and watched as the Queen of the coven stood on her perch of stones, raising her arms in the sky. "The one you seek is bound by the sea! They will all become shadows. They will become demons and bind those serving sentences with chains!"

The next stone appeared far as the waters crashed against the rocks, casting sulfuric spray upwards as arms and legs clung to the sides, slipping back downwards into the waters.

Do not let them touch you, LaDonna had warned. *Or they will drag you into the sea and you will become a shadow yourself!*

Ramiel lifted his foot, gasping at the heaviness.

"Ramiel!"

He turned and looked out at the sea.

The winds howled as the sea spray of white foam crashed against the rocks. The voice was feminine and familiar; one he had not heard in years. "Ramiel, look! Look out towards the sea!"

He squinted, scarcely seeing the countless, pasty white souls, thrashing limbs, clinging to a life lost and desperation in the waters. He looked outwards in the distance, ignoring the howling winds, and Queen Reynalda's deep, methodic laughter in the distance. He focused on the thrashing arms.

"I can't breathe Ramiel! I can hardly stay up! *The water*! Help me, Ramiel!"

It was her soft, feminine voice.

And then the vision pierced his mind.

Dominique lay in the darkness of the coffin and listened to the silence. She no longer had the sense of time; for the darkness enveloped, the eternal black void surrounded and muted her senses, and she prayed for a piercing of light…anything to make the coffin less of a threat. For the threat of an eternity of dark silence brought her the visions.

She opened her eyes, yet saw nothing.

Desperate to move, the chains bound her. Her resistance was useless. But she felt her heartbeat. Her chest pounded against the vice grip of the chains as she felt her desperation grow.

The hunger.

She felt it burn from deep within as it raced through her veins, and the thirst rose up deep within her throat. She opened her mouth as she felt the dryness tear into her tissue. Blood. She had to get blood.

But then she sensed the approach of footsteps.

The searing in her veins pierced through her body. She stopped as the coffin shook. She winced as she felt a rumble and a forward drag.

And then the drop onto the ground with a deep thud.

Muffled voices emitted from above her as the crackling of wood tore away from the edge of the coffin.

She opened her eyes.

A face in the shadows through the splintered wood looked down as the pale blue moonlight emanated from above. She watched as the mysterious dark figure remained a silhouette, and the cool night air blew across her face.

"Cristo," a male voice called from out of her view.

A second figure appeared in her field of vision shrouded with darkness. "I have her," he said.

"She will need the blood," the voice said. "Bring her."

Dominique watched as the shadowy figure retreated. The dark figure reached downwards and grabbed the chains, tearing them apart. She gasped for breath as the dryness of her mouth cast dust outwards.

The sea filled with deafening screams as Ramiel opened his eyes.

"Save us, Ramiel!"

Voices in unison charged towards him as he heard deep, rumbling steps. A dark figure loomed on the beach. He turned his head the opposite direction, towards the small mountain of rocks, and Queen Reynalda had again retreated. But the voices, he could not shut them out of his mind.

He heard the distant pleading from a male voice through the wailing and the winds. For an instant, he thought it might be Cristofano. Yet as he stared at the thrashing limbs, he watched and lost Dominique, yet her voice and memories had been all she had been able to offer. Had she perished in the sea? Was the dark figure on the beach the selector of the shadow demons which bound their penitent kind?

"Ramiel!"

The voice came again.

He scanned the area. "No!" the voice said. "Right below!"

He took a cautious step back towards the center of the stone and looked down, raising his arms to protect his face as the sea crashed against the side of the stone and sprayed foam into the air. When it cleared, he studied the faces which struggled to surface.

And then he saw the familiar eyes.

"Ramiel you must return!"

The voice was muddled with the water, in a desperate eternal attempt to tread and breathe above the surface, but he could see his features in the pasty skin clearly: Cristofano.

"Return to the coffin! The crypt!"

He fell to his knees, reaching his arm outwards towards the waters, and cried out as a torrent of arms reached up from the treacherous waters and grabbed his arm. He winced at the weight of the souls, the vice grip of their hands, tearing into his flesh.

"Get back on the rock!" Cristofano said as waves cascaded over the bodies.

Ramiel mustered his energy and tore his arm away from the writhing bodies, falling back on the rock on his back, gasping for breath.

"Don't let them pull you to the sea!" Cristofano pleaded. "But listen!"

Ramiel propped himself back onto his arms and saw that Cristofano had managed to grasp himself above the water, if only for a few moments. His skin appeared gelatinous, dead, yet his eyes were wide, filled with terror. "You cannot save me here no matter how hard you try! There will be no way for me to return."

Was this the fateful destiny of the immortals who were serving coffin sentences?

Cristofano coughed as the spray washed over his face. "You cannot save me," he said. "For I am bound and chained in a cage. Beneath the ground. *Within the coven.*"

Ramiel gasped.

He snapped his head back towards the beach, and watched as the dark figure moved back and forth; a faceless creature, a muscular demon. A shadow which stood guard.

"They will all become shadows!" Cristofano said. "It's our destiny! To bind and drag to hell!" Ramiel turned his head as Cristofano reached his free arm upwards and pointed towards the rocks. "It's her," he croaked. "She churns the sea into putrid hate. It's *unescapable*. For most. But go. Back to the coven. You will find me there! She casts her spell, weaves her hatred for us! *Save me, Ramiel!*"

Part Six – Act Three

BLOOD+CROSS

One

WHEN QUEEN REYNALDA had been bound by her own shadow demons, chained and dragged into a coffin for her sentence, Ramiel and Cristofano were still in Europe. When word reached Rome, the high council of the Inspiriti, and Monsignor Harrison, he insisted that there be as much immortal representation at the funeral as possible, in order to maintain a sense to the Reynalda coven that they were a peer, not at a lower ranking in the supernatural hierarchy. Both Ramiel and Cristofano received the time gift from Claret's ancestry, although both rarely used the gift.

The immortals all remembered when Queen Reynalda was issued her coffin sentence, and when the shadow demons, which she had created from her own spells and her own potions, had turned on her, and bound her in the very chains which she had reserved, until that point, for the immortal community. Still, when the sentence had been carried out for her own judgement, the immortal community, as dictated in the code, would assure the sentence be carried out without equivocation.

The Cathedral of the Gardens was a place of worship in the southern suburbs of Miami, near where Coconut Grove and Coral Gables wound into one another through small avenues with shaded oak canopies. It was a small, stone church, adorned with the accent of creeping green ivy and hibiscus plants, yet was called a Cathedral by the locals. And, over the years, it had become a center of guidance for some in the immortal community. After Queen Reynalda had been chained to the coffin, the cathedral was decorated with swags of hanging white tule, with scattered white roses, for the flower was Queen Reynalda's favorite.

Several pallbearers exited a long, black limousine and headed up towards the waiting hearse. The car was of a different era, it was a black Cadillac with a long, slender engine, thick white walls, and curtains hanging in the rectangular rear carriage.

A tall, lanky man emerged from the driver's door.

Ramiel watched as the man smoothed his jet-black hair, slicked back and always looking wet. He could be none other than Ned McCracken, the funeral director for the immortals. And now, of course, for the Reynalda Coven. Ramiel didn't understand Cristofano's insistence that he attend Queen Reynalda's funeral.

"It's political," Cristofano explained the previous evening.

"What about Antoine?" Ramiel asked. "Can't he go?"

Cristofano shook his head as the young Frenchman, Pasquale, Antoine's guardian of the Brickell condo which he had offered for Ramiel and Cristofano to stay in while in town for the funeral, started mixing martinis behind the bar. Ramiel watched Antoine's loyal, young, immortal friend pour vodka from a large, smoky glass bottle as Cristofano explained why Antoine was too busy with Club *Sacrafice*, and Darius was seemingly out of control, and with the strained relationship with the Reynalda Coven.

"They're quite powerful," Cristofano said as Pasquale approached with a tray. He took a frothy martini from a frosted, stemmed glass, and looked up and nodded at Pasquale, who approached Ramiel. He looked up at Pasquale, who stood above him, smiling. His brilliant smile stood out from his olive skin and dark black hair. "Your drink monsieur!"

Ramiel reached up, maintaining direct eye contact with Pasquale. "Maybe it's time we transform Pasquale, don't you think, Cristo?"

Pasquale beamed and his eyes widened. "Yes!"

Cristofano set his martini down on the table with a slight clank. He leaned back and gave an exasperated sigh. "Let's stick to the topic at hand, gentlemen."

He rose from the couch as Ramiel and Pasquale held their drinks, their eyes trained on him. "We must keep a positive relationship with the coven," Cristofano said, as he paced back and forth in front of a large, marble mantle. "Their powers through witchcraft run deep…and from many years ago. Queen Reynalda will walk these streets once again. Many years from now, for certain. We will receive a respite, for now." He looked at Ramiel. "But you must go to her funeral. Pay your respects. See where they bury her. That will be important to us."

"It won't be in the crypt at Resurrection?" Pasquale asked.

"It will be the choice of the coven," Cristofano said.

Ramiel nodded as Pasquale sipped his martini while his eyes looked up at Cristofano. "You are going to release her?" Ramiel asked.

Cristofano paused and draped his arm up on the mantle, letting out a sigh. "Claret would despise me for it."

Ramiel nodded as they locked eye contact. "Yes."

Cristofano looked up towards the ceiling. Ramiel knew that he was deciding how to process, thinking it over in his mind. But Ramiel knew what the answer would be.

"Yes, I believe so," Cristofano said.

And then Ramiel's thoughts were thrust back into the present, and he watched as the pallbearers gathered around the rear of the hearse as Ned slowly opened the wide door. The pallbearers lifted a golden casket from the cabin and hoisted it up on their shoulders.

"But you're not dead, are you Queen?"

Ramiel remained on the opposite side of the street as he watched the men carry the coffin through a massive crowed, the witches, Ramiel knew. A massive and powerful coven. "But you all don't know that she is bound and chained in there, do you?"

Ned closed the rear door to the hearse quietly as Ramiel watched him from afar. A friend of the immortals. He must have done the job, it seemed. A paralyzed Queen would not be a threat, and Ned would most likely have completed the job himself. But a witch, on an immortal coffin sentence, bore great speculation. When Claret continued her powerful reign, her ability to sentence any immortal to coffin time was undisputed. Ramiel did not know, however, when he was first transformed, that Queen Reynalda had been an immortal herself.

Had she been purposefully assigned to the coven?

Being sent by Cristofano to observe her funeral introduced more questions, but Ramiel knew, that it was the *magia de la bruja,* their witchcraft, that was sometimes more powerful than what the immortals could conjure. But in the past, Claret was able to overpower the Queen, and now, she was lying bound and chained, sealed in her casket, listening to the wails and cries of her coven.

Or, at least, that remained the assumption.

And as he watched Queen Reynalda's casket ascend the steps in front of the Cathedral, he also watched as the throngs of witches gathered around the casket and followed it through the massive, wooden doors. "If they only knew," Ramiel said. "There would be war."

Ramiel watched from afar as they headed into the darkness of the open cathedral doors, and Ramiel waited. And Cristofano planned to release her. There was a twinge of uncertainty that washed through him. For the Queen was the leader of the coven for a reason; a purpose of power, and for the time that Claret had been the Queen's greatest adversary, there had once been a union of their power.

And the Queen was transformed.

A clap of thunder sounded from above as dark clouds rolled in.

As Ramiel waited for the services to conclude, he approached Ned, who leaned against the hearse. His head was down, and he was rummaging through a stack of papers, brilliant white against the fading darkness of the sky. As Ramiel got closer, Ned raised his head and gave him a nod.

"Hello Ned," Ramiel said.

Ned nodded and returned to the paperwork, shuffling the papers. "You're attending the funeral for a prominent witch?"

Ramiel shuffled on his feet. "Well...Cristo sent me."

Ned didn't divert his attention from what he was reading. "Oh, he did, did he?"

Ramiel nodded, and leaned in closer towards the side of the hearse. "Yes."

Ned looked up and directly at Ramiel, yet remained expressionless. "And I know about what has been occurring between the immortals and the coven. I know all about that. But here...this coven...they contact me because I am the best at what I do. And they have money. Old money. For generations. And that talks. It keeps my business operating. And my employees paid, and well taken care of. So...what can I do for you?"

Ramiel sighed. "I need to know where she will be entombed."

Ned rolled the papers in one hand and leaned forward. He looked down at Ramiel with a stern look on his face. "And why do you need to know that?"

A flash of Queen Reynalda, lying in the casket, bound and gagged, locked in chains, frozen and unable to move, permeated his mind. He could hear her emit the smallest cry from the fabric wrapped tight across her mouth, but her expensive, golden casket, completely sealed, would conceal the slightest whimper.

But Ramiel dared not let on that he knew that the coffin in the funeral had a living immortal locked inside.

A flurry of chatter emitted from behind them as Ned turned around. The funeral procession had emerged, as the pallbearers carried the glimmering casket on their shoulders. A trio of sopranos nestled next to one another on the rising steps, joining in a chorus of song.

"You best not be intruding here, Ramiel."

A flurry of white doves was released as the casket neared the hearse. Ned rushed towards the back and opened the door. "We are only in the first part of her service," Ned said, looking back as Ramiel looked on. He moved closer to where Ned stood. Ned leaned forward and assisted as the casket was hoisted into the waiting cabin. "Queen Reynalda has connections to Paganism, of course, from running the coven. But also has connections to Catholicism, so her funeral comes in three stages."

"Where are you going, then, Ned?"

Ned looked up at him and paused. "You really want to go there? It will be you and hundreds of witches. Do you think you can be safe?"

Ned shook his head as the pallbearers closed the door. Several of the witches dressed in black, wore flowing necklaces of fresh flowers, which hung down towards their waists, and burned sage. Ramiel watched as the smoke rose up towards the darkening skies.

"They cross to another plane," Ned said, heading towards the front of the hearse. "They call it the Summerland."

Ned opened the door and flopped behind the wheel. "Look," he said. "I don't want to condone a war between the immortals and the coven. You've worked together for generations. Why start now?"

"Cristo has his purposes, and I am sure Claret does as well."

Ned fished for his keys and nodded. "Very well then. If you must, get in. I will take you. But don't say I didn't warn you."

Ramiel dashed around the long, slender hood and pulled the passenger door open. He looked up at Ned. "Do you listen to her?"

Ned looked up and shifted his face.

"Do you hear her in there? Whimpering? Crying?"

Ned scoffed. "No I do not. She does not whimper. She knows her sentence. I just carry it out."

The engine roared to life as Ned slowly pulled the hearse forward. The gathering procession tossed cut flowers towards them, and Ramiel watched and listened to the flowers thump against the windows and the sides of the hearse.

"She knows the rituals," Ned said, as he navigated the avenue. "And her heritage. She knows the coffin sentence is long, and tortuous. And that she will hear the dirt clumping on the lid. Sealing her away from the senses. But she *also* knows that there is absolutely nothing that she can do about it. Except wait."

"Wait..."

Ned nodded as he took a right turn. The hearse was crawling, as the women dressed in long, flowing black dresses, continued to toss fresh cut flowers at the car. Most landed in the street. But some caught Ramiel's attention with a thump on the glass.

"There's a crypt dancer, it's been told, among the lore of the immortals," Ned said. "Only one. A special appointment, and only by the most powerful, and the eldest of the immortals. Only he or she can release another immortal from a coffin sentence."

"And the witches won't save her?"

"Oh, they would, if they could. But they can't. Their power is great. And powerful. But this power is stronger. It goes far beyond paganism, or wicca. Or even magic. And spells. Because I am talking about the power that magic and spells has derived from."

Ramiel looked out the window and watched their long skirts blow in a passing breeze. The witches were together, holding hands, holding wreathes of fresh, colorful flowers in the air as he could hear their chanting.

"They are wishing her a safe passage towards the Summerland."

Ramiel watched in fascination. "We're not going far, are we?"

"No," Ned said softly. "We're not going far at all."

Ramiel noted their location. He recognized the start of the soaring and shady oak canopy at the end of the Cathedral property. "We're heading to Ascension, aren't we?" He looked over at Ned, and saw him nod.

"But," Ned said. "I cannot guarantee that she will be there when you and Cristo start looking for her."

Ramiel froze. Ned knew. He knew all along. There was no purpose in attempting to cover it up any longer. He took a breath and released it slowly, as he looked over at Ned. He was focused on the road.

"So…" Ramiel said. "Any thoughts on what's going to happen next?"

"You're not going to get any information from me."

Ramiel nodded and looked out at the witches as they followed the hearse on the sidewalk. "But I can deduce it for myself." He looked over at Ned.

Ned turned. And shrugged his shoulders. "I'm not here to stop you."

Ramiel watched as they approached the soaring statues and crypts that rose from the shaded grounds of Ascension. Spanish Moss drifted in a cooling afternoon breeze. As Ned pulled the hearse to a slow stop towards the side of a cracked sidewalk, Ramiel saw that there was a young man, dressed in a black suit, waiting for them at the edge of the sprawling, wrought iron gates. The man wore a black fedora low on his forehead, which concealed his eyes, but Ramiel could tell the mysterious man in the black suit was watching them. As Ned parked the hearse and prepared to display the casket at the crypt before the procession of flowers arrived, Ramiel kept the man in his line of sight. He had turned, now in a different position, still leaning on the tall, stone monument.

It was confirmed.

As they got out of the car, Ramiel kept his eyes trained on the man, who stood and stared right back at them. He slammed the door with a deep thud as he heard Ned open the back of the hearse with a creek, and the sliding apparatus drawing the casket outwards from the back. Ramiel broke his trance and walked to the back, looking down at the golden casket, covered with white roses.

"Aren't you going to wait for the pallbearers?"

Ned shook his head. "Just me and you." He nodded towards the foot of the casket. "Grab it, will you?"

They stopped as footsteps approached on the gravel.

Ramiel snapped his head around towards the crunching as Ned raised his head and looked ahead.

The man had decided to join them.

His fedora remained low, and his dark eyes were nestled in the shadow, despite the bright and brilliant Miami sun. His suit was tailored and fitted, clean and pressed, which served as a striking contrast to his hair, hanging low and stringy across both shoulders, and down the lapels.

"Don't take her to your crypt," he said, keeping his voice low. He looked over towards the entrance of the cemetery and they all looked, and noticed the procession was rounding the corner, their flowing white sun dresses catching the afternoon warmth and sun, and Ramiel thought for a moment that they must have an endless supply of petals and daisies, for they were still casting them in the air.

The man continued. "If you take her there, she will rob your souls. She rules the pass. And the sea. If she serves her sentence in Resurrection, she will thrust the immortals who share the crypt with her into the sea."

Ramiel shifted his face. "She has that much power?"

The man nodded and took a cautious step closer. Ramiel braced himself, but wanted to hear more. The knowledge of this man proved that he had a connection, not only to the coven, but also, possibly, to the immortal community.

"Her powers and potions made it possible for her to spend her sentence at Hades Pass rather than being chained in the coffin. Her tyranny will reign if she is taken to the crypt in Resurrection, I can assure you. She is the Mother of the Shadow Demons."

The man turned and took a few steps towards the procession, which was on the next block, marching up the small dirt road in the center of the sea of stone monuments. He stopped and turned for a moment.

"Don't say you haven't been warned," he said.

And then he turned and proceeded, walking directly towards the procession. Ramiel turned back and faced Ned, whose eyes were wide. Ned shrugged his shoulders. "Who was he?"

Ramiel focused on the man in the black suit, who disappeared into the throngs of witches in white summery dresses, dancing in circles, singing and celebrating the life of their Supreme Mother.

Two

THE CRYING never seemed to stop at Hadden House.

It came from the lower rafters; beneath the oiled hardwood, and the heavy rugs scarcely could absorb the distant wails.

Those in the coven had become accustomed to the nearly constant babbling, Emmaline and Giselle, the two leaders, sat across from each other in the front parlor, as Trudy pulled the heavy drapes back. Muted sunlight filtered through the shears, as the two senior witches stared at a carved marble chessboard.

"Check mate," Giselle said. She looked up at Emmaline and smiled.

Emmaline pursed her lips, scowled, and studied the chess board. After Giselle had captured her knight and her rook, there was no return. Nothing else she could do. "No more matches," she said.

The wail emanated from below as Giselle looked down towards the floor.

"You must learn to ignore it," Emmaline said. "How can you possibly advance to the level that you have been asking if you are so distracted all the time?"

Giselle raised her head and looked at Emmaline. "I can pray to the Queen. She will answer me from the summerland."

Emmaline slammed her palm on the table as the chess pieces clanked down on the hardwood. "She is *not* in the summerland! How many times must I remind you?!"

Giselle pursed her lips and rose from her chair, leaving the room without a word.

Trudy approached Emmaline slowly. "Can I get you anything, Emmaline? Something to calm your nerves?" Emmaline shook her head and waved Trudy away.

And then Emmaline thought of the Queen. She was the one they called Reynalda, and also the reason behind the babble which emanated nearly constantly from the cellar below. The Queen had been present when Emmaline was born; as the first to be born in Haddon House, she was told, from a young girl, that she was special because of that.

She had been given a specific and detailed account of her birth from the coven members.

And the images formed in her mind, as if it were a film, and she always thought of the Queen of the Coven. The Madame of Hades Pass.

She was Queen Reynalda, one of the few members of the coven who had a significant history backwards through time, and a deep connection with the immortals. She was the supreme of the coven before Miami had even been founded as a city; emigrating from South

America, through the Caribbean with a brief period in Port-au-Prince, before settling in southern Florida.

The picture had always been painted with long, sweeping brush strokes, in brilliant and vivid colors, for that is how Queen Reynalda chose to live her life: in vibrance. Her colorful personality matched her vibrant dresses, in bright yellows, blues, in a kaleidoscope of color each time she entered a room. Emmaline had been a mere girl when she first saw the Queen.

Her mother, Anastasia, had been initiated into the coven while still carrying Emmaline to term, and it was her destiny to be born in the Hadden House. She was given a room upstairs to rest until the term was complete, until Emmaline was ready enter the world of the witches. On the night when Anastasia went into labor, screams emanated from the room above, as Queen Reynalda had clasped her thick, meaty hands together. "There!" she said. "There it is! The night when one of our kind is born under this room! The goddesses are smiling upon us!"

Thunder crashed from overhead as Queen Reynalda barreled up the creaking stairs with heavy footsteps. "I am coming for the birth of our little one!" she boomed. Several of her assistants followed. "Bring the finest linens to wrap the babe in!" she said.

Emmaline opened her eyes and saw the sunlight fading.

She knelt down to pick up the chess pieces, placing the fawns first on both sides of the chess table, and then the rooks, knights, bishops and kings. She saw the two Queen pieces lying on the floor, next to one another.

Not enough room in this coven for two Queens, it seems.

But Queen Reynalda had a distinct advantage, which Emmaline had learned of while living in Hadden House once she was old enough to determine what the group of women were. And how they practiced magic, and confided with the earth, and nature.

Over the years, Queen Reynalda took Emmaline under her wing. Emmaline remembered the day quite vividly; she had entered the heavy, wooden door with the oval stained glass in the center, and headed into the foyer with the dark, smokey wood. It was near the end of the semester, and her school bag was light, as she had returned most of her books to the shelves. She still wore her blue plaid skirt and matching powder blue button down.

The house was silent, save the grandfather clock in the parlor.

She removed her necktie and undid the top button, as the nuns would never permit a more casual look. She craned her neck towards the parlor; Roman was dusting the piano, he looked towards her direction and gave her a nod. But there was no sign of anyone else from the coven. She dropped her bag and removed her shoes, and as she stepped on the bottom wooden step, she heard the authoritative, deep voice. "Emmaline, come here to me."

It was coming from the rear gathering room.

She sighed quietly, knowing that it was the Queen, and that her calls must always be answered. Emmaline glided through the foyer and down the rear hallway, pausing at the back room. The shades and curtains were drawn, and the glowing reflection of a roaring fire in the fireplace painted wisps of orange on the walls and artwork.

Queen Reynalda sat in a plush side chair, facing the fire, and Emmaline stood silently, watching her study the fire. She was wearing her white dress today, with matching headdress. Her heavy frame spilled over the sides of the chair, and she continued her stare ahead and did not turn to acknowledge Emmaline's presence.

"Come, sit."

She took a few steps forward, silent on the heavy floral rug, navigating overstuffed furniture and heavy, dark wood tables. She stood next to the fire and looked over at Queen Reynalda, who sat in the chair, her legs propped on a small ottoman, watching the fire. Emmaline could see the reflection of the flames on her big, round glasses. She reached out with a big, heavy arm and gestured towards the small chair.

"Sit."

She sat as the two women sat in silence. The fire crackled and warmed them, and if Emmaline listened closely enough, she could hear Queen Reynalda's slow and steady breathing. Emmaline waited, as she knew her place in the household. The senior witches were always in command, and although the Queen had adopted her since her mother died giving birth to her in the bedroom upstairs, she knew that she still must abide by the rules of the house.

And so she waited.

Queen Reynalda turned to face Emmaline. "You are almost fully schooled in our ways and cultures," she said. "Almost to the next level. I have been monitoring your progress quite closely, and I am pleased, dear Emmaline. Pleased indeed."

Emmaline smiled wanly and nodded.

"And you are the only member of the coven who has been here since birth," she added. "That places you in a very coveted position."

Emmaline turned her head towards the Queen as she turned back towards the fire. "I've never been much of a mother, it seems," she said. "But as my daughter, you must know more of my history. And the origin of where I came from."

Emmaline nodded. "Yes, I would like that very much."

Roman brought in a tray with a large ceramic pot and two small cups.

"Dandelion tea," she said, looking over towards Emmaline. "It helps with digestion."

Emmaline watched as Roman poured the steaming tea in a cup and placed it on a small wicker table in the center of the chairs. Queen Reynalda then removed the necklace she was wearing; a thin gold chain, with a purple crystal. She grasped the crystal and removed a small portion of the top. "The powder of our ancestors," she said. "This is how you will join me."

Emmaline watched Queen Reynalda's hands, removing the tiny, crystal top, placing it gently on the table next to the steaming cups of tea, gently shaking a touch of white powder into her hand, and brushing it into each cup. She placed the top back on the crystal and placed it back around her neck, where it hung, nestle between her breasts. She leaned over and gave each cup a stir with a small spoon. "It only takes a tiny bit. Sip the tea, it will relax you, and then you will enter the summerland."

"Enter? I don't want to die, dear Queen. I don't want to dear mother…"

Queen Reynalda leaned her head back and laughed. "You will not *die* sweet Emmaline…but you wanted to see how I became Queen, did you not?"

She nodded slowly.

"Then it's settled then. You drink the tea. And then you will join me on the journey…"

She picked up the cup slowly and felt its warmth through the ceramic as it heated her fingers and palm. She brought it up towards her nose and noted the delicate floral steam rising from the green liquid, held it up to her lips, and paused. She turned and looked at Queen Reynalda who was sipping her tea. "Will I one day be Queen?"

Queen Reynalda lowered her cup. "There is not enough room in the coven for two queens," she said. "Now drink your tea."

Emmaline held the two queen chess pieces and remembered the day with Queen Reynalda next to the fire. And what had happened next. The powder that she carried was powerful. A harbinger of death.

She stood and hugged her arms, listening to the babble in the cellar. The continuous and distant wail, the sound of desperation and loneliness. She knew that holding him there was against the treaty that they had signed with the immortal community and the Inspiriti, but now she was Queen since Queen Reynalda was gone, and the relationship with the immortals continued to be unsettled, she knew she had made the right decision.

But Queen Reynalda was the one who remained shrouded in mystery.

She was the one who governed the coven, and had for generations. Emmaline learned that the queen was an immortal herself, but on that day years ago when they had drank the tea, was when the mystery had deepened. She held the cup to her lips, and felt the steam rise from the hot liquid, and closed her eyes. She sipped it, swallowed it down, and felt it immediately warm her insides as the earthy notes remained in her mouth. She drew the cup to her mouth yet again, swallowed more, treasured the warmth again, and repeated the process until she looked down and saw the remaining leaves at the bottom of the cup.

Her head felt heavy, disconnected.

She could still hear the crackle of the fire before them, but there was a distance to the sounds. Her mind remained intact; she could hear Roman padding rummaging through the kitchen cabinets preparing dinner. But as she looked at the other chair, she saw Queen Reynalda slumped over the arm.

Emmaline opened her mouth to call her name, but nothing would come out, no matter how hard she tried to speak. *First it takes your voice and then it takes your sight,* Giselle had told her once about Queen Reynalda's secret, powerful powder.

Her heart pounded in her chest as she saw the world blackening; darkness surrounded her sight, closing inwards, as she slowly faded away…

She felt the dampness of dead leaves on the side of her cheek as the smell of burning wood was in the air. She opened her eyes to a piercing brightness, drawing her arms upwards and covering her face. "Queen? Are you here dear Queen?"

But there was no answer.

There was hammering in the distance. The sound of distant footsteps; the crunching of leaves and small twigs. Getting closer. She uncovered her eyes as saw the sun filtered through dead treetops. Each breath emitted a puff of vapor, the chill permeated her sweater, and as she scanned the area, no sign of the Queen.

Her heart pounded as she heard the footsteps stop behind her. The hooves of horses.

"Another one sir?"

She closed her eyes and heard the voice of a man. No placement of an accent. Her hands in her lap, her head bowed and eyes closed, she heard the thud of their dismount, and the footsteps, moving closer to her, and then stopping.

"You aren't from around here, are you?"

It was the same male voice.

She slowly opened her eyes, and turned around, looking upwards. The man was shielded in a silhouette, the sun haloing behind him, the chaos of his hair jutting outwards.

"Stop! Now!"

She felt relief wash through her as the tightness in her chest released. Queen Reynalda. She looked up as her queen mother glared at the men. "Head back to Ravenshire," she said. "You have no place here."

Emmaline looked up as the men retreated, mounted their horses, and turned back towards the forest. Queen Reynalda approached her, extending her hand outwards. Emmaline took it and eased herself onto her feet. There was a knowing look in the Queen's eyes. They weren't really there, the Queen knew, and now she knew; the men who approached her earlier couldn't have physically harmed her.

"Then how did they see me?" Emmaline asked, as the Queen led her down the path which she said would take them to town. "How did the men know I was there?"

She looked up at the sky for a moment, and Emmaline could tell that she was smiling. "That powder works in mysterious ways," she said. "It can place us in a different time, even in a different dimension. Most will not be able to detect us or our movements, for we still truly exist back in Hadden House, not here in the woods of Brazil. But yes, those two men could see us. It is rare, but it does happen."

"Why were they approaching me like that?"

The Queen put her arm around Emmaline as they walked. "You are special," she said. "A witch from the order of Reynalda. When you take the powder, you shine with an aura of an angel, soaring across the skies of the summerland, bathed in colorful flowers and the call of birds."

But there was a distinct characteristic to the Queen's potion and powders. Over the centuries, after she had received her own gift and transformation, she used the seemingly endless time to perfect her craft, her vision for her dark purposes. While many in the coven never fully understood her intentions, it was apparent that all knew of the powers which she possessed. Her gift, her immortality, allowed her to perfect her powder. Where it could be manipulated for her own agenda.

Emmaline's thought returned to the present, and although she only remembered snippets of her journey to Brazil with Queen Reynalda, there were consequences to their association. The power, Emmaline learned, lent a more distinct power to the Queen's motivations: the shadows.

Emmaline failed to remember much beyond the conversations in the warm and humid forests, but she knew that the powers behind the potion ran long and deep. And, perhaps, she didn't want her to remember.

But what Emmaline could recall were the shadows.

The shadows that formed once the tea had been imbibed; the wails, the deep growls and the pounding of her heart in her chest.

Three

IN MIAMI, there was a destiny of shadows.

Those dark, sinister spirits which crept across the sidewalks at night, under the hum of the streetlamps, when the children had all been put to bed, then the adults would come out to play. The shadows had been known throughout the immortal community as *The Dark Ones*, and Darius Sauvage was an immortal who experienced the shadows first-hand, while he lay dying in a hospital bed in Jackson Memorial, long before Ramiel and Cristofano had ventured outside of Europe.

By the time the dark ones came, from their shadowy corners in the nighttime chaos, Darius had already lost his gift. The dark gift was no longer bestowed upon him; no longer immortal, he felt the grip of aging grasping at him, tearing at his flesh and sanity, as he lay in the hospital bed he was a frail shell.

But Darius knew.

He knew about the dark ones.

He knew of the shadow of a streetlamp, its long, dark cylinder against the lighter shades of the night and sidewalks. He saw the dark figures move towards him as he would walk down the sidewalk, making a feeble attempt to remain in the light of shops and restaurants whose spilled out onto the pavement.

But the shadow pursued him.

Reaching across Ponce de Leon as he quickened his pace.

He turned his head and saw the dark cylinder slither closer towards him. He darted through groups of chatty night revelers, oblivious to his plight, unaware that the darkness pursued him. He paused for a moment at the edge a brick midrise, leaning against it catching his breath.

He scanned the area.

The alleyway was far too dark. Stay out of the darkness, that's what he was told. They can't leave the shadows, he was told. He turned around.

Movement towards Ponce de Leon.

Not far back, maybe half a block. It wouldn't take long. He turned forward and gasped. There was movement near the dumpster. The glow from the streetlamp on the opposite corner wasn't enough. The dark side. He could see it moving.

Lengthening.

His heart pounded as he looked behind him.

The darkness expanded as the lights of Ponce de Leon dimmed; he'd heard of it before but the true process of the dark ones had always been a mystery.

Destiny...

The hiss filled the air as he cried out. The darkness enveloped him, as the hum of the traffic silenced; the boisterous chatter of the night revelers was silenced, and the darkness dominated.

This is your destiny, Darius...

He fell to his knees as his heart pounded against his ribcage. Let me out! Let me out! He felt the sting of the pavement on his knees and the warm wetness of blood running down his legs as he dared not open his eyes. *Did you think you would feel physical pain from us?*

He wrapped his arms around himself and fell forward into a large putrid trash bag which stank of excrement. "No! No! Don't take me!

He buried his face in the trash bag and covered his head, holding his legs close to his chest. "No dark ones, no dark ones, no dark ones..." He murmured under his breath as he felt the chill approach.

The howl of the winds.

He dared not open his eyes for all he would see would be darkness. And pain. Loneliness and torment. But at one point, he knew he would have to open his eyes. Because he couldn't lay on the cool sand for all of eternity. For the street and alleyway had faded into darkness; there was no nightlife or trash dumpsters or bookstores or cafes.

He could hear the roar of an ocean's surf, the cool sand of a nearby beach. But opening his eyes would prove futile. His body would still by lying on the sidewalk in a haphazard mess, but he would no longer be there.

For the shadows came for him.

And he knew the shadows would come for him. From the moment he was transformed, he knew the shadows would come for him. And as he lay on the beach and listened to the surf, he knew that it was a fallacy. There would be no peace. There would be no solitude.

Because the shadows had come for him.

He felt no physical pain, not that he would from the shadows. An isolation; torment. Feelings of desperation and abandonment. That is what the shadows brought. And they dumped him on a beach. To lay with his face in the cool sand, the thirst building in his throat which may never be quenched, a desperate isolation from which he may never be unchained.

He knew exactly where he was.

He was in the place of torment; the place which only existed in nightmares from which one could never awaken; one of deception and lies, promising peace and delivering anguish. Other immortals who had encountered the dark ones likely had been dumped on the very beach on which he now lay, but he knew he likely wouldn't encounter any of them, no matter how hard he tried to find them.

The phone rang at club *Sacrafice* on the same night that Darius had gone missing. Antoine Nagevesh, the proprietor, had been counting the nightly drop as the staff was performing their cleaning duties. Antoine leaned against the bar and gestured for the bartender to grab his coat.

"He's been out of his mind lately," Antoine said, reaching for a band to tie his black locks behind his head. "Going on about these shadow demons, apparently. Have you heard of them?"

Delia sounded tired. "Yes, yes I've heard of them. They have a connection to Hades Pass. There's much speculation about their origins, but I have my suspicions. You don't want them coming after you, Antoine." And then there was a brief pause, as Antoine locked a stack of cash in a small metal box.

He picked it up and tucked it under his arm as the bartender handed him his long, black coat.

"We're going to return to Lyon, Delia. Darius and I already discussed it, and he's in agreement. We just can't continue governing this sector with him in this fragile state. We plan to head back to the chateau in the next few days, and I will make my best effort to nurse him back to health there. But you have to realize, Delia, is that his health is failing…miserably. He isn't even at a state where he could be transformed and given the gift back even if his sentence were communed. His body has truly caught up with his soul, and I'm not sure that he has much time left."

Antoine watched as the bartenders finished wiping the bar down, gathered their bags, and headed towards the timeclock and the rear employee entrance. "I think I am going to use my power," he said finally, after a few moments of silence. "Rather than attempt air travel."

"That will weaken you considerably," Delia said.

"I may have no other choice," he said. "Using the ascend gift will weaken me, yes, but we will be at the Chateau within moments, rather than using slow mortal transportation."

"What do you need me to do?"

Antoine locked the front club doors and walked around the corner towards his waiting coupe. "Go visit Ramiel," he said. "He is still in Paris, but has plans to travel to America with Cristofano, and will be staying at the estate while I am in Europe with Darius."

There was, in fact, a certain difference to understand, Antoine thought. Of what the shared purpose was…between those who took undiscovered journeys through the perpetual darkness of night. As if the shadows were formed for each individual, like the theories behind angels.

And there was a certain aura of despair in Coral Gables.

It was the days and the dreams on Ponce de Leon; when he had first arrived in the mystical city of Miami. And even as he cast his thoughts back to the chill and liveliness of Paris, he saw the picture in his mind. He looked towards where the Jefferson Majestic had stood, and each night in its glory, as the sun had highlighted a crimson painting across the fading sunset, each night at dusk, the performances would continue, despite the massacre. The building had been demolished, but the ghosts and the demons remained. The giant mirror beveled doors would swing open as the ushers, clad in black and white tuxedos, held the massive brass handles, and extend their arms as the couples dashed inside.

Antoine stood at the corner and looked up at the theater. It seemed to look nearly identical to the Jefferson Majestic he had remembered, and that was the point, clearly, he knew, because he had known, in the early days after his transformation, when he had traveled himself to Paris, with Darius, and when they met together at the theater after the performances, as Ramiel and Cristofano excitedly gave them a tour, and even took them down into the bowels where the coffins were stored.

There had been a call to return to the exquisite ballets of the previous century. Particularly from the immortal community.

Ramiel would be inside.

Taking care of the usual preparations.

But in Paris, the Jefferson Majestic, despite its sully reputation which it procured not long after it opened, continued its opulent opening nights of the latest and most coveted stage shows. "After the massacre the theater closed its curtains for at least a generation," Ramiel had said the last time he and Antoine were together at Antoine and Darius' chateau in Lyon.

Antoine lowered his head and nodded. "The ghosts remain," he said. "But Paris is full of old ghosts. They always remain."

When Antoine and Darius left Miami and arrived at their chateau in Lyon, Ramiel and Cristofano had visited them for a "passing of the torch", since Monsignor Harrison had insisted that Ramiel lead the sector through a time of healing, after the tumultuous period of the hooded man's wrath.

"I am writing a book about it," Antoine said quietly. "There's a number of stories to be told from that period, and how our own organizations have the power to – as it seems – possibly turn on their own kind."

Ramiel leaned forward. "Any interest?"

Antoine took a sip from a steaming cup of coffee and nodded. "A few in New York. But I've had numerous conversations with both Delia and Monsignor Harrison. They've told me that Parchman's Press has already contacted their offices in Rome and plans for an exclusive. So, that should be interesting."

Ramiel nodded. "You have a working title?"

"Yes," Antoine said. "I am calling it *The Blood Decanter.*"

Ramiel felt a chill run through his body, and his heart pounded for a moment. He could feel the sinister evil through that title; as if the book would chronicle the downfall of the immortals. And then he thought of Cristofano's obsession with LaDonna Mastuer, and the time at *Le Hotel Aristocrat* with the Mastuer dynasty.

They may be headed to *Pere Lachaise* later to release LaDonna from her sentence.

Could the witches – and the coven – somehow be involved with the wrath that would be chronicled in Antoine's manuscript *The Blood Decanter?*

Antoine grabbed his keys from the counter as his loyal house keeper Giovanni locked the cabinets. "And what of the fire?" Antoine asked, looking at Ramiel.

Ramiel paused, looking back at him, as he studied the keys. An image of the burning theater flashed through Ramiel's mind. "That was so many years ago," Ramiel said. "You must understand where I had been during that time, with Cristofano."

Antoine studied each key on the massive, silver ring, examining each etch closely for a few minutes, as Ramiel looked on, waiting for an answer, but Antoine did not give one. "This is the key for the crypt, am I correct?" Antoine held up the key as Ramiel saw a glimmer of light reflect on Antoine's face.

"Next one," he said. "The one you are looking for will never catch the light."

Antoine glided the key downwards on the ring and slowly drew a dark metal key, an elongated cylinder, into his hands. Ramiel watched as Antoine pursed his lips, drawing a breath in. "I can feel it's cold…"

"That is the only key which will do what you want it to do."

Antoine raised his eyes and looked directly at Ramiel.

"They had told me that you had the power," he said. "That you had the power to bring him back. Can you?"

Ramiel placed his hands on the stone countertop.

His long black hair draped across the sides of his face. He looked downwards, closing his eyes. What Antoine wanted to do was precisely what Cristofano had warned him not to. There was much wisdom in those words, Ramiel had remembered.

Too many lives had been lost.

And there was much uncertainty surrounding the practice of such things, but it did not matter. For raising Darius would require the help of the witches. Death as a mortal is a final death. The immortals did not possess that kind of magic.

But the witches did.

And what Antoine wanted, Antoine got. He was the leader of his sector, and Ramiel was only a second tier. He nearly caught himself when he heard the words come out of his mouth. "I have the connections."

He wished he hadn't said that, but Antoine's mere presence seemed to draw it out of him. That was one of his talents.

Antoine cracked a smile and leaned closer to him. Ramiel raised his eyes, watching the immortal. He had too much power in recent years. Once Darius had left, he had not returned to Miami. His estate had sat as a burned out shell the last time Ramiel had noticed, and the city had come close to condemning it.

"You have the connections, you say?" Antoine asked.

Ramiel scarcely recognized his voice when he heard the words. "You know about the coven of witches in Miami that rose to power shortly after you left the city. They control a great deal of the Miami supernatural underground."

Antoine slammed his fist on the counter. "That's *my* area!" And then his voice fell. "But yes. I've always been aware of them. And they've always been there. In the background. I know about their Queen, and their supreme Emmaline.

Ramiel stepped back and nodded. "Yes, we all know that, but you have been *gone*, Antoine! You've abandoned your sector!"

Antoine lashed forward and placed his hand around Ramiel's neck. "Be careful."

Ramiel felt his breath catch in his throat. Antoine released his grip as he took a step back.

"The witches have taken over," he said in between breaths. "I don't mean to be so rash, your highness. There is much desertion across America, but in Miami in particular. Ever since you left, we've received word from Rome that the immortals are losing their stronghold in that sector."

Antoine nodded. "I know, I know. And that's why I am holding this key." Ramiel looked as it caught the light, reflecting back on his face. "This is the key for the crypt here, in Lyon, at *Les Enfantes*. In Miami, it's an amethyst. A beautiful purple quartz. You're familiar with the crystal, yes?"

Ramiel nodded.

"Good then," Antoine said. "You'll find it on a shelf. On the landing of my cellar, at my mansion in Coral Gables. Call me if you need me to explain it to you, how it works. How it will grant you access to the crypt there. At Resurrection cemetery near the Waxley Mortuary."

Ramiel nodded again. "Cristofano and I have been told about the possibility of heading to America, for your sector in particular."

"And about Cristofano," Antoine said. "The Mastuer dynasty history is very long. Throughout time. Ask your maker. But LaDonna was placed under a coffin sentence for good reason."

Four

RAMIEL GASPED FOR AIR as he awakened.

He opened his eyes and remained in darkness, and the mustiness and claustrophobia returned, as if in an instant. He attempted to move, and felt the confinement. The wood. And the dust, darkness. The coffin. He was inside the coffin. As he squirmed in an attempt to move the coffin, he heard the scraping on the stone floor of the crypt.

Yet there was no response.

There was no opening of the lid; LaDonna did not come to his rescue when the effects of the powder wore off. As he felt the thin air penetrate the coffin, as he lay in desolation, he hoped that some of the cracks allowed enough air inside to breathe. But he was an immortal, wasn't he? He couldn't die, could he?

Yet why was he gasping for air?

For a moment, he stopped shifting himself against the sides, and waited. He listened, yet the only reply was silence. And solitude. There were no chains which bound him; there was no shadow demon which silenced him. He could cry out, but why?

Could he break through the coffin?

He reached up and felt the lid.

Torn and damp pleated satin. He felt movement along his fingers. A crawling. Perhaps an insect. Or possibly a spider.

But the wood. It felt thin.

He could easily break through it, he thought. And then he thought about Queen Reynalda. Lying in her casket – her golden monstrosity – at the cemetery across the city, and then, when it was removed, and brought to the crypt here, sitting next to him on the stone and in dark solitude, he wondered. Had her connection to him within Hades Pass been a result of the relocation of her sentencing?

He balled his fist and punched the lid.

There was a slight splinter of wood, but with the limited range, he knew he had to muster up more energy to break through, despite the slim composition, he had to feel the energy build from within; he thought about Cristofano.

His maker's desperate plea near the stones, as the putrid water crashed against them, spraying foam into the air.

You cannot save me here…but I beg of you, Ramiel. Find the fire within. It's a burning that I know you have. Break through. I'm in the cage below. Beneath the clap of footsteps on wood, in a deep cellar of isolation…

Ramiel felt the energy, pushed upwards and crashed through the lid, standing on his feet, ignoring the unsteadiness, and immediately looked around the crypt. Only a sliver of light emanated from the door, now closed, secured, possibly locked. There was no sign of LaDonna, and after experiencing Hades Pass, he wasn't much surprised.

The witches held too much power.

He had to restore the balance.

As he stood, and as he felt the splintered wood falling and crashing on the stone, he felt a wave of lightheadedness wash through him. *Go to Haddon House!*

The voice hissed through his mind, yet he failed to place it. It sounded masculine, but didn't sound like Cristofano. Ramiel fell forward and caught his balance, looking ahead at the wrought iron door. He stumbled forward and pressed against the iron bars. He felt the air, and the warmth of the setting sun, and the felt a sliver of confidence. He wrapped his hands around two of the metal bars. He'd once had the strength, but did he now?

For a mere moment, he peered through the bars, looking out at the cemetery. Mounds of dirt interspersed with rising, weathered stone monuments, and he could see the shadows and silhouette of the decrepit mortuary through the overgrown forest and fading light.

He grasped and mustered his strength, his arm and chest muscles tensed and flexed as he pulled; his nails dug into his palms as he felt the warmth of fresh spilled blood against his dusty, cold hands. The iron bars were formidable; a force of protection to keep the living out, yet nearly immobile from within. He tightened his grip, increased his force, and with a loud clank he fell backwards, spilling onto the splintered, dusty coffin.

The crypt...is broken. Filled with the terrors of dust and dancing, a determined threshold of hope wafted through those bars. There was a destiny of shadows. A weeping through stone.

The dancer; it was a pirouette of persistence, the threshold, crossed.

Ramiel scarcely remembered tearing out of the crypt, charging through Resurrection cemetery, spilling on the mounds of dirt, towards the shadows of the Waxley Mortuary and to his waiting car on the crumbling side street. It seemed as if it were a dream; there was the starting of his car, and he remembered hearing the engine roar to life. But then the period after that, until he was pulling up to Anastasia avenue and Antoine's estate, there was little else cemented in his mind.

As he slowly put the car in park, he looked up, and through the window, he saw Geret, their faithful friend, who flew in from Paris to join them once he learned that Cristofano was missing.

"Ramiel!"

Geret had the Mercedes waiting in the front driveway.

Ramiel rushed out of his car as Geret dashed into the Mercedes and blasted the horn. "Come on!" he called, as Ramiel rushed towards the other car. He yanked the passenger door open and slid into the seat and turned towards Geret. "Go! I will contact Delia now. Just drive."

Geret threw the car in gear and tore out of the driveway. As he charged through the Oak tree lined side streets, Ramiel hung his head down and shook his head. "We won't be able to go back there."

He looked over at Geret who alternated between watching the road and looking over at Ramiel, his face shifted and eyes wide. "What do you mean? Haddon Hall?"

Ramiel let out an exasperated sigh. "No, the crypt. Cristofano isn't there."

"Then where is he?"

Ramiel dialed Delia's number, spoke with her for a moment, and placed the phone down, looking back over at Geret. "His soul is in Hades Pass. And Queen Reynalda seems to...govern...that area."

Geret scoffed. "Wait a minute," he said. "Hades Pass? You mean what Monsignor Harrison told us to read about in *Code of the Immortals*?"

Ramiel nodded and sighed, facing forward once again. "That's the one. The supernatural realm. A sea of souls. Mostly lost wanderers. But many who are serving coffin sentences...seem to...appear...in that disgusting sea."

As Geret navigated towards the interstate, Ramiel took a deep breath and exhaled. He leaned his forehead against the glass and closed his eyes. The rumble of the pavement started lulling him closer to sleep, but he knew there would be no escape from the clutches of the darkness if he were to attempt rest. Very little time to do so, it wasn't that long of a drive to Haddon Hall.

Only in the crypt.

That is where his true rest would be.

He kept his eyes closed and in his mind, saw Dominque's coffin. It was as if he were buried in the crypt along with her; centuries had passed since she had been placed in the grave, yet the wooden coffin had little decomposition. The chains appeared tight around her torso.

Her eyes were open and wide with terror.

Dominique, we will save you.

The Mercedes arrived at Miami International Airport and Ramiel opened his eyes. The terminal was teeming with activity as travelers rushed with rolling suitcases, and young students carrying backpacks listened to headphones; Ramiel emerged from the car and Geret leaned forward. "Their flight should be landing at any moment," Ramiel said. "No reason to park the car. Wait here for as long as you can. Circle if you have to. But we don't have much time."

Geret pulled alongside a row of shuttle vans and parked as inconspicuously as he could, next to the sidewalk. He cut the engine and turned off the lights. They both watched as passengers rushed by with rolling suitcases, all heading to differing and distant destinations. And then, the familiar faces appeared through the sliding glass doors. Geret's face lit up as they approached the car. "Monsignor Harrison and Antoine?!" He became giddy.

Ramiel shot a glance back at him. "Stop! Please! Monsignor Harrison is one of our highest ranking. And Antoine. This is his *sector*! Get yourself together, Geret!"

Geret slunk down into his seat as Monsignor Harrison approached the car and flung the back door open. Antoine rounded his way to the trunk as Ramiel dashed out of the car and joined him behind the car. Antoine had a sour look on his face as he bent down and picked up the bags, hoisting each of them into the trunk. Ramiel assisted, and watched him.

"I knew this was going to happen," Antoine said.

They piled into the car as Geret's face brightened and he turned and nodded to Monsignor Harrison, and then over to Antoine.

"This is Geret," Ramiel said. "From the Atarah ancestry."

Monsignor Harrison nodded. "Oh! I see..." He leaned forward as Geret grinned, put the car in gear and eased into traffic.

"Let's just get to Haddon Hall," Antoine said.

The voluptuous black Mercedes turned onto the quiet streets of Coconut Grove; the sun filtered in spots through the soaring oak canopy, which appeared like swaths of delicate golden paint on a deep black canvas, which drifted as the wind filtered through the treetops. A dog barked in the distance, and the street was otherwise quiet.

The houses represented Old Florida; it was a far cry from the nearby stucco and Spanish Mediterranean architecture of Coral Gables and the opulence of Ponce de Leon. The homes on Ensanada Avenue had an eclectic mix of designs, and Haddon House was no different, withs its rising Victorian style and old Key West feel.

Unlike the neighboring homes, it was wood framed and had imposing large wooden steps leading up to the wraparound porch. The front doors were nestled int the background, with frosted glass and a colorful Brazilian rug in front.

Ramiel looked at the house behind throngs of colorful flowers, soaring oak trees and waves of hanging Spanish moss. He sighed as Geret pulled the car to a gentle stop.

"I see Delia's car parked on the opposite street," Monsignor Harrison said, as Ramiel turned his attention and saw the small red coupe. Delia was most certainly inside, waiting for them to emerge.

"Do I come in too?" Geret asked, as he cut the engine. Ramiel turned and faced Monsignor Harrison and Antoine.

Antoine nodded.

"Let him come," the monsignor said. "It will be good for him to see this type of conversation."

Antoine looked up at Geret. "Don't panic when they give us the powder." He looked at Ramiel. "This is the first time he will experience Hades Pass?"

Ramiel nodded, and turned to face Geret. "It will be like nothing you've ever experienced. But you won't die. Or even feel any pain. The pain and torment there is never physical."

"You are in danger of eternal madness and isolation," Monsignor Harrison said.

Geret yanked the keys from the ignition, dropped his hands in his lap and looked down. "Sounds like a great proposition…"

Ramiel let out a chuckle as Geret looked up and cracked a smile. Geret had yet been tested, but Ramiel had a warm spot in his heart for the young guy. He'd been fiercely loyal to both him and Cristofano since he walked into the Jefferson Majestic, with an intense desire to perform with the company, without even a pair of pointe shoes. Yet his talent proved to be extraordinary, along with his devotion to the immortals.

"Let's get inside," Antoine said. "I just sent Delia a message and she will join us once she sees us emerge from the car."

Five

THERE WAS THE CALL of angels and demons from a distant realm which Ramiel believed was where Cristofano existed; yet the soul, he knew, mattered, and had a peculiarity in and of its own. He knew that the soul was argued to have weight, an actual measurement, and if the body died, then, there were those spiritual scientists who would weigh the body, before and after death, and post mortem, the body typically would be lighter.

But if Cristofano's body were in Haddon House, somewhere, perhaps, like he suspected, in the cellar, would he be considered "dead" if he could babble and wail and cry for rescue? And if Cristofano was the source of the babble and wailing – which the coven's Supreme, Emmaline, had complained about throughout his and Delia's past visit, then how could be possibly be dead?

Ramiel pursed his lips, watched as the others got out of the car, and looked over and saw Delia approaching on the sidewalk, leaning on her cane. Her white hair blew in the passing breeze, and her flowing dress was colorful; wrapped around her waist like a tapestry. She looked onwards towards the group, and nodded and smiled. He knew that she had an angelic presence which no other immortal seemed to possess. But as Ramiel stood apart from the others, as they conversed in hushed tones with her, he thought of Cristofano.

Somewhere in that house, he would be, waiting to be saved.

He hoped.

There was always hope; yet he learned never to assume. Cristofano spoke to him at Hades Pass, yet Ramiel had no ability to save him. Now, with the others, there might be a force for reviving; a joined power, a combined destiny; a journey through the astral plane. The crypt dancer, he was the one who was transformed through the strongest blood ancestry. Through his maker Claret, the crypt dancer bloodline.

They quietly walked through the small, winding stone path, which cut through the brilliant lawn, leading up to the towering wooden house, the steps, the hanging colorful tapestries, delicately blowing in the light breezes, and the rocking chairs, which were nestled beneath the rising windows along all sides of the porch.

And the members of the coven.

They were most likely hovering inside, possibly parting the drapes, peering through, and monitoring their approach.

Ramiel and the others looked up and stopped as they heard a click towards the top of the steps.

And the heavy clump of footsteps.

Emmaline, the Supreme.

Her hands were at her hips, her southern hospitality had been abandoned, as her lips were pursed; her eyes, were intense and looking directly at Ramiel.

And then she looked over at Delia.

"We were expecting you, and Ramiel," she said. "But not the others."

Delia nodded and eased herself closer to the base of the stairs. She raised her free hand upwards. "Yes, yes, we know, and we planned to inform you before our arrival, but there was simply no time."

Emmaline sighed and lowered her head. She then looked back up and down at them. "You do know that what you are planning…only the Queen can achieve." She looked directly at Ramiel. "And you. We are in contact with our beloved Reynalda and she has informed us that you were there."

Ramiel felt his heart pound in his chest as the others looked at him. He ignored their looks of pleading, and he knew. He realized what they were thinking. Perhaps it was the mind gift; yet their thoughts, mostly, felt concealed. But as they stood, as Emmaline turned back towards the house and the group ascended the stairs, their shoes thumping on the wood, Ramiel sensed that the others felt a sense of betrayal; no words were spoken as they approached the large, wooden doors.

As he stood on the edge of the porch, letting the others pass as Emmaline stood at the threshold, extending her arm and guiding them in the house, Antoine stopped and leaned close to his ear. "Don't let those thoughts trouble you, Ramiel. We all know what you needed to do. That's why you have been helped in this journey. And now, we will provide the best form of assistance that we can."

The parlor looked familiar to Ramiel from their last visit; the small table remained in the corner where they had shared their tea with the other members of the coven; the piano in the far corner near the windows. Emmaline swung the doors open, and they slowly filed in. The grandfather clock in the corner chimed, and Ramiel noticed the remaining members of the coven were missing.

"Please sit," Emmaline said, gesturing over to the sofas.

Monsignor Harrison sank down in the edge of the large, overstuffed upholstery, grabbed a small side pillow, and placed it on the arm. Delia sat next to him, placing her cane neatly on the floor, as Antoine looked up at Ramiel. They took the opposite sofa, sitting next to each other, settling in.

Emmaline sat in a small side chair, set to face the others. She crossed her legs, placing her hands over her knee. She smiled; her lips were fiery red, her long blonde hair flowing across her shoulders. She waited as they settled, as they all listened to the tick of the clock, and then, she spoke.

"Now explain to me, please, one of you. The necessity for this meeting."

Ramiel fidgeted, and raised his eyes to her. "Cristofano is here, isn't he? He's here in this house?"

Antoine balled his fist and lightly punched him in the leg. Ramiel looked over at him, as Antoine shook his head slowly. Emmaline recrossed her legs and settled back into the chair. She looked at Monsignor Harrison and Delia, who both lowered their heads and remained silent, and then returned her gaze to Ramiel.

"And whatever has given you that idea?"

Ramiel looked down as Antoine placed a hand on his thigh. He took a breath, but said nothing, as Monsignor Harrison cleared his throat.

"It's my pleasure, ma'am," he said. "I represent the immortal community from Rome. I flew in along with Antoine here to discuss some of the events that have taken place in this community recently."

She reached for a long, slender cigarette as Antoine grabbed a lighter from his pocket and shot to his feet. He leaned forward, igniting the lighter, and held it out in front of Emmaline. She raised her eyes to him, looked down at his cupped hands and lit her cigarette. "Whatever are you referring to?"

Monsignor Harrison let out an exasperated sigh and leaned back in the sofa. Emmaline took a long drag from her cigarette, watching him, a grin on her face, and tapped her cigarette in the ashtray on the table below.

Delia glared at Emmaline. "You know exactly what's happened to us," she said. "Our population was nearly wiped out by a hooded figure. His deception lured immortals to their deaths!"

Emmaline sighed. "We had absolutely nothing to do with that. In fact, I am perplexed as to how you could even entertain such a thought."

Ramiel felt his chest tighten and his hands clenched.

There was a certain aspect of behavior which Cristofano had always taught him; that an immortal must always remain pragmatic. That every adversary might not be committing to a physical battle, but, quite possibly, a clash of minds, philosophy and interpretation.

"Very well then," Monsignor Harrison said, in a deep commanding tone. Everyone looked up at him as he slowly stood. "We are not here to place blame for an event which has afflicted our kind. What we are here for is your assistance. It's my understanding that our Cristofano has raised a certain LaDonna Mastuer from a coffin sentence in Paris, am I correct?"

Emmaline nodded. "The Mastuers are not affiliated with the Reynalda coven."

"I see," he said. "And so this release hasn't benefited the coven in any way?"

Emmaline drew on her cigarette but said nothing.

Monsignor Harrrison turned to the others, gave them a nod, and turned back to face Emmaline. He extended his arms, and then dropped them back to his side. She snubbed her cigarette out and stood, exhaling a cloud of sweet smelling smoke. "Very well," she said. "Come with me. All of you. I will get Giselle and Trudy, and we will accompany you to the cellar."

Ramiel stood slowly along with the others, and they headed towards the double French doors. Emmaline stopped and swung them open. She pressed on a small intercom and called the others to meet her in the cellar, and then turned back to face them. "What you will see may anger you," she said. "But you also must realize that we are all given free will, and this is the path that was chosen."

Ramiel felt his suspicions were confirmed when they met Giselle at the cellar door with Trudy. Emmaline crossed her arms as Giselle produced a gleaming golden key, and as he listened, he thought he heard a deep, distant moan.

Cristofano.

He snapped his head towards the others, and made eye contact with Antoine and Delia. Monsignor Harrison nodded. They knew. The witches knew. Yet no one was speaking.

And as Giselle opened the heavy, wooden door with a slight creaking, the damp musty air wafted up from below. Ramiel looked up as Emmaline took a step back in the foyer. She looked directly at him and smiled, extending her arm towards the darkness. "Please," she said politely. "After you, of course."

Ramiel felt his heart pounding in his chest as he stood at the threshold of the dark, decrepit cellar. Dirty red bricks lined the opposite wall of the landing; the light from the foyer caught them, yet failed to further penetrate the black void. He looked down, and saw the steps, made of stones. The stones in Hades Pass flashed through his mind for an instant; he saw the waves crashing up against them, he could still smell the pungent, rancid water.

They were nearly identical to the stones which comprised the staircase.

He turned for a moment, and Emmaline waved her hand, outwards towards the dark descent. A small torch ignited on the wall, bathing the small landing in a warm, yellow flickering glow.

"Just for you," she said with a sly smile, and stepped back. "Go on. The others can go for you, and you will find what you're looking for."

Ramiel looked back at the others and nodded.

They followed as he slowly navigated the stones. He thought he could hear the distant moans, the calls of wails, juxtaposed against the silence and the dull roar of an unseen surf. He felt the sea; he could smell the sulfuric air, yet only saw the descending stone staircase. As he walked, he heard the others' footsteps behind him; the small torches ignited, lighting the way as they passed, but only penetrating a short distance, keeping the lower bowels of the cellar shrouded in a dark mysterious cover.

He grasped a wooden railing, closed his eyes, and hung his head.

The waters crashed against the rocks; the limbs thrashed in the sea as the wails intensified. This was the source, the keeper of the sea. Hades Pass required a ruler; a gatekeeper, a force which conjured the dark shadows. The demons; the dark ones as they were known throughout the immortal community, required a ruler; an origin.

There was something about the cellar; a penetration of their minds. And as they set foot on an earthen floor, the mustiness returned, nearly overpowering. Ramiel turned for a moment, looked at the others, standing just behind him, and Delia looked up at him, the flickering torch light reflecting against her irises. Her eyes looked warm; understanding. She knew. And she was letting him know that she knew. He looked over at Antoine, and back at Monsignor Harrison and then he realized why he was always proud to be an immortal.

Ramiel heard the heavy clump of footsteps descending the stones; they each turned and looked up as Emmaline was followed by Giselle and Trudy, who was carrying a large tray with four pewter cups.

"Proceed down the corridor there," Emmaline instructed. As she pointed, torches lit a wide, dark lengthy corridor. The walls were made of stone and moss. Ramiel squinted a bit, and thought he saw the gleaming reflection.

A cage.

Bars, perhaps.

Was Cristofano there? In the dark, dank distance at the end of the corridor?

As they walked down the corridor, Ramiel led the way, maintaining his focus on the distant reflection, in the shadows and darkness. It was catching the light; the flickering, warm yellow flames. He tried to determine what it was, yet despite his attempts, he couldn't recognize it, yet assumed it was a cage, perhaps something metallic.

When they neared the end, he could see the reflection, much closer to them now, nestled in the darkness. He felt a hand rest on his shoulder, and he turned. Emmaline was right behind him, with a rare look of compassion in her eyes. "Are you ready?" she asked.

Ramiel looked at the others, who waited in silence, surrounding him. He looked back at Emmaline and Giselle, and then noticed the four pewter cups which Trudy carried. He looked back at Emmaline and nodded.

She closed her eyes and lowered her head as the room filled with flickering torchlight from larger torches on the walls which burst to life, ignited in brilliant fire. He turned slowly, and saw a familiar sight. His mouth slowly dropped open, as he shifted his posture closer to the reflection; glass, lined with gold.

A coffin made entirely of reflective glass.

He gasped quietly, and felt another hand on his opposite shoulder. He knew who it was in the coffin. And the hand on his shoulder was strong, familiar. He remembered the same hand on the same shoulder, when he stood in the catacombs in Rome, in a tormented scene of lost acceptance and remembrance; a glass coffin, which had ignited forgotten feelings of distance and the endless quest for love, which had never been realized.

Father, forgive me. Oh father, I have sinned.

Ramiel lowered his head and sighed, as Monsignor Harrison released his gentle grip on his shoulder.

"Go to him," Delia said softly. He turned and saw Antoine biting his lower lip. He noticed a single, solitary tear stream down his face, as Antoine lowered his head.

Ramiel took a deep breath and sighed, and trudged forward. The walk to the coffin had an aura of unwelcome familiarity; visions of his father, who lie in a glass coffin beneath the Sistine Chapel in Vatican City, had been a piercing reminder of his solitude, and yearning for love and acceptance. He closed his eyes as he approached the coffin,

406

and dared not open them. He could sense the coffin just before him, and once he opened his eyes, it would be past the point of no return.

He took another deep breath and sighed, feeling the waves of emotion building deep within his chest, and then, he knew that once he opened his eyes, reality would be thrust towards him.

And then he did; his mouth dropped open.

His clothes were familiar; wrapped in the very chains which bound his subjects, and as Ramiel looked up towards his head, the shadow bound him, yet the long dark hair had given the clue to his maker and confidant.

Cristo.

If only it were not Cristo.

He closed his eyes again, hung his head, and felt the silent tears begin to stream down his face, in warm, wet, tiny rivers; and then he saw Cristo's smile in his mind. He remembered the walks in Solerno near sunset, in the *degli Angeli*, in the catacombs, with thoughts of Claret and the Christ blood.

My cup runneth over...

Ramiel turned as the tears flowed. There was a quiver in his voice. "*What* did he *do*?!"

Antoine pursed his lips and then turned to face the witches. "Release him."

Emmaline took a few steps closer to the coffin and stood next to Ramiel. She placed her arm around him, and leaned close, towards his ear, speaking softly. "This was the choice that he made."

They turned as Delia raised her cane, shoving it between them. "Release him!" Emmaline took a step back as Ramiel watched her. Antoine and Geret stood in the background as Monsignor Harrison took a place on the opposite side of the coffin.

"Release him," Monsignor Harrison said, an urgent tone in his voice. "I don't care whether he chose this or not. You are holding him perhaps by his own accord, but this goes against *our* wishes."

Emmaline turned as Trudy stepped forward.

She picked up one of the small pewter cups, and help it up in front of Ramiel. "Only the Queen can release him," she said. "Cristofano made his choice. He received the powder, which is what he wanted. To help your kind recover from the assault which you spoke of."

Ramiel looked at Antoine, who returned a knowing glance.

"What will that do?" Delia asked.

Emmaline took another step closer to Ramiel and held the cup just in front of his face, and Ramiel could smell the floral aroma.

"Drink this," she said. "And you will awaken on the shores of Hades Pass. There you will find the Queen."

Ramiel reached for a cup and took a breath.

"I have a cup for each of you," she said, as Trudy passed the cups out to each of them, Emmaline continued. "Your heads will become heavy, and you will feel listless, but no harm will come to your body."

Ramiel lifted the cup to his mouth and took a breath. He looked one last time at the others who each held their cups. "I am doing this for Cristo. And I am doing this for all of our kind."

They each drank as the witches took a few steps back and waited behind the coffin. "Lie down, each of you," Emmaline said. "You will fall into a slumber; a death of sorts, until the potion's effect ceases."

As they each laid down on the cold, duty stone, Ramiel watched his fellow immortals place themselves in a desperate and vulnerable situation, placing trust in the coven, whose help, they hoped, would allow them to return Cristofano to his body, release the shadow demon which bound him, and unbind the chains.

"We will wait," Emmaline said, as Trudy and Giselle grabbed some small, metal folding chairs which had been stacked in the opposite corner. "We will watch and we will wait."

Ramiel looked at the others as they settled in and lay down on the floor. He watched as Delia placed her cane beside her, Antoine and Geret lying together, sides touching, and then he made eye contact with Monsignor Harrison, who lay next to him. "She won't release him without something in return," he said to Ramiel. "You know that, and I know that. So we must be prepared for that."

Ramiel nodded, and felt his head growing heavy, as the room softened. He remembered the grogginess of the power which LaDonna had given him, however this potion they drank was far more docile. If he had to die, he thought, this was the gentle, delicate way he wanted to pass through to the astral plane.

$\mathcal{S}ix$

RAMIEL'S THOUGHTS WERE PIERCED by the destiny which had been a flowing brightness in the dark scape; and his mind, conscious, remained aware. There was a feeling which washed through him, and thoughts of his soul.

Could it be so bright?

Had it been tarnished before...in a fierce parade of dark transgressions?

It felt as if he were flying, yet motionless; as the flickering of indiscriminate lights flashed by him. This was his dark destiny; the nightmare dream, yet now, as he was taking the same journey which he had experience before, yet now, with the others, it seemed somewhat different. But this, was him projected, beyond the physical realm, lacking a physical body, secured simply by his thoughts.

As he watched the lights in the darkness, he could feel the presence of the others, yet failed to see them. It was as if there was a unison of souls; a transmigration to another state of existence, one of spirit and destiny, intertwined together. And as the darkness slowly cleared, he saw once familiar shores; the call of the surf. It was a deep, methodical and gentle roar of crashing waves, on the desolate beach that he once remembered.

It was the sea filled with lost souls, the sea where he knew Cristofano would be, and Claret, and the others, desperate to remain above the water as waves flowed over their faces, silencing their wailing pleas.

Hades Pass.

The similar aggressive clouds charged across the skies with storms which brewed eternally, and as he looked outwards, towards the waterline, he saw the stones. And how each stone reached farther outwards, deeper into the sea, towards the distant, angry horizon filled with shadows.

And then there was a dark figure, outwards. He looked behind him; no sign of the others. The waves crashed against the stones, spraying white foam across the rocks as if there were an unseen orchestra commanding them, achieving successive crescendos.

It was the darkness; he knew, the feeling washed through him.

This was his destiny.

He took several steps forward, as he felt a wave on confidence pass through him. His destiny, remained. It tugged at his soul, reminding him that this was spiritual; there could be no physical pain in Hades Pass. But as the figure came closer, he saw the details in her presence.

She wore a long, flowing gown of skulls, drifting towards the waters. Pasty, white souls emerged from the water, crying desperate screams, reaching outwards to clutch the ropes of skulls which drifted into the waves, yet they failed. She wore a crown of thorns, as blood dripped down the sides of her face.

"You have a choice," she said.

Thunder rumbled above.

"Those who have been cast in this sea had a choice as well," she continued. "You have your own free will. They made their choice, and now their destiny is of shadows. You will choose. You will decide your own destiny with the free will you have been given."

Ramiel stood and clenched his fists. It was no use; aggression would not harm her. This was not a physical battle, but rather one of negotiation. Queen Reynalda, it seemed, had known precisely why he was standing on the rocks, why he had been in Hades Pass before, and why he had come again.

"Your beloved Cristofano made *his* choice," she said. "He wanted the power to give renewed life. To resurrect. He came to us and received that power. But with that power, there comes a price. And he made his choice."

Ramiel thought of Cristofano's eyes wide open in terror, as the waves crashed over his pasty limbs, covered in oozing red sores. Had he made the choice for desperation to have the power to restore life to others of their kind?

Queen Reynalda approached again and came closer as Ramiel noted that her hair blew in the increasing winds, it had great length, down towards her ankles. She dragged the many skulls, and stood at the edge of the shore. "You have free will, as I told you."

Ramiel nodded. "At what price?"

She cracked a smile. "Oh, well that is quite obvious, don't you think?" She extended her arm outwards towards the sea as the lost soul rose up through the churning waters; the cries and wails intensified as Ramiel covered his ears and shook his head. He looked up at her with wide eyes. "What kind of a choice is that?!"

She crossed her arms.

"These decisions are sometimes made in desperation," she said. "The thoughts of living without your maker consume you. Without his instruction. And guidance. And you don't see the others, do you?"

Ramiel turned and looked back at the beach; there was a thick, dead forest at the edge of the sand, but no sign of any of the others. Queen Reynalda took a few steps closer as she stood on the beach.

"So now you choose," she said. "You can assume Cristofano's liability if you would like him back in the physical realm, with your kind, and his body rests in the coffin that you saw in the coven cellar. But his sentence remains. You can choose one of the others to take his place in the sea."

Ramiel fell to his knees and hung his head. Thoughts of the others pierced his mind; he remembered watching Monsignor Harrison at the Sistine Chapel in Rome, as he spoke with Claret. He saw Madame Arsenault, charred and burned in the back gardens of the theater in Paris; was she held captive by the raging waters?

He stood and looked out towards the sea; the waves remained furious and steadfast, yet, from a distance, it appeared as if it could be any beach from those which he had experienced before.

Queen Reynalda waited patiently for his answer, standing on the stones in the middle of the waters, close to the shore, away from the distraction of the wails and the thrashing limbs and punishing waters, and clasped her hands at her waist, watching him. It was the sea to where souls had been destined; and then, as he stood and watched, he had an opportunity to save a soul. To bring him back to the others, the one they called Cristo, the crypt dancer.

He raised his head and looked at Queen Reynalda. Her eyes were intense, beckoning for a decision.

"If I take his place," he said. "Then you must release the others."

She remained silent, watching him as the waves relaxed and the winds calmed. She turned, slowly, without saying a word, and started walking farther out towards the sea, towards the distant horizon; as he watched her figure darken and become smaller, he waited for the resolution, and prayed that it would come.

Had she given her answer?

He turned, for a moment, and saw four waves of light appear on the beach, in the distance, far from where he stood, towards the genesis of the dead and decrepit forest. As he returned to watching the sea, as the waves approached the shore with a delicate roll, he saw a distant figure. Farther out than Queen Reynalda had been; he struggled to discern who it might be, who the approaching figure, lost in the call of waves and spray of foam, and as he approached, the bodies in the sea retreated and calmed.

Ramiel recognized his face; his smile had a warmth he hadn't remembered, as if the state of this brightening had been a dream, a call of his soul, a unity of shared destinies. Cristofano walked towards the sands in tattered clothes, his hair was disheveled and mussed, but he was there. Released from the torment of the sea.

Cristofano stopped in front of Ramiel, and placed his head on his chest, as Ramiel placed his hand on his head, and closed his eyes. There would be no further purpose to remain in Hades. As they turned towards the dark forest, the four beams of light faded.

Cristofano opened his eyes and looked up at Ramiel. "You have the power to stop them," he said. "It's been in your blood since I transformed you. It's been in your blood since you were mortal. That's why I pursued you. Not just because Claret wanted to continue the lineage, but because I saw it in you. The witches are waiting in the room where I lay in the glass coffin. Hold on to me tight. And you will know what to do."

Ramiel wrapped his arms tightly around Cristofano's frail body, holding him close to his powerful, muscular chest. As Cristofano placed his head back on his shoulder, Ramiel looked out towards the sea, as three writhing bodies shot upwards from the sea, up into the clouds, transforming to darkness, charging above them and back through the forest. He closed his eyes, holding on to Cristofano with increasing intensity, as wings crashed outwards from his back, carrying them both upwards into the skies.

The wings were illuminated, powerful, equally muscular to his torso, as he carried them across the skies, in pursuit of the shadows, through the darkness, towards the coffins. He watched as the darkness drew chains searing forward.

The witches shot up from their chairs, their eyes wide as each of the them backed up against the wall.

"Oh blessed Queen have mercy on us!"

Emmaline fell to her knees as the chains wrapped around her, dragging her across the stone floor; the next binding Giselle and Trudy. They crashed into coffins as the shadows emerged, groaning, wailing, wrapping around them, thrusting them into coffins as the bricks exploded from the walls. Dirt flew into the room as each lid slammed into place, and the remaining darkness crashed each coffin into earthen holes of rock, each sealing themselves from light and air.

Ramiel felt his breath return and slowly opened his eyes.

The room was silent; the witches were gone. He slowly eased himself up on his elbows, scanning the area, as the fuzziness in his head lessened.

He was surrounded by glass coffins.

As he slowly stood, and felt his heartbeat return, he maintained a focus on the one which was raised on a slab. Cristofano. Had his efforts worked?

He looked down at the coffin.

He felt a twinge of relief wash through him. The chains were gone. The shadow demon was gone. He reached down and lifted the lid, pushing it off as it shattered on the floor. Cristofano remained motionless, his eyes closed. Did he truly return with him?

He turned and focused on the four remaining coffins, lined up neatly against the wall where they each had lay. As he walked back to the others, they each lay in a coffin; he gasped as each of them appeared luminescent; angelic and radiant. Still, motionless and silent.

He turned as he heard coughing, and he watched as Cristofano slowly sat up, grasping the edges of the coffin. If there had been a more determined outcome, he thought, there couldn't have been an equally uncertain journey. Cristofano looked over at him, his eyes warm, and he smiled wanly. He didn't need to speak.

Ramiel rushed over to the coffin and assisted Cristofano, who placed his arm around his shoulder. He looked up as Ramiel lifted him and stood him on the stone floor. "Thank you," he said softly. "For saving me."

Ramiel closed his eyes and nodded. "You would have done the same for me."

They turned as Ramiel took him to the glass coffins. They leaned on each other and looked down at the others, lying in the coffins, motionless yet appearing radiant.

Cristofano raised his arm and pointed at Delia. "Do you…see that?"

Ramiel kneeled down and took a closer look.

Behind her back, there were wings. He gasped and snapped his head back to where Cristofano stood. He nodded over towards Monsignor Harrison's coffin, and Antoine's. Ramiel rushed over to examine the others. "What about Geret?" he asked. "He is glowing!"

Wings; of an angel.

It could only be.

But Ramiel had believed, throughout his mortal – and immortal – lifetimes, that the immortals were dark; sinister; sinful. That there was a preconceived dark destiny for each of them. But Antoine, Ramiel knew, had a longing for a greater sense of purpose. Had it been within all of them...and just needed to be awakened?

Were all of the immortals angels, fallen or otherwise?

He looked back at Cristofano, who had eased himself closer to Geret, the only one remaining from the other three empty coffins. Ramiel watched as Geret slowly rose to a sitting position, coughing into the crook of his arm. The luminescence had vanished, and he appeared like Geret had always appeared since they first saw him in the Jefferson Majestic theater.

Cristofano turned to face Ramiel, with a knowing smile.

Ramiel thought of the beach in Hades Pass; of the beams of light, the radiance near the dark, dead trees.

We were there with you. We are always with you.

Haddon House was empty and eerily quiet.

As they left the small room with the coffins, Ramiel turned and looked back at the three empty coffins which had contained Delia, Monsignor Harrison, and Antoine. He felt a twinge of hope that they were not in Hades Pass. He longed for a confirmation that Queen Reynalda had kept her word, and that his three beloved friends were not writhing in the putrid sea, being tormented under endless fierce skies.

He felt a hand on his shoulder. It was Geret. "Relax, Ramiel. They are absolutely, perfectly fine. They are on a mission which was assigned to them."

Ramiel shifted his face, shook his head, and looked over at Cristofano. He nodded. "Geret is correct," Cristo said. "They are in Rome. You were not transported with them because you still have more to consider on your own mission."

"The witches are bound in chains," he said. "What is there left for me to do here?" He looked at Geret. "Where are you planning to go?"

Geret shrugged. "Back to the estate, I suppose."

"They will find you there," Ramiel said. "LaDonna is still unaccounted for. Don't go there."

"I cannot accompany you to France."

Ramiel nodded. "I know."

As they climbed the stone stairs and emerged into the foyer, they heard the grandfather clock ticking in the parlor. Just as Cristofano opened the door, he looked at Ramiel. "You know you're not going to France, right?"

The clock chimed midnight as the bells rang through the otherwise silent house. They emerged from the doors, out towards their waiting cars, and Cristofano pulled the door shut, and Haddon House was empty.

Part Seven – Act Three

THE CRYPT
DANCER (III)

RAMIEL FELL SILENT as he felt the warmth of a single tear stream down his cheek.

Cristofano felt strong enough to drive, and he took the Mercedes sedan while Geret drove Delia's tiny red sportscar. They headed to Antoine's estate, but Ramiel knew what Cristofano had been referring to. Queen Reynalda had presumed that there would be retribution for saving Cristofano, and now, perhaps also, for casting the three witches into coffins bound with chains and shadow demons.

The tear flowed down his cheek, in silent mourning not for what may become his fate, but for a longing for the others who, he felt, were left in Haddon House. There wasn't any reason to miss the others, yet he felt an eternal emptiness grasp his heart like a vice. There wasn't so much of a damnation, of sorts, he knew, everyone could be redeemed. They all would.

But the others – Delia, the monsignor, Antoine – they all appeared to be the redeemers, were they?

Would they be, perhaps?

He looked over at Cristofano as he pulled the car into the driveway which circled by the front door of Antoine's estate, and considered what he must be feeling. Claret was his maker. An image of her in the rancid sea flashed through his mind. Ramiel wondered if Cristofano could save her.

From the days in Solerno, when Cristofano had watched and waited for someone to rescue him from his torrents of uncertainty, Claret found him. But Claret had not been the quintessential parent; she had shown the exuberance of tough love, and Ramiel knew that Cristofano had known that she did care for him, deep down, although rarely showed it.

And now Cristofano, The Crypt Dancer, was planning to sentence Ramiel to the coffin himself. The one who had the power and the authority to raise the immortals from their sentences had completed the ultimate error in judgement, and now, Ramiel was destined to pay the price.

I will acquiesce. Place me in my crypt. The doctrine of the code is law and I will comply.

Cristofano looked over at Ramiel with knowing eyes.

Geret pulled behind the black sedan and ran up towards them, taking the steps two at a time. "Hey guys!"

They both looked at Geret, who stood before them with an anxious look on his face. He looked back and forth at each of them, and could sense that something was amiss.

"I must go to the crypt," Ramiel said. "In order to save Cristofano, I had to bargain with the Queen." He stepped closer, and placed his hands on Geret's cheeks. "I will miss you, but I will see you when I return."

Geret's eyes welled up with tears. He reached up and grabbed Ramiel's wrists, flinging his arms down. Geret's mouth quivered as he paced back and forth on the porch. He pointed at Ramiel. "How do you *know* you will be back?!"

Cristofano took a step closer to Geret. "Because *I* have the authority to amend his sentence!"

Geret dropped his head, shaking it back and forth. He placed his hand over his eyes, and started to cry. "I cannot be in this house alone," he said. "I am not ready. *I am not ready!*"

Ramiel and Cristofano exchanged glances as Geret sat on a flower pot. Tears streamed down his face as he hung his head, draping his arms over his knees. Ramiel knelt down next to him. "Look," he said. "We will figure something out. But you must understand the code. It is law with us. It must be upheld, and I made a choice."

"And I will not abandon you," Cristofano said.

Geret looked up at each of them. He reached up, wiped his arm across his face, and stood. He then looked over at Cristofano. "Don't forget about me here. I can't stay here all alone. I don't know Antoine. And he isn't even here anyway."

Cristofano nodded, reaching forward, placing his arms around Geret. He looked over at Ramiel, who reached into his pocket and produced a set of keys, and handed them over to Geret.

"Cristofano will return shortly, and you will see me soon."

Geret looked down, studied the keys for a moment, walked to the door and thrust the key into the lock, opened the door, and disappeared into the darkness.

Cristofano looked up at Ramiel and placed his hand on his cheek. Ramiel thought that Cristo's eyes were wide, inviting. As he placed his other hand on Ramiel's cheek, they started to levitate, they rose upwards, over the mansion and above the treetops. Ramiel did not notice the rising skyscrapers from downtown, or the spire from the cathedral, the architecture or the clouds. He remained focused on Cristofano's eyes; and as they soared across the city, and started to rotate, they drifted away from the buildings.

It was if they were spinning, yet focused on each other's eyes; the intensity of their staring pierced their minds.

They descended, downwards, and Ramiel saw the rising stone monuments, and the small crypts. It was not Resurrection; they were nowhere near the Waxley Mortuary. They gently landed on the grass, and the moonlight bathed the masonry in pale blue light.

Cristofano placed his arm on Ramiel's, looked at him as they locked their eyes, and shook his head. Ramiel heard the moans and the approach of the shadows, the rattle of the chains preparing; Cristofano raised his open palms and they quieted. He lowered his arms and the cover to the crypt.

They stood…and waited.

The night faded as the sun rose with a brilliance of pink and auburn light. They stood, staring into each other's eyes, as the sun ascended higher into the sky, until the sky turned bright and blue and brilliant. Cristofano finally moved; he withdrew the casket which was inside the small crypt, and placed it gently in front of them, sitting it on the grass. Several cemetery workers approached them, and Cristofano nodded to them.

Ramiel watched as the workers bent down and placed the casket in the stone mausoleum. The two cemetery workers in stained cover-alls hoisted the massive casket; and as Ramiel stood, he watched them lift the square cement block and shove it into place. One of the men pressed against it with both palms as the other leaned down and grabbed a tube. He reached up and smoothed sealant over the edges as the other worker gradually eased up on his pressing.

And as Cristofano watched, and listened, he leaned in closer. He didn't hear anything. But the cemetery workers knew. The sound wouldn't escape the crypt. And the shadow demon would inhibit screaming. And the chains prevented movement.

So the cemetery workers remained blissfully ignorant.

They would be entirely unaware that the grave they were sealing contained what they thought was an immortal – a being that, despite having dead blood coursing through the veins, no heartbeat or discernible brainwave activity – had continued to exist.

They would assume that the immortal who was supposed to be sealed inside the coffin would be bound and chained, and would hear the coffin scraping the bottom of the crypt as it slid into place. And that the immortal would see a tiny sliver of light emanate through a tiny space between the side of the coffin and lid…until the crypt cover was sealed into place, until an appointed immortal could raise them from their coffin sentence.

The Code of the Immortals. That was the directive, it seemed. Ramiel looked at Cristofano watching the cemetery staff leave after the crypt was sealed with an empty casket.

Ramiel wondered that if there was a way, he hopefully could follow in the same footsteps as Cristofano.

Would the immortals initiate a second crypt dancer?

He was a dancer as well, but Cristofano had the bloodline of apparent immortal royalty, and Ramiel did not.

Yet when Ramiel watched as the workers smoothed the sealant over with dirty white rags, he also watched as Cristofano reviewed their work.

As if there were an agreement between the immortals and the cemetery.

Bound and chained.

Lying in the constricted confines, the dark solitude of a coffin, Ramiel wondered what those sentenced might think as they heard the heavy, cement cover hoisted into place, banging against the masonry.

And then, Ramiel wondered what Cristofano must be thinking now, as the cemetery workers gathered their equipment, leaving the grave. Maybe the coffin itself listened as their footsteps faded away…to silence.

Ramiel watched as the day grew quiet.

He pictured the others alone in the dark coffin; alone with their thoughts, a racing mind, chained and unable to move, constricted in the confines of small wooden boxes. They would be destined for torment for a period of desolation and isolation, leading up to eternity.

With their souls in the rancid sea of stones among the writhing pasty limbs.

Ramiel hoped that wasn't the case; the punishment, the loneliness, the isolation was far more than he could ever expect to endure. But his being part of the immortals was his own reality, his own private uncertainty. It was a common bond; a fear that they all shared.

And he wondered if he might ever truly commit an offense to warrant such a torturous penance. But as he looked out into the cemetery, he watched, and gasped as he felt the warmth of a hand on his shoulder. He turned around.

"Cristo! What – you are –?"

"I am The Crypt Dancer. You didn't think you would stay in that coffin for long, did you?"

He winked.

Ramiel smiled, watching as his beloved maker closed his eyes, feeling the warmth of the sun against his face. "I haven't experienced this for many years," he said. "Always a creature of the night, it seemed." He opened his eyes, and looked back at Ramiel. "My destiny, I believe. It's apparent."

"And what of the coven?"

Cristofano took a breath, held it for a moment, and seemed to be considering his answer. "The Queen has her shadows. And her sea of souls. But there's one missing piece of the puzzle."

Ramiel leaned closer towards him.

"The Mastuer dynasty," Cristofano said. "We can assume she's there. Down in Port-au-Prince, perhaps in New Orleans. Back in Paris even. They are powerful, Ramiel, but are a force within our community. The powder she holds…"

"LaDonna has a presence which cannot be denied," Ramiel added.

"Yes."

THE CURTAIN FALLS

The End

11/4/20 2:48pm

11/24/20 1:41pm second run

If you enjoyed Ballet of The Crypt Dancer, please consider leaving a review.

Reviews are most helpful for independent artists such as myself.

Many thanks,

A.L.

OTHER TITLES FROM
PARCHMAN'S PRESS

Excellence In Fiction

FIND US ON FACEBOOK

ASHES

An abandoned immortal raises his maker from a centuries old grave to hellish consequences and uncertainty about his maker...but also himself: is he good...or evil?

ANTOINE GATHERED HIS EQUIPMENT - a shovel, brown tarp, pickaxe (in order to pry open the casket) and a flame oil lantern; carefully and quietly he entered the graveyard through a layer of swirling, early morning mist - the type of white cloudy mist that would leave a layer of dewdrops on the earth like a cool, wet blanket. The plot Antoine headed toward, located in the center of the graveyard, housed Darius' casket, encased for two centuries now in layers of earth - sealed by six nails, and placed in a thick cement liner with a crest of a lion on the marble-topped cover.

It was Antoine who put Darius here two centuries ago, and Darius has been in this graveyard ever since. In this cemetery and dead, yes – Darius was dead. But Darius had been dead before Antoine had ever put him there. And when the coffin was nailed shut, when the darkness enveloped satin interior, there was more of changing a state of existence.

It was Darius who had heard the nails being pounded into the edges of the casket; he had felt the shaking as the coffin was picked up – most likely with ropes tied below the bottom, but he couldn't know for sure – and lowered into the deep, dark grave. He had felt the sides of the coffin scraping the cold, hard earthen walls. The dirt fell onto the lid of the casket – each shovel of earth inundating the coffin further with a deep clump.

Blackness.

The sounds from above now seemed more distant. The coffin had been buried. Darius knew that. He even felt the weight of the dirt above him, as if the entire casket would fall on top of him in a cascade of splintering wood and falling sand. But it held. The coffin was holding fast against the pressures of the earth, and would prove to be his holding place for…how long?

The stagnancy of the air inside the small confines grew more insistent, as the heat overtook the darkness and caused him to cough and choke on the thickness of the air that was so quickly fading. But Darius knew. He knew that no matter how fast the air would dissipate, no matter how faint the sounds of the earth above would be – no matter how dead he would be – he would be just that.

Dead.

But death is just a state of existence. And Darius knew - all too well - that his death had been many, many years ago – and not so recently in his foyer.

His death had been much earlier when he was a very young man passing into his newfound immortality. Not at the hands of Antoine.

As time passed, he became more aware of his surroundings, although all he saw was total darkness. He could feel the softness and smoothness of the satin liner, the pillow at the head of the casket - which grew hard and cold over time and dusty with mold.

Above where he lay, Darius on occasion could hear the faint, muffled voices above the cold ground expressing words of condolence, the grating of a casket being lowered into a freshly dug grave, or the pitter patter of children's feet; ceremonial instruments would play from time to time, signifying the passing of a loved one. All this, he experienced, lying in the cold darkness of the casket, as time passed by above.

Time passed with an eternal slowness until Antoine returned.

At one point, Darius knew the time had come. He continued to lie in the casket as he felt and heard snippets of the outside world over time, but there was one quiet day when he heard those familiar footsteps; the methodic, determined stomps coming closer and closer to his unmarked resting place. The footsteps stopped, just above. Darius could sense it. He knew who it was. No one knew of his grave except one soul. Only one.

Antoine.

THE QUEST FOR IMMORTALITY

An immortal who lost his gift races against time to avoid a final and permanent death.

DOUGLAS KAHN AWOKE with a start.

He shot up in bed, covered in sweat, and rubbed his eyes, burying his face into his hands. He had been dreaming of the bodies again.

He swung his legs over the side of the bed, and looked at the clock. It was still hours before dawn, and he knew that shortly he would have to put on the black suit that was hanging in the hotel room closet. He closed his eyes and exhaled, running his hands through what was left of his silvery, stringy hair.

He got up, slowly, and walked over to check the air conditioner. He felt the cool air blowing from the vents, but it stopped there. The humidity in the small, boxy hotel room was just stifling.

He poured himself a small glass of bourbon from the mini-bar, and picked up the phone. But he didn't call the front desk.

"Jim?" He took a sip and set the glass down on the bedside table. "Sorry to call you, Jim, but I had the dream again."

"What do you mean?"

"I mean it was just liked it had happened when I was in Miami…the streets…everything. I had passed out in the limo, and when I woke up, the bodies were just everywhere. I couldn't even get out of the car."

"And where was I?"

Douglas stopped for a moment, as his eyes scanned the room. He saw shadows against the wall, set by the warm, pale glow of the exterior hotel lights. "You…I think you were dead."

Jim laughed. "Doug, you have been having this dream for a while now. Doesn't mean a thing."

Doug closed his eyes and shook his head. "Look, Jim. Let's just cancel this trip. I have no idea what it means, but I have known Sheldon for a long time."

"Sure you have."

Doug reached for a cigarette, placed it in his mouth, and flicked the lighter. It wouldn't light after several attempts. He tossed the unlit cigarette back on the table. "Look, Jim, I don't want to go. I have talked with Sheldon so many times before he died, and I know about all the weird shit that he was into. I mean, The Astral was one of the strangest things he ever did. And that Antoine guy…I don't even know what to say about him. But this dream, Jim…I just don't know how to explain it."

"Like it was a prophecy?"

"Exactly."

"So we don't go then. When you go down to the lobby at 8am, like you always do, I will make sure not to be there."

Doug placed his hand over his chin. "I don't know if that's the solution. I still have a lot I have to do down here. The reading of the will, everything."

"So then I should be there? Waiting for you outside the lobby as usual? You need to decide whether you're going or not, Doug."

There was a moment of silence on the line as Doug attempted to light his cigarette again, now with a book of matches he had fished out of the drawer next to the Holy Bible. "Doug? Are you there?"

Doug waved the match and treasured the hot smoke as it flew to his lungs. A small trail of smoke rose to into the air. He exhaled deeply, closed his eyes, and sighed. "Yes, that will be fine. That will be just dandy. Be there at 8. I have an appointment at 9. You know how the Dolphin gets."

Jim chuckled on the other end of the phone. "I sure do, Doug, I sure do. See you then."

They hung up from the call. Doug looked down at the cigarette as it burned in the ashtray; the cherry red tip shone through a plume of ash as the sweet smoke continued rising towards the ceiling. Doug had not touched the cigarette since his initial drag. He didn't even want it anymore. He looked at the clock. It was almost 4am. Jim would be here in four hours.

He extinguished the burning cigarette and slid back under the covers. He desperately wanted to fall asleep, he wanted rest without dreams; he wanted it to be how it was when he and Sheldon were in college, back in the days in Boston, back when life was simpler, before Sheldon followed the path beyond theology and into the darkness.

But Douglas knew better.

THE BLOOD DECANTER

The immortal community bands together against a hooded figure who is determined to wipe them out of existence.

THERE WAS A CERTAIN TIME, and in a certain place, that they knew when they were being hunted.

The rumors had, in fact, been true. They had been

circulating for decades, but were never taken seriously.

Until the one precise moment when the revelation came.

But the knowledge of their potential demise did not come so easily; for it was months, if not years, of research, relationship building, and foraging trust missions where the truth had been revealed: the immortals were, undoubtedly, being extinguished.

And a small, bulbous crystal decanter was the culprit.

The decanter was thought, for a great while, to be the key to eternal salvation. There were many who had talked about it, and about the mysterious one who carried the decanter, who would visit the immortals in time of need; and the one who carried the decanter visited those immortals who were stripped of their gift, who lay dying and aging, heading towards a quick and final death. The decanter was viewed as the ultimate salvation; a catalyst to continue the gift, to add to the dark destiny for which they had been chosen.

But that was a fallacy.

Those who drank from the decanter did not find the solace that they desired; they did not receive the expected gift. They did not regain their immortality or strengthen or increase their intelligence. There was an utter agony which propelled itself on them. An infection filled with anxiety, torment, and a slow and painful death.

There were no gifts. There was no salvation from the decanter.

One of the most recent who drank the swirling, hot, red potion lay motionless on the sidewalk outside the Ponce de Leon after sunset, when the night was still in its infancy; lying still and motionless, eyes closed, and the blood still dripped from his mouth.

But he was still as if dead, eyes shut tight, and the young man, and his unkempt hair and sullied clothes, did nothing to represent the individual he had been in life – for he had once been quite fashionable. The torn, dirty pants, should they have been removed, sewn and cleaned, would be seen as of the latest fashion, and could be seen hanging in one of the upscale boutique shop windows that were a mere few steps from where the man lay.

Above where the man lay stood the one who wielded the decanter, who appeared to be a man – a 'Hooded Man' in a long, flowing, dark cloak – who would visit, shortly before death (as it was argued). Here, above the motionless, bloodied man, the 'Hooded Man' stood, watching and waiting, as the white mist that swirled around him abated. As the cloud retreated, so did the man. He walked without motion, with no bending of the knee; as if he were floating or levitating along the ground, and once his duty had been complete, he left.

He was the one who had crossed the world for decades, undetected until recently, the one who had been, for so long, a mythical figure who was thought to bring life eternal, and now was found to bring death.

WAR ANGEL

Can the immortals be redeemed? The story of a warrior, a protector, and confidant: a battle of Good versus evil.

THERE ONCE WAS A STORY of a 'War Angel'.

When the story had first been told, there were the many questions that followed. There were those who did not understand who the War Angel could be. While many wondered, there was an equally significant amount of people who were entirely unaware. But the questions remained, particularly in those societies who had a spiritual and cosmic connection. They asked the questions, over and over. Who is the angel?

Who is this mysterious, mythical angel of battles?

Was the angel male?

Female?

Did the War Angel walk among us? Protect us?

Stories had started to circulate among the populace. There were some people that claimed to have seen angelic figures and spirits, particularly at night. Pale, white ghostly apparitions in trees, watching them.

As if waiting for something.

Or someone.

But no one could be for certain if the phenomenon were a product of the War Angel. No one could tell if he (or she) were simply observing.

Or protecting.

And then there was the story of the immortals.

And their similar musings of the War Angel, and those same supernatural phenomena. The immortals, who had been peacefully coexisting with the humans for centuries, had come to a precipice in their existence: for they were dying and close to extinction. And so the same rumors of the War Angel started to circulate through their communities.

The same dinner table talk that the humans discussed penetrated their existence.

Initially, they were just stories.

Stories of angels.

And of demons, and of ghosts.

Throughout time, the stories had fueled the dinner table chatter among the immortals and humans alike. The immortals were on the brink of extinction after dealing with years of torment at the hands of the 'hooded man'. Some of the immortals had wondered who the War

Angel could be. Perhaps a warrior to protect them? To triumph in their pursuit of goodness?

But the immortals had not been the harbingers of good. And there was no rest for the wicked. For centuries, the immortals were connected with sin.

And evil.

Debauchery and poison.

The humans who befriended them often found untimely deaths. And when they did not, those humans typically had great misfortunes befall upon them.

People started to talk about the immortals.

That they were sinful.

And that those humans who befriended them were courting evil; that those people who became embroiled in the wickedness deserved their fate.

Over time and recent decades, as the immortal society neared total collapse, there had been the advent of a mythical figure called The Hooded Man, a malevolent destroyer of the immortal foundation.

While no human being had ever been reported to have seen the robed figure, the rumors, which had initially circulated through the immortal communities, filtered over towards the human population, and not long after, were discussed in government meetings, on news stations, and media.

Immortals Targeted for Annihilation the headlines screamed. Artists painted renditions of The Hooded Man from long discussions with their immortal friends.

In Miami, which had long been thought to be the central battleground of The Hooded Man's wrath, immortal Antoine Nagevesh, who headed that "sector" of their society, had led a local effort, in joint conjuncture with the human population, to hunt down the hooded figure and destroy him before the immortals were wiped off the face of the Earth.

His drive made it across the Atlantic to France and Rome, where a large concentration of immortals lived, but it became futile. For The Hooded Man cast a seductive spell, and Antoine saw that the immortals were destined to wind up where they did: near extinction.

And so came the mystery of the War Angel in the society of the immortals. At the council of The Inspiriti in Rome, an enlightened society thought to be governed by a council of immortals, there were many discussions. Several members of the high council met over the course of decades to confer the possibility of a warrior, of an angel, and whether the angel posed a threat to the immortals or if it could be an ally.

And others, immortals and humans alike, argued about the mystery.

The War Angel.

Who could it be?

The apparitions continued.

Many during times of great distress.

Why the apparitions now? At this time? At this moment when the immortals were on the cusp of extinction? Certainly this being could not be sent to combat the immortals.

Could it have?

And so the questions circulated.

Did he or she travel along the sidewalks, and take a similar journey as the immortals and the people...or did he or she ride a horse?

Or was the story of the War Angel possibly in a modern time?

And did he or she sit in automobiles, ride on trains and ships and airplanes, and travel next to us...watching us...without our awareness of their presence?

Many questions permeated minds throughout the world.

And then, after the period of speculation, would follow the mystery of the angel's existence.

There were rarely answers, but the questions would always remain, regardless of the time period or amount of technology in the search: Would the angels only be seen in fleeting moments in times of distress?

Or could they be engaged with human beings in mundane, everyday situations, without our knowledge? Could the next interaction one were to have with another person be a conversation with an angel?

Or even a war angel?

The phenomenon remained a mystery.

There were those who did not understand who the War Angel was — nor did they choose to believe in something that they could not see nor prove.

And then, due to the lack of conviction, the world continued to evolve; man discovered science, and evolution. Industry, and technology.

The idea of a spiritual journey — and spirits who were sent from the celestial dimensions to protect — seemed increasingly foreign.

So the questions remained.

Was the war angel really there? Or was it an idea of stories and prayers?

For he or she who the angel was called to protect – would they see the angel? Would they even know the angel was there fighting a battle in their name?

Initially, there was no acknowledgement.

And complacency reigned, within the immortal populace but the human beings as well. Stories of the War Angel faded as time wore on.

Over the years, some did not believe the war angel actually existed. Man adopted the scientific mindset, and the world evolved. The Industrial Revolution proved to man – at least to a degree – that man was the 'Supreme Being'.

That man ruled the Earth.

God was not the ruler.

God was not the spiritual entity He once was; for man became increasingly self-absorbed.

The seven sins were prevalent. And because of that, man suffered the consequences.

According to Biblical history, Adam and Eve, after committing the first sin, were cast out of Eden, and ever since that time, a time which man had been birthed in the created World, there had been the stain of sin on man, like a fingerprint on a clean surface.

But the stain could be wiped clean.

It could be absolved, there was a method of cleansing.

Of redemption.

Man was given "free will" by God. And man, as a general entity, chose to focus on themselves. But that did not mean that man denied God, but, perhaps, rather, did not acknowledge Him. But He was always there, and He still gave man the tools needed for their survival – both physical and spiritual.

And then came a war angel.

A battle assigned angel.

One given to each and every living soul; in many cases (most, if not all cases) the presence of the war angel was completely undetected.

Their presence was ignored, and all spiritual connection was extinguished – and those who were to be protected continued their lives without any awareness of the war angel. But, and it was argued over generations, the war angel was still there, fulfilling their duties.

The story of the War Angel was told through generations – it was told again, and again, and again; over the centuries, no matter how many times the story had become diluted, it always reached the same conclusion.

And left the same questions.

Did the war angel actually exist?

THE WANDERING STAR

Stranded colonists in a post-apocalyptic world seek a habitable zone after the Earth's rotation has stopped.

MANY OF THOSE who remained living on the planet Earth could still remember the days when the oceans shifted towards the poles, and when the sea levels rose, higher; seemingly before their eyes; but certainly within a generation.

For the citizens of the United States of America, their memory of the water shifting was real and recent, and even years and decades later, many would recall the Great Shift. It became dinner table talk; bedtime stories. Those who were too young to remember the period of the Great Shift were told of the days when the wave came.

And in those days, it was when the mass exodus from the Northern states was plastered over every news channel; every blog; throughout the internet and on every street corner. In the years during which the shift took place, and as the rotation of the planet slowed, the coastal population was forced to relocate to inland cities. Those in the Northern Hemisphere (and equally so in the Southern Hemisphere) would relocate a short distance from their previous coastal residence, and then, several years later, would be forced to move once again, as the sea crept closer…and closer…to the population. As the planet slowed even further, and it became inevitable for those located nearest to the poles that their cities were slowly being inundated and swallowed by the Earth's waters, it came to a point that entire countries had to be abandoned as great cities were reclaimed by mother nature.

The people of the planet recalled watching in horror as the waters retreated from the tropical zones and spilled towards the north. It wasn't until the northern cities were completely swallowed, and each metropolis would fall into memory and would lie beneath vast depths of seawater, that the inhabitants of the remaining dry areas towards the equator felt the twinge of uncertainty.

Until then, when the cities were lost, it had simply been disbelief. Some cites, like Atlanta or Rome, with a more southerly location, were not spared entirely from the assault of the waters, but the skyscrapers, and some crests on taller buildings rose from the sea. Those cities were partially inundated and still abandoned. Others, closer to the poles, were completely submerged – under a mile of water in some cases, and sentenced to decompose in a watery grave.

London, New York, Toronto, and Moscow – all were lost. Santiago, Sydney, Cape Town…all underwater.

Forever.

THE EUROPA EFFECT

*Space explorers band together on a mission to excavate through Jupiter's moon
Europa's layer of ice to search for life.*

THE STUDY OF THE COSMOLOGY of the Universe had been overlooked in the latter days of the planet. It was when the days on the Earth had turned away from the exploration of the distant and the interstellar; and on the planet, the appreciation of music, and of art, and of philosophy, had waned.

It was during those years when there had been a transformation of such. A transformation of the human minds; but also, physically, of the planet; not only in the geology and the geography of the world, but also a change in the thought process of the people who populated the planet. Their beliefs, motives, and culture.

The long period of the shift had continued for generations...the subtle changes were initially ignored. But over the years, and as the generations progressed, the planet gradually re-terraformed itself. The period of the shift, which had been considered "long" based on the percentage of a typical human life, was insignificant on a cosmic scale.

And that period had become a quest for survival.

After the period of what became known across the planet as the Great Shift, those who remained had been labeled "the survivors" and those who perished were remembered. And the world changed drastically in the generations that followed.

During those years, man rarely looked up towards the Heavens. Those times on Earth had become a period of survival, and the thoughts of the cosmos were forgotten.

Until the day when a man had arrived unexpectedly to a colony known simply as "Sector B". He had been disheveled and dirty, physically near death as he had staggered towards the colony's outer doors. Those who had witnessed his approach recalled watching his silhouette against searing sunlight, which had cast radiation on the planet in those days. The man, the scout, had collapsed on arrival, seemingly near death. The colonists risked exposure and rushed to his side, saw that he was still living, and had him taken to medical. Over the following weeks he was nursed back to health, and was known through the colony population as 'the scout'.

Rumors traveled through the colony about what the scout's purpose was.

And when the scout was well enough to speak with them, the people of the planet were urged to look up towards the sky once again: for there was a message.

There was a beacon of hope; of light.

There were those who claimed they had seen a star; and also rumors of those who were thought to have spoken to a mystical star with a message.

And the message was survival.

They believed that the human race could live on, if they looked upwards and outwards. Their destiny was not to remain living underground with dwindling rations, heading toward extinction.

It was to journey outwards.

To reach beyond.

To trust, and to take a leap of faith.

But the aura of the planet had indeed changed. Culture had vanished; no longer were there orchestral performances in city centers; many artistic masterpieces were lost forever under the sea in cities that had been swallowed by oceans.

And it was then, quite unexpectedly, that the people of the planet had the visitor. It was he who was called the "scout". After the colonists spoke with him, he was regarded as a messenger of sorts.

But not everyone trusted the mysterious man. Some thought he had been a warrior, or perhaps a pirate.

But there were others who did trust him.

And even others still who thought he could be a 'messiah'.

But he had a message to deliver, and that was his purpose.

People were given the free will to choose to accompany him, or stay behind. But those who chose to stay behind, he had claimed, would experience a fiery death as the planet was destined to perish.

After the scout had come, after the people looked up towards the stars, and after the people's journey, there had been a feeling of despair that washed over those who waited for what was to come next.

For the journey that the people took had been a quest for survival. Leaving the safety of Sector B, out into an increasingly hostile, now foreign world.

The people, though, learned to trust the scout.

They followed him as he led them to salvation.

The masses of people found themselves standing in the midst of a large, sandy desert, on a planet which had become dangerous and uninhabitable. Radiation threatened from above during six months of sunlight. It had only been safe to venture out during the six months of darkness.

Half the world was flooded, and the other half was a barren desert. Forests and agriculture had slowly died off after the physical transformation of the planet took place once the rotation had slowed to a stop.

But the scout brought the people hope.

As they stood exposed to cosmic rays in a large desert clearing, underneath a rapidly lightening sky, they felt a twinge of the unknown. Dusty, sandy hills rolled along the plains around them towards the horizon. The sky was starting to turn from black to dark blue.

But they still felt safe, at least to a degree. For they didn't quite remember much before seeing the massive, dark cylinder in the sky that hovered over the dry and dusty landscape. As they looked up at the dark hovering spacecraft, the rest of the thoughts of the dying planet gradually faded away.

It was a massive ship; one that was miles long and wide, one that would travel vast distances at speeds that mankind had never been able to achieve.

COLONIA VOLUME ONE:
THE ARRIVAL OF DESTINY

In the beginning…there was nothing. Until there was something.

Throughout history, the theory of life beyond was explored. Until it became fact.

THE COSMIC DUST of the fallen Donada Explorer showered through the skies of Colonia.

Fiery rain of a melted hull crashed downwards in bright orange flames; the burning tails fleeting through the atmosphere; white, hot, glowing. Steel embers dove from the orbit against the rose-tinted skies, igniting the forests of blue on the planet surface.

But the Vegans did not mind the burning of the foliage; for it would quickly regenerate.

Their eyes remained focused on the skies; the pastel pink, the pale over-blanket, the layer of protection for which it had come to be known.

And then it was the starship, the grand explosion, which caused their mouths to gape open and their eyes to widen. Colonia hadn't seen a starship so massive, one that reached across their skies and from their planet to the Ion moon base. Even the two familiar Vegan starships – Vega One and Destiny – hadn't been so gargantuan as the Donada Explorer.

It was as if it were a massive cylindrical rock…a floating planet, perhaps?

The speculation tore through the population like wildfire.

A massive section of the hull crashed in the forests before them. Several of the Vegans rushed forward to investigate. Some of the Humans followed. The leader snapped her head in the direction of the falling hull segment.

"Get back!" she barked as they timidly retreated.

Flames engulfed the forests as the gargantuan segment continued burning. But they could see it through the trees.

An unknown metal and rock covering – it was like nothing they had ever seen in the Lyra Constellation or the Milky Way. From where the ship had originated continued the mystery.

The starship had nearly blended into the dark skies beyond the orbit of Colonia, yet the firepower was significant. A massive cylindrical hull matched those of both Destiny and Vega One – but it was the Destiny that had been the most enigmatic of the three, at least in purpose.

It was argued, though, that the Donada Explorer had never been seen within the realm of the trinity across the cosmos; that the reach of the spacecraft had been well beyond the interstellar regions. A foreign metal which they had never seen blanketed the exterior; it could have – perhaps – been geological in nature; rock-like, protective…but the origin was unknown. The hull provided undeniable protection, absorbing heat and energy from passing magnetic fields.

The interior, initially, had been an enigma.

There was a rumor which had circulated among the Vegans, but also the Human survivors, that the interior had a monstrous, demonic influence; the vultures of the galaxies. And that they traveled from galaxy to galaxy, destroying any life they found by consuming resources.

But before the Donada Explore had fallen from the skies of Colonia, they found the mysterious hull could be penetrated.

The explosion rocked the planet as the oceans' waters tore towards the lands from the winds. The global event was like nothing Colonia had ever seen; the waters generally were peaceful, lapping at the shores with a gentle flow across the sands.

A shock wave tore down through the atmosphere, igniting their shallow, lifeless ocean, as a towering wave charged towards the rising sleek amphibious buildings of the city center.

The Vegans scattered, but actively protected the Humans.

Cries ensued as the massive fireball reached downwards and ignited taller buildings.

The Donada Explorer was no more.

Just a fiery remnant of scrap metal and flaming chards floating across cosmic skies; and the shrapnel plummeting to the blue forests below.

"Were there any of us on there?!" was overheard through the chaotic clatter of indiscernible voices. The Vegans, those protective Vegans. The worriers; the protectors of the cosmos. An enlightened culture; scientifically advanced; yet emotionally vague.

Even the Humans, who were looking up towards the skies, appeared to process the event with somber tears falling across cheeks and hands covering mouths agape.

"I know there were Vegans on board! I just know it!" A voice was heard again above the chaos and cries. But the Vegans knew. There had to be sacrifices for salvation. There was a price for redemption. And there would always be an eternity to consider the alternatives.

But there was one who they all looked up to for guidance and direction, who stood and watched the starship's demise next to them. As the Vegans and Humans watched in horror, the wave crashed through the buildings, destroying city center; gasps were heard as the Administration Building fell.

But there was one who they would look up to, for guidance and direction, if not protection.

The leader.

She was the one who stood at command, her hands balled into fists, resting against her hips, watching upwards with the others as she stood on the clearing. The continued explosions reflected on her dark helmet visor.

Colonia was falling.

The Vegans gathered on the hill below where she stood, huddled together, hugging and crying. Heads rested on shoulders as two members of the trinity watched the villainous wrecking fall from the skies, igniting their planet.

But the Vegan who stood above them, piercing her energy up towards the skies, was the one they had hoped for. In the times of uncertainty, the Vegans had once thought a leader would never arrive.

Her mystery was omnipresent, but they knew who she was. And the chatter discussed her origins.

Both the Vegans and the new Earthly arrivals – the "Humans" – knew.

They respected her leadership.

Her protection.

They shared the same awe for her acceptance of her calling.

"You are the battle angelica!" they would chorus when the starship fell from the skies. "You protect us!"

COLONIA VOLUME TWO:

BATTLE OF THE TRINITY

A return to a lifeless Earth. A story of destiny, a battle for truth. A rescue mission across the cosmos leads to a battle with an unclear adversary.

IN THE COSMOS, destiny is born through stardust and supernovas. And a propensity to eternally recreate. Through a sense of purpose, the chorus of songs amidst the silence of space might never be heard...but the music remains.

The showering of carbon on rocky worlds birthed with water inoculated with purpose; that sense of the chaos of rising life within the steadfast cosmos. And within, throughout millennia, the purpose transformed to a search for meaning.

Life begot life; yet in the chronology of the evolution, there had always been a sense of wonder: was life shared on other planets, peppered throughout galaxies? Rocky worlds with breathable atmospheres which orbited similar stars that Humans had been familiar with?

Was life aware of the existence of other life that surrounded them? Were supernovas in distant realms of the Universe showering similar stardust and carbon on habitable planets…leading to life forms which resembled one another?

Those who were bestowed The Stardust Gift would share the same wonderment. On distant planets separated by light-years, similar species would gaze up towards the skies; where the distant sentinels watched: the stars, the governors of the galaxies.

And protectors.

The stars would hold the same mystery for all. As if they could reach up towards the sky, hold their fingers up before their line of site and touch them…one by one; the tiny white pin-points peppered across the dark, nighttime sky.

But the stars remained distant, yet close and guiding.

They provided a sense of meaning and direction to worlds across the distance of space and time. For those who gazed at the purple skies of twilight might have been separated by galaxies…yet connected through a shared purpose.

Through the destruction of stars births the creation of life; not withstanding to singular planets. For the life which had become known to one another – the 'Trinity of Life' as it had been called over the multiple worlds – there had been a shared destiny.

A shared sense of purpose, if not to protect then at least to preserve. The Trinity must be protected.

Destiny dictated the movement.

As the bright pastel plumes of gases continued their outward reaching, in that singular moment when space and time began; towards the distant, beyond the interstellar…in the deep blackness of the void beyond the known…there had been a shared dream. Of other worlds, and different species.

Had there truly been life beyond their own existences?

Would their share of the skies across the distance of space and time reveal the secrets of the cosmos?

There hadn't been an awareness of one another's existence for generations on each of their home planets. But the mystery remained, throughout millennia, as the cosmos were explored in their home galaxies.

Lyra had been the most advanced by far, followed by the Milky Way.

However those in the Milky Way, the Humans on planet Earth, had a different destiny. And the Andromedans on Zylcon, in the Andromeda Galaxy, surpassed them in technology and exploration…despite the hostility of Zyclon.

And in the midst of this Trinity there arose a chosen warrior.

Her mission had not been revealed to her throughout her life; her destiny had been written by the stars yet executed by the Trinity. She had once been thought to exist without fault, and remained true to her destiny; her presence, still, could not save the destruction that had been written by the cosmos.

For the Universe was quiet about its intentions.

Their speaking was never in words; it was a noble intention of destiny.

Of the dreams of the creation. And the determination of stardust and interstellar gaseous outbursts which formulated creation…and destruction.

But destinies unfounded would make an easy scapegoat for an arrival of a planetary destruction. For creation would ultimately lead towards annihilation; and the collision of purpose and meaning was unable to thwart the inevitable.

A dead, lifeless planet.

For the destination had always been the same.

Sanded beaches, in front of the dull roar of a pounding surf, or gently lapping waves at the shore. The destination was shared by the Trinity and soared towards the stars.

For the warrior, there was the fable of thoughts that permeated her mind; the cosmos were unfaltering. The scribbles of destiny pierced her mind.

She hadn't dreamed of this outcome. Or what had become the fabric of her existence.

And there was the star.

The simplicity of its presence tore through her thoughts; a fragment of purpose which examined its own existence. For she had been there. During the times when she had seen and spoken with the star on the shores of Earth, now many light-years away.

Yet still she knew her true purpose.

And her destiny.

For time would wrap around her; as she traveled, her destiny, carved between the wisps of interstellar reaches of colorful cosmic gaseous clouds. The darkness enveloped her; wrapped around her as if it were a cool blanket…yet she felt adrift. Floating in the frigid outer recesses of the cosmos.

There hadn't been a wormhole, had there?

She struggled to remember, and when she fought to see, to view the tiny white stars set against the dark pallet, there was nothing. A distance of the darkness had been enveloping.

Have you discovered it yet? Your destiny? What you have been chosen to do?

The voice.

It came again, its whisper searing through her mind like the pierce of a sword. The deep penetration within her consciousness. It appeared to her…but what was it trying to tell her? There was something soothing about the voice. Something special.

And directive.

But it had always seemed distant.

Mysterious, yet suggestive. A mystical fragmented dream, which penetrated her mind during the unpredictability of scattered moments, which would challenge her thought process, rob her of her confidence and interject discouragement and self-doubt.

It was during those times that the star would appear to her.

But it was there.

She could sense it, although not always see it.

Even in the days when she had been on Earth…as she had stood on the shores, staring at the angry ocean as its crest of foam crashed against the rocks, when the seagulls called and retreated.

A deep male voice had called from behind her. "Your destiny! It lies within the waters!"

She snapped her head around and looked out towards the far end of the beach, but saw no one. Just the strengthening winds tearing through the blowing tree tops.

And the howl of the atmosphere as the waters retreated, the impending tsunami suctioning the sea outwards in the torrent of its approach. But the voice had come, despite the churning atmosphere nearly drowning it out.

For that she was certain.

She could scarcely hear it against the roar of the surf and the howl of the increasing winds, when the voice came again. "Your destiny is everything that is and ever was!"

She turned but all she saw were the approaching winds tearing through the palm fronds.

And she had still been alone.

The call of the cosmos was certain; it was a deep, determined, methodical voice which sought its rhythm within her mind.

And it was persistent.

"Discover the call of your destiny! The arrival of which from within your true heart soars!"

Yet still there was no one.

She turned and faced the angry surf.

This was the moment, she had known that much. This was the time from which her soul had been born; and discovered its true purpose.

There was something about the time of the wave. When many places on the Earth had been swallowed by the sea.

The wave, she wondered, could it be her destiny?

THE MORTICIAN

Three students explore an abandoned mortuary and discover the secrets within.

JUST DAYS BEFORE HIS THIRTIETH BIRTHDAY, and nearly twenty-seven years after it happened, Jacob Benjamin could still remember standing on the stepstool next to his Grandmother's coffin.

He clutched his blankie in his small, determined hands, and looked at Gramma. Her eyes were closed; there was a slight smile on her face, but it was just that – slight.

She looked like she was sleeping.

Was she going to wake up?

Despite the passage of time, his mind had still painted a perfect picture: as if she were the subject of an oil painting. A sleeping beauty of sorts. And when he remembered the scene over two decades later, he knew, that when he had stood on the step stool as a small child, all he wondered about was when Gramma was going to wake up and do the choo-choo.

As he remembered the visual of her body in the casket, he reminisced every tiny detail, as if each tiny detail of the scene before him were a specific and determined stroke of the brush; and the crimson tinged palette before him was noted despite his young age: it had been an artful presentation.

She was a sleeping beauty surrounded by white lilies and roses, bathed in a rose tinted light. An equally warm look to her skin. He hadn't known, in those days, that it was the makeup and creams that added a more lifelike appearance.

That the formaldehyde which was pumped into her veins was tinted to make it appear as if she were still alive.

But he knew it twenty-seven years after the viewing when he stood on the stepstool next to the casket as a three year old little boy.

Nor had he known that the tint applied to the lightbulbs on the standing lamps on either side of the coffin actually had a purpose: to make her skin look like blood had still flowed through her dead veins.

But twenty seven years later, he knew the purpose of the hue of the lamps.

Her body lay meticulously in the center of the casket, surrounded by soft, supple, creamy satin. The lid was propped open. Her face had a peaceful expression; as if she were sleeping, as if she had just dozed off, perhaps while watching television, or after a shared family meal, or board games with the children.

Her mouth had a slight smile; not overly so, but a subtle translation of euphoria. But there was not the slightest depiction that she was anything other than a sleeping beauty.

He looked at her lifeless, yet peaceful looking body, lying in the middle of a sea of cream colored satin, underneath a golden hanging crucifix, which was nestled in the center of the pleats of satin on the propped open lid.

She could have been merely sleeping. In her elegant surroundings. That was all, really.

Just sleeping.

On display for everyone to see, but simply off in dreamland, and she certainly was going to awake at any time, sit up, and ask everyone why they were so somber and dressed in dark suits.

Although he was still a toddler when his grandmother had passed, the memories were still vivid, as if the funeral had been just yesterday. The sweet, wafting smoke of the incense still rose into the air and the perfumed smell of the flowers flowed through his nostrils as he inhaled; he could still hear the muffled conversations at the viewing, and he could still remember the cold, firm feel to her cheek after he had touched it with his finger. And the organ was playing in the background. Then, to him, it just sounded like music. And twenty-seven later, he still did not know the name of the hymn.

But when he gazed upon Gramma, he could remember, even at his young, tender age, the days when she would carry him in her heavy arms. When she would cook him dinners that only a Gramma could make. But the thoughts that swam through his mind swirled with ferocity: she just had to be asleep. He didn't know the answers to the questions that added in number: why wouldn't she wake up?

He leaned on the edge of the casket, his brown penny loafers falling off his heels as he placed his weight on his toes. He could feel the cool air through his thin black dress socks. He turned and looked around the room.

Mommy and Daddy were talking.

He turned and looked at Gramma again. And then he reached out with a pointed index finger, slowly, and lightly touched her cheek.

He gasped and drew his finger back quickly. His face fell, his mouth agape, his small, wide child eyes open and wondering.

He turned around and saw Mother and Father standing nearby, hugging some other adults, their eyes red rimmed, tears streaming down their faces.

"Mommy?"

She released her friend, who dabbed at her eyes with a tissue. Mommy opened her eyes and looked down at her young son. She held a wadded up tissue near her cheek and tilted her head to the side.

Her voice was soft and defeated. She leaned down closer to him and whispered into his ear.

"What is it, Jacob?"

He frowned but his eyes remained wide. "Mommy? Gramma won't wake up…she keeps sleeping…"

Mommy covered her mouth with the tissue and closed her eyes.

She bent over and picked him up, but he kept looking at gramma, lying in the casket, her hands folded at her waist, holding a small, black Rosary.

"But she's so cold mommy!"

Even after the passage of time, he still remembered the bite of the wind against his face as he stood in the dim, grey February afternoon under a blanket of clouds and snow flurries. His father's hand felt so big, wrapped around his hand. His fingers felt warm in his tiny, knitted mittens, and his Father's fingers held tight as they enveloped his little hand as they watched the funeral motorcade approach the vestibule of the church.

At the beginning of the procession was a long Cadillac limousine, which pulled off to the side. The driver, dressed completely in black, rushed to the back door and opened it. He saw his grandpa step out.

And then Jacob turned and looked at the other cars which approached the doors. A black hearse followed the limousine, and pulled up right in front of where they stood, waiting.

Small puffs of white vapor flowed across the chill of the air as they breathed.

Jacob saw the brown casket inside through the side windows. He recognized the white flowers from the funeral home last night.

He tugged at his father's coat lapel.

He could still remember the look on his daddy's face when he looked down at him. His eyes, red-rimmed, puffy. "What is it, tyke?"

"What are those little orange flags for, daddy?"

Jacob pointed at the hearse. There was a small flag above the passenger door that read FUNERAL and then he pointed at the other cars in the motorcade, which all had the same bright orange flags above the passenger door.

Daddy closed his eyes for a moment and Jacob noticed a tear stream down his cheek. "They're to let everyone on the roads know that there is a funeral, Jacob. They are there so the other cars on the road let the line of cars by."

"Do we have one of those flags on our car?"

Daddy nodded. "Yes, we do."

The memories of his grandmother's funeral were burned into his tiny, inquisitive, three year old mind. Throughout his childhood and into his teenage years, years after his grandmother had been buried, he could still remember the February day. In his mind, he could still look down, remember the blue winter boots that he wore, the tiny black suit and red bow-tie; and even remembered slipping on the cracked ice while walking into the vestibule into which his grandmother's coffin was being wheeled.

He could still remember watching in wonder as the funeral director (back then, he just saw a man in a suit), as he opened the casket lid, gently unfolded the satin linings, draped it over the outer sides of the casket, and straightened his grandmother's dress. He watched as the man pulled a shiny, silver looking crank from under the head of the casket and turned it. Jacob watched as gramma seemed to rise up and become more visible.

The image of gramma lying there was a memory he would never forget. The first image of death in his life; just a toddler of three when she had passed, and with his parents seemingly inconsolable, he was there to experience it on his own.

There was a slight smile on her face.

But not too much.

He remembered overhearing the phone conversations his mother had. "Don't make her look like she's laughing, that would be strange. But we certainly don't want a frown. Just make her look like she's sleeping. At least as best you can."

When Jacob was standing on the riser, his small hands gripping the satin, he looked at his grandmother. Where did you go, gramma?

Just a week ago, he had been sitting on her lap in the kitchen. She was peeling a banana, getting ready to do the choo-choo. She'd held him in one big, meaty arm, as she laid the half peeled banana on the table. She looked over at Jacob, and smiled her warm, grandmotherly smile as she started to tug down on the peel with one hand. "Get ready for the choo-choo!"

EXCELLENCE

IN

FICTION

ALL TITLES AVAILABLE WORLDWIDE FROM
PARCHMAN'S PRESS

Made in United States
Orlando, FL
27 March 2022

16187882R10286